Praise for Alice Clayton's

LAS...

"The hilarious conclusion to a series that made me laugh until I cried, swoon until I sighed, and reminded us all that there's always time for one *Last Call*."

—*New York Times* bestselling author Colleen Hoover

"This is everything we ever wanted for Simon and Caroline. *Last Call* is the perfect nightcap for a couple who belong in the romance hall of fame."

—*Heroes and Heartbreakers*

"Witty dialogue, engaging scenes, and the ever-present smoking-hot chemistry once again prove that Clayton is a master at her trade."

—*RT Book Review*

MAI TAI'D UP

"Clayton's a master at balancing heart, humor, and plenty of action between the sheets."

—*People*

"Alice Clayton is a genius! *Mai Tai'd Up* is sexy, steamy, and totally hilarious! A must read that I didn't want to end."

—*New York Times* and *USA Today* bestselling author Emma Chase

"Alice Clayton never fails to charm me. Her humor pops up in the oddest and most entertaining ways."

—*ebookobsessed*

"Clayton's trademark charm and comical wit saturates the storyline, which features engaging dialogue, eccentric characters, and a couple who defines the word 'adorable.'"

—*RT Book review*

SCREWDRIVERED

"Cheers to Alice Clayton! *Screwdrivered* is a hilarious cocktail of crackling banter, heady sexual tension, and pop-your-cork love scenes. The heroine is brisk and lively (can we be friends, Viv?) and the hot librarian hero seduced me with his barely restrained sensuality. I've never wanted a nerd more."

—*New York Times* and *USA Today* bestselling author Kresley Cole

"I don't know how Alice does it, but she 'nailed' it again with this book for me. She has this amazing ability to make me laugh and swoon."

—Bookish Temptations

"If you plan to read only one book in Alice Clayton's Cocktail series it MUST be *Screwdrivered*!"

—The Book Nympho

"*Screwdrivered* has sexual tension, romantic longing, and fantastic chemistry."

—Fresh Fiction

RUSTY NAILED

"We want to bask in the afterglow: giddy, blushing, and utterly in love with this book."

—New York Times and *USA Today* bestselling author Christina Lauren

"Clayton's trademark wit and general zaniness shine through in abundance as readers get an intimate view of the insecurities one faces while in a serious relationship. Steamy playful sex scenes and incorrigible friends make this a wonderful continuation of Wallbanger and Nightie Girl's journey to their happily ever after."

—RT Book Reviews

"For fun, sex, and strudel, make sure to spend some time with these wallbangers."

—Heroes and Heartbreakers

"A great follow up to *Wallbanger* . . . just as funny and HOT as the first!"
—Schmexy Girl Book Blog

"Humorous, sizzling hot, romantic, and not missing dramatics. If you weren't a fan before, you certainly will be after reading *Rusty Nailed*."

—Love Between the Sheets

"Excuse me, I need to catch my breath. Either from panting or cracking up. Because I was always doing one of the two while reading *Rusty Nailed*. Alice Clayton, you never disappoint."

—Book Bumblings

WALLBANGER

"Sultry, seXXXy, super-awesome . . . we LOVE it!"

—Perez Hilton

"An instant classic, with plenty of laugh-out-loud moments and riveting characters."

—Jennifer Probst, *New York Times* bestselling author of *Searching for Perfect*

"Alice Clayton strikes again, seducing me with her real woman sex appeal, unparalleled wit, and addicting snark; leaving me laughing, blushing, and craving knock-all-the-paintings-off-the-wall sex of my very own."

—Humor blogger Brittany Gibbons

"From the brilliantly fun characters to the hilarious, sexy, heartwarming storyline, *Wallbanger* is one that shouldn't be missed. I laughed. I sighed. Mostly, I grinned like an idiot."

—*Tangled Up in Books*

"A funny, madcap, smexy romantic contemporary. . . . Fast pacing and a smooth flowing storyline will keep you in stitches. . . ."

—*Smexy Books*

And for her acclaimed Redhead series

"Zany and smoking-hot romance [that] will keep readers in stitches. . . ."

—*RT Book Reviews*

"I adore Grace and Jack. They have such amazing chemistry. The love that flows between them scorches the pages."

—*Smexy Books*

"Steamy romance, witty characters and a barrel full of laughs. . . ."

—*The Book Vixen*

"Laugh out loud funny."

—*Smokin Hot Books*

ALSO BY ALICE CLAYTON

The Cocktail Series

Wallbanger

Rusty Nailed

Screwdrivered

Mai Tai'd Up

Last Call

The Redhead Series

The Unidentified Redhead

The Redhead Revealed

The Redhead Plays Her Hand

NUTS

Alice Clayton

G

GALLERY BOOKS

NEW YORK   LONDON   TORONTO   SYDNEY   NEW DELHI

Gallery Books
An Imprint of Simon & Schuster, Inc.
1230 Avenue of the Americas
New York, NY 10020

First Gallery Books trade paperback edition October 2015

GALLERY BOOKS and colophon are registered trademarks of Simon & Schuster, Inc.

For information about special discounts for bulk purchases, please contact Simon &
Schuster Special Sales at 1-866-506-1949 or business@simonandschuster.com.

The Simon & Schuster Speakers Bureau can bring authors to your live event.
For more information or to book an event contact the Simon & Schuster Speakers
Bureau at 1-866-248-3049 or visit our website at www.simonspeakers.com.

Manufactured in the United States of America

10 9 8 7 6 5 4 3 2 1

Library of Congress Cataloging-in-Publication Data

Clayton, Alice.
  Nuts / Alice Clayton. — First Gallery Books trade paperback edition.
     pages ; cm. — (The Hudson Valley series ; 1)
  1. Women cooks—Fiction. 2. Man-woman relationships—Fiction. I. Title.
PS3603.L3968N88 2015
813'.6—dc23   2015025020

ISBN 978-1-5011-1813-5
ISBN 978-1-5011-1814-2 (ebook)

*To Peter—for becoming my husband
four days before this book became real.*

Acknowledgments

$\mathcal{J}$his entire series came into being one afternoon at the Schlafly Farmers Market in St. Louis, Missouri. Mr. Alice and I were there on our regular Wednesday with our reusable bags, cash in hand, ready to support our local farmers and get some fantastic food to boot. And, as it quickly does where I am concerned, it dissolved into debauchery. Debauchery because standing behind the table in a new stall was the cutest mother-lovin' farmer I ever did see. He was tall, handsome, and scruffy in that adorable way, and he was holding the largest cucumber I'd ever seen.

No joke.

By the time I got up to the front of the line, Mr. Alice wondering why I was giggling so, I'd outlined a brand-new series centering on farm to table . . . and farmers on tables. In my head, I began to rifle through a catalog of possible titles.

Lettuce Do It.

Beet It.

Hey That's My Cucumber You're Holding.

Thank goodness, I went with the slightly less embarrassing but no less ridiculous *Nuts*. By the time we'd gotten into the car, bags full of beautiful locally produced vegetables, fruit, bread, poultry, sausage, and these adorable little hand-held apple pies (you know I love an apple pie), I'd begun thinking of possible places I could set this new series. Hudson Valley, New York, seemed like a perfect fit. The more research I did in the area made it feel even more perfect, and other stories began to suggest themselves. I spent a week playing up there with my bestie Nina Bocci, and we explored beautiful little towns like New Paltz, Hyde Park, Tarrytown, Sleepy Hollow, and were introduced to one of my very favorite places on the planet, Mohonk Mountain House. More on that later. . . .

We also had the privilege of touring an absolutely incredible farm in Pocantico Hills, just outside Tarrytown. Blue Hill at Stone Barns, a restaurant and agricultural center, is a place everyone should get to explore at some point in their lives. This place is 100 percent the inspiration behind Maxwell Farms, and it's a truly magical place. They're innovative, they're driven, and most of all, they're respectful of the land they farm and the animals they raise.

The next time I visited the Hudson Valley, I took the Metro North train out of Grand Central, and was blown away at not only how beautiful a rail line it is but how quickly you can go from being in the most exciting city on earth to the perfect quiet stillness of sleepy river towns. I was hooked on All Things Hudson.

Back at home, I was getting to know more and more of the farmers that I would see each and every week at the farmers market. I know the guy that raises my chickens. I know where to find the absolute best blueberry jam around, and I know the woman who makes it. And I know a guy who can make a kielbasa so good you'll want . . . well . . . another kielbasa. This farm-to-table thing, it's not just a trend—it's the way it used to be, a community knowing where its food is coming from and making the choice to support it. It's better for us, better for small farmers, better for the land, and holy shit does food taste different when it's grown with love and thought and respect.

And good-night nurse, there are some great-looking farmers out there . . .

Thank you to everyone who helped me bring this book into the world. The usual suspects like Nina and Jessica, Micki and Christina, who listened to me panic and pushed me through it. Thank you to all the experts in their field who patiently answered my private questions, my farming questions, my would-this-grow-together questions. Thank you to the people who grow our food and make it wonderful for us.

There are farm shares and CSAs in cities and towns around the country. Look for them, google them, seek them out. Try something new, cook something in a new way, and ask questions. And if you see a great-looking farmer holding his cucumber, for the love of God send me a picture.

Alice
XOXO

Chapter 1

"Okay, let's see. Dashi broth is done. Bok choy is roasting; shrimp are a'poachin'. Gluten free as far as the eye can see," I told myself, leaning on the stainless steel counter in the most beautiful kitchen ever created. If you liked midcentury California modern. And who didn't? Miles and miles of stainless steel and poured polished concrete.

Countless appliances and chefs' tools sat against the herringbone subway tiles, shiny and untouched by their owner's hand. Touched only by my hand— private chef and banisher of the evil gluten in this land of blond and trendy. Specifically, Hollywood. Specifically, Bel Air. Specifically, the home of Mitzi St. Renee, wife of a famous producer and chaser of that most elusive of brass rings . . . never-ending youth.

And at thirty-two (who would have thought that someone only five years older than me could talk down to me like it was her job), in a town where thirty was the benchmark for older men marrying for the love of tits, Mitzi was obviously concerned about her age. Holding a honeydew, I paused to consider said tits. Said tits were attached to a beautiful woman. Said tits were attached to a not-very-nice woman. Said tits were attached to an asshole, truth be told.

I shook my head to clear it, and started to cut up the melon. One-inch cubes with crisp edges; no rounded corners here. Next up were cantaloupe balls, rounded and plump. No ragged hollows; simply perfect balls. I heard how that sounded in my head, snorted, and moved on to the watermelon triangles. Acute. Obtuse. Did Mitzi appreciate the knife skills that went into her fruit bowl? Doubtful. Did she notice the culinary geometry that composed her a.m. energy burst? Probably not. No one noticed the perfection of my melons—but everyone sure noticed hers.

My inner dialogue and I moved on to assembling Mitzi's plate—she liked her dinner served at exactly 6:30 p.m. Some people hired private chefs just to do the cooking. Some even took the credit, while the chefs were hidden in the kitchen. And others assumed that because I worked in a kitchen and was paid for cooking, I also was a butler of sorts. But with the kind of money Mitzi paid me, I was okay serving her trendy Asian-fusion, low-calorie-but-high-in-taste dinner on a tray in her dining room.

As I was pulling the bok choy from the oven my phone suddenly rang, surprising me and causing me to bump my hand on the inside edge of the oven. Hissing in pain, I set the pan down on top of the range. When I saw who the caller was I quickly pressed decline, then gave the bok choy a once-over. Selecting the greenest and the most pristine, I carefully placed it in the center of a white porcelain bowl, creating a tiny green tower just as the egg timer went off, alerting me to my shrimp.

Poached in a court bouillon with the faintest hint of Thai chili and cinnamon, they were pink and perfect. Stacking three on top of the bok choy trio (symmetry, always symmetry), I then sprinkled bias-cut scallion, pickled garlic, and shallots that had been ever so slightly browned in peanut oil (a secret that would never be disclosed to Miss Fat Gram Counter) all around.

Setting the bowl onto an enameled tortoiseshell tray, I then poured the dashi broth into a white porcelain pitcher, and put exactly three-fourths of a cup of kaffir lime–scented jasmine rice in a matching bowl. Portion control is essential to maintaining a size zero lifestyle in a size zero town. Just as I was gathering up the tray to take into the dining room, my phone rang again. I hit Decline once more, noticed the time, and internally cursed myself for letting it get to 6:32 without noticing.

In the dining room, my client was perched at the head of the table, eating alone as usual. Her husband was always working, though whatever momentary soft spot I might have had for her disappeared when she made a show of looking at her watch.

"So sorry it's a little late; the bok choy needed just a bit extra tonight," I chirped, setting down the tray and serving her from the left.

"Why, Roxie, what's four minutes? I mean, four minutes here, seven minutes there, let's just relax all the rules, shall we?" she chirped back as I poured the broth from the pitcher, circling around the center.

She pays you well. Very well.

Gritting my teeth, I smiled at her Botoxed forehead and whisked away the empty pitcher. *Why, Roxie* indeed.

I headed back into the kitchen to finish up her "dessert" and her coffee, box up her breakfast and lunch for tomorrow, and clean up. Dessert had giant neon quotation marks around it inside my head, since it was hard to visualize such a lovely word applied to sugar-free carob-based wafer cookies set just so into shaved lemon ice. I wasn't opposed to the lemon ice, or the "cookies"—which, let's face it, also needed the quotation treatment. But they were not so much dessert.

The one thing I could get on board with was the way Mitzi took her coffee. Kona blend, dark roast, with one—and only one—tablespoon of full-fat, honest-to-goodness homemade whipped cream. She let herself indulge in this one treat, each and every day. Hey, it's not up to me to tell anyone where to spend their "cheat calories." Wow, lots of quotations tonight.

I fired up the stainless steel artisan KitchenAid mixer, retrieved the bowl from the freezer, and poured in a little over half a cup of fresh heavy cream. The bottle was almost empty; I'd have to add that to her market list. I made a shopping list for her each week, then came over several days to prepare meals that she could have on hand. Twice a week I cooked for her.

Adding a teaspoon of Madagascar vanilla and exactly two teaspoons of sugar to the cream, I let it whip while I tidied up the kitchen, ignoring the beep coming from my phone from the two calls I'd missed while on dashi duty.

Keeping one eye on the whipped cream and one ear toward the dining room, I tamped the coffee down, readying it to brew exactly four ounces of espresso. When my phone buzzed against the stainless steel counter, I saw who was calling *again* and slammed the trap shut on the expensive Breville machine.

"For heaven's sake, can I call you back?"

"Well, that's a fine howdy-do to your one and only mother," a cheerful voice sang out.

I closed my eyes in frustration. "Howdy-do, Mother. I'm working. Can I call you back?"

"That depends. Will you call me back tonight?"

"I'll try," I replied, struggling to get the foam nozzle locked into the espresso machine.

"You'll try?"

"I *will*, okay?"

"You promise?"

"*Yes*, I promise that I'll— Oh, man . . ."

"What's the matter? Are you okay, Roxie?"

"I'm fine—just a little kitchen mishap. I'll call you later." I hung up, staring into the bowl.

I needed to figure out how to explain to Mitzi St. Renee, a woman whose lifestyle hinged upon her ability to look beautiful and maintain an exquisite body, and whose *only* indulgence was her evening coffee, that instead of making billowy soft whipped cream . . . I'd made butter.

Fired.

Fired?

Fired.

F O R. B U T T E R.

I sat in my car outside Mitzi's house, tucked high up into the hills. I'd packed up my knives, plucked my last check from her perfectly manicured gel tips, then trudged to my 1982 Jeep Wagoneer.

Fired. Over butter. I should have known better than to turn my back on cream being whipped. It can go from stiff peaks to buttery squeaks in seconds.

My phone rang again and my mother's face appeared on the screen, with frizzy brown braids and a daisy behind her ear. Second-generation hippie. Woodstock Part Deux. I'd inherited my hair from her, but my eyes came from my father. I'd never met him, but my mother said she could always tell our moods based on our eye color. Hazel when I'm calm, a little blue when I'm blue, and a little green when I'm frazzled. I was very celery at the moment.

I heard the front door shut and saw Mitzi coming down the driveway, likely to tell me it was time to leave. Starting the engine, I waved good-bye with a specific finger and left.

Unprofessional, but I didn't have to care about what she thought anymore.

I grumbled to myself all the way home, down from the hills, across town to the other side of Highland, where the homes were considerably smaller, giving way to blocks and blocks of apartment buildings filled to bursting with hopeful young beauties. As I approached my building, my phone rang. *Again*.

"You really couldn't wait for me to call you back?" I said as her voice came through the speakers. California's hands-free law meant that I got to hear my mother's voice ricocheting off every corner of the car, in stereo.

"Who knows when that would be? I'm literally bursting to tell you my news!" my mother cried out, giggling excitedly.

I chuckled in spite of myself. My mother was many things, but her enthusiasm was always hard to resist.

"It must be big news; it's late back there. Why aren't you in bed?" It was almost eleven back east: way past her bedtime.

"Eh, I'll sleep when I'm dead. Listen, Roxie, I've got something fantastic to tell you!"

"Phish is touring again?"

"Roxie . . ." she warned.

I bit my lip to keep from saying something snarky. "You found a new brand of wheat germ and you can't hide your excitement?" Lip biting does not, in fact, always work.

"I'm so glad you enjoy making fun of your mother, especially with your generic hippie quips. You're very quippy tonight," she replied, her voice getting a bit sharp.

I needed to ease off a bit. After all, it wasn't entirely her fault that I'd been fired.

"Your news?" I asked sweetly, before she could go off on a tangent about maybe the reason I was so quippy is that I wasn't getting enough iron. Or sex. Typical mother-daughter stuff.

"Right! Yes! My news! Are you sitting down?"

"Yes, I'm sitting down."

"I'm going to be on television!" she burst out, ending in a squeal.

"Oh, that's nice. Is *Craft Corner* back on the air again?"

Our little town in upstate New York had its own public access channel, and Mom had been contributing ideas for years. Every now and then, when the budget hadn't been cut in half to seventy-five dollars, they'd ask her to come on and demonstrate. How to make a sweater dress, how to make a ceramic birdbath, etc. Her segment on Jiffy Pop paper lanterns generated the most calls the station had ever received. Three.

"No, no, not *Craft Corner*. Ever hear of *The Amazing Race*?"

"Sure, sure. Is Channel 47 doing a local version?" I asked, turning into my parking lot.

"It's not Channel 47, dear, it's the actual show! I'm going to be on *The Amazing Race*—the real one!"

"Wait, *what*?" I asked, swinging wide into my spot and almost taking out a trash can.

"You heard me right! I auditioned for the show last fall when they were in Poughkeepsie, with your aunt Cheryl, and they picked us! We're going around the world!" she yelled.

"Okay, stop shouting. Mom, seriously, stop—okay. Okay, hello?" I tried to get a word in edgewise, but it was impossible. She was spouting names of cities and countries right and left, her voice getting ever more excited. Cairo. Mozambique. Krakatoa.

"Krakatoa? You're going to a volcano?"

"Who knows, that's the whole point! They could send us anywhere! I'm going on a quest!"

"With Aunt Cheryl? She got lost in the new A&P. What good is she going to be on a quest?"

"Oh, don't be such a pill, Roxie," my mother said, and I could feel my shoulders tensing up—like they always did when she took this tone.

My mother was a "free spirit," and she couldn't for the life of her understand why her daughter was such a stick-in-the-mud. A stick-in-the-mud who, since she was fourteen, had made sure the lights stayed on, the gas didn't get turned off, and there was always food in the pantry. Still, I was happy for her.

"Sorry—it sounds awesome. Really, I'm excited for you," I said, envisioning my mother and her sister trying to navigate a bazaar in North Africa. "When does all this happen?"

"Well, that's the thing, sweetie. We leave in two weeks."

"Two weeks? Who are you going to get to run Callahan's?"

"Who do you think?" she asked.

She wasn't— No, she couldn't possibly think that I'd leave my— No, she would never . . . Hell yes, she would.

"Are you insane? Like, 'check you into a place without forks' insane?"

"Just hear me out, Roxie—"

"Hear you *out*? You want me to leave my business, which is finally starting to get somewhere, to cook in a run-down diner in Bailey Falls, New York? While you go off on some geriatric 'around the world in eighty days' bullshit?"

"I can't believe you would call me geriatric—"

"*I can't believe* that's *the word you heard!*" I exploded. As I sat in my car, eyes bugging out of my head at my mother's audacity, my phone vibrated with a text. "Explain to me how you think this can work. How can I do this?"

"Easy. You take a leave of absence out there, you drive to here, and you run the diner while I do this."

I took a breath, held on to it for a moment, then let it out slowly. "A leave of absence." *Breathe in. Breathe out.* "I work for

"We don't make that casserole anymore."

"We have to discuss your selective hearing sometime," I said
as my phone vibrated with another text. "Mother, I have to go.
We can—"

"We *can't* talk about this later. I need to know if you can do
this or not."

"You cannot call me up out of the blue and ask me—"

"Wouldn't be out of the blue if you called more often," she
sneaked in.

Breathe in. Breathe out. I suddenly understood the phrase
"my blood was boiling": I could feel bubbles of stress forming
inside my veins, knocking around and heating me up from the
inside. I was a little past simmer, getting close to parboil. Before
I could go fork tender, I tried once more.

"Here's the thing, Mom. I need you to be reasonable. I can't
do this every time you get into trouble or—"

"I'm not in trouble, Roxie. I'm—"

"Maybe not this time, but it's the same thing, just dressed up
in a package from CBS. It's not going to work anymore."

"I paid for your college, Roxie—two years at the American
Culinary Institute. The least you could do is this."

Okay. That's it.

"You know what, Mom? *No.* I'm not doing it," I said angrily,
just as another freakin' text came in. "And you only paid for ACI
because you'd just won the lottery. And you've gone through the
rest of that money already, which is ludicrous."

She remained stubbornly silent. This was usually the point
in the conversation where I'd cave. But not this time.

"Okay, Mom. While you're figuring out the real meaning of life and jumping into a shark tank off the coast of South Africa with Aunt Cheryl—who can't swim, by the way—I'll be here. In Los Angeles. Working my ass off, trying to build a business and keep my *own* lights on so I don't have to live in my car," I snapped—as yet *another* text came in.

"You really think they'll make us go in a shark tank?"

"Oh, go smoke a bowl, Mother!" I hung up, steaming, wondering how in the world she could be ludicrous enough to think I'd drop everything to go home and run her diner. Unbelievable. I had a life, I had clients, I had . . . good lord, *another* text?

I looked down at my phone, which showed six messages waiting for me. Nope, seven—another one just came in. What was going on? Opening the first, I saw it was from Shawna, a client.

> Roxie: I won't need you to cook for me next week.

Huh. That was weird. I opened the next bubble.

> Sorry for the last-minute notice, but I'm going to have to cancel the meals you have planned for next week, and the week after that. I'll contact you in the future, perhaps.

Wait, what? Miranda was another client. She'd been with me for a few months, referred by . . . Mitzi. Ah shit.

I opened the next text bubble. By the time I'd read them all, every single client Mitzi had referred to me had canceled. Backed out. Quit me.

Over B U T T E R???

Or maybe over the obscene finger gesture?

I fucking hate this town.

Referrals were everything in a town like this, and because of Mitzi St. Fucking Renee, I was now a culinary pariah. Vapid, plastically beautiful women with more money than actual God had had decided to make my career into a game of herd mentality. The few clients I had left only used me occasionally, for events or as their schedules allowed.

Though I loved California, I really was beginning to hate LA. The money was great here, but what it took to live here, to deal with these people—it was almost too much sometimes. And the money was only good . . . until it wasn't. I'd just spent most of my savings on a new engine for the Jeep, and I was temporarily light in the cash-flow department.

All those clients, all those dependable dollars, gone in the span of one phone call. My stomach knotted at the thought of having to rebuild my business. A bubble of worry floated up as I mentally ran through my client list, wondering who might be able to use me on a more full-time basis.

Then my phone beeped with another text. Oh, God. Was someone else getting in on the butter gang bang?

I'll be back in town the middle of next week. Let me know if you're up for some company.

Thank God, it wasn't culinary related. Although there was that one time with a jar of peanut butter . . . never mind that. I sighed as I let myself into my apartment. Mitchell was my . . . hmm. Not my boyfriend, that's for sure. He was my . . . plaything. My latest in a string of men whom I enjoyed for the sexing, not for the vexing. Emotionally invested? No. Interested in long walks on the beach and a partner for life? I'll pass. Sweaty, writhing, panting bodies a phone call away with a minimum of fuss and muss? Now you're talking.

No *how was your day, dear?* No *hey, Roxie, we'll get through this hard time.* The kind of hard time he'd bring would be me bent over the easy chair, one of his hands full of my hair and the other hand full of my . . . Too bad he wasn't here tonight— I could use something to take the edge off. My brain was churning, my career was potentially imploding, and there was a guilt trip barreling west from Bailey Falls, New York.

I needed peace. I needed quiet. My eyes scanned my apartment—which I couldn't afford unless I got every single one of my clients back—and settled on the Patrón. Besides peace and quiet, I needed a lime. . . .

Chapter 2

I woke up the next—hmm, let's say afternoon, so I'm not a liar—with my face covered in lime pulp and stuck to my leatherette easy chair. I checked the clock. Nice—I'd managed almost four hours of tequila-assisted sleep. A good night, when I usually only averaged about three hours a night. Suffering from intermittent insomnia since grade school, I'd adapted to less sleep than your average chicken.

I stumbled to the kitchen, reached blindly for the coffee, refusing to think about being fired. For *B U T T-* —oh, forget it. Yawning as the coffee percolated, I scrambled eggs with some tomatoes, garlic, spinach, and a touch of crème fraîche. I grated a little pecorino over the finished product, snatched a piece of perfectly toasted challah bread from the toaster, then grabbed my coffee and went back to the leatherette.

As I munched, a tabloid magazine on the table caught my eye. My guilty pleasure. I propped them up on a recipe stand while I was cooking sometimes. As I deboned a roasting chicken, I'd catch up on who was boning who in Tinseltown. But this morning, I realized I knew the person on the cover. She was a client. And I'd like to think maybe a friend?

I first heard of Grace Sheridan when the entire world was focusing on her other half, Jack Hamilton. An incredibly good-looking young British actor, he'd been the darling of the media world for a few years now, and just as his star was beginning to really rise, the press was constantly speculating on who the hot new movie star might be dating. As the world discovered that this unidentified redhead was actually Grace Sheridan, an actress as well, the media flurry became a storm, especially when she announced to the world they were a couple by taking him by the hand and publicly claiming him as hers on a red carpet. I knew all of this from what I'd read online. But when she called me one day to ask me to cook for her while getting ready for a new season on her hit TV series, I began to know the woman behind the magazine covers.

She was funny. She was sweet. And she loved food. And— I was cooking for her later today. Crap! I'd completely forgotten about my actual existing client, one who was expecting me for dinner tonight. I took five minutes to scrub my face, pits, and bits, threw on some clean clothes, grabbed my knives, and raced to the market.

I'd cooked for Grace on and off for the past year. She was a big foodie and loved to cook, so she only used me when her schedule got too demanding. Two actors in one house, both working crazy hours when they weren't on location—having a private chef was a perk to some people and a lifesaver for others.

Grace had been very outspoken in the press about her up-and-down weight, and she took her figure very seriously. Jack? Took it even more seriously . . .

The first time I met Jack Hamilton he'd been stealing as many kisses from his fiancée as he was carrots from the salad bowl I'd been working on. I was a bit giddy, being so close to such a big movie star, but giddy and a paring knife don't work so well together, so I sucked it down and cooked an amazing meal. So amazing that I became their occasional private chef.

I power shopped through the market, grabbing things I knew she'd like. Arugula. Frisée. Shallots. Lemons. Hanger steak. Jerusalem artichokes. Prosciutto. Bosc pears. A lovely slice of English cheddar. Because, bless my buttons, Jack and Grace liked dessert. In a town that frowned on dessert. So into the cart also went flour, sugar, eggs, and gorgeous, wonderful butter.

An hour later found me in the sunny kitchen of two of Hollywood's brightest stars, spooning pound cake batter into two loaf pans and shooshing Grace over to her side of the island.

"It doesn't make sense for you to pay me money to cook if you're doing half the work."

"I'm like your sous chef," Grace protested as I pulled out a kitchen stool and pointed at it.

"Sit down, relax, stay on your side of the kitchen, and I'll let you lick this." I held up a beater.

"It's a good thing Jack's not home yet; he'd never let a line like that go by," she said with a chuckle. "But I *do* want to lick that, so I'll stay over here."

I smiled as I thought about how I held sway over one of television's biggest stars with just a battery beater. Why couldn't all my clients have been like her? It was silent for a few minutes while she read through a script and I worked on my lemon cakes. But she couldn't keep quiet for too long . . .

"So they all just canceled on you? Just like that?" she asked, looking up from her papers.

I kept my eye on my loaf pans. "I shouldn't have told you. That was incredibly unprofessional."

"It was also incredibly unprofessional when Jack offered you a threesome for another serving of spotted dick. Unprofessional is how we roll."

I snorted in spite of myself. I'd made a traditional English pudding one night, and Jack the Brit was beside himself. So beside himself that he really *had* offered his body in return for future proper English sweets.

I really shouldn't have unloaded everything on Grace, as nice and as welcoming as she was. But somewhere between the grocery unpacking and the artichoke pruning, she'd guessed that something was bothering me. And before I knew it, the entire story had poured out.

"So your mom wants to go on *The Amazing Race,* huh?"

"Ugh, yes. Ridiculous idea."

"I don't know, I've seen the show a few times. Always looks fun."

"Oh, it's not that it doesn't look fun. It's just . . . hmm . . . how to explain my mother." I paused, rapping the loaf pans against the counter to coax any air bubbles out before placing them in the oven. "She's an eighties hippie. She got caught up in that whole second-wave thing."

She nodded. "I remember that. Buy your peace sign earrings at Contempo Casuals."

"Exactly." I handed over the promised beaters and she began to lick. "But it stuck with her. She'll tell you she's a free spirit. I have another word for it."

"Flakey?" she asked.

"Yep. Irresponsible. She means well, but when you're all about the moon being in the seventh house, it's hard to remember things like paying the electric company to keep the lights on in the *actual* house. Luckily, she had me. Not to mention the countless 'uncles' who were constantly around."

"Ah," she said, switching to the other beater.

"They were all nice guys; she just hated being alone. So she made sure she never was. She fell in love with any man who bothered to look twice at her." My mother was convinced that every single man she met was The One. Or at least The Next One. And I'd seen the aftermath countless times when the guys eventually bailed, the carnage that was left behind. The crying, the yelling, the sugar bingeing, the Van Morrison playing endlessly on the record player. And then the inevitable mooning over the next guy who wandered into her hippie love snare.

"So she's a romantic?" Grace asked.

"You say romantic, I say codependent." I rinsed the pears in the sink. "You say romantic, I say afraid to be alone. You say romantic, I say why in the world would someone put themselves through the hassle and the heartache?"

This is exactly why I liked my relationships simple, full of sex and free of love. My trouble sleeping was a great reason to ensure men never spent the night, since it was hard enough for me to fall asleep when I was alone. Compound insomnia with another snoring human in the bed, and I'd literally never sleep. Plus, I saw no reason to stare at a man awkwardly all night after the exercise portion of the evening had concluded, so I sent them on their way. They didn't seem to mind, and I avoided all the bullshit.

Grace looked thoughtful for a moment, and I could see her mind working. "Okay, so you don't approach things the same way . . ."

I shook my head. "Besides my mother's search for love everlasting, the only constant in our lives was the diner. I need a better handle on my life than that."

"Your family's diner?"

"Yes, my grandpa opened Callahan's a thousand years ago. I started washing dishes there when I was ten, maybe? Gotta love that child labor. When my grandpa died, it went to my mom. It's nothing special, just kind of a meeting place in a small town."

"Sounds great."

"It totally is—that's where I realized I wanted to make cooking my career. But I never wanted to run it, not even for a short period of time. Do you have any idea how much goes into running a barely successful family restaurant? Forget vacations. Forget freedom. Forget a peaceful evening. And even if you're home, you're fielding calls about a broken-down mixer or a walk-in fridge that's leaking, or a waitress whose nail broke off in the salad bowl and should we close the place down until we find it?" I sighed, exhaling the tension that always set up shop when I thought about our charming slice of Americana.

"Plus forget about having any kind of privacy—in a town like Bailey Falls, everyone knows everything about everybody. You are who you are, and they don't let you forget it. I spent my entire childhood living in my mother's flakey shadow, waiting to be eighteen and move away from home just to get the chance to be a kid. So for my mom to think I'd just drop everything and run home . . . oh, it just pisses me off."

"I can tell. You've peeled that pear down to the core," she said gently, and I looked down. I had indeed.

"Oh for the love of—" All the peel was piled up in the sink, along with all the pear. "I'm so sorry, this is terrible. Let's talk about you—what's going on with you?" I swished all the peel down the drain and started on a fresh pear.

She gave me a look that told me we weren't done with this, but she'd play along. She told me all about the new season of the show, then told me a few secrets from the set of the new Time movie Jack had just finished, a successful film franchise based on a series of erotic short stories. A time-traveling scientist schtupping women across time . . . not a bad way to spend an evening at the movies. By the time dinner was almost ready, I'd almost managed to forget that other than this wonderful client, I was now a private chef without a private kitchen.

I was just taking the steak out of the pan and setting it to the side to rest when headlights shone through the back window as a car swung into the driveway. I turned to see Grace beaming as bright as the headlights, even blushing a little. "Jack's home." She seemed so genuinely happy that I had to smile too, even if she did remind me of my perpetually lovesick mother for a moment.

I looked around the kitchen, with its warm honey wood and giant marble island. Pictures of the couple and their friends hung on the walls, not fancy artwork. Flowers spilled casually out of mason jars and Bakelite pitchers—no enormous florist arrangements in this house. Because it wasn't just a house, it was a home. Unlike any of the other houses I'd cooked in. Grace and Jack were that impossibility in this plastic town: *real people*. I missed real people.

But I didn't need to be the third wheel for the remainder of their real-people evening. So as Jack banged in through the back door, I gathered up my tools.

He immediately called to his fiancée, "C'mere, Crazy, I've been waiting to get my hands on you all—oh! Hey, Roxie." Jack smiled lazily over the top of Grace's red curls as he tucked her in for a hug. "I forgot you were here tonight. Smells great, what is it?"

"Sliced hanger steak marinated in a little coriander and soy sauce, sliced on a bed of baby arugula and frisée, with roasted Jerusalem artichokes tossed lightly with lemon juice and pecorino cheese," I said, taking their plates to the table. "Jack, you're also getting prosciutto-wrapped bosc pears and a big slice of your favorite English cheddar. Grace, you just get pears."

"How come she doesn't get fancy pears too?" he asked, sitting in his chair and trying to pull Grace onto his lap.

"I don't get fancy pears because I have a sex scene to shoot in two weeks," she said lightly, planting a kiss on his cheek and barely escaping his grabby hands.

"And since I'm skipping the fancy pears, I get to have cake later on," she said, digging into her salad. "And I might have licked the beaters."

"Wish I'd been here to see that," Jack said under his breath.

I shook my head and quietly finished cleaning up the kitchen as they ate their dinner. Which they loved.

After I poured lemon honey glaze over the still-warm pound cakes and prepared to go, Jack and Grace began imploring me to stay.

"You should have some cake with us," Jack said, moving easily around the kitchen.

Jack Hamilton with an armful of Tupperware: I could sell that picture to a magazine and never have to work again.

"Can't, but thanks for the offer. I've gotta get home and figure out some stuff," I said, sliding my last knife into its sheath just as my phone rang. Unreal timing, my mother. I'd deal with her later.

"Everything okay?" he asked, concern in his warm eyes.

Unbelievably, I felt my eyes burning a bit. I swallowed hard around the sudden lump in my throat.

"She's good. I'm going to walk her out," Grace said, looping an arm through mine and heading toward the back door.

"Brilliant dinner, Roxie, really excellent. Thanks again," Jack answered, whistling as he turned his attention back to rearranging the inside of the fridge.

I breathed in a huge, watery sigh as I headed out into the night air. "I'm so sorry about that. I don't know what came over me just now." I sniffled a bit, dabbing my eyes as we walked out toward my car.

"You've had a shitty day—it happens. Talk to your mom."

"She's just going to talk me into doing this for her," I said, setting my things in the back of my car.

"I hate to say this, because it'd mean your pound cakes are

leaving—but maybe you need a break. Maybe this would be a good idea. Get out of town for a while, clear your head."

"If I leave, I'm leaving everything."

"You already lost most of your clients, Rox," she said. "Except for us, of course, your favorites."

"Of course." I sighed. "You know why I love cooking for you?"

"Because you get to stare at Jack?"

"Obviously. But other than that, I miss cooking real food. Homey food. Calories be damned."

"Real food in the real world. I hear that." Grace laughed. "Call your mother, talk it out, and decide what you want to do. Even if you leave, you can always come back."

"Oh, I'd come back. It took me eighteen years to get out of that tiny town—there's no way I'd stay there for good," I said, shaking my head. Population two thousand and thirty-crap?

"Great! If you come back—sorry, *when* you come back—I'll put the word out. We know tons of people who could use a great chef, none of them plastic. It'll all work out."

"Go eat your cake. I presliced some for you, exactly three ounces. No more," I said, climbing up into my Wagoneer.

"We'll see," she said with a wink.

A few minutes later, I was halfway down the canyon. As soon as I had reception, I called my mother.

I listened to what she said.

Then I went home and looked at my stack of bills, and compared that to my now nonexistent income.

I called my mother back.

"Roxie, it's after midnight."

"I'm coming home, Mother. I'll run the diner. You'll pay me your salary. For exactly as long as it takes for you to run around the world on your quest with Aunt Cheryl. And then I'm done. No more favors. Ever. Clear?"

"Oh yes! Thank you, you fantastic daughter of mine, thank you! When will you be here? Can you be here by—"

"I'll call you in the morning and we'll work all that out, okay? You won, Mother—enjoy it." I sighed, hanging up and lying back onto my bed.

Shit. I was going home.

A week later, I had sublet my apartment, packed up the Wagoneer, told my boy toy that I'd be gone for the summer and sadly without his *company*, and pointed the car right.

I mean, east.

Chapter 3

Driving across the country alone can be boring, especially at the beginning of a trip. Sorry, Nevada. Sorry, Utah. I enjoy what you offer the world, the gambling and the Osmonds, but when you're feeling unsure about your life choices, the desert isn't a great place to drive through alone for hours on end.

On the other hand, with only the cacti, the sand, and an actual buzzard to bear witness, the desert is the perfect place to roll down the windows and sing "Sweet Caroline" at the top of your lungs. I even did my own backup vocals, giving each *bah bah bah* my all, with some swerves across the yellow line as a dance element.

It's possible the desert was getting to me.

But it kept the memories at bay. Memories that were fluttering around the edges between the songs. Thinking about spending some time back east, and maybe seeing my best friends Natalie and Clara, got me thinking about when we all met and that particular time in my life.

I'd left home for the American Culinary Institute in Santa Barbara, convinced it would be the cannon that would shoot me out into adulthood. The place where I'd finally find the life and the life's work that fit me. I could focus on myself without my mother's perpetual disasters or the awkwardness of high school holding me back.

I'd been a shy kid, embarrassingly so. Belonging to neither the jocks nor the geeks, the freaks or the brains, I lived in a kind of interstitial no-man's-land. It's not like there's a high school clique comprised of food snobs. It's not like there's tons of kids spending their weekends perfecting goat cheese tartlets, or holding olive oil tastings in their backyard.

I did both.

I was shy; I was all elbows and knees and blushing as soon as someone looked at me. I fumbled my way through my first serious make-out session with a foreign exchange student from Finland after getting tipsy on smuggled aquavit. He touched my boobs and I liked it. But then I threw up. He never called again.

I once managed to get the zipper of my coat attached to a knot in my hair at lunchtime and spent five minutes trying to free myself, before calmly (I hoped it looked calmly; it felt anything but) eating the haricots verts tossed with almonds and Gruyère that I'd brought from home, trying not to notice the staring from classmates. I once tripped and fell down a flight of stairs in front of my entire class, landing with my skirt around my waist.

I once checked the wrong box on my elective class assignment, and instead of signing up for the Taste of the World parade of culinary delights, I signed up for debate class, and spent an entire semester fearing an egg timer and flop-sweating my way through "The Missouri Compromise—Or Was It?"

When I graduated, I was determined to shed my wallflower persona and redefine who Roxie Callahan was. To decide what kind of person I wanted to be, how I wanted to present myself to the world. And the beauty of going away to school is that no one has a preconceived idea of who you are.

Plus, at ACI I was in the exact environment I was supposed

to be in. I was with people like me. We got excited when a new box of foie gras arrived, we salivated when truffles were in season, and we got downright horny when we learned how to caramelize chicken skin for a garnish.

And speaking of horny . . . Let's speak of horny. I enjoyed the horny times. Culinary school was a fondue pot of sexual tension, and we were all dying to get speared and forked. Along with the confidence that came from learning to cook well, I gained confidence in my body. I might still be elbows and knees, but I finally gained some cleavage and a sweet ass, thanks to the freshman fifteen.

The frizzy brown hair became sleek and bouncy after being introduced to some smoothing treatments. The California lifestyle gave me a nice tan year-round, and the freckles that I'd tried to fade with lemon juice when I was a kid became a nice frame for my eyes.

I had friends, and some of the friends were boys. And boys were fun. After seeing my mother moon over every guy with a passing resemblance to Tom Selleck (no idea), I did the opposite. I flirted and flounced and enjoyed the shit out of my newfound empowerment to become physically, but never emotionally, entangled with whichever guy I set my fancy on.

Because Roxie Callahan wasn't going to go down the same path as her mother, bouncing from relationship to relationship with a kid in one hand and a Harlequin romance novel in the other, saddled with a usually in-the-red diner and waiting for the next man to sweep her off her Birkenstocked feet. Uh-uh. *I* had a career to craft.

Which I did. When my instructors gave me feedback, I thrived. I saw what they saw—the little tweaks here and there to make the difference between executing and mastering a technique. To understand how a splash of champagne vinegar at exactly the right time could elevate a recipe, but if added only a moment later it would muddy and cloud an otherwise acceptable dish. That was pure perfection. I spent hours in those beautiful stainless steel kitchens, blending ingredients, playing with flavors, savoring the process: all the things you don't actually get to do when you're working in a restaurant kitchen.

Though I knew what a diner's daily grind was like, I believed that once you raised food to an art form, the artist had time to work. But not so. Being an executive chef in a Michelin-starred restaurant—the goal of every culinary student—was not all it was cracked up to be. It was staffing, and payroll, and management, and critics, and reviews, and front of the house, and back of the house—and yeah, occasionally you got to get lost in your kitchen and *cook*. So I found myself adrift: in love with the process of creating food, but convinced deep down that the restaurant life—that hectic schedule, cooking under constant pressure, never having any freedom—was not for me.

But I sucked it up, enjoyed the opportunity to cook beautiful food while it lasted, and graduated with honors. And offers. Offers to apprentice and work in some of the finest and most innovative restaurant kitchens in the country, even abroad.

But I knew I wouldn't be happy. It wasn't glamor and fame I wanted, it was the opportunity to create. I hated the stress of the day-to-day operations of a professional kitchen, so with some guidance from a professor, I chose the quieter life of a private chef.

It was the best decision I could have made. There, I could excel, let my food speak for itself. Sometimes I'd find myself giving a client tips here and there: tricks of the trade on how to make sure piecrust always came out flaky, how to caramelize but not burn onions, and how to carve a chicken. In the age of the boneless and the skinless, people under forty had never learned the things that now only chefs and older people knew how to do. And I enjoyed the "teaching" aspect of my job a lot. It was the "something extra" I could offer to make them feel like hiring a private chef wasn't just a luxury, but something invaluable.

I stayed in California, moving all over the Golden State whenever the mood struck, or a new client beckoned. Santa Barbara, San Diego, Monterey, finally settling in Los Angeles. I'd always heard you learned how to say no in your thirties, so my twenties were all about saying yes. To a new job, a new town, a new experience. Unless it was illegal (mostly), dangerous (really), or had to do with butt sex (not going to happen), I rarely said no.

I rarely returned to Bailey Falls, preferring to have my mom visit me out west. I liked my life, I liked the new Roxie, and I was determined never to return to Wallflower Roxie again.

But while I sidestepped the stress of working with overbearing executive chefs and the drama of bartenders sleeping with waitstaff, I didn't sidestep the stress of being solely responsible for making sure that the checks kept coming in. My livelihood depended almost entirely on referrals, and though I'd worked my ass off to build my business, I had no security. No automatic paycheck every week. No medical. No dental. No promotions. No family. Restaurant family, I mean.

This thought brought me back to the present, where I was driving across the country to bail out my mother. I turned up the radio and concentrated on staying between the lines.

On day three I pulled into a roadside restaurant that proclaimed it had the World's Best Pork Butts. I was familiar with the marketing; every diner in the world had a claim to a particular culinary fame. World's Best Coconut Cream Pie, World's Best Fried Pickles, World's Best Scrapple . . . that last one belonging to our diner. You don't even want to know what scrapple is; it's about three rungs below Spam on the evolutionary scale.

But I appreciated the way this dive threw their Butts right up onto the billboard, and I was hungry for some good BBQ. I was halfway across Kansas, close enough to Kansas City that it should be good.

It *was* good. Sweetly spicy like all KC barbecue should be, the butts were shredded and piled high on an open-faced roll, the meat tender with the right amount of chew, the flavors balanced perfectly.

On the side? Burnt ends. Find them. Seek them out. Go to the middle of the country right *now* for a plate of them.

The diner was old-school Americana. It had the right smell of chili seasonings, home fries, and that faint scent of grease that hung in the air no matter how thoroughly the grease traps were cleaned out. And the diner came complete with something that was almost impossible to find these days, but used to be a staple: a "Flo." An honest-to-goodness, pencil-in-her-hair, pantyhose-wearing Flo.

"You want anything else, sugar?"

I smiled at the little old lady who had walked a million miles in those Reebok sneakers and never slipped on a mushed pea. "I'm good. Thanks for the recommendation on the cake; it was terrific."

"Sour cream. That's the secret," she smiled, placing my check on the table. "Makes all the difference in the world. It's not just for baked potatoes, you know."

"You don't say," I grinned, letting her tell me her diner wisdom.

Twenty minutes later I was back on the road with a full tummy, a new recipe for mocha chocolate fudge cake, and a sudden soft spot for a good old diner.

❦

By the time I made it across the New York State line, I was in a very different state of mind. I was sick of driving, sick of peeing in truck stops, and already sick of being home—even though I wasn't technically home yet. Two hours later, when I began the slow, gradual climb into the Catskill Mountains, I was so tired and cranky that no amount of chirping birds or late-season tulips bordering the two-lane country highway could lift my mood. And when I turned off the highway and onto the main drag of Bailey Falls, the quaint banner that hung from city hall, proclaiming that the annual Memorial Day parade would be held in just a few days, and the charming red, white, and blue bunting draped across porches and hung from telephone poles and lampposts, failed to charm me.

On autopilot, I drove past the grand homes on Main Street, the still-grand homes on Elm and Maple, past the smaller but neat-as-a-pin cottages on Locust and Chestnut, past the quiet ranch homes in the subdivision on the outskirts of town, over the railroad tracks, and back out into the country. The houses were farther apart now, some with adjoining farms, some stranded in a sea of rusted and busted-out cars forever on blocks.

Finally I turned onto the long winding driveway, gravelly and pitted, lined with flower boxes painted in Day-Glo yellow, orange, purple, and pink. Here and there, signs propped up in the flower boxes shouted motivational messages in neon green:

LESS TROOPS MORE HUGS

A WOMAN NEEDS A MAN LIKE A FISH NEEDS A BICYCLE

NO DAY BUT TODAY

Pretty sure that last one was a line from *Rent*. My eyes rolled, a conditioned response. As I bumped down the driveway, reading the new signs mixed with the old, I tried to see her as others might see her. Happy. Positive. Eternally optimistic.

I still saw the woman in overalls with a flower behind her ear who brought me my lunch bag when I deliberately left it at home, telling me in front of all of my friends to make sure I *didn't pick off my bean sprouts from my sandwich, that I needed the fiber for my constitution.*

Mortifying.

I drove around the last bend in the driveway and found myself in front of my childhood home. Though it had been a few years, it looked exactly the same. Two-story clapboard with peeling white paint. Expansive front porch covered in half-finished art projects. Whirlybirds and pinwheels scattered across the front lawn, which could use a good mowing. At least three different paint colors had been tried out here and there on the side of the house, all abandoned when something else had caught my mother's attention. Knotholes where woodpeckers tap-tap-tapped right on through, and occasionally brought their friends the squirrels. Always nice to wake up to a scurry in the walls.

But home was home. I parked the car, dragged my luggage onto the porch, and debated whether to knock. On the front door of the house I'd lived in since I was three days old.

Screw the knock, I thought, and turned the handle.

It was locked.

So I knocked. No answer.

Are you kidding me?

I marched through the backyard, past the signs encouraging me not to worry but to be happy, and dug for the key that still lived under the planter by the back door. I knocked once more, then let myself in.

Every house has a smell. You can smell it when you visit someone's house for the first time. Sometimes it's good, like cinnamon and clean laundry. Pecan rolls and pipe tobacco. Sometimes it's bad. Febreze and cabbage. Curry and hamster cage. Stale pizza and dead skin cells. (If you've ever been to a college guy's apartment then you're familiar with the latter. Like I said, every house has a scent.) And that scent tells a story. You usually can't smell your own home, unless you've been on vacation for a while and manage to get a quick whiff when you first come home. Or if you moved away for several years.

One deep breath and I was home. Steel-cut oatmeal. Borax. And patchouli. I looked around and found it exactly the same as it always was. Same Camp Snoopy water glasses drying by the sink. Same white-and-brown ceramic mushroom canisters lined up on the counter. Same bicentennial plates hung from the wall, although Rhode Island seemed to be missing.

"Mom? You home?" I called, knowing she wasn't.

And suddenly I was pissed. I'd driven across the entire country, walked away from my own business (my fury didn't care about facts), and shown up so she could race around the world. And she wasn't. Even. Home.

I banged back out the door, jumped into my car, and headed back into town. It was Monday morning. I had a good idea where she was.

When I pulled into the back parking lot of the diner, I swung into the slot beside her car. Wood-paneled cars ran in the family, and there was no mistaking her 1977 station wagon with the Darwin bumper sticker. And the faded Vote Mondale/Ferraro! sticker that still lingered.

I grabbed my purse and barreled through the back door into the kitchen, straight into a scene I'd seen a thousand times. Tickets flying. Bells dinging. Feet running. The door to the walk-in fridge banged as people ran in and out. Vegetables chopped. Pans sautéed. An army of retro-looking waitresses (we had our own Flos) barking orders and bringing food, dressed in pink and green polyester dresses that perfectly matched the seat covers. There was a certain rhythm. There was a certain madness. There was also laughter—and mostly from my mother.

She stood in the center of the *Fantasia*-like storm, her dirty apron tied back expertly, her frizzy, gray-streaked hair whisked back into a bun, wearing a broad smile as she expedited orders, ran food, and shouted special requests left and right: "For Table 16 I need two dots and a dash, two eggs wrecked, a club high and dry, and a cowboy with spurs."

She caught my eye over the chaos, and a second later I was wrapped in a bear hug that would take out a quarterback. I hugged back, unable to stop the laugh that popped out. Mostly because all of my air was forced out at once. Mostly.

"Roxie, you're early! I thought you'd be here this afternoon, or even tonight. When did you get in?"

"Just now—I was so close last night that I just decided to keep going."

"I'm so glad you got my note."

"What note?" I asked as she pulled back to look me over, eyes assessing.

"On the front door, that I was working the early shift. How else did you know I was here?"

"I guessed. And there wasn't a note, Mom." I shook my head.

"Sure there was. I taped it to the front door on my way out this morning, when I . . . Oh shoot, here it is," she said, shaking her own head at the piece of paper she pulled out of her apron.

Roxie—I'm working the early shift, come on down. So glad you're here!

"Oh well, you're here! That's all that matters! And not a moment too soon; we are in the weeds. Carla called in sick at 4 a.m. so I had to come down to open up this morning, and one of our dishwashers quit last week and I haven't had a chance to replace him. Did you bring your apron?"

"Bring my— Mom, I literally came straight here after driving all night and—"

"No trouble, just grab one off the wall. I need to get moving, those beans have been sitting in the window too long as it is, talk when the rush is over? Thanks, sweetie!" she called out, turning to yell to Maxine, one of the oldest waitresses. "Those whistle berries are getting cold, get those out to Table Seven on the double!"

"Stuff it, Trudy! Hiya, Roxie! Great to have you home again!" came the response, and the chaos resumed.

I stood in the center, wondering what had just happened.

"You remember how to peel potatoes? We're getting low on fries and I'd love to get ahead before the lunch rush," my mom chirped as she sped by me, turning me toward a mountain of potato sacks.

"I know how to peel potatoes, for goodness' sake," I mumbled testily, realizing there wasn't any way I was getting out of this. My mother was already heading back to the front counter, shouting over her shoulder to "Burn one, run it through the garden, and pin a rose on it."

"It's faster just to say burger with lettuce and tomato," I told the potatoes, which looked back at me blandly. Because they had eyes, you see.

I grabbed a clean apron off the wall, grabbed the least dull and least likely to cut me knife from the block, and started filling a hotel pan with water to soak the cut potatoes. We served steak fries at the diner, thick cut and big enough to fill a hot dog bun, should someone choose. But that didn't mean they couldn't be perfect steak fries. So I settled in with my paring knife, peeling and slicing and lining them up with perfect uniformity. I dug out eyes, trimmed away green, and lost myself in the details.

As shouts of black cows, Eve with a lid on, and burn it echoed around me, I concentrated on the slippery right angles, making sure they were perfectly edged before going into the water bath.

My mother buzzed over to grab the first pan of ready-to-go spuds, and she looked on curiously as I concentrated on removing a stubborn peel. "They're gonna get covered in gravy or dipped in ketchup—they don't need to be a work of art, Rox."

"You told me to peel potatoes. This is how I peel potatoes," I replied, tossing it into the pan as she turned to go.

"Light a fire, or we'll never get ahead of this," she instructed, and I rolled my eyes. "I saw that!" she called out.

"I meant you to!" I pulled another pan down and filled it full of water. "Light a fire," I mumbled.

Now *I* had a quest: to make a perfect steak fry, fast. I shut out the noise and the clatter and bent my head to the task. Hands flew, pruney fingers danced, and the pan filled with starchy, pointy art. Time flew by as I filled pan after pan, the sacks dwindling.

When one of the other waitresses patted my shoulder in greeting it startled me, and my knife slipped from my hand, landing in the back of the water pan. Leaning across the pan to retrieve it, I overbalanced and managed to submerge my front in cold potato water. "Bleagh," I said, feeling the cold water running down the inside of my shirt and across my belly. Paused from my fry frenzy, I looked around. There were pans of fries on every work surface in my corner. Huh. Might have gone a little overboard.

"Land's sake, Roxie, how many fries did you think we need?" my mother asked as she came around the corner.

"They'll keep until tomorrow—the next day, even," I replied, a little sheepish.

"It's fine, I'll make some room in the walk-in. How about cleaning some sugar snap peas?" she asked, thunking down a big pan of pea pods. "Cut off the end, strip out the stringy part."

"I know how to clean a sugar snap," I grumbled. "Cut off the end . . ." I filled the pan with water, huffing, "Strip out the stringy part. No shit, strip out the stringy part."

"You start talking to yourself out there in Hollywood?" my mother teased, sticking her head around the corner and very nearly getting hit in the face with the snap pea I threw at her. She laughed and disappeared back into the kitchen.

I sighed, stretched, and went to work again. After this, I was taking a nap.

After a while I became aware of a tingling on the back of my neck, and I looked over my shoulder to find the source. Then several things happened within mere seconds, though I saw them in super slo-mo:

1. A man was standing right behind me.
2. He was holding a basket.
3. The basket contained some lovely walnuts.
4. I shrieked, because he was standing right behind me.
5. I dropped my pan.
6. Snap peas shot out in all directions.
7. Some of the peas landed on his work boots.
8. I looked above the boots. Jeans.

9. I looked above the jeans. Vintage Fugazi concert tee. Green flannel shirt.

10. I looked above the flannel. Two weeks' worth of shaggy blond beard. Mmm. Country hipster.

11. I looked above the beard. Lips.

12. I looked at the lips.

13. I looked at the lips.

14. I looked at the lips.

15. COME ON.

16. I looked above the lips.

17. I was glad I looked above the lips.

18. The eyes and the hair were a package deal, the hair was falling across his eyes in a careless way that said "Hey, girl. I've got peas on my shoes, but who cares, because I've got these eyes and this hair, and it's pretty fucking great."

19. The hair was the color of tabbouleh.

20. His eyes were the color of . . .

21. Pickles?

22. Green beans?

23. No. Broccoli that had been steamed for exactly sixty seconds. Vibrant. Piercing.

24. I stood—and slipped on the snap peas.

25. At his feet, I stared up at him.

26. One corner of his mouth lifted for the tiniest moment.

27. He looked at my nearly transparent wet T-shirt for the tiniest moment before decency dictated that he not do that.

28. He set down his basket of nuts and extended a hand to me. Callused. Rough. Both corners of his mouth now lifted.

29. I took his hand to stand. Slipped again on a snap. Worlds collided when my skin met his. Heads collided when my forehead conked his.

30. One of my pea pods wedged under his boot

31. He fell down too.
32. His nuts went everywhere.
33. Our legs tangled.
34. His head fell into my . . . lap.
35. Sugar snap peas were my new favorite vegetable.

The guy with the nuts was named Leo. I know this because when my mom came around the corner and caught him face-down in her daughter, she cried out, "Leo!" and rushed to help him up. *Him.* She never could resist a good-looking man. And once the man was extricated from between my legs . . . mercy . . . he reached down once more to try to help me up.

"For goodness' sake, Roxie, what're you doing on the floor?" my mother interrupted, lifting me up underneath both arms and plopping me back on my feet like a flour sack.

"I . . . uh . . . well . . ."

"I think I surprised her, Ms. Callahan," this Leo said, his voice smooth and rough at the same time. How is that possible? "You okay?"

"I . . . uh . . . well . . ." Where was this coming from? I don't stammer.

He grinned, a look of curious amusement spreading across his entire face.

"She's totally fine, aren't you— Oh dear, it looks like the turkey's done; you might want to cover up," my mother said, looking at a very specific part of my chest.

I looked down, remembered that I was on full transparent display here, and quickly crossed my arms over my wet chest. Where my nipples had popped like Butterball turkey timers. My mother, ladies and gentlemen.

"Roxie, go get a fresh apron, and then come sit with Leo here and have a cup of coffee. You've got time for coffee, don't you, Leo? It's the least we can offer you after you ended up on our floor!"

Coffee suddenly sounded like the best idea in the history of best ideas. Coffee? Yes. Lay on top of me again? If you must.

"Sorry Mrs. C, can't stay for coffee today. I've got a truck full of deliveries to make before five. Rain check?" he asked, unleashing the grin of the ages on my mother, and then turned his grin on me. "You sure you're okay?"

Absolutely okay. I didn't get weak in the knees anymore just because a cute guy looked at me, even if my turkeys *were* done.

I looked up at him through lowered lashes, cocked my head to the side, and let loose my own grin. "Sorry about your nuts." Then I slowly walked toward the walk-in fridge, putting a tiny extra sway in my hips.

Inside the walk-in I allowed myself ten seconds of teenage cute-boy-freak-out, getting caught in a fist pump when my mother poked her head inside to see if I was okay.

"If you're done in here, there's a bunch of snap peas on the floor that aren't going to clean themselves up," she said with a knowing grin.

Face flaming, I left the walk-in.

But spending the summer back home just got a little more interesting.

Chapter 4

After the lunch rush was over, I sat in the corner booth to take a break. Leo. Who was named Leo these days? And why was he carrying all those nuts?

"He brings me nuts every week, dear. I'm on his route."

"Pardon me?" I asked, swiveling in my seat.

"You asked why he was carrying all those nuts. I assume you mean Leo, the young man you wrestled to the floor this morning."

"I said that out loud?"

"You did. It's either sleep deprivation from the drive, or your trip to the floor knocked something loose, but you're out here talking to the vinyl seats."

She came to sit with me, now that the doors were locked and the staff sent home. Monday through Thursday the diner closed after lunch; it was only open for dinner Friday through Sunday. Afternoons at the diner were one of my favorite memories from childhood. It was quiet and peaceful, I could build towns out of the napkin dispensers while my mom worked on her orders and invoices, and I'd get to eat as much pie as I could sneak.

We had this quiet time together almost every day when I was young—my elementary school was just a few blocks up the road and it was a quick walk after the bell. Me and my home-work, her and her workwork, and an afternoon in the late-day sunshine. Somewhere between 4:30 and 5:30 we'd pack up and head for home, since whichever "uncle" my mother was cur-rently dating would be arriving home soon, hungry for dinner. So in the evenings, I'd lose her a bit. In the same way any child has to share her mother with a dad or other kids or PTA or whatever else take up her time.

She dated nice guys, cool guys, so there's no need for the *Afterschool Special* music. But they never stuck around for very long. She'd loved my father, I knew. His picture was on the mantle as long as I could remember, no matter what uncle hap-pened to be circling at the time. He died when I wasn't even a year old, and she was forever chasing that heartbreak with another one.

Anyways, though, afternoons in the diner had always been nice.

Apparently now they involved me talking out loud to myself. Not even back in town one day, and I was losing my mind.

"You're not losing your mind, dear," my mother offered, and I looked at her with wide eyes.

"Did I say that out loud too?" I asked, shrinking down into my seat. "What the hell did you put in this coffee?"

"You didn't, but I know my daughter. You're thinking this small town is already making you crazy, right?"

"Possibly," I allowed. After a moment of inspecting the flecked linoleum top of the table, I nonchalantly asked, "So, what route?"

"Hmm?"

"You said route."

"When did I say route?"

"A minute ago."

"I don't think I did."

"*Mother*."

"Oh, you mean Leo's route?"

"That'd be the one you mentioned," I said, nodding. Her memory was fine, by the way. Her sense of humor, however, was twisted. "So, the guy with the route . . ."

"Yes, dear?" she asked innocently.

"That's it, I'm going home." I started to pull myself out of the booth.

"Oh, relax. Stay and drink your coffee; I'm just teasing," she said, waving me back down. "So, what do you want to know about the guy with the route? Although I like to think of him as the guy with the eyes—did you see his eyes?"

"His eyes are an interesting shade of green, I'll give you that," I admitted, knowing that until I did, I'd get nowhere. "Who is he?"

"He's from the Maxwell Farm; he sells produce to all the local restaurants. Every week, he brings something special by. This week it was walnuts."

"*The* Maxwell Farm?"

"The very one."

"Someone is actually farming that land now?"

"Oh yeah, they've turned that entire place around! He's got the orchards back on line, the greenhouses, the fields are producing again—oh, it's just wonderful."

"When did all this happen?"

"You haven't been here in how many years, Roxie? Things haven't exactly stood still just because you weren't here." Her face was neutral, but her voice was a little sharper than normal.

"I realize that," I said, twirling my coffee cup in its saucer. I felt a small tug. I *had* been gone a long time. But I tamped it down, keeping my attention on the farmer.

The Maxwell Farm was legend in this part of the country. Hell, the Maxwells were legend, in *all* parts of the country. Old New York. Old money. Old banking family. Have a mortgage? It was probably held by a Maxwell bank at some point. Lease a car? Probably guaranteed by a Maxwell bank at some point. Invested in mutual funds? If it has to do with the stock market, the Maxwell Banking Family of Greater New York is likely involved.

And like all old wealthy families, they occasionally like to leave their Manhattan apartment, or their Hamptons seaside "cottage," or their Palm Beach winter house, and head up for some good old-fashioned rustic country life on their "farm."

Farm in the loosest sense of the word imaginable. What do you think of when you hear the word *farm*? Ten or twenty acres around an old family farmhouse and a weathered red barn, somewhere in one of those states you fly over? Perhaps a lazy barn cat. Perhaps a chicken or two. Perhaps if you're very lucky, and also adorable, you might even envision a moo cow.

If you're slightly less romantic and slightly more aware, you might imagine a different vision entirely. Hundreds and hundreds of acres farming one crop, probably feed corn or soybeans, with no old farmhouse or barn. There'd probably been several on this giant property at one point, but they all sold their land in one huge land consolidation, and the structures have been torn down or left to the elements. There's maybe one large equipment "barn," and definitely no moo cow.

But Maxwell Farm? It's an idyllic, look-how-salt-of-the-earth-and-how-cute-are-we-in-these-overalls "farm." In the late 1800s, when the Maxwells were already firmly entrenched into New York's social elite, they purchased a large plot of land in the Hudson Valley. This was not uncommon back then: the Vanderbilts, the Rockefellers, the Carnegies all owned farms. Enormous acreages, beautiful and elaborate stone "farmhouses" complete with equally beautiful stone barns, riding paths, teahouses, fountains, and gazebos. And occasionally, these farms might actually plant a crop or two.

It started out as a place to get away from the daily grind of being wealthy—as one does. The main house and the barns were situated high on a bluff overlooking the Hudson River. The enormous stone barns were mostly used to house cattle, as it was once a working dairy farm. The land was used for some farming—mostly vegetables and fruit orchards—but most of the acreage was set aside as a nature preserve. Some fields were cleared for hunting, as the Maxwells hosted large parties for their city friends, the men scaring up quail and pheasant, while the ladies visited the gardens and the orchards and the orangerie.

The Maxwells were in residence only a few times a year. The rest of the time the land was worked by hired hands and groundskeepers, making sure it was always ready for the city folk. As time passed, most of the land went fallow, the fields were retaken by the woods, and the house was shuttered for years at a time. I suppose the Maxwells had found other places to "get away" to.

The home and barns fell into disrepair, and the property became a lonely estate on the edge of town. In the 1970s, the new Mrs. Maxwell became interested in the history of the family she'd married into and began a restoration of the house. No one ever lived there for any length of time, but tours were given on special occasions, and my own fourth-grade class trotted up there on a field trip to marvel over the views and the house and the grandeur.

I saw all that land not being used, all those barns not filled with livestock, a cold stone house filled with flowers but no other form of life, and always felt it was a waste.

"Well, I'm glad to see it's going to good use now," I said.

"Agreed."

"And Leo is the guy that delivers all the produce? Well, that's great. Just great."

"Agreed."

"Do they have a stand at the farmers' market?"

"They do."

"Well, maybe I'll check it out. It's still on Saturdays, right?"

"Mmm-hmm."

"Might be a good idea to see what they've got in season, for the diner."

"Agreed." My mother sipped her coffee, a dreamy look on her face. Must be thinking about her amazing race.

"Let's go home," I said. "You can make me some of your vegetable soup, and then I'm going to bed as soon as the sun sets." I dragged myself out of the booth and grabbed my bag. My jeans literally creaked as I walked, stiff with dried potato and snap pea water, reminding me of the tumble I'd taken with the cutest farmer this side of *Little House on the Prairie*.

"Why are your jeans creaking?" my mother asked.

Nothing, and I repeat nothing, gets by her. Except final due notices from the electric company. And property taxes. And renewing her driver's license. But walk in the kitchen and find your daughter spread-eagled on the floor with some random guy's face in her lap, while nuts and sugar snap peas skate around? She won't miss that. Or the subsequent jean creak.

"It's nothing. Let's go home."

I'm assuming she also didn't miss my blush.

I drove in my car, my mother drove hers, and despite my exhaustion, I used the few minutes of quiet (quiet! I'd almost forgotten what it sounded like, after the diner chaos) to take stock. Some things in town had clearly changed since I was home, and I tried to really see it.

It was beautiful, actually. Drive through Bailey Falls pretty much any time of the year and you'll convince yourself that there's not a prettier town on the planet. Autumn in upstate New York? Forget it. The flames of orange and yellow and red that raced through the forest and turned everything into a blanket of crispy, crunchy, kicky leaves—there's nothing like it. Except maybe the winter. When the snow piles for miles, and everything takes on a hushed quality, all stars and silver and moonlight. Then again, spring was pretty extraordinary, when the apple blossoms pillowed out, and the air was soft and warm and filled with that gorgeous growing green scent. Yeah, plenty going for it in the scenery department.

So why was I always so reluctant to go home, and why was I so adamant about making sure my mom knew this was temporary? It wasn't to be hurtful . . .

My eyes swept over the quaint and cute once again. It was just that Bailey Falls was like quicksand to me. Like stepping into muck in your Wellies, and trying to get out of it left you with a cold, wet foot and your shoe behind you in the puddle. It was like a whirlpool, a black hole, a Norman Rockwellian Suck-Space that was nearly impossible to escape.

That small-town Americana that everyone seemed to want nowadays? I'd grown up in it. And for a shy, dorky, apt-to-trip-over-her-own-feet teenager, I was beyond ready for an adventure when it was time to leave home. And though I hadn't lived there since I was eighteen, there was like a tiny rubber band tucked into the back of my pants, and no matter where I went or how far I traveled . . . *Helloooo, Roxie . . . your past is calling . . .* that small town was ready to snap me back eventually. And sure enough, here I was.

I certainly can't say I had a bad childhood. But I grew up early and fast, and over the years the resentment grew. The classic child-becomes-the-parent scenario. Flaky parent and studious child: watch the disconcerting yet sometimes charming storyline unfold on tonight's episode of *What'd Your Parents Do to You?* I knew it, I recognized it, I could see my issues coming a mile away. Especially when I was halfway through my twenties and my mother was halfway through her fifties, and I was still cleaning up her messes.

I was California Roxie now, but I was secretly scared to death that I'd morph back into Bailey Falls Roxie here. I'd defined *myself* in California, and I was extremely reluctant to live again in a town that defined me only as Trudy Callahan's daughter, the one who blushes a lot.

This really couldn't have come at a better time, though . . .

Okay—so I just wouldn't let it get under my skin. I'd do this for her, but this was it.

"It's good pie. Really good pie. Lard?" I asked my mother later that evening. She'd brought home the last of a pie from the diner for dessert.

"Pardon me?"

"Is there lard in the crust?" I asked again.

I'd come outside after dinner to clear my head, get some fresh air, and of course, she'd flitted after me like a moth. I realized shortly after I entered the house that my dream of going to bed with the sun was a pipe dream. But I had to admit, there was great air in the Hudson Valley—far better than that in Los Angeles.

"Oh, you'd have to ask Katie about the pie, dear; she makes it." My mother scraped her plate clean with the back of her fork, getting the last little bit.

"Have you ever asked her why she only makes cherry?" I asked, also scraping the plate clean. It was *really* good.

"No."

"Why not? Didn't you ever think that maybe, since the cherry pie is so fantastic, she might make other pies? Just as good, if not better?" I asked, licking my fork.

My mom just shrugged.

I exploded. "But you *run* the place! It's your diner! Why in the world wouldn't a business owner ask the pie woman if she *makes more pie*?" I thumped on the arm of my Adirondack chair for emphasis, and my fork clattered to the porch floor.

She looked at me for a moment; my hand was still clenched in a fist. "Just how pissed are you?"

"Pretty pissed." I sighed, setting my plate on the floor. So much for not letting it get under my skin. Evidently this was a splinter the size of a telephone pole. "I just — ugh." I set my head down where my plate had been.

"Say it, Roxie," she said.

"I'm here. And I'm going to hold down the fort while you're gone. But like I said, I'm not bailing you out again." I lifted my head to look up at her through tired eyes.

"I hardly think coming to help at your family's diner is bailing out. Not when I have a chance to go on TV and try something really new and exciting," she said.

I closed my eyes. I was feeling the effects of my drive, and not up to a fight right now.

"I agree that this time has a different feel to it. CBS programming isn't usually the method you use to get me to come home, or fix something, or make a call, or *literally* bail you out when you flood the basement because you forget to turn off the hose. But I'm talking about in the future. When these things happen again? Not going to come running. I've got my own life to take care of. I have a career—or I'm trying to, anyway. We clear?"

She opened her mouth. Then closed it. Then opened it again.

"When will you be back?" I asked quietly.

"The main producer said I won't be able to check in, something about a nondisclosure, but that in an emergency I'd be able to contact you or vice versa, so don't think that—"

"When will you be back?" I repeated.

"It depends on how well I do, how well Aunt Cheryl does, if we're able to stay in the game until the end, so—"

I used literally every ounce of patience available to me to calmly ask one more time, "When. Will you. Be back?"

"September. Hopefully by Labor Day."

Three months. I'd be here the entire summer. Wow. Would I have totally morphed back into my high school self by the time she returned?

I sat up tall. I wasn't that socially awkward girl anymore. I was a graduate of the American Culinary Institute. A private chef in Los Angeles. California Roxie, a chef so talented I once made a spotted dick so good that Jack Hamilton made a face I'm pretty sure only Grace Sheridan usually gets to see.

I took a deep breath, centered, and nodded. "Okay. The summer. That's fine."

"Really?" she asked, looking surprised and relieved.

I forced a smile. "I'm sure it will be just fine. And I'm exhausted, so I'm going to bed."

I settled into my childhood bed, surrounded by everything important to me as a teenage girl. Instead of posters of Justin Timberlake and Edward Cullen, I had a shrine to Eric Ripert and

Anthony Bourdain. Those two would make a heavenly sandwich for any woman to slip in between. If asked, I'd be their meat.

Instead of cheerleading pom-poms and pictures of the prom, I had framed menus from some of my favorite restaurants in New York City. The NoMad. WD-50. The Shake Shack. Pok Pok NY. Union Square Café. Of course Le Bernardin. See above-mentioned Ripert/Bourdain sammich.

While other girls in my high school were planning which sorority to rush next year in college and what dress to wear to prom, I was daydreaming about chanterelles and geoduck. Of the American Culinary Institute in beautiful, sunny Santa Barbara. A world away from my hometown.

And here I was, back in the house I'd grown up in. I pulled back the comforter, smiling when I smelled the homemade lavender laundry soap my mom made each summer, when the herb gardens in the backyard were thick with spicy scent.

She forgot to leave me a note on the door, but she made sure I had fresh sheets.

I slipped between them, turned off the light on my nightstand, and watched as the shadows became familiar. The glow from the old shed still shone through the back window, making the sequins dance in the blue ribbon I'd won in the pudding contest at the county fair. The dolls on the shelf above the desk were still lined up, their shapes changing a bit as the moonlight settled over them. Blue and silver, they waited to be pulled off the shelf again. I could hear the crickets, ending their first symphony of the evening, but knowing they'd only take a brief intermission before their till-dawn concert continued. I flipped and flopped in the twin bed, taking comfort and a bit of melancholy in the knowledge that nothing had changed.

The nights I spent in this room, fighting to fall asleep, fighting to relax and will myself to get a few hours in before the alarm went off—it felt exactly the same. And right on cue, that last train from Poughkeepsie heading down the Hudson sounded its lonely horn. On its way to Grand Central in the city, that sound marked the beginning of the loneliest part of the night. When I knew everyone else was asleep, and I couldn't pretend anymore that I wasn't the only person still awake.

I hated that sound.

I flopped one more time, feeling the edges of pure exhaustion begin to pull me under. I still couldn't believe I was back here.

But only for the summer. And then I'd take Grace Sheridan up on her promise to introduce me to some better people to cook for.

And if I was lucky, I'd find some *company* in the meantime.

When I woke the next morning my mother was already gone, and I was immensely thankful not to be officially on the diner work schedule yet, since my brain remained on Pacific time. As I struggled to feel even remotely alert, the specter of high school Roxie emerged again—so I called in reinforcements. Literally.

My best friend Natalie and I had met years ago when we were both freshmen at ACI in Santa Barbara. Wild-eyed eighteen year olds, away from home for the first time, we bonded, and met our other friend Clara in Basic Baking and Pastry Technique class the first day of school. Natalie and Clara both left ACI after their freshmen year, not having the passion for food as I did, but we'd remained close even though we were spread across the country. Natalie returned to her hometown of Manhattan, while Clara headed back to Boston.

"Girl. What's up?" Natalie answered on the second ring.

"Oh, the usual. Cooking. Sharpening my knives. Lounging in my childhood bedroom."

"You got a gig cooking in New York or something?"

"I got a gig cooking in Bailey Falls," I said, preparing myself for shrieking.

Natalie did not disappoint. Ten seconds later, the shriek was still ringing in my ears.

"Wait a minute, just wait a goddamned minute. You're in New York? When? How? When? Why? When? Awesome!" Another shriek. "Okay, okay. Stop yelling and tell me what happened!"

"Pretty sure I'm not the one that's yelling," I reminded her, laughing.

"Fine, fine, I'm calming down. Tell me what's going on," she said in a singsongy voice. Natalie excited meant singsongy. Although come to think of it, Natalie anything meant singsongy.

I regaled her with stories of butter and texts, lemon pound cakes and Hollywood hunks. Amazing races and bailing out Mother. She sympathized with the client loss, but didn't hide her excitement that I was closer now. At least for a little while.

"You have to come into the city as soon as possible! Or I could come see you; I never get a chance to get out of the city."

"You *choose* never to get out of the city, Nat." I laughed. A born-and-raised Manhattanite, she thought the country stopped at the West Side Highway and didn't start again until you touched down at LAX. With an occasional trip to the "country," meaning Bridgehampton.

"All the more reason for me to get off my island and come see you. Besides, after hearing you complain about your hometown all these years, the chance to actually see you in it? That's worth a Metro North ticket."

"Save the ticket. Actually, don't save the ticket, send me one. I'm already dying for a chance to get back into actual civilization.

If I'm wearing a big floppy hat and waxing poetic about aroma-
therapy by the time you see me, go ahead and tie me to the
tracks."

"Big floppy hats are totally back in, Rox," she replied promptly.
"Don't sell yourself short. You're hipper than you know."

I harrumphed in response.

"And it can't be that bad there, right? I mean, you're at least
in the same time zone now. Isn't there anything—or anyone—
that seems promising? By the way, how long have you been
there?"

"I'm just now passing the twenty-four-hour mark," I told her.
"And very few of those hours have been spent sleeping, so there
could be hallucination involved, but I did have an interesting
encounter in the back of the diner . . ." I trailed off, thinking of
slippery nuts.

"And?" she demanded.

So I filled her in about Leo and his route, perhaps leaving
out a few of the more embarrassing potato-water-related details.

"Ooooh, a summer boyfriend seems promising!" she crowed,
launching into a rendition of "Summer Lovin'" from *Grease*.

"Whoa, sister. My position on dating has not changed."

I didn't one-night-stand per se. More like . . . enough nights
to get to know the guy's body and what he liked, and to make
sure he knew what I liked, but not long enough to get into anything serious. Easy. Simple.

"Yes, but you're going to have some free time this summer.
Maybe Leo would be good *company*." I could practically hear
her waggling her eyebrows.

"Who knows? My career is still my focus, so if I need a little
something to take the edge off, I'll get a guy on standby. No
strings, no attachments. Just easy breezy fun times."

She was quiet for a moment. "That's totally how a guy would
set things up."

"Yeah, if a guy bangs chicks all over town, he's just being a guy. But if a girl does it, she's slutty, right?"

That's probably how Bailey Falls people would react. I wondered again if this was a huge mistake. But as usual, Natalie knew what I needed.

"I think it's kind of brilliant, actually," she said. "You'll make it work. Just find a way to run into him again."

"This is silly to even talk about—it's hardly the focus of my life. Now, what's up with you? Break anyone's heart lately?"

We chatted for over an hour, until I began to feel more awake and more like myself. And guilty for not maximizing every moment to figure out the diner before my mother headed off into the sunset. I promised I'd check in with Natalie again once I had things under control, and we hung up.

Chapter 5

$\mathscr{I}$ spent the next few days reacquainting myself with the family diner, picked my mother's brain about everything I needed to know to keep things afloat. Who her vendors were, when she placed her orders, who had keys and could lock up, when deliveries were made, and was she absolutely, positively married to the idea of a blue-plate special? Married she was. But she didn't say I couldn't try out something new if I was so inclined. Excellent!

As I headed toward the prep table, I heard someone say Leo's name. There was a small window between the kitchen and the station where the waitresses tended to hang, where they kept all the side items for their tables, like lemons for iced tea, extra napkins, etc. I sidled closer, staying out of sight ninja style. Sandy and Maxine were always good for local gossip, and I wanted to hear as much about Leo as I could. I was determined to redeem myself next time I saw him—as in carrying on an actual conversation.

"He's just—dammit, he's just . . . *dammit!*" Ruby said, swooning.

Maxine agreed. "I know, I hear what you're saying. Did you see that cucumber he brought last week? Gave me ideas."

"Girl, if Roy ever had a cucumber that big, you think I'd have left him?"

"Hell no! You're better off though, you know that."

"I do. I also know that I've never seen Leo around town with anyone. Maybe he's just waiting for the right gal."

"And you think the right gal for him is a fifty-seven-year-old waitress from Bailey Falls?"

"Point taken. But if I were thirty years younger, I'd be throwing myself at him."

Maxine snorted. "You'd *have* to be thirty years younger. A cucumber that size would kill you now."

"But what a way to go!"

No girlfriend in the picture. Hmmm . . . I definitely needed to be on the lookout every time a delivery dude came through the back door. Strictly for redemption's sake.

And that might also be why I found myself at the farmers' market on Saturday morning.

I mean, maybe not. I was looking to see what was in season, who had the freshest produce. After all, excellence is my area.

Okay, and perhaps I *was* looking to see if a certain someone with a certain pair of eyes and a certain pair of strong and capable hands was there. So I could speak to him as an adult this time.

He was indeed there, and he had the biggest, longest line of all the vendors. Of course.

I also noticed how different the farmers' market was from while I was growing up. Back then my mother and some other granola heads kept it alive, doing the local-food thing way back before it was hip. It was literally a few tables with giant tomatoes and the Jam Lady (best jam ever), and occasionally someone would bring in some eggs. It was held in the parking lot behind the Methodist church; there were never more than ten people at a time, including the farmers; and it usually ended with everyone sitting in the back of a truck, eating all the left-over caramel corn.

But this place was booming! The market had been relocated to the edge of town, in an old barn that was older than the town itself, from back when everything in the Hudson Valley had been farmland. Soaring high with white oak beams and rafters, it still held honest-to-goodness barn dances. And it was now home to the Bailey Falls farmers' market, with permanent vendor booths set up inside the old stalls.

Each booth had the farm's name proudly displayed over its table, which displayed whatever they were producing. Late spring greens were everywhere, turnip and mustard greens the most prominent. Lettuce of all varieties. Carrots in a riot of colors, not just orange—ruby red, purple, and vibrant yellow carrots spilled over their baskets and into customer's waiting hands. One farmer had plates of sliced fresh radish set out, with piles of coarse salt and soft butter ready for dipping. Root vegetables, spring onion, garlic, and garlic scapes, that wonderful delectable that was only available in the late spring. Asparagus stalks, thin and tender, begged to be barely blanched and then tossed with the greenest olive oil. Early strawberries, still with their vines attached. And rhubarb for days.

But farmers' markets were no longer just the territory of produce. A good farmers' market could offer almost everything you needed for a week's worth of great meals. Eggs, chicken, pork, sausage, beef—you name it, someone local was producing it. I circled the stalls, taking note of everything I wanted to try while I was in town. And as I circled, I found myself right back where I started. The big and the long—yeah yeah yeah.

Since Leo delivered to us, it would only be polite to say hi. Using the anonymity of the crowd, I give him a proper checkout. He was at least six feet two, long and lean, like someone who swam and ran track, rather than played football. He had an easy smile, and he was quick with it. I watched as he interacted with people he knew, people he didn't as he stopped to shake hands, and when he came around the table to help a little old lady carry a basket out to her car, I couldn't help but smile. Country Hipster was not only hot, but he was sweet. Lethal.

As I was getting in line to say hello I heard my name being called, and I turned to see a very good-looking man approaching. Chad Bowman?

Oh boy. Captain of the swim team Chad Bowman. Senior class president Chad Bowman. Voted Best Looking, Best Body, and Most Likely to Succeed Chad Bowman.

And he's walking toward me. The last time I saw him was at graduation, after he signed my yearbook. Then he walked away with Amy Schaefer, the prettiest girl in my school, probably to have the sex. The last time I saw him, I may have been drooling.

"Roxie? Holy shit, Roxie Callahan!" He caught me in a giant bear hug, pulling me off my feet. "I haven't seen you since, oh man, was it graduation?"

He smelled like sunscreen and honey and something intangible. Was it the scent of success? The scent of perfection? Of the good life, the incredible lightness of being handsome? The scent of knowing who you are and what you want and how to get it? Because a guy like this doesn't take no for an answer. Doesn't know the meaning of shy or nervous. He just knows awesome.

I inhaled another hit of high school royalty before he could put me down and his stunningly gorgeous wife would no doubt appear and ask why he was hugging some town girl wearing a T-shirt that said That's Not Cream Filling.

"Chad, it's great to see you, how've you been?" I managed as he finally set me down. I wasn't stammering; California Roxie had returned!

"I'm good, really good actually," he said with a wide grin. God, he even had perfect teeth. "How about you—what're you doing back home?"

"Oh, just helping out my mom. She's heading out of town for a while to do—"

"*The Amazing Race,* I heard about that!" he exclaimed, looking over his shoulder, doubtless for his wife.

"She's told half the town, I bet." I sighed, enjoying this moment in the sun with Chad Freaking Bowman. I peeked over his other shoulder. Would she be petite and brunette? Tall and blond?

"She told half the town, and that half told the other half," he chuckled, waving at someone over *my* shoulder. "Roxie, I'd love for you to meet—"

I turned to finally see—

"—my husband."

Tall and blond it is.

I ended up having coffee in a small café in the barn with The Chad Bowman and his husband, the equally charming and handsome Logan O'Reilly. Actually, I bet he was someone's *The* Logan O'Reilly. And while my high school self would have been incredibly nervous about sitting at the cool kids' table, I found myself surprisingly at ease. Perhaps I could remember who I was this summer after all.

"I can't believe how easy it is to talk to you," I admitted, taking a big bite. Bagels on the West Coast had nothing on these. Nothing.

"Why wouldn't it be?" Chad asked, looking confused.

"You're Chad Bowman," I replied simply, licking a glob of cream cheese from my thumb.

"And?" he asked after a pause.

"You're, like, the guy. And I'm sitting and talking with you like I'm a cool kid from way back! If we were still in high school, I'd assume you wanted me to help you with homework —which doesn't actually make sense, since you were in honor society. I mean really, how blessed can one guy be?"

"Oh, very. Blessed," Logan added, which made me giggle.

"I remember you were a little shy back then," Chad said, ignoring Logan's comment despite the color creeping into his cheeks.

"That's like saying you were a little gorgeous. Fortunately I've moved past most of that, though I admit I had a little nervous pang when I drove into town yesterday, wondering if it would all come screaming back." *Not at all, scrambling for nuts and peas on the floor.* Changing the subject smoothly, I asked, "So, how are you? What have you been up to since high school?"

"Things are really good. We moved back into town about a year ago from the city."

"And where are you from, Logan?" I asked.

"Iowa, then Manhattan."

"Wow, that's a big difference."

"Totally. Which is why, after Chad brought me up here to meet his folks and I got a look at life along the Hudson, I knew this is where I wanted to live."

Chad picked up the conversation. "We're renovating a house on Maple. Remember the old pink house on the corner?"

"The one with the lace curtains fluttering out of those broken windows?" I made a face. That house was hideous.

"That's the one, though you should see it now. It's come a long way. We're having a painting party next week—you should come!"

"A painting party?"

"Yeah, all the new Sheetrock just went in, and the floors

are being sanded this week. Now it's time for paint," Logan explained. "Please come."

I smiled and raised my bagel in solidarity. "I'm in."

And just like that, I had a date with Chad Bowman. And his husband. I had a sudden mental snapshot of what an actual date with these two gorgeous men might entail, and I filed it away for a lonely night with a deliciously naughty shiver.

I visited with the two of them for another half hour or so, catching up on all the high school gossip, town gossip, and gossip in general. Chad had gone from our small town to Syracuse, then on to grad school in the city, getting his MBA. He was working for a financial firm on Wall Street when he met Logan at a competing house. They'd dated, fell in love, and decided to move upstate. Investing everything they had, they opened a financial advisory company and now The Chad Bowman helped little old blue hairs with their retirement plans.

"So now you're back from LA to run the diner while your mom's out of town. Are you here just for the summer, or . . ." Chad asked as we were finishing up our snack.

"Is there a town crier?" I asked, making a show of looking around.

Chad rolled up his menu and held it to his mouth like a megaphone. "Oh please, like you don't remember how fast news travels in this town. For instance, how in the world did you manage to catch Farmer Leo between your thighs?"

I choked on my chai. "Keep your voice down!" I whisper-yelled, horrified.

"Oh please, you've got all the single ladies in this town pissed, not to mention half the married ones. Everyone wants to know how you made that happen, on your first day back in town, no less!" Chad exclaimed, and Logan nodded agreement.

"Okay, seriously, stop. I slipped and fell, and took him out as well. I don't know anything about him, except that I heard that he works over at Maxwell Farm—"

"*Works* over at Maxwell Farm?" Logan interrupted.

I nodded, continuing, "—which I think is great. I can't believe those blue bloods let that land just sit around for so many years. What a waste! And if he works there and is helping that family do something good for a change, instead of just sitting back and counting their money, then good for him."

They grew silent.

"Owning a farm, ha! It's not like a Maxwell is ever going to get his hands dirty—that'll be the day."

As I paused to sip my chai, two hands suddenly appeared in my field of vision. Rough. Ready. And . . . dirty? These hands set a small basket on the table, filled with . . . sugar snap peas. Oh man. I looked at Chad and Logan, both of whom looked positively delighted at the turn this morning was taking. Dammit.

I sighed, then turned slowly in my seat to find Leo standing behind me, wearing an equally delighted look.

"Your last name is Maxwell, isn't it?" I asked, looking up into his eyes.

"Oh yeah," he replied, making sure to wave his "dirty" farmer hands. "Brought you some sugar snaps. I picked those with my very own blue-blood hands." His eyes danced.

I picked up the peas, prepared to eat crow. Standing up, I turned toward him to apologize for the other day and the snarky comments I'd just made. But as I turned, I tripped on the leg of the chair, my forehead hitting his chest as I pitched forward into him, taking us both to the floor once more, sugar snap peas flying everywhere again. Only this time I landed on top of him.

Facedown. Between *his* thighs. As you do.

The Chad Bowman and The Logan O'Reilly applauded and took pictures.

The next moments unfolded in slow motion: those rough hands on my shoulders, lifting me off and brushing my hair from my face, one corner of his mouth raising again as he surveyed me from this reverse vantage point. He groaned as he sat up, no doubt because my frozen body was still draped across his. His chuckle as he brushed off the peas that clung to his farmery chest muscles. And then the flash of mischief in his eyes as he watched me look around wildly, trying to figure out how to get any shred of dignity I may still have left.

I could see people watching, faces I recognized, that knew me. I knew the story would be all around town within the hour, with nothing better to do in Bailey Falls on a Saturday morning than to tattle on Trudy's daughter, back in town one day and as klutzy as ever. The Hippie and the Trippie. Still on the floor, tangled with this gorgeous man, I could feel my old self telling me to run, to hide, and pretend this never happened.

Fuck all that noise.

"So, was this your idea of a *peace* offering?" I asked, plucking a pea pod from his sandy blond hair and twirling it between my fingertips. For the record, I was still draped across his lower half.

"I suppose so," he chuckled. "Although technically, you've now literally thrown yourself at me twice. Shouldn't you be offering *me* something?" His eyes were warm, and a little challenging. He seemed to be asking me to play.

Okay Farmer Boy, let's play.

I propped myself up, hand under one chin, like I was sitting at a desk instead of hovering over his plowshare. "I've got half a bagel on that table up there. You're welcome to it."

"Before I eat your bagel, we should be formally introduced, don't you think?"

He licked his lower lip. I very nearly did the same. I'd lick his lower lip till the cows came home.

"Roxie."

"Leo."

"Dying!" Chad proclaimed from the table above. I looked up and grimaced as Chad and Logan peered down, gleeful. Understandable. We were covered in peas.

Spell broken, we untangled, then retrieved the sugar snaps that were scattered across the barn floor. Leo helped me up, keeping his hand at my waist a half second longer than he needed to. We faced the peanut gallery, who hadn't helped retrieve a single pea, watching with wide grins.

I looked at my plate. "Whoops, more like a quarter of a bagel. But say the word and it's all yours."

"I'll pass," he replied, lifting one eyebrow. "For now."

"Can I at least buy you a cup of coffee, to say sorry for all the falling down?"

He looked over his shoulder toward the Maxwell Farm stand. The line was still long. "I should get back—Saturday mornings are always busy." He looked genuinely sorry to have to turn down my offer. "Rain check?"

"Sure. I'll be here all summer," I said. For the first time, without a hint of grumble.

He grinned, then nodded good-bye to the guys. As he strode off through the crowd, I sank back into my chair with a sigh, poking at my bagel.

"He's single, you know," Chad murmured, making me look up from my plate.

"Not a concern, but thank you," I said primly. "You're as bad as the waitresses at the diner. I received a similar report from them." A report they didn't know they were sharing with me, but still . . .

"He doesn't date," Chad added, his face impassive.

"Perfect. Me either," I purred, watching Leo make his way across the barn.

"Sure."

Neither of them offered any further information, so I pulled my gaze off Leo's backside, which was magnificent, and back to my bagel mates.

I sighed. "Okay, I'll bite. He doesn't date at all? You know this, how?"

"He hasn't since we've been back in town," said Logan.

"And that's why so many of the ladies here are always flocking to his stand at the market. Not just for his veggies," Chad added.

"I hadn't noticed," I told them.

"Look at your nose just grow and grow," said Chad, eyes dancing.

"I may have noticed his line was a wee bit longer than most," I conceded.

"God willing," Logan mumbled.

"Stop it." I suppressed a giggle.

"For the record, when I said he doesn't date, that doesn't necessarily mean he doesn't . . . you know . . ." Chad said meaningfully.

"He may *you know* all the time, but keeps it very quiet," Logan chimed in.

I managed to remain silent, but under the table, I dug my nails into my palm. All three of us now looked across the barn at the stall where Leo was charming the hot pants off Mrs. Sherman, an eighty-year-old retired Rockette and the local Elizabeth Taylor. Did I neglect to mention her full name was Mrs. Kitty Chase Bocci Billings Cole Billings Hobbs Sherman? She liked Mr. Billings so much she married him twice. And now she was flap-ball-changing herself right around Leo.

Who at that moment looked up with a sheepish grin and locked gazes with me.

"Hmm," I said, chewing on this and my bite of bagel. Had I found my summer *company*? I'd always had a farmer fantasy, a holdover from watching reruns of *Little House*. And holy Almanzo Wilder, this farmer was a looker.

I said good-bye to The Chad and The Logan and headed for the diner, where I was due to work the lunch shift. Doesn't date, huh? As I drove, I hummed a little song.

Summer lovin', had me a blast . . .

But all thoughts of summer lovin' went bye-bye as I pulled into the parking lot behind the diner, because there was my mother standing at the back door, dish towel in hand and a shit-eating grin on her face. "How was the farmers' market?" she asked, her voice full of mirth.

"Full of vegetables," I replied, feeling my cheeks burn as I wondered how in the world she knew already.

Small towns. For the love . . .

Chapter 6

Over the next few days, every knowing glance and furtive look reminded me how much small towns loved to gossip. My mother delighted me each day by telling me what she'd heard. I'd pushed Leo behind a snap pea display at the farmers' market and wrestled him to the ground. I'd offered him my bagel repeatedly, refusing to take no for an answer. I'd been seen out behind the market, helping him load up his vegetables and been caught holding his cucumber. That was my favorite.

But while my mother wanted to focus on whether I'd be able to remain upright this summer wherever Leo may be concerned, I was trying to get things ready at the diner so it'd be a smooth transition when my mother left. I was also fielding all sorts of questions from the intrigued public about what it had been like to be a private chef in LA. "Do they eat more than just bean sprouts?" "Have you ever met Jennifer Aniston?" "Is it true you see movie stars everywhere, even at the gas station?" Apparently retirees watched a lot of *Access Hollywood*. But no problem. Because here I was, determined to make the best of it.

As I mixed up meat loaf and shredded Velveeta to make cheesy cauliflower bake, I said, "Mom. Seriously. All the incredible cheese you could be using, some even from literally right down the road, and you're still using Velveeta?"

"People like what they like, Rox," she said, shredding cabbage for a coleslaw that she'd drown in a thick mayonnaise dressing. "You can't be such a food snob."

"Using real cheese makes me a food snob?"

"That, and the fact that your eyeballs are about to come out of your face because of the way I'm making my coleslaw," she said, not even having to turn around to see my face.

I put my eyeballs back into my face. "I have a great recipe for coleslaw. Maybe I could try it sometime?" I offered.

"You do realize my coleslaw is my mother's recipe, and her mother's before her, right?"

"I do know this, and I know people love it, Mom. I just thought that maybe we could try something new for a change and—"

"Hey, Albert!" my mother called to an older gentleman sitting at the end of the counter.

"What's the good word, Trudy?" he answered, not looking up from his newspaper. Albert had been coming in every afternoon as long as I could remember, lingering after lunch to read the funnies.

"What's your favorite side dish here?" she asked.

I rolled my eyes at the pile of Velveeta shreds.

"Coleslaw," he replied, and she turned to smile prettily at me.

"Hey, Albert!" I shouted back.

"What's up, Roxie?"

"If there was a new side dish on the menu, maybe a different kind of coleslaw, would you try it?"

"Sure, I love all kinds of coleslaw," he answered, never taking his eyes off his newspaper.

My mother's pretty smile became one with teeth.

"Hey, Albert?" she called out, voice considerably more aspartame.

"Yes, Trudy?"

"Would you say that while occasionally you might like to try something new, there's something to be said for consistency? Having what you like when you like it?" she asked.

"Sure thing," he answered.

My mother is the first person in history to swagger while shredding.

"Hey, Albert," I called out.

"Yes, Roxie?"

"Would you say that sometimes we all tend to get a little complacent and order the same thing every day, simply because it's what we're used to, and that perhaps, if someone created something new and innovative, it might be exactly the new something you were looking for, without even knowing you were looking for it?"

"You betcha."

A head of cabbage was thrown down on the counter, causing my pile of neon cheese to topple over.

"Hey, Albert!" my mother called out.

But Hey, Albert had other ideas. "Now, both of you just cram it! I'm trying to read my funnies. If I wanted to hear this kind of squabbling, I could have stayed home with my wife!"

A rustle of newspaper. A clatter as an annoyed coffee cup hit an innocent saucer. Cabbage and cheese shredding were resumed.

"Just so you know, you can make changes if you like," she said a few minutes later.

"Thanks."

"Who knows, maybe some fresh blood is just what this place needs."

"Mom—"

"When I took this place over from your grandfather, they were still serving tongue on the menu. Can you imagine?"

"Mom—"

"So when it was my turn I kept some of the old recipes, of course, but I added a few things here and there, tweaked a few ingredients now and then, and over time I revamped almost the entire menu! So you see—"

"Mom. I'm not staying," I said quietly, moving around the counter to make sure she saw me. "End of the summer, that's it. Okay?"

She looked like me like she wanted to say something else, but in the end simply nodded. "Hey, Albert—want some more coffee?" she called.

"I thought you'd never ask."

I smothered a laugh as she went out to kibitz with him, stirring the cheese sauce. My phone vibrated and I saw that I had a Facebook alert. A new friend request, from The Chad Bowman! I quickly friended him, and just as quickly got a message from him.

Painting Party Friday Night, and you're invited! Bring old clothes and some booze. We'll provide the paint and food! Love, Chad and Logan.

Awesome.

I'd always marveled at girls who could walk into any room without knowing a soul and own it. I'd watched my friend Natalie make friends with almost everyone in our class. She could talk to anyone, and did talk to everyone, and everyone gravitated toward her. Clara was quieter, a bit more serious, but still fully capable of meeting new people. Most people had the small-talk gene.

I wasn't born with it, but I'd cultivated it over time. Away from home, I'd learned from my new friends how easy it could be to socialize. Now I could go to a party where I didn't know anyone and be okay, even have fun. I'd met some of my best *company* this way. I wasn't the life of the party, but I no longer felt like the death of it.

However, knowing *everyone* at a party could be even worse than not knowing anyone—so I was a little nervous as I approached Chad's house Friday night. I knew every family and every kid and every cousin in town, and every single one of them knew me. Especially after my triumphs, winning cooking contest after cooking contest as a kid, started to make me stick out. Being emotionally invested in things like Vietnamese cinnamon versus Cambodian cinnamon tended to draw attention in your average American high school. And though Chad had been a "nice" popular kid, some of his friends sometimes fell over into the "mean" category. And some of them might be here tonight.

I was excited to be invited to a party; it made the prospect of spending the summer here more fun. But I'd be lying if I said there wasn't a little bit of High School Roxie lingering as I reached the doorstep. I reminded myself that was then, this was now. Besides, I was carrying my famous Tuscan white bean dip, studded with lemon and garlic and accented with perfectly bias-cut brioche crostini. So there. I took a deep breath and rang the doorbell.

Logan answered the door with a big hug and a smile, took my dip, handed me a brush and pail, and just like that, I was at a Cool Kids Party. And yeah, there were people there whom I remembered, but they were actually glad to see me. They asked if I was still cooking, and expressed admiration at my graduating from one of the top cooking schools in the country and envy at my living in Los Angeles, a place that was still considered very exciting and "cool" and "awesome" and "dude, that's fucking great!" No one knew how butter had sunk my career; they were just impressed I was doing something most people would never do, and they were curious.

It had never seemed hard or adventurous to me; it was just what I supposed to do. So now, chatting with people who thought I was brave for venturing out and doing something different from everyone else? Dude. I was cool.

I mingled happily, seeing more of the house. A big and sprawling old Victorian, it was in rough shape but beautiful. The main floor had gorgeous wide windows, wainscoting, and an enormous fireplace with built-in bookshelves on either side. The kitchen had been recently renovated, and Chad told me that when they knocked down an old closet to gain more room in the new kitchen, they found old newspaper clippings from a hundred years ago. The house oozed charm, even in the state it was in.

Everyone was assigned a room to paint, with each part of the house telling a different color story. I was trotted up to the third floor, where there was a giant converted attic space, with a small room off to the side with a curved exterior wall.

"Oh my goodness, is this the turret room?" I exclaimed.

"Yes, it's my favorite room in the house. The rest of the attic will be sort of a second living room, but I thought I'd make this into my home office," Chad said as I explored.

"It's perfect, I love it! What color will it be?"

He opened up a can and showed me the deepest, silkiest slate gray I'd ever seen. "I know conventional wisdom says a room this small shouldn't be this dark, but I thought it'd be cozy."

"No no, I think it's perfect," I said, laying down a drop cloth. "Now get outta here and let me paint your office."

"Knock yourself out, sister. There's more people coming over, and I'll send a few up to paint the rest of the attic so you're not alone up here for too long," he said, then headed back downstairs.

I started pouring the dark, inky paint into the paint tray. This would be a great room.

I was lost in painting when I heard someone coming up the stairs. I turned around to say hi with a smile on my face, confident I could make whoever it was feel welcome.

And of course it was Leo. And the third time was the charm apparently, because after falling down and pea flinging the first two times, *this* time I got to just slow turn and take him in. This guy was some kind of handsome.

Even better than the tall was the broad shoulders. And those eyes were going to be the death of me. Green, oh so green, and fixed solidly on me. With that twinkle. He filled up his space with an easy confidence. Not cocky, just self-assured. Now I could see the Maxwell edge that had been softened by the delivery-guy first impression. He assessed, calculated, and appraised, wearing a ten-dollar plaid shirt with an impeccably designed submariner watch. Richie Rich with a green thumb?

"Hey, it's the girl with the sugar snap peas," he said, setting down his roller and paint tray.

"Oh no, no no no, stay right there," I instructed.

"Why?" he asked, puzzled.

"Are you kidding?" I asked, looking at the minefield laid out between us. "Open paint cans, rollers, brushes—this could end very badly."

"Good point," he admitted, shrugging out of his jacket and setting it on a ladder. "But I think I'll risk it."

"I practically went down on you in public. Now, *that* was risky," I said, crossing my arms and popping out one hip with a little swagger.

Then I heard what I'd just said. I might have been overcompensating just a bit.

He began to laugh. "Where the hell did you come from?"

"LA," I said with a carefree wave of my hand, getting paint across my boobs. He laughed harder, leaning against the wall for support. I didn't have the heart to tell him I'd just painted that wall.

"So, how do you know Chad and Logan?" he asked, picking up a paintbrush.

"I went to high school with Chad, and Logan I just met. How about you?"

"They're part of the CSA out at the farm," Leo said. "I usually see them once a week when they pick up their box."

"CSA, CSA—why does that sound familiar?" I crinkled my forehead as I thought about it. "Oh sure! Community Supported Agriculture, right? They're popping up in Los Angeles too—all over California, actually. I've never belonged to one, though; how exactly does it work?"

"It's really simple. A group of people pay an agreed-upon fee before the growing season, and in return, each week they get a box of whatever's fresh from the field. The farmer gets the money in advance, which is great when figuring out a budget ahead of time, and the consumer gets a price break on the weekly box, paying less than he would at the farm stand, and much less than at a conventional grocery store."

The way his eyes had lit up told me he enjoyed educating people on what he did for a living. It also was fascinating information, and anytime someone wanted to talk food with me, I was willing. But right now, I was having a hard time concentrating because of how close he was. How good-looking he was. And thinking that if he was so passionate when he was talking about his farm . . .

"Slow food, right?" I said, aware that my voice was taking on a dreamy quality. Slightly less aware that I was rubbing a paint roller.

"Mmm-hmm. Slow." His gaze narrowed, and then he narrowed the space between us, taking just one step but doing it *slowly*. He was close enough that if my shirt somehow popped open and my bra flew off, he could likely make me come just with his mouth on my breasts.

But then I remembered I was here to paint. And paint I did.

In that small room, Leo and I painted, and we listened to everyone having a grand old time chatting in the next room. But in that tiny office? Pheromones were bouncing off the walls.

We only said things like "Can you straighten out that drop cloth?" and "Do you have one of those stirrer sticks?" and "Does this look runny to you?"—but whenever our eyes met across the empty room . . . tingly tingles. The tension was so thick that when Leo broke the silence, I jumped a little.

"So your mom said you're a private chef in California, right? She told me you cook fancy food for fancy people," he replied, dabbing paint along the windowsill. "She seemed pretty proud of you."

"Really? She used the word *proud*?"

"No, but she *seemed* proud."

"Huh," I said.

"You're just home for the summer, right? Then back to the fancy?" he asked.

I nodded slowly. Ooh, perfect opening to tell him *yeah, I'm*

here for the summer, I'll be heading back out to California in the
fall so, you know, if you want to be my company . . . . Guys usually
loved this conversation. No strings, just pure fun. I opened my
mouth to say this, but he continued before I had a chance.

"LA is great and all, but I'll take Bailey Falls any day of the
week." He saw me frown. "You don't agree?"

"I'm not big on small towns," I replied. "Everyone knows
each other's business. Everyone knows each other's history."

"They watch out for each other," he insisted.

"They gossip about each other," I corrected.

"Some people would call that charming."

"Some people would call that infuriating." I laughed, shaking my head. "Listen, I totally understand the appeal of a small
town; it's just not for me."

"Bright lights, big city?" he asked, suddenly right next to me.
His paint roller had been getting increasingly closer to my paintbrush.

"Something like that," I replied, feeling my heart thud in my
chest. "Sometimes it's nice to be just a face in a crowd."

"Not possible," he murmured, and I looked up into his eyes.
Thud. "*Just* a face? Not possible." *Thud thud.*

My pulse was racing, and it would be so easy to lift up onto
my tippytoes and surprise him with a kiss. Instead, I fumbled,
I blinked. This guy was exactly the kind of guy I normally went
for—easygoing, good-looking, funny. But he made me . . . nervous.
In a way that I hadn't been in a long time. If I was going to turn
this into anything but a painting party, I needed to get back the
upper hand.

But before that happened, I needed to clear something up
first. "I'm sorry again about that crack I made about your family,
at the market the other day," I said sheepishly. "I didn't really
mean it; I don't even know your family. I only know what the

rest of the town knows." He blinked, his face taking on an edge I hadn't seen before.

I hurriedly pressed on, my racing pulse making my words come out a little jumbled. "Obviously you've got tons of cash and old New York family and all that, and you've got all that land. And now you're working the land, and you seem as passionate about growing food as I am about cooking it, and you're all hot farmer guy, and I'm sure that's a helluva story—and holy shit, I need to shut my mouth right now."

"Roxie?"

"Uh-huh?" I responded, mortified.

"You seem very strange. But definitely . . . " There was a grin in his voice.

"Definitely . . . what?" I looked up at him.

I have never in my life wanted to ravish someone. Kiss? Sure. See naked? Sure. But when my eyes met his, I felt a powerful urge to ravish. His mouth, his neck, his chest, his stomach, and everything beneath those frayed blue jeans. And the funny thing is, I felt like he was thinking the same thing.

And if Logan hadn't come up the stairs at that moment to announce a snack break, it might've happened.

"Definitely," he repeated with a grin.

I started tidying up my work space as Logan admired the room. "You guys are speedy. You want to work on that giant sunroom on the main floor next?"

"Actually, I've got to take a pass. Got a long day tomorrow," Leo said, wiping a little bit of paint onto his shirt.

In the process, it rode up a bit. In the process, I got to see the stomach. In the process I tingled, and may have gasped the tiniest bit.

Logan noticed. Leo luckily did not. I turned quickly toward the wall to cover my blush, squeezing my paintbrush within an inch of its life. As Leo and Logan chatted behind me, I told myself it was just a stomach. A tan stomach, sure. Tan and flat and dusted with a little bit of happy trail, but it was just a stomach.

As I tried to convince myself of this, I realized that the room had grown quiet. And my skin, which was tingling again, told me Leo was standing right behind me. I turned.

"Nice working with you, Roxie."

"You too, Leo," I said. "Good painting."

Good painting? Good grief.

"Good painting to you," he said with a laugh. "I'll see you around, I'm sure."

"It's a small town," I replied. "Maybe you'll show up at my back door with your nuts again."

Leo shook his head as he turned to go, and I could hear him chuckling as he went down the stairs. I still didn't have the heart to tell him about the paint all over the back of his shirt.

I grinned at Logan, slapped him on the shoulder, and said "I'm starving. Let's go have some snacks!"

Chapter 7

That week sped by, and before I knew it, I was helping my mother pack for her reality show. And *that's* a sentence rarely uttered. The producers had given her a list of things she couldn't bring, including a phone or laptop. She'd need to be totally cut off from what was going on at home, and while that would have driven me batty, she was excited to unplug. She went through her final to-do lists with me, made sure I had everything I needed for the diner for the summer, and then was ready to go.

The trait that annoyed me the most about my mother was also one that I admired: her ability to go with the flow. Growing up, it was frustrating as hell to have my only parent be so easygoing. I wished for the kind of mom who made sure I did my homework, made sure things like permission slips were signed and bag lunches packed for field trips. But her flight-of-fancy brain also caused her to wake me up out of a dead sleep at night to make sure I didn't miss a meteor shower, and sing Christmas carols in July at the top of her lungs as we barreled up the highway because she just *had* to go to an antique fair in Albany she'd just read about.

This same attitude made it possible for her to enjoy the

trip she was about to go on and truly see it as an adventure. I watched her buzz about the kitchen, searching for a chopstick to stick into her hair bun while we waited for the car that was picking her up and taking her to the airport. Aunt Cheryl lived in Dayton, Ohio, and was meeting her in New York City. Since Aunt Cheryl was short, squatty, and cantankerous, the two of them were going to make for great television.

"Okay, is there anything else you need from me? You've got the phone numbers for all of the employees in case you need to get hold of them, and did you ever find the insurance papers in that stack I showed you on the desk?"

"I do and I did. We're good, Mom." And I was ready to take over.

"And don't forget—if the walk-in seems like its leaking, just shove a few towels under there and it's good to go. It usually only does that on really hot days, and you know how it can get in July," she said, buzzing by in a cloud of neroli and peppermint. Mom was a big fan of essential oils. Hmm, was that a hint of clary sage? She might just be a little nervous.

"I got it, Mom," I said, handing her the passport she'd just set down and now couldn't find again.

"Oh, thank you, dear, thank you." When a horn sounded outside, she almost jumped out of her skin. "Oh! That's my car, it's time to go!" She hooted, then ran out the front door. I couldn't help but laugh as I watched her excitement, helping her get her bags into the car. I doubted any of the other contestants would be traveling with a vintage army knapsack embroidered with the phrase Make Biscuits Not War on the side.

"And you've got the contact information for the producers, so if you need me, you call, right?"

"I've got it. Don't worry about a thing."

She stopped loading her bags and looked at me. "I *don't*

worry about you handling things, Roxie. That's never something I have to think about,"

"So go have fun. I'll be here when you get back," I assured her, patting her on the arm.

She caught me in a close hug, holding me tight. "You have some fun this summer too. Enjoy, okay?"

"I will, Mom."

"Use mitts if you're baking; that old oven is testy."

"I will."

"Use citronella oil if you're in the woods."

"I will."

"Use sunscreen if you go swimming in the lake."

"I will."

"Use a condom if you have sex with a farmer."

"I will—Jesus, Mother!"

She snickered, then climbed into the backseat, blowing me a kiss and telling me that she loved me. She told the driver to take her away on an adventure, and then she was gone, leaving me shaking my head. Honestly.

Ears and cheeks burning, I headed back inside and took a good look around. I had the day off, and I knew exactly how I was going to spend it. I cleaned.

I'd always been the housekeeper, and always would be. I enjoyed cleaning, and clutter made me nuts. So I stacked and straightened, dusted and swept. I didn't throw anything away, since it wasn't my house, but I did file and box up much of the stuff and nonsense. Once the living room was done, I tackled the kitchen, making the wood floors gleam and the countertops sparkle.

Taking a load of boxes out to the shed, I decided the garden could use a good weeding and made that my afternoon project. The annual beds were a tangled mess of honeysuckle vines and old shrub roses, the blooms thick and the thorns thicker.

As I was dragging a mess of cut vines back toward the trash heap, something caught my eye. Something that had been part of the backyard for so long that it was just part of the scenery: the old Airstream trailer, parked behind a row of straggly pines.

It had belonged to my grandfather, who'd used to it to travel the country on the original hippie train, Woodstock not being far from Bailey Falls. After he passed away, it was put out to pasture. It was always far down on the list of things to do, with something else always taking priority for where to spend those few extra dollars each month, and it gradually became a giant starting-to-rust elephant in the backyard, so big it was unnoticeable.

But today I noticed it, and went in for a closer look. I'd always thought these old trailers were kind of beautiful, in a retro kitschy kind of way. Very Rosie the Riveter meets the open road. But this one was half covered by weeds and listing to one side on bald tires, doubtless a home for critters as well. Someday it could be fun to look inside the trailer, but not today.

I returned to my garden work, finished it up, and then headed inside. After my mother's constant chatter for the last week or so, the small house felt big and empty.

Another day, another breakfast rush. I kept my eyes and ears open as I worked my first managing shift at the diner the next day. The employees had mostly been there for years and the place really was capable of running itself, but I knew why my mom wanted someone in charge. It was her baby, it had been her father's baby, and she was hoping it would one day be mine, no matter how many times I'd told her pigs would fly first. But that was a thought for another day; I had a breakfast shift to run. So I played short order cook, cracking eggs and slapping toast down for *Adam and Eve on a raft, wrecked*.

A steady flow of orders, constant gossip from the people doing the ordering, three burned fingers, two quarreling waitresses, and one very small grease fire later, I had successfully made it through the breakfast. And found myself once more on the business end of a potato peeler.

Concentrating on the perfection that would become my steak fries, I almost didn't hear the back door opening. But this time the farmer was smart enough to announce himself before spuds went flying.

"Are you armed?"

I peeked over my shoulder to see Leo, wearing a teasing grin. I answered it with my own and held my hands up in the air, potato in one and peeler in the other.

"I am; you may not want to come much closer," I said very seriously. I nodded toward the basket on top of the boxes he was carrying. "I can't believe you brought nuts to a potato fight."

"I'll admit it didn't go well for me last time," he said, walking over to my station and setting down the boxes he was carrying. "Or it went *very* well for me last time, depending on the point of view."

"Point of view is important," I said, setting down my peeler. He was closer than I expected and I found myself staring up into the incredible green eyes, bright and curious. "So what did you bring me today?"

Without taking his eyes from mine, he thumped lightly on the stack of boxes. "Lettuce—a few different kinds, including a new blush variety. Big mess of fennel and garlic bulbs. Leeks, celery, and a big fat rutabaga. And a special treat, the first strawberries." He lifted a small paper bag from the top of the pile, opened the top, and I peered inside. Nestled at the bottom were a handful of plump strawberries, pinky red and speckled with fragrant green leaves.

"Mmm." I breathed in. "That smells like summer."

"Doesn't it?" he answered, pulling out one of the tiny fruits. "It's a new variety we're trying this year—brown sugar strawberries. A low yield so far, but it's about the sweetest strawberry I've ever tasted."

"Yeah?" It looked the same as every other one I'd ever seen.

"Go on. Try it," he said, offering me the strawberry.

"I don't take candy from strangers."

"It's not candy, and we're not strangers. We painted together."

"And fell down a few times."

"Exactly," he nodded, holding it out once more. "Put this in your mouth."

"That's exactly what a stranger might say," I said, but opened up.

He dropped it onto my tongue, his eyes crinkling when I let out the tiniest sigh.

"That's a *great* fucking strawberry."

"I like to think so," he replied. We looked at each other exactly two seconds longer than was necessary, then moved on.

"So what's with all the walnuts?" I asked, looking at the big basket.

"There's an old grove on the property, and we're always rolling in them. So I started adding them to the foodshare, and people love them."

Suddenly inspired, I said, "I'll make a black walnut cake! I haven't made one in ages, and I could make a few, based on how many nuts you've brought me."

"I feel like so many of our conversations have been nut based," he said.

I tilted my head sideways, my thoughts drawn back from visions of thick frosting to the very handsome farmer in front of me. "Agreed. How can we change that?"

"You wanna come see my farm?"

"Hell yes. Should I bring some walnut cake?"

He nodded, and I made him feed me another strawberry.

Summer lovin', happened so fast . . .

After the lunch shift, I got out some cake pans and went to work. I'd found the recipe in an old church cookbook that I came across at a flea market when I was in school. I frequented them and garage sales for exactly this kind of thing—especially old cookbooks from bake sales and church socials. Spiral bound and usually well used, they contained recipes that stood the test of time. Meat loaf, chicken and dumplings, brisket—they were still around for a reason. But I particularly loved the desserts, especially the cakes. Good old-fashioned cakes like triple coconut. Hummingbird. Spice. Black walnut.

I'd gone straight to the black walnut cake recipe in this cookbook because it was on the most worn-out page. The pages with the spatters and the spoon rest stains were the ones used most often, so you knew they'd be good. And this one was no exception. Given to the First Methodist Church cookbook by a Mrs. Myra Oglesby of Latrobe, Pennsylvania, this black walnut recipe was "in my family for generations. My mother used walnuts from her mother's trees, picked by hand and shelled by the fire."

I loved this idea. I loved that the cookbook had grease stains and chocolate speckles throughout. I loved that someone a hundred years ago sat by a fire and shelled walnuts. In much the same way a quilt could tell a story, so could a recipe. You could approach an old recipe like a detective and whittle out clues about the people who had written it. Did a recipe call for shortening or butter? Margarine or oleo? The term *oleo* was used only by people of a certain age, so I could often date the recipe based on this one word. Occasionally, I'd get very lucky and find an old recipe box that contained handwritten index cards, and I'd marvel over the penmanship. People used to write! In cursive! On purpose!

And how charming, albeit frustrating, to find that some of these handwritten recipe cards included measurements only the family would understand. "Two spoonfuls of vanilla using the old blue enameled spoon." "Three dashes of vinegar from the green glass cruet." "Add salt till Uncle Elmer's face pinches."

The black walnut cake was a labor of love for Mrs. Myra Oglesby, and for anyone who used her recipe to bake for their family and friends. Of all the recipes I'd come across, this one was my favorite. Thick, rich, stacked high with three layers, and flecked with walnuts and cinnamon. The surprise was the slight tang from a cup of buttermilk, and the flecks of coconut that were spread throughout the cake. But the highlight? Delectable cream cheese frosting, whipped fluffy with egg whites and creamy butter.

As I pressed the final touch of chopped walnuts onto the outside edge of the cakes, I glanced out the diner's big front window and saw that it was almost dark. Where had the time gone? I quickly hurried the cakes into the old-fashioned glass display case by the cash register, where the desserts had lived since the thirties, and turned off the lights. Letting myself out the front door and into the soft early summer evening, I stopped, suddenly overcome by how truly beautiful my hometown was. Had I been taking it for granted all these years?

The streetlights were just coming on, adding another layer of gold against the sunshine peeking over the old elm trees. The streets in the downtown area were a bit higgledy-piggledy, as many of the small towns in the Northeast were. Old Indian trails, post roads, even cow paths had over the years become the roads we see today. The town was built at the foot of the Catskill Mountains, and some of the oldest homes were built almost directly into the hills themselves, with tiered porches spilling down along Main Street.

After being inside all day, I walked the long way around the block to where I had parked, breathing in that special June twilight, where even the air seemed gentle, cushiony on tired arms and legs. Kids were outside, taking advantage of those extra hours of sunshine, riding bikes and yelling back and forth in that unconcerned way all kids have of being present in the moment, and your entire world is whether you can talk your mom into having a Popsicle. I walked a little further, cutting down Locust and down along the river walk, the Hudson sparkling gold and orange. A marshy scent rose as I got closer to the water, clean and a little silty from the oozy mud.

It really was a great little town. If you liked that roll-the-sidewalks-up-at-eight kind of thing.

The next afternoon after the diner had closed, I headed over to Maxwell Farms with a slice of walnut cake as thick as my bicep riding shotgun. Mountain laurel and spiky chokeberry trees dotted the woods, and here and there the pines thinned enough to get a glimpse of the rocky stone below the surface.

I bounced along, humming a very specific song from *Grease*, feeling the sun bake into my bones through the windows. I felt a little like I was on a field trip, heading up to see the farm with the rest of my class. But this time I'd be escorted around by the farmer himself.

The very cute farmer.

This would be the time to elaborate on my farmer fantasy.

I read the *Little House* books cover to cover when I was a child, over and over again. I loved everything about this little family, and their struggles with pioneer life. I'd marvel at the fact that Ma and Pa left Laura and Mary alone, on the prairie, while they went to town . . . for hours! They were six and eight years old, and they were building fires, milking cows, and sewing on their nine-block quilts! That was free-range parenting at its finest.

When I got a little older, I'd pile onto the old couch with my mom and watch reruns of the *Little House* TV series, booing at Nellie Oleson and wondering what it must be like to have a Pa who would cry at the drop of a hat.

And then somewhere around season six, a certain blond farmer made his appearance and changed Laura's life, and little Miss Roxie Callahan's life as well. He was my first crush. Almanzo was strong, and lean, and cute as a button, and I sighed along with Laura whenever he drove his buggy through town. Even as an adult, if I was flipping through the channels late at night and an episode of *Little House* was on, I'd watch long enough to see if Almanzo was going to show up. And if he did . . .

Let's just say that if I was driving my buggy alone that night, he was a helpful addition.

And in tonight's fantasy, ladies and gentlemen, the part of Almanzo Wilder will be played by Leo Maxwell.

I shivered a little as I bounced along over the potholes toward the Maxwell Farm. Mmm, bouncing . . . more daydream fuel . . .

An enormous sign stretched across the driveway, proclaiming that I had arrived at Maxwell Farms. Stone pillars on either side held up the old oak beams spelling out the family name. It'd been here as long as I could remember. I suppose when you have more money than practically everyone, a simple name on a mailbox just isn't enough.

The property was fronted by the rural highway, and once you turned down the driveway you were enveloped in a tunnel of trees, planted to feel majestic yet protective. It was an impression, that's for sure. Tremendous live oaks, soaring proud and tall and arching across the drive toward their friends on the other side, their branches tangled together, shaking little acorn hands and making sure the sun was dappled and soft below. Signs appeared intermittently, pointing the way toward other destinations on the property. Hiking trails, turn left. English maze, head straight. Pond, turn right here. I stayed on the main road, marveling at how large the property was. It was a whole other world, living back behind this green tunnel that separated the real world from this rich one.

Now and again I'd see patches of sun on either side of the road, giving way to a meadow here, an outbuilding there. And finally, around one last curve, there was farmland as far as I could see. But not the kind of farm I'd seen as I drove across Kansas, Missouri, and Iowa. There the land was wide and mostly treeless, green corn or soybean marching away in uniform rows. But here, I saw an explosion of color. Small fields, plants of all shapes and sizes. Between the fields were bushes and small scrubby trees. There was activity everywhere I looked: people kneeling in the dirt, workers with baskets carefully picking over what looked like pole beans, someone spreading mulch on a freshly planted bed.

I even had to stop my car to let a flock of chickens cross the road. (Insert your own joke here, please.)

The main house was at the top of the hill, the highest point for miles, looking down on everything like a genteel old lady (beautiful but stone-faced). Signs pointed me to parking by the main house, and as I pulled into a spot I looked toward the enormous stone barn, where Leo told me he'd be waiting for me. And there he was, towering above a gaggle of Cub Scouts.

He caught my eye and waved, and a teeny tiny butterfly batted her wings in my tummy. I waved back, grabbed the slice of cake I'd brought for him, and set out across the yard. The barn was set up in almost a U shape, wrapped around a central yard shaded by an enormous oak tree. The fieldstone walls were half-timbered and two stories high. Wide beams were visible through open windows, their sashes painted bright red. The original hay bins now contained offices and classrooms. Maxwell Farms was not only a working farm but a teaching farm. I was hoping to learn more about what they were teaching on my tour today.

Boyish laughter made me turn from admiring the window boxes on the second floor, spilling over with brightly colored flowers, to the group clustered around Leo. The boys were jumping and shouting as he held what looked like patches over them, doling them out and calling the kids by name. As I got closer, I could hear him laughing along with the kids.

"I hear you, Owen; you'll get your activity patch too—don't worry. Who else? Here you go, Jeffrey, you earned it when you picked the biggest eggplant we've had yet this year! Who else? Let's see . . . oh boy, we can't forget Matthew—here you go, buddy. You guys are the best Webelos around."

His smile really was contagious, and I found myself grinning as I crossed the gravel, admiring his high cheekbones, the curve of his lower lip as he laughed, and the green eyes that, when fixed on mine, turned my belly all butterflies.

And that beard. What constituted a hipster beard? Is it the length? The shape? The proximity to flannel and Mumford? We were within twenty yards of an heirloom tomato; does that count as hipster cred?

I hadn't been a fan of facial hair beyond two-day sexy scruff, yet Leo was sporting an actual beard and I liked it. I more than liked it, I wanted to touch it. Was it scratchy? Soft? Coarse? Touch it, hell—I'd like to look down and see it, and his face, between my thighs. With significantly less clothing than in our previous encounters.

As my breathing speeded up, another image popped into my brain: sweaty, naked parts and grasping, clutching hands. Whew, it seemed hot out! Christ, the farmer was now affecting me physically. Which was good— I wanted physical. I needed physical. So when I saw him pick up a bottleneck squash that mimicked something very specific in my mind, I covered my moan with a cough.

"You okay?" he asked as I reached him.

"Yeah. Why?" I said, tugging at my T-shirt. Air, please—just a little air.

"Sounded like you were—"

"Just clearing my throat," I said, and quickly changed the topic. "I made the black walnut cake, with cream cheese butter-cream frosting." I thrust the white box into his hands.

"Wow, you really made me cake?" he asked, looking quite pleased.

"Well, I made it for the diner; the rest got sold today."

"Is it good?" he asked.

I grinned. "It's fucking great."

Leo closed his eyes and shook his head, and I realized I'd just F-bombed a Boy Scout troop.

"Ah shit," I muttered, then clapped my hand over my mouth.

Leo just snorted, and rallied. "Hey there, Jason, you still need your badge, right? Roxie, maybe you could run this cake over to the cooler inside the store there, huh?"

I grabbed the cake and quick-stepped away, heading for the farm stand. I had no idea how to talk to kids, but I was pretty sure swearing in front of them was high on the list of things *not* to do. I found someone to stick the cake into the fridge, took a breath, and decided to act like it never happened. I headed back to the troop.

"I didn't know you were playing with friends today," I said, nodding at the scouts.

"Actually, we've got people visiting almost every day, whether it's a class field trip, new interns rotating through, or a bunch of—"

He was suddenly knocked toward me by a riot of Webelos fighting over the final patch. The wind was nearly knocked out of me as roughly two hundred pounds of Leo collided with me, making me gasp. I was once again in his arms, but this time upright and tucked in, almost hugged. And he. Smelled. Fan. Tastic.

All around us birds chirped, dogs barked, farmhands handed, and Webelos rumpused. But in the moment, all I was aware of were his arms, snug around my waist. His hands, initially on my hips just to steady me, were now kneading like a cat, nudging underneath my defenseless T-shirt, and spreading wide to touch my very lucky lower back.

And hey look, are those my hands, pressed firmly against his flannel-covered chest? Sliding higher, higher, curling over impossibly strong muscles and moving north, around the back of his neck, feeling the tickly ends of his hair . . . And those green eyes are smoldering . . . and interested . . . and hey, I'm up on my tiptoes now, and I bet my boobs look fantastic crushed up against his—

"I'm gonna kick you in the balls!" a Webelo shouted, and I instantly backed away from the muscular chest. And the mouth, which was now tipped up at one end. And his head was nodding, saying oh yeah—this'll get finished later.

I love getting finished.

Chapter 8

But first I had a farm to tour. And once the Webelos vacated, the tour began. Just me and Leo and seventeen other people who'd signed up to be shown around what I was now learning was the premier organic teaching farm in the Hudson Valley. Some say the state. Some say the Northeast.

Some say it should have been hard for me to concentrate on things like cover crops and rotational crop planting, now that I'd had my hands in that luscious honey-blond hair. But to his credit, Leo gave a helluva tour.

What he'd done with the land since taking it over several years ago was all new to me. The estate had evolved from a house for one family into an entire business community, employing not only a year-round team but a host of summer interns, eager to learn what Leo had to teach them. In the two hours that we walked around the property, I learned more about organic and sustainable farming than I had in my entire lifetime.

"So, when you started to convert the fields back to—what did you call it?" one of the guys on the tour asked.

"It's called fallow syndrome, when fields haven't been tended to in a while. You'd think letting a field rest a bit would naturally replenish it, and that's somewhat true. But if you let farmland just sit for years and years, there's not a lot of action going on under the surface. So when we first started getting things going here, we turned the earth over, aerated and tilled it, and then planted a green manure crop in all the fields we wanted to be able to grow on."

A couple of young boys, tagging along with their parents and bored out of their minds judging by the fact that their iPhones hadn't left their hands since we left the barn, snickered. "Green manure? Is that like vegetable poo?" one of them asked, to the delight of the other.

"Nah, the poo came later," Leo fired back, clapping the kid on the back and nodding toward the iPhone. "You planning on playing on that thing the whole time?"

"Um, no?"

"Great answer. So, back to the poo—"

"Wait, the poo is real?" the kid asked, looking at his friend in disbelief.

"Dude. This is a farm. There's poo everywhere," Leo said seriously. Every single one of us did a discreet quick lift and check of the bottom of our shoes. "Green manure is a cover crop we sow to put some nitrogen back into the soil. Clover's also great for cows, which works out perfectly, since the next farm over is a dairy farm. The owner's a friend of mine, and we help each other out. I provide the grazing land, Oscar provides the four-legged poo machines, and pow."

"Poo?" the kids asked.

Leo nodded. "Nature's way of ensuring a good harvest."

Everyone nodded like this made sense.

"We usually don't have so much poo talk this early on in the tour, but every now and again we get someone in the group who can't let the word *manure* go by without a chuckle. I get it," Leo said, patting the kid on the shoulder. "Who wants to see the compost pile?"

Both kids forgot all about their iPhones for the rest of the tour, and I heard them telling their father that Leo was "awesome."

We hiked up and down hills, tucking in and out of hedgerows and along the naturally worn paths between the fields. We saw rows and rows of vegetables, almost every kind imaginable. Pole beans grew vertically up green wood stakes, teepee'd over frothy catnip plants, designed to deter pests in a natural way. Carrots were planted alternately with leeks, which encouraged growth and discouraged something called carrot fly. We stopped periodically to taste, nibbling chive flowers and the first tiny yellow pear tomatoes, planted alongside bushes of purple basil.

We visited the greenhouse, where trays and trays of seedlings were in various stages of growth. Tiny potato seedlings grew next to enormous heads of butter lettuce. We spent some time out in the fields that were deliberately resting from crop production, but hardly dormant. We were up higher on the hills now, the barns and the main house far below in a sea of green.

Just as we were leaving one of the fields, three tractors appeared, towing what looked like . . . outhouses?

"Perfect timing, here come the chickens," Leo said, herding us into a corner of the field as the tractors made their way out into the middle. "If you look at this field, compared to the one next to it, what do you see?" He looked at everyone, encouraging the kids to answer.

To my left, a field with sheep grazing. To my far left, a field with the aforementioned borrowed cows grazing. And the current field? As each tractor stopped and disengaged its little towed house there were chickens everywhere. Beautiful big birds with glossy feathers, fat and sassy and tumbling out onto the waving grass. Grass. Hmmm . . .

I looked from field to field. "You're moving the animals to mow the grass," I piped up. Leo looked straight at me, his expression lighting up at my correct answer, and a feeling of warmth started in my tummy and spread outward.

"Exactly right: the animals are mowing the grass for us." He pointed toward the cows patiently chewing their cuds. "On that field we've got a tasty cover crop of alfalfa grass, with a bit of clover mixed in. The cows chew it, crop it down to about knee high, then we move them on to the next field."

"And the sheep move into the first field, right?" I pointed to the fluffy snowballs.

"Right again, Roxie," he said, walking through the group to stand right in front of me.

For a moment, I thrilled at the sound of my name on his lips. And for another moment, I imagined him saying my name over and over again. And then for a particularly naughty moment, I forgot all about my *name* on his lips, and just imagined *me* on his lips.

And just like that, he licked them. His lips, I mean. And that sweet feeling of warmth headed straight between my legs. No longer sweet, no longer content. Just lust.

"So what do the chickens do?" someone asked.

Leo was silent, lost in studying . . . me?

"Why do you move the chickens behind the sheep?" the asker repeated.

Leo's jaw clenched. I stopped breathing.

"The chickens?" the guy repeated.

I started to tell whoever was so worried about the chickens exactly where to go, when Leo luckily intervened.

"The chickens finish the job the sheep and the cows started," he said, appearing to ground himself in the familiar material. "And in turns, they all fertilize the field. The chickens help to finish aerating the soil and feast on all the bugs left behind, making them fat and happy in a completely natural and stress-free environment. The chickens produce eggs with yolks so orange you've never seen anything like it. And the chickens"—he started off down the hill toward the main house—"are at the end of the tour. Let's head back."

The group followed dutifully behind him, and I could hear him telling them about how they could help out in their own community, or join the farmshare if they were local. Were we moving faster than normal? We sure seemed to be, as he hurried us down the hill and back to where the tour began, wrapping things up.

He caught me by the elbow as he said, "Thanks for coming out today, folks. Hope you enjoyed your tour. Anyone interested in purchasing anything we've made here on the farm, including those orange-yolked eggs I was telling you about, just see Lisa over in the store on your way out."

He waved good-bye, keeping me close to him with the other hand. My heart sped up a bit at the feel of his hand clutching my elbow. Lucky, lucky elbow. He was touching my wenis. It's a word—look it up.

"What's up, Farmer Boy," I murmured, leaning a little closer to him, grazing my breast against his arm. Now my right boob was as lucky as my right wenis.

"Didn't want you to run away with the herd. I wanted to show you something," he murmured back, smiling and nodding and still with the waving. Once the group had left, he steered me across the courtyard and around the back of the stone barn.

"Oh, the employee parking lot," I remarked as we emerged into the shade of the building, where cars with Maxwell Farms mirror tags were parked. "This is the man-behind-the-curtain stuff, where all the magic happens, right? Gee, thanks for showing me this."

"You're a bit of a smart-ass, you know that?" he asked, letting go of my wenis and climbing into an old black Wrangler. "I'd open the door for you, but I took them off last spring and haven't bothered to put them on again."

"Maybe this fall you'll get around to it?" I said, climbing in. "And yes, I've been told I'm a smart-ass. Where are we—whoa!" I'd barely buckled my seat belt before he'd backed out of the spot.

We drove down a dirt road behind the stone barns that was equal parts gravel, loose soil, and bone crunch. As we bounced along at kidney-shattering speed, he somehow managed to keep us on the road and plug his iPod into a dashboard that, when originally installed, had likely contained a tape deck. I know this because my mother still had one in our living room. This also happened to be one of her favorite albums.

"U2?" I asked, holding on to the roll bar.

"Oh yeah," he replied. "Best band in the world."

Somewhere in the world, my mother was punching the sky like the end of *The Breakfast Club*. "My mother used to play this album for hours when I was a kid."

"Did she have a favorite track?" he asked, turning us onto another dirt road, which ran along some of the fields.

"Nine," I said, knowing the *Achtung Baby* track list by heart. I smiled as soon as I heard that opening drum beat. And I waited for the annoyance that usually accompanied a thought about my mother, but it didn't come.

"Good song," he said, thumping his hand on the steering wheel in time with the music. I thumped too, while holding myself in the Jeep as we went around a tight turn. I caught him looking at me, and he unleashed a huge grin. The sun was low in the sky, a big ball of red highlighting the tall crops out this way, deeper onto the property than I'd known existed. Out here, cornstalks were climbing, wheat was waving, and . . . what was that?

"It's rye."

"As in bread?"

"As in grass—ryegrass. Great as a winter crop, cover crop, or as livestock feed, which this field will end up being. I'll put it up as hay at the end of the season, and sell it to some of the dairy farmers around here."

"Like Oscar, from the farm next door?" I asked.

"Someone was paying attention," he teased, and before I could tease him back, he made another crazy turn and we were suddenly headed into the woods.

"Where the hell are we going?"

He pointed toward the road. "This way."

I snorted. "This feels very fairy tale—into the woods and all that. You're not going to take me to a cabin made of candy and try and eat me, are you?"

"Not today," he said, giving me the side eye.

I gave it right back. "Well, isn't that too bad," I said, keeping my voice low. And just like that, he slowed down. "I was kidding! Don't go all *Children of the Corn* on me," I joked, scooching as far over as I could.

"Relax. We're here."

"Where?" We were in an entirely indistinguishable part of the woods we'd been driving through.

He walked around to my side of the Jeep and reached across me to unbuckle my seat belt. As he did, his hand brushed against the outside of my thigh, and I inhaled sharply. He turned toward me at the sound, his gaze knowing. I wrinkled my brows at him, trying to cover. But his hand on my thigh. *Oh* to the *my*.

"So where are we?" I repeated.

"Come on out of there, Sugar Snap," he said, taking my hand and pulling me out of the doorless door. He dropped my hand as soon as I was clear but I could still feel it, like a phantom hand hold. Not to mention the delight that surely showed up in my cheeks at him calling me Sugar Snap. Oh, this shit was *on* now.

He set off on a barely there path through the woods. We'd gone maybe a hundred yards when he stopped and I almost ran into his back. Recovering, I peered around him.

"What are we looking at?" I whispered.

"Why are you whispering?" he answered back.

"I don't know," I said, still whispering. "And you didn't answer my question."

"It's on the other side of that big tree." He pointed at a tree that allegedly concealed something I was supposed to be able to see.

"Leo, I hate to tell you this, but I sometimes need things spelled out for me. So if there's something I'm supposed to be seeing? I don't get it."

He pulled me in front of him and leaned down, his chin almost resting on my shoulder. He pointed with one hand, turned my hips with his other, and murmured in my ear. "See it now?"

And I did. After I got over the riot of butterflies in my tummy at the feel of Leo curving against my back, I could see the remains of an old house on a crumbling stone foundation. Trees grew up through the old walls, and the second floor had fallen into the center years ago. A chimney of fieldstone, leaning precariously, shaped the far wall, while the wall facing us was gone.

"Wow," I breathed.

"You know what's all around that house, right?" he asked, right in my ear.

Mercy. I loved the feeling of him behind me. I could so get used to it.

"No?"

"Your walnut trees." He nudged me forward on the path, his hand moving from my hip to the small of my back. "Whether the trees were here before the house, or the trees took over after the house was abandoned, I have no idea."

"Oh, now that is seriously cool," I said, delighted at the idea I was meeting the trees that made my cake so delicious. He nodded back at me, in sync on this. I loved knowing where my food was coming from. I let him lead me toward the house, picking my way carefully across fallen rock and downed limbs. The sunlight filtered through, creating a little pocket of dappled green. "This is still your property, right?"

"Technically it's my family's property, but yes. We're not even halfway across the preserve," he said, walking over to the biggest tree, knotted and gnarled.

I marveled at the idea that this family had owned so much land for so long. "So this is a walnut tree, huh? I never would have known."

"I wouldn't have known either, until I was out here one day in the fall and found all the husks on the ground. We've got another grove over by the main orchards, but we still come in and harvest here every year."

"And the house? Was this one your family built?" I asked, looking back toward the stone foundation.

"I don't think so. I've looked on a bunch of old maps and surveys of the property, and it seems like it's part of an older farm that was abandoned long before the Maxwells arrived." He said his family name with a trace of bitterness. But before I could ask anything else, he turned toward me. "Anyway, I just thought you might like to see it."

"It's nice back here. It's quiet, peaceful. There's pockets of peaceful where I live now, but you have to drive pretty far to find them."

"I've been to LA many times. *Peaceful* isn't the first word that springs to mind."

"Hmm," I said, leaning my head back against the tree and staring up into the canopy. The green overlapped, leaves and limbs weaving together, swaying high in a breeze that didn't make it down to where we standing. Leo leaned against his tree, I leaned against mine, and we were content to drink in the stillness of being so deep in a forest. I breathed in the smell of the dusty, crunchy leaves, the grassy scent of growing things, exhaling in a long slow sigh.

"Was that a 'this place is boring' sigh?" he asked from across the clearing.

I shook my head. "Hell no. That was a 'what a good day this turned out to be' sigh. Perfect weather, perfect temperature, perfect setting. I got to see why chickens cross the road, and see where walnuts come from. Compared to what my days have been like in LA lately, this was exactly what I needed."

"A good-day sigh," he repeated, pushing off from his tree and walking slowly toward me.

"A *great*-day sigh," I amended.

"An upgrade? Why the change from good to great?"

He was close enough now that I could see the bit of faint red in his beard along his jaw, the spot on his T-shirt where it was worn thin from years of washing, the veins on the inside of his tanned forearm, and how strong his hands must be.

"It's on its way from great to awesome," I answered, wrapping my arms around the tree behind me, looking for all the world like a damsel in distress. I gazed up at him through lowered lashes, California Roxie on the case. "Especially if you keep coming this way."

The grin that crept across his face was less friendly neighborhood farmer and more sexy neighborhood pirate. Then he was suddenly there, inside my dance space.

It was time to kick this summer romance into gear. There I was, leaning against a tree in a forest with my arms behind me, my breasts thrust forward in the international signal for *kiss me, you fool*. I looked like the prow of a ship. And there *he* was, all slow amble and eyes blazing and forearms temptation, a little bit stranger and a little sexy danger.

And then there *it* was—a huge bumblebee, bobbing on the unseen flower highway. It buzzed my ear, dive-bombed my neck, laughed in my face, and flew right down between my outthrust boobs.

I instantly became a flailing, screaming, beating-at-my-chest ball of freak-out. I tore off my shirt to get at the bee and ran in circles around the tree, slapping at my bra while shrieking at the top of my lungs.

"Roxie? Roxie! What the hell are you—"

"*Beeeeeeeeeeee!*" I shouted as he stopped me cold, closing his hands around my arms and trying—but not hard enough—to not look down at my tits, now struggling to stay inside their cups.

"Okay, calm down. It won't sting if you calm—"

"Yes it will! Bees are assholes!" I screamed, shimmying like Charo and trying to break away.

"Are you allergic?"

"No!"

"Then stop squirming!"

"No!"

"Settle down, please."

"Fuck off!" I thrashed as the bee buzzed inside my bra. "Beeeeee!"

My primeval brain kicked in, and suddenly a vertical escape

seemed to be my only option. I climbed Leo like a totem pole. He got a mouthful of abdomen as I surged onto his shoulders. I wrapped my legs around his head, thighs to ears, and arched backward into the tree. With bark at my back and a scream at my lips, I struck at my bra again. The bee looked at me, and I looked at him, and he glared.

Though I've never been stung by a bee before, I've always had a fear of all things buzzy. I've left garden parties, eaten inside at barbecues, and refused to hold flowers at an outdoor wedding once, all because of one tiny buzz.

I swatted at my boobs again once more, and finally succeeded in knocking him clear. He zigged and zagged drunkenly a few times, throwing me a nasty glance over his bee shoulder, then buzzed off into the forest to do whatever he was doing before the crazy lady decided to implode. "Ugh," I said, shivering.

"Ugh?" a voice said from below.

I remembered where I was, what had happened, and where Leo now had his face. Looking down, I brushed his sandy blond hair back from his brow to see his eyes staring up into mine.

Oh. I was so mortified. "I'm so sor—"

"Ah gawna seh oo donna," came the muffled reply, and I scooted further back against the tree, freeing his lips from my rather short shorts.

"Sorry?" I sang out, trying to make this not at all awkward.

"I said"—he grasped my hands—"I'm gonna"—giving me a little bounce to get him out from under—"set you"—I flew up in the air before he caught me neatly—"down now."

I stood in his arms, shirtless, hair full of bark, my chest red from my slapping. He was covered in mud from my scrambling shoes, breathing heavily, and keeping his hands firmly at my waist, holding me at a safe distance. He shook his head. "You're a bit of a train wreck, aren't you?"

I puffed a bit of hair away from my face. "Choo choo?"

Thank goodness, he laughed.

Then he gallantly turned around while I put my T-shirt back on, which was sweet, considering he'd already had a substantial peek at the goods. Then we began walking back toward the Jeep.

"So what's with the bees?" he asked.

"Where?" I asked, automatically ducking. My heart rate spiked at the thought that the bee had returned to get his revenge.

"Easy there, he's long gone."

"Good," I said, scanning the area.

"He's probably telling all of his buddies to steer clear of the lady in the woods in her underwear."

"Hey!" I said, giving him an elbow. "It was just my bra."

He just shook his head and chuckled. "No more nature for you today." He placed his hand on the small of my back again and guided me toward the road.

It was quiet, just the sounds of our feet crunching through the underbrush. I looked up at him, his face almost in shadow. It was past dusk; we'd been out in the woods for a while. The fireflies were beginning to turn on, sparking here and there in the twilight. We'd spent the better part of the afternoon together, and it had flown by.

"Bees aside, thanks for bringing me out here. And sorry again about the climbing. And the screaming."

"Next time, less screaming. Climbing is fine; just gimme a heads up," he replied with an easy smile.

By now we'd reached the Jeep. "Climbing," I announced in warning, stepping up high and settling into my seat. He stood next to the car a moment longer, and I looked at him curiously. "What's up, Leo?"

"You're only here for the summer, right?" he asked, his eyes staring intently into mine.

I felt the tiniest of jolts running through me.

"Mmm-hmm." Maybe this would be easier than I thought, if we both wanted the same thing. Did this mean . . .

He leaned into the Jeep, one hand grasping the roll bar over my head, the other resting on the dashboard. Caged in by his strong arms, I looked up into his face. The edge of his mouth lifted in a sneaky grin. "Then I should probably get going on this."

Then his lips were on mine, warm and soft. Mmm. My eyes were still open, searching his. Thrilled and emboldened by his sudden move, my mouth molded to his. The kiss was quick, too quick—before I could close my eyes and begin to revel in it, he pulled back, licking his lips and grinning like a cat.

"Hey, get back here," I insisted, slipping my hands behind his neck, my thumbs grazing his cheekbones. I pulled his mouth back to mine, luxuriating in the feel of him. His beard tickled a bit, raspy and soft at the same time. I liked it. I more than liked it. I could see how I would very quickly begin to *crave it*. I leaned into the kiss, rising out of my seat a little, brushing his lips with mine. We kissed again and again, little light lip explosions and soft teasing brushes. I sighed into his mouth, and he pulled back slightly. I tried to follow his lips, and he chuckled.

"Was that a 'this is boring' sigh?"

"Are you kidding? That was a 'please to be kissing me more' sigh." I pressed another kiss to his lips.

"'Please to be kissing me'?" he asked, his eyes full of laughter.

"Uh-huh," I nodded, placing a kiss on his forehead, his nose, his chin, and one final one on his mouth. "Is that how every farm tour ends?"

"I'd say that's a first." He laughed, leaning across me and clicking my seat belt.

"Good," I replied as he walked around to his side of the Jeep. "I like being an original."

"Oh, I'll give you that," he answered, starting up the car and giving me a sexy grin.

My toes pointed. I couldn't help it. We drove back to the main house, where he put me in my car, then kissed me once more before I left.

And as I drove home, I fiddled with my music, scrolling through songs until I found *Achtung Baby*. I'd forgotten how awesome this album was.

Chapter 9

When the alarm went off the next morning at 4:30, I began listing all the reasons I should throttle my mother. By 4:37 I had seventeen well-thought-out reasons that would be hard to prosecute under New York State law. But by 4:57 I was in the car, wet hair tied back into a bun, travel mug of coffee in hand, ready for a day of blue plates and blue hairs.

I hated being up this early, as any human would. There was nothing worse than being dragged out of bed before the sun had even thrown back its covers, to clean out grease traps and chop seventy heads of iceberg lettuce for "salad." This was my life from about the age of eleven through high school graduation. Same thing, day after day. That was part of the reason I'd chosen the private chef route: there was always something new and exciting to play around with, new menus to create, new taste buds to tantalize. Nothing ho hum there.

I squashed that thought as I headed into town. As the sun crept over the mountains, I moaned and groaned about how early it was the entire way to the diner. Yet there was something about the air this early, especially in the summer. It was clean and fresh as I drove with my windows down. Though the forecast called for rain, right now the skies were clear, without a trace of humidity.

I yawned as I pulled into my spot behind the diner. I'd slept particularly poorly last night. Was it because I'd had a farmer ambling in and out of my dreams? And in and out of . . . Well. Yes, indeed. I touched my lips in remembrance of the feel of his mouth on mine, and with a secretive smile, I unlocked the back door and started my day.

By 8 a.m. I had veggies prepped for the day, six batches of blue-ribbon meat loaf mixed up and ready for the oven for the lunch service, and I was barking right back at Maxine and Sandy when they asked for *four on two over easy*, and *fry two, let the sun shine*. I ran the griddle until Carl came in at 9, then I headed into the walk-in fridge to see about something new for tomorrow's lunch special. Wednesday had been Beef Stew Day since time began, but I thought I might try something a little different. If Albert was willing to try something new, some of the other stalwart customers might be open to it as well. Modifying the stew wasn't exactly negotiating a peace treaty in the Middle East, but it could be my own little victory.

Propping the door of the walk-in open a bit to avoid becoming trapped, I perused the shelves, noting my mother's disorganization. "Carl, you good if I work in here for a bit? Rearrange some things?" I called out.

"Sure, sure Roxie, leave me alone out here," he grumbled good-naturedly.

I knew he was happier when he was left alone. Carl had worked here as long as anyone can remember; even my mother wasn't sure how long he'd been there. One of my earliest memories was Carl flicking water on the griddle to clean it off. I liked working with him. He was quiet, he didn't let the waitresses pull him into any drama, and he never lost his cool, even when we were at our busiest.

I stepped back out into the kitchen to grab my sweatshirt.

"Call me if you get in the weeds, okay?" I stepped back into the walk-in, grabbed the clipboard from its hook, and started doing an inventory.

As I did, I rearranged everything so that like went with like. Proteins on one side, vegetables and fruit on the other. The menu was so heavily dependent on the standard diner items (Salisbury steak, chicken pot pie, burgers, etc.) that the fresh selection was a bit sparse; most of the fresh deliveries went directly into the freezer for later. As I reorganized, I started thinking of ways I could repurpose some of these ingredients. I was deeply engrossed in calculating how many pounds of potatoes I needed for fries and if I'd have enough left over to do a fennel and potato gratin when I heard a knock on the propped-open door.

"I'm coming, Carl," I called, setting down the clipboard and starting to push open the door.

"Why am I suddenly jealous of Carl?" Leo filled up the doorway with his big body and grin.

"What are you doing here?" I asked as he took a step toward me. "It's not your normal delivery day."

"Would you believe me if I said I had some beets to bring by?"

"It would depend on the beet," I said. "What else you got?"

"What are you wearing?" he asked, taking another step.

I backed up into the lettuce. "This?" I opened the sides of my very attractive gray zip-up hoodie.

"It's pretty fucking great," he said, taking the last step and slipping his hands inside my sweatshirt, settling low around my hips.

"You didn't really bring me beets, did you?" I said, not feeling the cold around me at all. I let my hands come up to his chest, sliding up and around his neck.

"I did," he murmured, his thumbs sliding underneath my T-shirt the tiniest bit. "I brought mad beets."

"Oh man," I snorted, which changed to a snort*mmm* as he nuzzled my neck. "Did you bring me anything else?"

He brought his face back to mine, tinged with the slightest of blush. "I hesitate to say it now."

"What did you bring?" I asked, shaking his shoulders.

He buried his head once again into my neck. "A really big zucchini" was the muffled reply, and I threw my head back and laughed. He continued on his nuzzle path, now sweeping kisses back up toward my ear.

"I'm taking my beets and going home," he whispered, and my laughter stopped as he licked my skin.

"No, no, you went to all that trouble to bring me that zucchini. At least let me see it."

He groaned into my neck. "Now you're just killing me." He made to pull away, and I tugged him back.

"You should stay just another minute," I said, turning my head to allow him better access to my sweet spot. Well, the sweetest spot accessible right now. "Oh yeah . . . you should definitely stay another minute . . . or seven."

He answered with a kiss on my collarbone. "Is that the diner version of Seven Minutes in Heaven? I feel like a teenager."

"I'll go you one better," I said, arching up into him, feeling my breasts press against his chest. "My mom's out of town; you wanna come over for dinner tonight?"

"Now you're talking," he told my bra strap, which he was pushing aside to dance little kisses on the skin underneath. My shoulder was in heaven. He gathered my hair back into his fist, sweeping it off my shoulders. He inhaled deeply. "Did anyone ever tell you that you smell like honey?"

"It would certainly explain the bees."

He lifted his head. "Are you aware that the second you said the word *bees,* your entire body froze?"

I sighed. "I truly believe 'so goes the colony, so goes the planet'—but bees are assholes."

He dropped his head to my back to my shoulder. "You're twisted."

I smiled. "But you still want to lick my honey, don't you?"

He groaned.

Approximately six and a half minutes later, after running his hands through his hair to smooth out the furrows my hands had made in it, and straightening my bunchy shirt, Leo backed out of the walk-in, saying, "Okay—so I'll bring you beets as long as I have them in season."

I knew he was making sure people knew he was just there for business—and not monkey business—but I couldn't help giggling.

Tonight, I was having Leo. Over for dinner. Yes, that period was intentional. It was rare that I sat down with a guy and shared a meal I had prepared. But with Leo providing so much of the food, and little potential for strings attached, it only seemed fair. And more to the point, I liked the idea of cooking for Leo. I wanted to cook for him.

I waited a few minutes, getting my giggles under control and zipping up my hoodie, wondering if my lips looked used. God *damn*, the man could kiss.

When I returned to the kitchen, clipboard in hand, everything was normal—the world had continued to turn.

But lunch was approaching, so my curiosity about the basket he'd brought me—I needed to see just how big this zucchini *was*—would have to wait. As I prepped the stew, I realized I was curious to get to the bottom of the Leo Story, as I'm sure it was a good one. And now I was off on a daydream tangent about his bottom, which was considerably cute.

I pondered this and other ponderables throughout lunch,

and during the hour afterward roasting mad beets. I had some ideas of what I wanted to make for dinner tonight with Leo, and beets would be figured prominently. And speaking of prominent, I finally peeked in the basket he left me and saw the zucchini. He should have been arrested for carrying that thing through town. Honestly.

⬿⬾

After I closed up the diner and collected my beets, I went shopping for the rest of what I'd need tonight. Being so close to the Culinary Institute of America in Hyde Park, this area had always had its share of impeccable palates. But with the farm-to-table explosion, the number of shops selling local and homegrown foods had multiplied significantly.

I'd spent the last few years being spoiled by the riches of living so close to the San Joaquin Valley, one of the greatest agricultural areas in all of the United States. Access to locally grown fruits and vegetables was something I took for granted.

But here, it was homegrown New York style. The Hudson Valley had always had a mix of people making it home. Take some hippies and richies, add a dash of old school, a sprinkle of blue blood and a dollop of millennial, with a generous helping of city professionals who owned weekend homes, and you had an eclectic melting pot.

So it made perfect sense that on Main Street, you'd find a high-end clothing store next to a shop that sold crystals promising you inner light and peace. A Realtor with pictures of multimillion-dollar "farmhouses" in the front window, next door to a dive bar advertising dollar pitchers and quarter wings.

But I was focusing on the return of the small-town butcher. A cheese shop. A bakery. An actual general store selling everything from two-dollar belt buckles to nine-dollar artisanal pickles. Ooh, and a wine shop. Locally grown, sustainably sourced bubbly to make us a little tipsy? Why, thank you, sir, I think I'll have another.

I spent the afternoon popping in and out of stores, saying hello to people I hadn't seen in ages, and stocking my summer pantry in a major way. I'd left so many of my things in LA, bringing only the basics: clothing, makeup, knives, chopsticks, a rasp, a bamboo steamer, and a fistful of saffron.

Now I filled the back of the Wagoneer with fresh pumpernickel bread, aged balsamic vinegar, and local maplewood smoked bacon. I snatched up armfuls of spices, bunches of fresh herbs, and a wedge of the stinkiest Stilton I could find, imported by a cheesemaker here in town. The cheese shop featured a wide variety from a nearby creamery, and I was willing to bet Leo would know more about those cows.

And as I shopped, I was reminded several times of things that Leo had told our group on the farm tour. What he was doing wasn't any different from how family farms had been run a hundred years ago; he was just doing it on a larger scale than most. "What grows together, goes together" was a phrase I'd heard my entire culinary life. Sometimes it applied to wine pairings with specific foods, and often it applied to herbs and the like. Take tomatoes and basil. Everyone knew they tasted great together, but I learned from Leo that they literally *grew* better when they were planted together—something about the soil and a particular pest. It was hard to pay attention at that point, because he was kneeling down, which pulled his pants tight over his very cute caboose—but the point is that tomatoes and basil planted near each other actually tasted better. Mother Nature had her shit together.

So as I shopped, I was even more aware about what went

with what, and who produced it. And why it was nice to find an honest-to-goodness butcher who not only could tell me what was the best cut of the day, but when I mentioned I needed some fresh ground pork, he lopped off a piece of tenderloin and ground it for me personally. His name was Steve. My new butcher's name was Steve.

I caught myself whistling a happy tune on my way back to my car, and for one tiny moment I found myself a little homesick. For my hometown.

But for now, I sped off in the direction of my mother's house. I had a boy coming over tonight. Thank goodness I'd cleaned the place up.

Chapter 10

A few hours later I'd opened all the windows to let the late afternoon breeze blow in, and I was back to thinking about Leo. I enjoyed being around him, and was looking forward to enjoying him naked at some point. But beyond that I wanted to get to know him, to find out what made him tick.

What would Leo think of my tiny childhood home? I wasn't ashamed of where I'd come from, but it was striking to think of how different our backgrounds were.

But I couldn't marinate on this too long, I had actual marinating to do. Tossing together some Meyer lemon, fresh tarragon, olive oil, and a pinch of salt, I poured this over the beautiful diver scallops I'd picked up at the fish market—something else new in town. I set the scallops and their marinade in the fridge, assembled the Stilton with some early cherries I'd picked out, then set about peeling the beets I'd roasted at the diner.

I was slicing the beets when I heard a car coming down the drive. A glance through the curtains showed Leo's Jeep pulling to a stop, kicking up dust. Even under his shirt, his muscles were evident as he swung down, his back strong but not rippling in a beefcakey way. Just plain awesome strength, honestly come by. I'd seen how hard he worked on his farm. And speaking of awesome, he'd ditched the T-shirt/flannel workingman's combo and was rocking the shit out of a white button-down and comfortable-looking jeans.

That beard was still there, gorgeously scruffy yet neatly trimmed, and I wanted to kiss him just to feel the tickle. I felt a thrill run up and down my spine as I imagined what it would be like to be the girl he came home to every night. Whoa. Where did that come from?

Shaking it off, I leaned out the window and called out, "The door's open, go ahead and let yourself in!"

I had the pleasure of watching his face light up at my voice. Wow, look at that.

"Well, hey there," he said, coming around the corner with a bottle of wine. "I wasn't sure what you were making, so I went with a Riesling from—wow, did you murder someone this afternoon?"

"Ha-ha," I replied, holding up the last beet I was slicing and showing him my pinky-purple hands. "Someone brought me beets, and that same someone knows exactly what they do to your hands when you mess with them."

"If I made a joke about catching you red-handed, would you laugh?"

"I think so," I said, blowing a piece of hair out of my face.

He waited a moment, looking at me expectantly.

"What'd I miss?"

"You're not laughing," he said, setting the wine down and moving a little closer.

"I was waiting for your joke," I said, blowing again at a piece of hair sticking to my face. I didn't dare touch it; the beet juice would stain almost anything it touched.

His cheeks crinkled as he laughed. "Forget it. Can I help you with that?" He leaned in and plucked the piece of hair from my face, tucking it neatly behind my ear. "Better?"

"Better," I agreed. "You hungry?"

"Starved," he replied, stepping even closer. "Famished." His hand lingered on my neck, fingertips dancing across my skin as he skimmed around to the nape, warm and heavy. "Can I kiss you without you getting my shirt all beety?"

"You can sure try," I answered, letting him pull me into him. I kept my hands straight out to my sides, trying to keep from marking him. He kissed me slow and sweet. Little fleeting brushes of his lips, first on one side of my mouth, then the other. By the time he made it to the middle of my mouth, I was rising up on my tiptoes to get closer, still keeping my beet hands out to my sides. He held my face in his hands, thumbs sweeping across my cheekbones, feathering and light. In the walk-in this afternoon, there was surprised passion. Now it was a slow burn.

His kisses swept down along my jawline, and right about the time he got to my earlobe, I had to warn him that my hands were beginning to have a mind of their own.

"If you want to keep that shirt from being ruined, you better quit while you're ahead." I groaned, lowering my head and beating it against his chest a few times.

"For the record, I'm not at all concerned about my shirt," he said as I extricated myself and headed back over to my cutting board.

"*Now* you tell me." I finished slicing the beets, washed my hands until the water ran clear, then started assembling the salad. I stacked frisée and endive leaves on two plates, topped them with wedges of the purple beets, added a handful of Leo's walnuts (for which I got an approving eyebrow), and finished with a few crumbles of good feta. I drizzled syrupy balsamic vinegar over the whole thing, added a little walnut oil, then dusted salt, pepper, and a few sprigs of fresh parsley across the top.

As I assembled, he told me about one of his heritage pigs that had gotten loose from the paddock in the woods, and how he and some of his interns spent the afternoon running through the forest, trying to tackle a hog.

"I really wish I could have seen that," I said, setting the plates down on the table while Leo opened the wine he'd brought.

"Come back again sometime and I'll show you the pigs. They're great."

"And you raise pigs for . . ."

"Pork. Bacon. Chops. Everything."

I turned from the stove, where I was getting the cast-iron pan sizzling hot for the scallops. I'd fried some bacon earlier, and it was chopped and ready to go in at the last moment. "Can I ask you something?"

"Sure," he replied, pouring wine into the glasses I'd set out.

"Is it ever weird, getting to know the animals you're going to end up killing? Do you ever get attached?"

I held my hand over the pan, testing the heat. I flicked a drop of water in, watched it sizzle and pop. Good to go. Too hot, and the scallops would burn. Not hot enough, they would just steam.

"Hmm. Not sure *attached* is the right word. How can I explain without sounding callous?" He came to stand next to me while I started the scallops. "On the tour, I talked about how everything at the farm has a purpose, right? The animals live the most stress-free life I can give them. Not just for humane reasons, which I feel very strongly about. But it's also better for me, and the rest of my farm, to let the chickens, the sheep, the pigs, even the cows that graze on some of my land live as normally as possible. When I move sheep onto a field, I get the benefit of their hooves aerating the soil. I get the benefit of the naturally occurring compost that happens when animals do their business. They get the benefit of eating clover all day under a gorgeous sky and moving around as freely as they want to. They're incredibly happy animals."

"They did seem happy," I said, watching the scallops. I resisted the urge to move them, knowing the longer I let them sit still, the more caramelized and sticky good they'd be.

"It's amazing how much better a pork chop is from a pig that's been rooting through the forest, rolling in the mud, sleeping in the shade, and living a full life. We try to produce as much as we can on the farm, try to be as diverse as we can and still maintain the quality. It's a balancing act, one I'm still learning."

He was so full of passion for what he did, his entire body perked up when he talked about it.

I checked one of my scallops—charred and gorgeous on the underside. Using tongs, I flipped each one over.

"I wonder if this was happy bacon," I said, taking the plate I'd cooked up earlier.

"Where'd you get it?"

"In town. Steve, my new favorite butcher, recommended it."

"That's very happy bacon," he said proudly. "That's from Maxwell Farms."

"Well, look at you." I grinned, watching him puff up a little bit. And why shouldn't he? It seemed like he was doing exactly what he was supposed to do.

The scallops only needed a moment on the second side, so I lifted them out of the pan. "Might want to lean back a little bit," I warned, then splashed a tablespoon or so of brandy into the pan, which I tilted slightly. The fire caught the alcohol, flames dancing furiously before dying down just as quickly. Was

I showing off a little? Maybe a touch. It was nice, cooking for someone I was . . . getting to know.

I let the brandy deglaze the pan a bit, added a pat of butter for shine, then tumbled the bacon back in. Swirling for just a moment, I finished the sauce and poured it over the line of scallops on the plate, sprinkling fresh-cut chives over the whole thing. "Well, I'm ready to eat this happy bacon, and these totally blissed-out scallops, and those supremely thrilled-to-be-here beets."

"This looks amazing—thanks so much for cooking tonight. I'd say I'd return the favor, but saying I suck in the kitchen would be the understatement of the century."

"You help me with my mother's kitchen garden out there, and I'll teach you some basic recipes. How would that be?" I offered before I thought about it. I didn't teach guys to cook. That wasn't how I operated. But what could it hurt—right?

He set the plates on the table, then looked back at me, eyes dancing. "I'd say it's going to be a busy summer."

The beets were good. The scallops were lovely. The wine was fantastic. The farmer was lickable. We chatted as we ate, and he praised everything lucky enough to be brought to his exquisite mouth. Never in my life have I been more jealous of an endive leaf. But in between my fantasies of being devoured, I actually learned a little more about Leo. I say little because he didn't share all that much.

Ask him about crop rotation, and you'll hear more than you ever thought you could. Ask him about the phrase *slow foods movement* and you'd think you were in church, listening to a testimony. But ask him about his parents, how this all happened for him, or how often he saw anyone with his same last name, and the guy clammed up like a littleneck. Thank God for Chad and Logan—and Maxine the gossipy waitress.

"But you didn't grow up here, I would remember that," I said, leaning back in my chair and allowing Leo to pour me another glass of wine. I wasn't tipsy yet, but the edges of the room were becoming *juuust* the tiniest bit fuzzy.

"Why would you remember that?" he asked, finishing off the bottle with his own pour.

"Are you kidding? When the big house got opened up again, people knew. It's like the queen: when the flag is there, she's in the house."

"*The Maxwells*. That's really how people see us, don't they? The name?" he sighed, his eyes looking tired as he swallowed his wine.

"Well, it's a bit of an institution, you have to admit." I traced the lace in the tablecloth. "I always wondered if you guys were the coffee people too."

"Very distantly related. We're just the bankers. Well, *they're* the bankers. I'm not involved in the family business anymore," he said, watching my fingertips on the table. "You were born and raised here, right? Why'd you leave?" he asked, the change of topic coming so swiftly I had to shake my head. "Other than wanting brighter lights and a bigger city."

"Uh, yeah. Born here, raised here, Bailey Falls through and through. I left right after I graduated because I wanted to add something else to the Bailey Falls. I knew what would happen if I stayed here."

"What were you so sure was going to happen?"

"It was pretty much written into the town law books that I'd inherit the diner and run it for the rest of my life. I'd like to actually have a life first."

"You didn't want the diner?"

"Do you have any idea how hard it is to try on a new hat, when everyone in your family assumes you want to wear the same one they're all wearing?" I asked, feeling some of the old weight I used to carry around, taking care of everything including my mother, beginning to pile back on.

He grimaced. "Yeah. There's a bank in Manhattan the size of a city block with my last name on it."

It was quiet except for the *plink plunk* of the faucet dripping. Of course he knew what I was talking about. There was more to that story, but he seemed content to sit in the quiet, and I wasn't about to push him.

I sipped my wine, then drained it. "So yeah, away I went to culinary school in California."

He seemed glad to turn the conversation back to me. "Even with the CIA right up the road?"

"The Culinary Institute of America is an amazing school— one of the best. But it was here, and I wanted to be there."

"California specifically?" he asked.

"Yes and no. I was intrigued by the West Coast because it was on the other side of the world, kind of. And I really liked being out there—liked the weather, the people, especially in Santa Barbara. But I think mostly it was because it was *not* here."

"But it's so great here," he said, looking puzzled. "It seems like the perfect place to grow up."

"Spoken like someone who's actually gotten to live a little," I said with a chuckle. "Where did you grow up?"

"Manhattan, mostly. I was born there, went to school there through eighth grade, then I went away."

"To prep school?"

He nodded ruefully, rolling his eyes a bit.

"Let me guess, Andover?"

"Exeter."

"Ooooo, you rowed one of those boats, didn't you!"

"You mean crew?"

"Crew! Yes!"

"I did," he replied, his face reflecting confusion and delight at my obvious enjoyment. But before I had a chance to ask him about anything else, he swung the subject back to me. "So, was there a reason you wanted out of here so bad?"

"Let's just say my mother had a lot of boyfriends, and leave it at that."

He looked a bit horrified. "Wait, you mean— did they—"

"No, nothing like you're imagining! It was just . . . my mother believes in love at first sight."

"Well, that's . . . romantic?"

"It's exhausting," I said, holding my head in my hands and peeking at him through my fingers. "It meant every new guy was the one and only, her soul mate, her be all and end all. And if, in the middle of this new exciting romance, she forgot to pay the electric bill and the lights got shut off by the power company, true love would conquer all, right?"

"True love versus electricity?"

"Well, that only happened once. But there was always stuff like that. Missing a school play because Bob had a tractor pull, or no cupcakes to bring to school on my birthday because Chuck ate them all at midnight. But the worst was the break-ups. She met her Prince Charming over and over again, and when Prince Charming inevitably left, there was the aftermath. She'd be emotionally decimated. And yet, ready to go when the next guy in shiny armor showed up."

"Sounds like she's what they call a—"

"Crazy person?"

"I was going to say *hopeless romantic*," he said, arching an eyebrow at me. "So I take it that gene wasn't passed down to you?"

"Not so much," I answered, shaking my head. "Love is messy, painful, and emotionally draining. It hardly seems worth it." He was studying me carefully: time to lighten things up a bit. "But blah blah blah, boring boring boring. Let's talk about crew some more, because now I'm imagining you on a boat without a shirt on, and hello, I'm enjoying that image!"

He grinned. "You are, huh?"

"Yeah, tell me all about your oar. What position did you play?" I asked eagerly, wanting to flesh out this fantasy with some real-life details.

He laughed. "You know nothing about crew, do you?"

"I know there's a guy at the end that chants or something."

"The coxswain?"

"Now you're talking." I sighed, playing at swooning. Emboldened by his chuckle, I hopped out of my chair and right onto his lap. He was surprised, but also seemed delighted. "Please keep saying more words like coxswain."

"You're besmirching one of the oldest traditions in American prep schools, and I won't have it," he scolded as I wriggled a bit, prompting him to push back from the table a bit to give me more room. Which enabled his arms to wrap around my waist, his thumbs tracing little arcs on my skin.

"*Besmirch* isn't nearly as good as *coxswain*," I teased. "Give me more pretty preppy words, like Izod or Perrier."

"What year do these preppies live in?" he asked, watching me with an amused grin as I played with the buttons on his shirt.

"The Year of the Coxswain has a wonderful ring to it." I leaned in and rubbed my cheek on his beard. "Did I mention how much I like this beard?"

"You haven't, but thanks. I was thinking of shaving it off, though."

"Don't do that yet, there's something I want to try first." I let my hands come up to his beard, roughing it up a bit with my fingertips.

"What might that be?" he asked, scooting the chair back a bit more. I took the opportunity to rise up a bit, throwing one leg over to straddle him.

"I can't tell you. Not yet," I said, feeling my cheeks heat up.

He held my face in his hands. "Look at you blush. I wonder what you're thinking about," he teased, happy.

"Shush," I said, laughing. I rocked forward a bit, tipping my hips and arching my back, and his face went from amused to instantly focused. "Why aren't we kissing yet?"

"Hell if I know," he replied, then kissed me strong. He kissed me hot. And when his tongue teased, my lips parted—hell, my thighs parted . . . more . . . And he kissed me wet.

And he kissed me . . . slow. Agonizingly, maddeningly, painfully slow.

I loved kissing. I also loved what it usually led to, but I was especially loving this part with Leo. The beginning, when everything is new and exciting, and everything in the entire world boils down to sweet feathering lips and quiet sighs. When the stars fade and the earth ceases to turn, its axis forgotten in the wake of things like: which way will you lean and which way will my neck naturally turn, and is it possible that I can actually detect your fingerprints, because my skin seems so alive right now and my nose just brushed yours and the tiny groan that just rumbled from deep in your chest is the most erotic sound imaginable, and gee your hair smells terrific.

I kissed him and he kissed me, and in that country kitchen we kissed for a thousand years. Or at least fifteen solid minutes. That's a long time for just kissing . . . or not nearly enough. No above-the-shirt or below-the-buckle action, no thrusting or grinding. Just kissing. My hands stayed on his shoulders. And a little bit in his hair. His hands stayed on my waist. And a little bit on my bum. Except for that glorious moment when they came up to cup my face in his hands, tracing his thumbs over my cheekbones and turning my face so that he could tickle my neck with his lips.

Slow and lazy, unhurried and some kind of wonderful, his tongue dipped against mine again and again, and I could feel little prickles and tingles all along my spine. And by little prickles and tingles I mean Katy Perry–sized fireworks, my body waking up under his hands and wanting more, needing more. If his mouth alone could do this, what might happen when other parts were involved? I felt lust tug low in my belly, pooling in my blood, threatening to run wild across my body.

I pulled back from him, my lips swollen, the area around my mouth tickled hot from his beard. My head tipped back a bit, seeming to float along, my body knowing what to do even if my mind didn't quite understand exactly what I was feeling. The feeling underneath all the swimmy and silly and tipsy from the farmer, the feeling that something epic and unusual was happening. Leo followed me back, his lips tracing a path down my neck, licking and sucking and groaning as his hands now came up to carefully thumb open one button on my shirt, and then the next.

He looked up at me, his eyes heavy and dark and thrilling. He raised an eyebrow, I nodded, and he began to peel the edges of my shirt back, revealing an edge of lace. And as he bent his head back to me, his lips barely brushing the tops of my breasts, I knew exactly where I was hoping this would go—and exactly the conversation I needed to have before it went there. Losing myself, and my fingers, in his hair, I murmured in a low voice, "Leo?"

"Mmm?" he replied, his lips tickling my throat.

"Remember what we were talking about earlier, about love at first sight, and relationships and Prince Charming and all that?"

"Mm-hmm," he said, turning those blazing eyes up toward me. "Prince Charming, sure. Were you going to ask to see my sword or something?"

I could feel his grin; it was wide enough to touch the tops of both my left and right breasts. I giggled in spite of myself, then tried to use my big girl voice. "You know I'm only here for the summer, right?"

"I'm aware. Were you aware you had a freckle in between your—"

"I'm aware," I said, groaning, my skin buzzy and tight. "But, the summer—"

"Yes, you're here for the summer. And only the summer. You mention that a lot. Do you turn into a pumpkin in September or something?"

I grinned, but then turned serious again. "I mention it a lot because I like things to be clear-cut and aboveboard, with no messy misunderstandings later on. So, you should know I don't really get involved. Actually, I don't at all get involved."

He stopped the kissing and the awesome, and lifted his face to look at me. Really look at me. He seemed to be studying me, trying to figure out what I was thinking, and what I wasn't saying. And even though I'd had this conversation with men before, this time I felt a . . . curious sort of twinge. But before I could marinate on it, he nodded. Then he returned his lips to my collarbone, and I twinged no more. And as his mouth grew heated across my skin again, as I felt my hips begin to move against his, my phone rang from across the room.

I groaned, leaning back against the table as he looked across the kitchen.

"Do you need to get that?" he asked, his hands slipping

back down to my waist and tugging me against him, holding me closer. *Yes, closer!*

"No, I don't think so," I replied, sinking my hands into his hair. Thick and silky, it curled naturally over my fingertips. We played a silent waiting game as the phone rang three times before finally going to voice mail. And in that time, we breathed together, my chest rising in time with his.

I bent over to kiss the top of his head, and he moaned. "You should do that again," he murmured into my skin.

"Do what?" I asked, repeating the motion.

"That," he answered, kissing the top of my breast. "It lets me see all the way down your shirt."

Laughing, I smacked his back, letting my nails dig in a little as I dragged my hands up toward his shoulders. In retaliation, he squeezed my waist a bit harder, his fingers digging in to a borderline tickle.

And the phone rang again. Oh, for the love . . .

I tried to reach my phone without leaving his lap, but couldn't. I huffed as I lifted myself off Leo, taking two steps forward then one step back for one more kiss. He leaned in hungrily, and one kiss became eight. Eight became thirteen. My phone stopped ringing.

Thirteen was on its way to a very magical twenty-seven when my phone rang for the third time. I literally had to pry my lips from his, using my thumb as a crowbar. "There better be something on fire," I said, finally retrieving my phone. I didn't recognize the number.

"Is this Roxie Callahan?" a man's voice asked.

"Speaking."

"This is the fire department."

Nothing was on fire. The local fire department also fielded calls from the alarm company, and the back door on the diner was open, bells going off like crazy. By the time I had my shoes on and was ready to go down there, they'd gotten hold of Carl, also on the call list, and he'd headed down to check it out. A sticky lock and a stiff breeze had worried it open, but the crisis was over. Leo volunteered to head over to the diner with me to follow up, but Carl assured me everything was okay, and I'd call a locksmith in the morning to make sure it didn't happen again.

We walked out toward his truck, his hand on the small of my back heavy and warm and . . . comforting? Hell, comfort felt a lot like horny, so I'd go with that.

"Thanks for having me over tonight. I'd say the scallops were the best part, but I think it was—"

"If you say the beets, I'll—"

"Obviously it was getting to peek down your shirt," he said deadpan. "But the beets *were* pretty great."

"Just wait till I get to work on your zucchini," I said with a wink.

"You're a little bit dangerous, aren't you?" he asked, catching me into a loose embrace and gazing down at me. The moon was full and bright, making shadows across the lawn. And in the moonlight, he was the dangerous one.

Instead of answering, I brought his head down to me and kissed him. Once more, with feeling.

Chapter 11

A few days later, Chad Bowman came waltzing into the empty diner just after the lunch shift.

"What's up, Teen Dream?" I asked as he swung himself onto one of the counter stools.

"What's up with you, Teen Dreaming of Me?" he replied, and I laughed.

"You got me there—I think I had your schedule memorized sophomore year. I knew exactly what halls to be slinking down at exactly the right time to catch a glimpse of you," I admitted, exaggerating a beating heart with my hand.

"I did that too, sophomore year," he said. "But I was hall slinking for Coach Whitmore."

"Oooh, that's a good crush," I replied, thinking of the varsity basketball coach who wore the tightest, whitest athletic shorts he could find. I wiped down the counter, noticing the time on his watch. "Yes! Closing time!" I fist pumped and headed for the front door. "High school crushes get special permission to stay, so you're good while I'm cleaning up."

"It won't take that long; I just came in for some cake. I heard a rumor that after a thousand years, this diner was serving something other than cherry pie?" He craned his neck to see into the dessert display. It was empty.

"You heard right, but I'm totally sold out of everything except"— I hurried back into the kitchen—"this." I held a plate with the last two pieces of southern caramel cake.

"Oh my God, that's gorgeous," he whispered, and I had to agree. Impossibly tall, the cake towered at three layers high. Fluffy, puffy ivory layers of butter cake, slightly tangy with buttermilk and flecked with Madagascar vanilla. Hidden between the layers was a slowly boiled homemade caramel glaze, which I'd also poured over the top and dripped down over the sides, the top crisp and shiny sweet.

"I was taking these home with me tonight, but I'd rather sit at the counter with my favorite high school crush and watch the fork go in and out of your mouth."

"I'd say that made me feel a little creeped out, but not until you give me that cake," he said, eyes not leaving the plate.

"Want some coffee to go with it?" I laughed, setting the plate down on the counter and grabbing two forks.

"What's coffee?" he asked, charmed like a snake.

"Noted," I said with a laugh, handing over a fork. I loved watching people enjoy my food. I needed coffee to go with my sweet treat, however. Before I'd finished pouring my cup, half of his cake was gone.

"What do you call this?" he asked, his mouth full. I leaned over and wiped a crumb off his chin with my thumb, brought it to my lips, and licked it off. He looked sad that I'd stolen a crumb.

"Triple Layer Southern Caramel Cake."

"Now it's the Chad Bowman Special."

"Understood," I answered, and dug into my own slice.

When I'd baked these the night before, I had no idea they'd

be such a hit. I'd made four cakes, and these two slices were all that was left. I'd started thinking about other cakes I could make, wondering how Italian Cream Layer Cake would go over. I was used to constantly testing recipes, changing and adapting them, and now I was stuck making the same spaghetti and meatballs recipe that had been on the menu since before I was born. I'd be bored out of my gourd if I didn't try something new on the menu soon.

I sighed as I tasted the caramel cake. This was an instance when an old recipe was still just as good as the day it was written down. The only thing I'd changed? I added buttermilk for a little extra tang, and used actual vanilla bean instead of just grocery store extract. Same recipe, slightly elevated. I sighed once more, tasting the sweetness of the caramel, the richness of the brown sugar.

"This is good," I admitted, and Chad nodded in agreement, his mouth full of cake. It was quiet, just the clinking of our forks as we finished our cake.

"So, how are things going with the farmer?" Chad asked, after literally licking the plate clean. I'd done the same thing to the bowl when I made the frosting.

"What farmer?" I asked innocently, taking our plates back to the kitchen so he didn't see my blushing cheeks.

"What farmer," he said with a snort. "Aren't you cute."

"Oh, *that* farmer," I answered. "I assume he's doing just fine."

"I heard a rumor he was seen driving away from your house a few nights ago. Care to comment?"

I snapped my dish towel toward him. "Where are these rumors coming from? First the cake, now this."

"My husband likes to think of himself as a small-town newspaper reporter—very *His Girl Friday*." He laughed, pretending to type furiously. "'I'm gonna break this story wide open, see?'"

"I'm the least interesting person to gossip about," I said, wiping off the crumbs from our snack. Then I grabbed the last few sugar containers from the counter stations and began refilling them from the giant sack.

"Oh, I don't think that's true at all. Shy little Roxie Callahan comes home from La-La Land with her ladle in hand to rescue the family diner, and finds something other than a ladle to grab on to at night?" he said, still in his newspaper voice.

"You are so twisted. Were you always this twisted?" I asked, handing him a container of salt and pointing him at the shakers.

"Always. I just hid it under a football helmet back then," he answered, going to work.

"You sure were cute under that helmet. And without the helmet too." I sighed, giving him my best eyelash batting.

"True, all true. But enough deflecting—what's up with the farmer?"

"I'm not deflecting. Hey, look what I found last night!" I said, holding up a canning jar I'd found in the basement. My mom's canning equipment was sitting around getting dusty since she was away, and I'd brought a few jars in to run through the dishwasher. I was craving early summer green tomato pickles like nobody's business.

"Deflect all you want—I just need know when you get into his overalls."

"I seriously doubt Leo wears overalls. Holy crap, do you think Leo wears overalls?"

"Holy crap, are you making moonshine? What's with all the jars?" he asked as I lined them up all along the counter.

"I'm making pickles, silly." I laughed.

"You know how to make pickles?"

"Chef, remember?" I said, pointing at myself. "I've even got the tall funny hat somewhere."

"Teach me how to make them. Logan is always going on and on about learning how to do stuff like that."

"Stuff like pickles?" I asked.

"Pickles, jelly, stuff in jars." He filled another shaker. "He watches a lot of *Walking Dead*."

"Not sure I get the connection between zombies and jelly."

"Like, if there was a zombie apocalypse and no one was making food anymore, eventually someone would have to start making that stuff. Except no one knows how to do that kind of thing anymore—except hippies and chefs. And what are the chances they'd make it through without getting eaten?" He said all of this as he went about filling the salt shakers, as if it was perfectly natural.

"But you're pretty sure you and Logan would make it through? Without getting eaten?"

"Exactly. We both ran track. Plus he learned how to fence in school, so he'd be like that badass woman with the swords. And when he comes home from a hard day at work killing zombies, it'd be nice to have some J on the PBJ."

"And a pickle on the side?" I asked, my forehead wrinkling as I tried to follow this train wreck of thought.

"Exactly!"

"Huh" was my only answer.

A moment later, he looked up from his pouring. "So will you teach us?"

"Sure," I said. "Be glad to. For zombies' sake." I made a mental note to pick up some vinegar at the market. *I wonder if Leo has dill weed?*

My phone rang. Hmm, speak of the farmer, and he doth appear. I mean, doth call.

"Do you have any dill weed?" I asked by way of a greeting.

"If I had a nickel . . ." Leo's deep voice trailed off. Cue shiver.

"I'll give you a nickel, I'm making pickles." I laughed, stifling the second round of shiver. I quickly focused. "I require dill weed."

"Pickles, huh? So would it interest you to know the first baby cucumbers are just about ready to pick?"

"Nothing would interest me more than your cucumber," I murmured into the phone, keeping my voice low. The Chad Bowman was now holding up the funnel like a low-tech listening device.

Leo snorted. "I'm so glad we've moved on to my cucumber, instead of talking about my nuts all the time."

"Oh, I'm sure your nuts will be fair game again soon enough."

"What was that loud noise?" Leo asked, sounding a bit concerned.

"Sorry about that, a customer just fell off his stool," I replied, shaking my head as Chad's head popped back up over the counter, his eyes still wide from the nuts. I held my finger up to my lips, warning him to keep quiet. "Nuts aside, what's up?"

"Funny that you mentioned you need dill weed, because I was calling to see if you wanted to join the CSA for the summer. You can come out and either pick up your box, or you can pick your own. I usually don't let people do that, but, you know . . ." He trailed off.

"But, you know, *I* know the farmer." I grinned, swatting at Chad's hand as he made two salt shakers kiss.

"You *could* know this farmer," Leo said, his tone darkening a bit, his voice getting a bit lower, more heated. Speaking of heated . . .

"When should I come?" I asked, mimicking his tone.

Chad bit down on a dish towel. Then spat it out, as I'd been cleaning with bleach.

"Hmm, I feel like I'm supposed to say something like . . . often? Repeatedly?"

"Good man."

"Tomorrow?"

"I can come right after the lunch shift is over," I purred, and he laughed.

"Dangerous," he said, then hung up.

Laughing to myself, I turned around to see that Chad had written OH MY GOD in salt along the counter.

"You're totally cleaning that up," I said.

Chapter 12

The next afternoon I headed out to Maxwell Farm again, with even more anticipation this time. I was looking forward to the picking of the vegetables, the signing up for the farmshare, the kissing of the lips. Mostly the kissing of the lips.

I hadn't seen him since the night I'd made him dinner, since the fire department interrupted something that was already smoldering. I'd been busy with the diner—working double shifts, replacing the back door lock, and getting back into the swing of cooking in a professional kitchen. I had new burns on my forearm from wrestling with a meat loaf, a Band-Aid on my thumb when I mistook it for a carrot . . . and a girlish urge to giggle every single time I went into the walk-in. I fought the giggle right now, just thinking about it.

When I arrived at Maxwell Farm, the fields and parking lot were a flurry of activity. I grabbed the square of ginger spice cake I'd brought Leo from the diner and set off across the gravel. It was the day everyone came to pick up their farmshare box, and I nodded to several people I knew. It was late afternoon, the sun shining down through a cloudless sky, and groups lingered around cars, almost like a farm-to-table tailgate.

Kids played with barn cats, parents chatted leisurely with other moms and dads, and the easy community feel was palpable. It was a feeling I was familiar with, but I'd never really felt it . . . on the inside before. Since my family owned the most popular diner around, if anyone should feel like they belonged, you'd think it'd be me, right? But now, as a few familiar faces smiled in my direction, and a few casually friendly waves were sent my way, I felt something suspiciously like hometown pride. Interesting.

People were leaving the main barn with large baskets filled with all kinds of produce, cartons of eggs, paper-wrapped cheese, and walnuts. Smiling, I headed inside.

There, in the middle of everything, was Leo. I was struck once more at how truly handsome he was. Women around me were similarly struck, and I felt an odd urge to strike them myself, as a matter of fact . . . He chatted easily with everyone as they came up in line for their box, asking questions about their kids, making recommendations on how to pair this with that, telling them what would be in season in the next few weeks.

The women understandably hung on every word. He was kind, his grin was warm, and his forearms were spectacular. A vintage long-sleeved Beastie Boys T-shirt was shoved up to his elbows, his skin tanned from working outside, faded, ripped jeans hanging low on his hips. When he lifted a box of rhubarb down from the truck behind him, a sliver of skin peeked out, and I saw a woman fan herself with a leaf of romaine.

His eyes rose toward the crowd, and then found mine. His easy smile changed, one corner of his mouth lifting in a sexy grin that made my pulse skippy. He waved me up through the chatting throngs, past the romaine lady, and I felt my cheeks warm at being singled out. He pointed over toward the side, where wooden crates were stacked.

"Hey, Sugar Snap," he said in a low voice, and my pulse skipped again.

"Hey, Almanzo" was all I could answer. And he called *me* dangerous.

He leaned in. "*Little House?*"

"Busted. Are you a fan?"

"Kid sister. She used to make us play Little House in the summer in the big barn," he replied, his eyes twinkling. "You hiding something behind your back?" he asked, and I proudly produced the sweet treat I'd brought for him. "For me?"

"You seemed to like the walnut cake, thought you might like something a little spicier," I said. Loudly enough for romaine fanner to hear me? It's a fair bet.

He grinned, lifting the corner of the parchment and peeking inside. "Smells good."

"Tastes even better," I answered, giving him an honest-to-goodness eyelash bat. He nodded, set the cake inside the cooler behind the table, and then turned back to me with an expectant look.

"You ready for this?"

"I think so? Not sure exactly what we're doing here." *Liar. You knew exactly what you were hoping was on tap for the day.*

"Simple," he replied, stepping out from behind the stand with a crate. "We're going shopping. Take over here for me, will you?" he asked, slapping the guy next to him on the back and handing him a clipboard.

As he led me out of the barn, he pointed out the giant deep freezers and coolers behind the workers. "Depending on the share you purchase, you can get everything and anything you want, when it's in season. Some people opt in for a small share—just produce and sometimes specialty items like mushrooms or canned tomatoes. Some people go in for the full share, and they get protein each week. Sometimes pork, sometimes beef, always chicken, either whole roasters or already cut up. Usually eggs, and sometimes cheese."

"You guys make cheese here too?" I asked, surprised at the scope of the operation.

"We don't, but we work with other farms in the area to make sure the shares are really well rounded. We partner with Oscar Mendoza, the guy who runs the creamery the next farm over, to bring cheese, milk, butter, and all that for our customers."

As I looked around, I noticed several baskets with big glass bottles of milk, smaller bottles of thick, heavy cream, and paper-wrapped butter, all stamped Bailey Falls Creamery.

"It seems like you don't even have to go to the grocery store if you're a member," I said. This was how shopping used to be, back in the day.

"That's what we hope. For the most part, you can feed your family entirely from locally sourced, clean-eating food," he said, his voice full of pride. "Supermarkets have their place; that's never going to change. But we like to think this can be just as convenient, and over time, it costs less than conventional stores."

"And you know the guy who's growing your food," I said, warming to the idea that I would be preparing food that Leo's hands pulled from the earth. Granted, I seemed to have special access to his hands this summer, but I was still tickled by the general idea. Also, his mouth. I'd like to be tickled by that mouth. Dammit, where was that romaine leaf? I needed fanning.

And speaking of his mouth, his was now turned up in a mischievous way. "What are you thinking about right now?" he asked.

"Honestly? Food."

"Just food?"

"And your mouth," I admitted.

His eyes widened, then narrowed. "C'mere." He dragged me and his basket behind the barn, into a tiny cleft of the rock wall. And then his mouth pressed into mine in a flurry of licks and nibbles, and soft little moans and sighs.

"If I said I was thinking about more than your mouth, what would that get me?" I panted between fiery kisses.

"Trouble," he replied, looking to his left and seeing a few people wandering close to where we were. "Come on, let's go fill your basket."

"I feel like that might be farm code for something way more fun than picking vegetables, but I'll indulge you." I laughed, straightening my dress, making it look like I hadn't just been pressed between a rock and a hard farmer. "This would be the time to tell you I want the full share."

"You got it." He winked and, grabbing my basket, led me out into the fields.

We wandered up and down the rows of the vegetable patch, and I marveled at everything that was just coming up. I tasted lemony sorrel and snappy fennel, and picked handfuls of tiny baby eggplant, a Japanese variety striped purple and white. In this week's share everyone was getting new lettuce, more of those brown sugar strawberries, some rhubarb, and, new this week, the first blackberries. I was mentally testing recipes, deciding what else I'd need to spice up my home dinners, and what else I could use at the diner.

And as we walked, Leo pointed out various landmarks. Where they'd tilled an unused field and discovered a hundred-year-old coffee can filled with old pennies. Where an original well was still hidden by rotting wood planks, but was now safely fenced off. The well was repurposed and used now for irrigation in the herb garden. He'd laid raised beds in the same pattern originally planted, using an old landscape blueprint he'd found in the attic of the big house, when gardens were plotted to exacting standards.

"Back then, marigold would have been planted all the way around. It's a great insect repellent," he explained as we made our way through the herbs. "You needed dill, right?"

"Yeah, I'm turning some of those little cukes and green tomatoes we picked into zombie pickles," I said.

"Should I know what that means?" he asked, kneeling down and picking a handful of dill.

"I'd hope not. Chad asked me to teach him how to make pickles. So he and Logan are coming by the diner after we close this weekend, and I'm going to show them how. The zombie part is harder to explain."

"They want to learn how to pickle?" he asked, incredulous. He bundled the dill together, wrapping the ends with a bit of kitchen twine. "Is this enough?"

"Perfect," I said as he offered it to me like a bouquet. And like a bouquet, I sniffed it. Mmm. Nothing smelled like warm, fresh herbs. "And you'd be surprised how many people want to know that stuff. The most popular class at the Learning Annex at UCLA is canning and pickling. A bunch of my clients used to take classes there. All these gorgeous plastic women with more money than they know what to do with, and they're learning how to make fifty-cent fridge pickles."

"Seriously?"

"Oh yeah. Your slow foods movement here is all about getting back to the land and local and sustainable, but it's also a rampant food trend. And nobody knows trendy like LA wives. It makes sense, though. No one in our generation knows how to do much of that stuff."

"Stuff like . . . ?"

"Pickling. Canning. Putting up preserves. Also sewing. If I

lose a button on anything, I'm screwed. My mom knows how to sew, but I never bothered to learn. And she's in the minority— most women these days are at least two generations away from those skills. Does your mom know how to sew?"

He threw his head back and laughed. "You're adorable."

"Exactly. But I bet *her* mom did—money had nothing to do with it. People used to know how to do these things, and now they don't."

"The Learning Annex. Interesting," he said thoughtfully, rubbing his beard. "Can I come to the pickle class?"

"It's not really a class," I said, playing with the dill fronds. "But, sure. If you want."

"I want."

I ran my fingers over the frothy green herbs, feeling the silk slide across my skin. *I want.* I enjoyed the way that sounded, more than I cared to admit. But what I *didn't* enjoy was the tell-tale buzz that suddenly zoomed by my ear.

"No! No no no!" I shrieked, dropping my dill and my basket and running halfway across the field before Leo knew what had happened.

"Rox! Hey, Rox!" he yelled after me, but I was running full out. "Roxie!"

I looked over my shoulder to shout back, "I told you, bees are assholes!" And because I looked over my shoulder, I tripped over a left-behind bucket, and down I went into the softly tilled dirt.

Catching up to me a few seconds later, Leo crouched down next to me. "Are you okay?" he asked, scanning me hurriedly.

"Of course." I sighed, holding my hands over my face. "I really have this thing with bees."

He pried my fingers loose, but didn't release them. He inhaled deeply. "Must be that honey."

I held my breath, aware of every point of contact between

us. On the ground, surrounded by walls of green ruffling in the breeze, we seemed cut off from the world, and asshole bees— just me and this farmer and a skirt rucked up around my thighs.

He leaned down, releasing my hands to brush my hair back from my forehead. "If you get stung, guess what happens?"

"The world ends," I answered promptly, and he gave me a pointed look.

"You get stung. That's it. It hurts, sometimes worse than others, but then it's over."

I raised up on my elbows, deliberately pushing into his space. "I'd rather not get stung at all." And then I kissed him. My lips brushed his once, twice, and I was gearing up for a third when I heard a rumble nearby.

He groaned, but held me to him for one more kiss. "Unless we want the afternoon tour to catch us taking a tumble in the catnip, we should probably get up."

"Probably." Reluctantly, as I could hear voices getting closer, I let him pull me up and we went back to where my fifty-yard dash had scattered vegetables every which way.

After Leo helped me gather them back up, he sneaked one more kiss just before the tour crested the top of the hill. We waved from where we stood, and headed in the opposite direction. We wandered from this field to that, chatting about anything and everything. He told me all sorts of trivia about the property, asked me endless questions about different ways I might use certain products from the farm, and we laughed more than I can remember doing in a very long time.

"It's great that you have access to all this history, knowing the hows and whys of how this estate came into being," I remarked as we started back toward the barn.

The day was winding down. From up high on the ridge, the only thing we could hear was the wind and the birds chirping.

My hands were dirty from digging in the beds, fingertips stained green from tugging on a stubborn parsnip.

"We didn't come here that often; mostly in the summer," he said, stopping and looking down at the big house, silhouetted against the setting sun. The Hudson was just on the other side, wide and unhurried, and he pointed in the opposite direction. "I'd spend hours out here, running through the woods, playing with the dogs. There's a creek on the far side of the property, and I can't tell you how many arrowheads I used to find along the banks. I'd come home covered in chigger bites and absolutely filthy, usually to the horror of my mother and her friends."

"My mother used to run the hose in the backyard to make a mud pit, and we'd sit there and make mud pies." The mud felt so cool on those hot summer days. "She always said mud was good for the skin. And I quote: 'All kids should get dirty, especially little girls.'"

"I can hear her saying that." He laughed, catching my hand. He examined my dirt-embedded fingernails. "So she would love this."

"She'd be thrilled," I confirmed as he turned my palm up and ran his thumb across my love line. I shivered. "I bet your mom thinks all that playing in the dirt paid off in the end. Look how awesome this place is."

He traced another line down the center of my hand, then looked off into the distance. "Let's go make sure there's some eggs left for you, before they're all gone."

He didn't say anything else about his mom, and I didn't ask. We headed down the hill toward the barn, Leo carrying my basket for me, our arms brushing occasionally.

It felt nice.

ᴇᴏ◯

There were a few cartons of eggs left, and I was delighted to see that they not only were a beautiful speckled brown, but there were a few pale blue eggs tucked inside. My share that week also yielded a big wheel of local farm cheese, a pound of fresh butter, some locally raised trout, and two roasting chickens. And some of that thick-cut Maxwell bacon. I did enjoy a thick-cut Maxwell.

By the time we finished up, the parking lot was nearly empty. It was almost dusk, and as he said good-bye to the last stragglers, I wandered into the back corner of the original dairy barn, with its enormous stone silo. It now housed a reading bench, a bookshelf, and a collection of framed photographs spanning the history of the farm. I stood in the doorway, marveling at the workmanship that had gone into the silo. How perfectly constructed it was, with a nod here and there to design, even though it was made to simply store grain.

I heard Leo saying good night to some of the guys who worked the farm, then heard his footsteps. Which came to stop just behind me. I walked through the old oaken doorway of the silo, and he followed. Once the door closed behind us, it was quiet. And dark.

"So which came first, the barn or the silos?" I asked, looking at the soaring stone walls. Perfectly cylindrical, the four silos were almost three stories tall and could be seen from all over the farm.

"The barn," Leo answered, walking toward me.

I backed away slightly, letting my gaze linger on the stone walls, and not the farmer who was now circling behind me.

"And when did you say the barn was constructed?" I asked, moving closer to the curved wall.

"Weren't you paying attention on the tour the other day?"

I traced the line of one of the fieldstones, fitting my fingertip into the groove between it and the one on top. Though the day had been warm, inside the silo the stones were cool. "I was mostly paying attention," I admitted.

"Mostly?" he asked, now directly behind me.

I shivered a bit, and not from the cool rock wall. I could feel the heat of him on my body, not yet touching, but fitting against my skin.

"I was a little"—I inhaled sharply, as those strong hands lifted my hair off my left shoulder, leaving my freckled skin exposed—"distracted," I finished weakly.

Because now he bent his head down to my skin, nuzzling into my hair. Little flickers of desire were starting to smolder all over. Thinking someone felt the same attraction you were feeling was one thing; *knowing* that it was mutual was an entirely different kind of awesome. His nose brushed against my shoulder, and my fingers opened wide against the stone.

He pressed one solitary kiss into the hollow between my shoulder and neck, and my brain went a bit fuzzy. His lips, warm and wet, continued a path up along my neck, dragging his mouth, a little bit nibbling and a lot bit incredible.

His hands settled on my hips, curving around and up as his thumbs brushed the skin exposed by the dip in my dress. My back arched as my body reacted to having him so close. Once again he nuzzled at my neck, his breath now heavy in my ear.

"If you still want to talk about construction dates and historical significance, I'm happy to oblige," he told me, then swept another line of kisses along my jawline.

I turned my head to let the man do the job he was clearly so good at. "I like history," I replied, my voice husky.

"History . . ." he said, closing his mouth around my pulse point. Pretty sure my heart tried to move closer to his lips. ". . . has its place."

"I like the present too." My hands finally tangled in his hair. "The present can be just as interesting."

And in the current present, Leo's hands were sliding up the sides of my torso to splay his fingers wide across my rib cage, just barely brushing underneath my breasts. I stopped breathing. I also stopped caring that I was unaware of how many people might be outside that heavy oaken door. A door that, while extremely thick, might not be thick enough to muffle my cries if Leo touched me where I needed him to.

Every part of my body shivered as his fingers slid up, up toward my breasts, which felt heavy and full. I sighed when the tip of his pinkie grazed my nipple. I sighed when I arched into him and felt him at my back, strong and hard and *oh* . . . hard. I sighed when his teeth nibbled just behind my ear, his teeth and his tongue and his sweet scruff rasping my skin. And I sighed when one of his hands left my breasts to sweep my hair back again, rolling my head to the side to expose the base of my neck. And I cried out when he left a trail of openmouthed kisses down the center of my back, and then licked my spine on the way back up.

He. Licked. My. Spine.

That night I tossed and turned for a different reason than usual. The breeze had dissipated, leaving the night warm and sticky. I had all the windows open with a fan blowing, trying to bring in a breath of wind. I tossed and turned because I was hot, I tossed and turned because I was an insomniac, and I tossed and turned because I was horny as hell after Almanzo Wilder very nearly worked me over in a century-old silo. And if it wasn't for a tour group very nearly catching us in flagrante de*silo*, I'd have totally let him.

I turned over onto my stomach, burying my face in my pillow as images scorched my overheated mind. His hands, sliding my dress halfway up my thighs. I exhaled loudly into the pillow, and rolled over onto my side. A minifilm played out in my mind, where Leo and his torture beard tickled my spine as he kissed a path straight down from the base of my skull down to where my dress began, *and then licked my spine on the way back up.* A dress that was one of my favorites, but if he'd torn it off and left it in a heap on the floor, I'd have shouted hallelujah and made sure that he found my bra and panties equally as offensive.

He licked my spine.

I huffed over onto my back, right leg bent up and left leg stretched to the side, trying to feel some kind of breeze, some kind of air, some kind of relief from the way my brain was burning up with fantasy flashes of sweaty, sexy bodies frolicking through a vegetable patch and doing the naughty next to some peeping tomatoes.

How do you spell relief?

T-O-U-C-H M-Y-S-E-L-F.

Well, a girl's gotta do what she's gotta do . . .

My left hand was clenched into a fist up by my head, and my entire body was clenched in a ball of tension. I forced it to unclench, forced my fingers to relax and waggle back and forth a little bit, rolling my wrist as I let my hand come down down down, ghosting along the white sheets, along the edge of my tank top and my overheated skin.

I ruffled the little bit of lace, feeling my skin pebble. I dipped my hand underneath the fabric, arching into my touch.

He licked my spine.

A moan escaped my mouth as my nipples instantly hardened, sensitive and tight. I tugged at my shirt, and my breasts tumbled out. As my left hand danced across my skin, my right hand dipped below, sliding inside my panties.

He licked my spine.

What was it about that that made me go stupid? There were certainly other body parts, much more secret, wicked, and certainly more intimate, parts. Or maybe the spine was my new erogenous zone. Maybe my entire body was my new erogenous zone. Maybe I was now zoned solely by Leo Maxwell.

But meanwhile, back on the ranch, there was only me touching my . . . mmm.

My breath caught as I felt my body coming alive under my hands. Desire pooled in my tummy, spreading all through me. What did he sound like when he came? Did he shudder, silent and strong, or did he groan, panting my name as his hand slid back and forth over his rock-hard—

I was fantasizing about what he looked like when *he* was touching himself . . . while *I* was touching myself? *So* hot.

I was on fire. I slid my fingertips down, finding my own heat. Slick and wet, I almost arched off the bed, my hips rolling as I moved my fingers, seeking that perfect balance of pressure and—*sweet Christ, that was good*! I cried out *his* name as I danced right on the edge, the pressure building in my belly . . .

Buzz.

Buzz. Buzz.

I looked to the right, saw my phone light up with an incoming text. Leo's name flashed across the screen. Leo was incoming—if only! I groaned at the interruption, but in case he'd happened to text me a picture of his prize-winning . . . rooster . . .

I snatched up my phone.

I'm outside.

Oh.

And I can hear you.

Ohhh.

You said my name.

Oh. My. God.

Let me in.

Chapter 13

I ran down the stairs and threw open the door. Leo stood in the yard, staring up at my window. Jesus, he really *did* know what I'd been up to. I went out onto the porch in my underwear, and as the screen door closed behind me, he looked my way.

His eyes widened when he took me in, barely clothed and flushed pink from what I'd been doing. He was across the yard in three strides, and had me up against the door in one more.

I should have known when he licked my spine that this guy was going to ruin me. "What are you doing here?"

"I couldn't sleep," he said, his arms caging me in, one leg nudging between mine. "Couldn't stop thinking about you." His mouth came down on my shoulder, kissing a path toward my neck, up along my jawline to my mouth. He hovered there, his breath mingling with mine. I grasped his hips, angling him toward me, the energy between us sparking and electric.

"I was thinking about you too," I whispered. As he pushed his leg farther in, his thigh into my heat, I gasped.

He nodded. "I heard."

He kissed me hard, my teeth and his colliding, heads turning this way and that. If I could have climbed inside his mouth,

I'd have done it. "Roxie?" he said, lifting his mouth from mine for the briefest of seconds. I swooped in to kiss him again, not wanting his lips to get away from me.

"Mmm?" I managed.

"Fuck," he hissed as I pulled his hips into mine once more. "I'm dying to see you."

"Me?" I asked, arching against the door to get more leverage. "What did you want to see?"

He tugged the strap of my tank top. "This." He kissed between my breasts. "You. All of you." He spoke to my skin, his breath warm.

And just like that, every sense filled with Leo. The scratch of the wooden door against my back as he thrust his hips into mine, grinding and winding me up. The way my skin reacted to his body, goose bumps rising even through the heat of the night. The way the light from the shed lit his profile, showing me hints of cheekbone, and tousled hair, and that sexy, raspy beard. The raspy beard sliding between my breasts, his nose and teeth already shoving my shirt high around my collarbone to allow him access to ravage. The groans from the back of his throat as he licked my belly button.

"You smell like honey and taste like heaven," he murmured, his rough voice reaching my dizzy ears before he rose back up my body to plant kisses over every inch of my neck.

I forgot my name. I forgot his name. I knew only that I had a doorknob in the small of my back, what felt like a doorknob between my thighs, and I was once again climbing Leo like it was exactly what I was put on earth to do.

And then the doorknob between my thighs shifted, felling much more like a door knocker. Like the kind you'd find on a really big church.

And speaking of seeing God, Leo's right hand slid up my

thigh, slipped underneath, and pulled it around his hip. That rough, callused hand on my soft inner thigh made me want to weep, it was already so good. While I was still able to speak, I lifted his head from my shoulder looked him in the eye.

"If this happens—and I *need* this to happen . . ." I paused, because though his lips had stopped, his hips had not, and the slow grind was brain melting. My own hips circled, aching, needing.

"*Need* is a curious word," he murmured with a slow circle of his hips. "You need food. You need water. You need shelter."

"Sex. Sex is also a need," I panted as his lips moved down to bite my neck. With one hand—one hand!—he tore my camisole from my body. I blinked. The poly/Lycra was now tatters and shreds. I blinked again. Holy shit.

"I was getting to the sex," he replied, using the same hand to flick open the back of my bra and toss that over his shoulder as well. Eyes flaring as he took me in, he now spoke directly to my breasts. "I was thinking that the word *need* was curious because right now, I needed to see your tits more than almost anything else in the world. Not *would have liked to*, or *gee that'd be great*—I *need* to see your tits."

Laughter bubbled up from inside me, spilling out over him, washing the sticky hot night with a tiny dose of silly, which was mirrored in his eyes as he raised them from my chest to my face, his mouth lifted slightly in the corner.

I settled into his good, strong hands, which were already so at home on my body. *At home? Dangerous.*

"I'm glad you're as happy with our arrangement as I am," I said, dodging his gaze. Why did using that term feel strange with Leo? Distant. Detached. Lonely?

I felt his gaze on me and forced mine up to meet it. He held it for a few seconds, looking carefully at me, and I could feel my resolve start to crumble. But then he nodded his head, his mouth returning to my skin, urgent, wanting, and needing. And I gave myself over to it all.

Suddenly we were lying on across the threshold, half inside the house and half out on the porch and where did my panties go? Everything was Leo, everything was his hands and his lips and his mouth and how perfectly my heel fit into that dip just above his ass and how insanely amazing his skin felt against mine and where did his shirt go? Everything was my back arching and his tongue moving and my hands grasping and his hands splaying and my hips lifting and his beard scratching and where did his jeans go?

It was an eon. It was five seconds. I have no idea how we came to be on the floor or to be naked, but all I know is he whispered, "I have a condom," and I whispered, "You were awfully presumptuous," and he whispered, "Was that wrong?" and I whispered, "Hell no, I've got one in my purse just in case you wanted to do exactly this," and he whispered, "It's been a long time for me," and I whispered, "That's okay," and he whispered, "I don't know how long I can last," and I whispered, "Fuck me furious, then," and he groaned and I moaned and. He. Pushed. Inside. He was thick and hard and I was wet and warm and he kept his eyes on mine the entire time, not letting me look away, not letting me shrink away from this intimate contact. For an age he pushed inside, as he panted and I gasped, and holy hell, it felt like the world slowed down and then stopped spinning altogether, becoming only the feel of him, pulsing low and deep and I could feel my heart literally beating around him.

Once he was inside, he didn't move. He just rose over me, his strong arms on either side of my head, and gazed down at me, something like relief on his face, something almost sad. But then the corner of his mouth lifted, and lust crowded back into his eyes, and his hips thrust into mine. "Fucking hell, Roxie," he groaned, and he laid back down on me, my legs wrapped firmly around his waist.

It was furious.

On the porch, in the middle of the night, under a cover of darkness and to the delightful sounds of mosquito zapping, I lay tangled in a heap of naked farmer. Limbs splayed, heads lolling, hands still roaming in that sweet lazy way after orgasms rocket through and turn everyone into goo. Happy goo. Intensely satisfied goo.

Leo slapped my ass.

"Pardon me?" I asked, raising my head and looking at him strangely.

"Mosquito," he grinned, showing me his hand.

"Ew." I grimaced, pushing his hand down to the porch floor and wiping it for him.

Wooden planks aren't exactly the most comfortable location for a first time. But would I change it? No way. I'd wear this doorknob imprint on my thigh proudly. I lay in the circle of his arms, one leg still wrapped high around his hips. Fast and furious it had been, the opposite of the way Leo lived his life. But I wasn't complaining. The three trips around the world had clued me in to the fact that Leo was killer in the sack. And up against the side of a house . . .

I nuzzled into his neck, smelling the warmth of his skin. Describing his scent as earthy seems too easy, but truly, it was. A bit like green growing things, loamy but clean. Accented with a tinge of Lava soap. He had a bit of hair on his chest, which was nice. Not thick in a seventies porn way, but in this day and age of manscaping, it was nice to discover some fluff under the vintage concert tees.

What could *not* be described as a "bit" of anything was what was between his legs, and I could feel it already stirring again against my bottom. I rolled over slightly to look at him, and found him watching me with lazy eyes.

"I should get you off this porch," he murmured.

I nodded vigorously. "And into my bed?"

His response was to scoop me up, throw me over his shoulder in one quick motion, and carry me into the house. "I thought you'd never ask." Inside, he looked for the stairs. "Which way?"

Laughing, I kicked up a foot and pointed. With one hand firmly wedged between my thighs, he headed toward them. "I hope you're up for round two, because I plan on going slow this time."

"And you heard me complaining . . . when?"

"I'm just saying, I hadn't planned on fucking you on the front porch," he replied, planting a kiss on my right cheek as he ran (oh my god, he ran!) up the stairs.

"If you weren't planning on fucking me, then why the late-night visit?" I giggled, pointing toward my room now with my foot.

"Oh, I planned on fucking you." He dropped me onto my bed, where I bounced back into the air. "The front porch was just the surprising part."

"How did you know I'd let you?" I asked, coming to rest. Still naked as the day is long, mind you.

Leo, also still naked and in possession of his own long day, leaned over me. Planting a kiss in between my breasts, he groaned into my skin. "I was *hoping* you'd let me fuck you." Another kiss. "And then when I heard what was going on up there—aw, hell, Sugar Snap. You were already up here fucking me, all by yourself."

A decent person would blush now. I had blushed when I fell on him, twice. I'd blushed when I thought about his beard, and where else I'd like to feel it tickle me. Occasionally I blushed when he talked so freely about his walnuts. But now? When I legitimately could and should blush?

I simply took him by the neck, pulled him down to me, and kissed him slow and sweet and long. As his tongue dipped into my mouth, I shivered. The initial itch had been scratched, and now I longed to explore, to taste, to luxuriate in getting to know his body, and how it responded to mine. We fell back onto the bed, lazy and close, the air still thick and still, but now filled with quiet kisses and the insistent creaking of my bed as we rolled and rocked.

"I think I've got some WD-40 in my Jeep," Leo murmured, and I giggled into his throat. He rolled me on top of him, and I kissed his Adam's apple.

"You think I haven't tried that before? It's just a squeaker."

"You're kind a of a squeaker too." He scooted me higher on his body, nibbling as he went. As his lips closed around my nipple, I did indeed squeak a bit. "See?"

"That was a squeal, not a squeak," I protested, beginning to pant as he surrounded me with his teeth. I squeaked and the bed creaked and the farmer laughed into my breast.

"I knew the minute you screamed at that poor bumblebee that you were going to be mouthy."

I sat up in pseudo-indignation, crossing my arms over my naked chest. "For the record, that bee and I were going to have trouble the minute I set foot in the forest. They always see me coming."

"I'd like to see you coming," he murmured, running his hands up and down my thighs, encouraging me to sit astride him. "I still can't believe how tense you get when I mention bees. Are you even aware how tight your thighs are right now on my hips? You're like a nutcracker."

"You really want to talk about bees right now?" I replied, forcing myself to relax.

"Nope." He rolled me over once more and slid down my body. "But I'll take some of that honey."

"Honey? Oh—"

I gave myself over to the feel of his lips trailing down my tummy, pausing to lick lightly just below my belly button. His mouth, planting little kisses from one hip across to the other, his hands sliding up, cupping my breasts, teasing the peaks. I gasped, my back arching again under his touch. He moved farther south, nuzzling at the very top of my thigh. I had been fantasizing for weeks what that beard might feel like between my legs.

He rested his chin about three inches above where I was dying for him to go. I bumped my hips. He pressed a kiss about two inches above where I was dying for him to go. I moaned, closing my eyes, ready to burst out of my skin at the slightest touch. I was buzzing, crackles of tension beginning to run wild across my body. And yet . . .

"Do you remember that night in your kitchen?" he asked, and my eyes flew open. Raising up on my elbows, I peered down at him. He once again rested his chin on me, looking perfectly natural and not at all concerned to find himself at the juncture of Please Oh Please and For the Love of God.

"Kitchen?" I said, trying to keep from squeaking again. I was becoming addicted to his touch, and right now, being so very close to it and being denied? It was maddening.

It was incredible.

But mostly, it was maddening.

"The night you made me dinner, and you sat on my lap and

turned the same color as the beets I brought you? Something about liking my beard?" He dipped his chin, running the length of it up and down my *yesrightexactlythere*. "Something about wanting to try something, I think. Before I shaved it off?"

"Really? Hmm, I don't remember." I nonchalantly slid my ankles down a little farther, bending my knees slightly, and oops. I bumped him with my *yesrightexactlytheredammit*. "Oops."

His grin widened at my oops. My knees widened at his grin. There really was only one way this was going to end.

"See now, I'm amazed you can't remember. Whatever made you blush that night, you sure seemed to be thinking about something fairly specific." He dipped down, running the tip of his nose across my skin, over a valley and a couple of dells. The farmer was very much in the dell. I was panting. I very deliberately slipped my heels across his shoulders, maintaining an air not so much of nonchalance but of . . . whatever was the opposite of nonchalance. My heels and I were the epitome of chalance. "Sure, you can't remember," he breathed, his lips mere centimeters from the center of the entire world.

"I might . . . remember . . . something . . ." I said, feeling a rush of heat spreading through me. The only part of him touching me was his breath, and I was feeling more and more sure I could get off on air alone, providing it was Air Leo.

"You say it," he offered, brushing his lips across mine. "And I'll do it."

I was past playing games. As he slid his eager hands along the underside of my thighs, pushing my legs higher over his shoulders and anchoring my hips with his palms, I squeaked. "Please, your mouth. I need your mouth!" I cried. And he complied.

At the first stroke of his tongue, I fell back against the pillows. At the first nibble of his teeth, I threw the pillow from the bed. At the first moan from his lips, deep into the center of that world, I bowed so hard off the bed I pulled the fitted sheet free. And when he sucked me into his mouth, burying his face and licking furiously, I could feel that beard tickling the very softest part of my thighs. And it was so. Very. Good.

Worth every squeak.

"So who are the two old guys?"

"Old guys?" I asked, not sure where this was going.

"Over the desk," he said, referencing the bulletin board. "One of them looks familiar, actually."

"They're Ripert and Bourdain. Celebrity chefs."

"Sounds like a French cop show."

I laughed. "Anthony Bourdain was a chef in Manhattan for many years; now he's got a couple of shows on traveling, eating, et cetera. Eric Ripert runs Le Bernardin, also in—"

"Aha! That's why he looks familiar."

"Makes sense; he's been on TV forever."

He shook his head. "No no, the other guy. Le Bernardin is my father's favorite restaurant. My parents have a standing reservation; they're there at least twice a month."

Somewhere in the world, tiny chef heads exploded. The idea that there could be a life where you could regularly go to Le Bernardin even once a month—but twice? At *least*? That was the most decadent morsel of that entire sentence.

I stifled my own envious head explosion and took the time to admire his posterior from where I was curled up in a comfy ball. Leo had about the cutest butt I'd ever seen. Round and firm, like two scoops of sexy. It walked, er, he walked, over toward the front window and looked out. "The wind finally picked up again."

"Oh yeah?"

"Our clothes are all over the backyard."

I chuckled, and started to get up.

"No no, you relax. I'll go get the clothes."

"And I'll let you get my clothes," I said, heading over to join him. "I'm going to make us something to eat." I added a slap to his sexy scoops and headed downstairs.

Soon we had a few layers of clothing back on, and I was swirling a pan of hot olive oil and garlic. Leo, looking all kinds of rumpled soft sexy in just his jeans, leaned over my shoulder to see what I was making.

"Smells good."

"My favorite smell in the entire world is garlic, exactly twenty seconds after it hits a hot pan," I said, breathing in the heady aroma. A pinch of crushed red pepper went into the pan next, and a pot of boiling salted water bubbled away on the back burner, filled with big handfuls of linguini. "There's half a baguette on the counter over there—want to tear off a few hunks? Plates are in that cupboard." I pointed with my wooden spoon. Technically it was my mother's wooden spoon. Even more technically, it was my great-aunt Mildred's wooden spoon. She'd been gone from the earth for many years, but her spoon remained. Stained dark brown from millions of sauces, it was angled on one side, the result of years of stirring.

I'd thought about that angle many times over the years, often when using it to stir something myself. How many times had she stood in a kitchen stirring a Sunday sauce, or making sure a batch of mashed potatoes had just the right amount of golden butter and milk? How many times had she cooked even though she was exhausted? How many times was she yelling at Great-Uncle Fred while she was stirring something with this spoon? How many times had she used it to punctuate a statement, pointing it into the air as she emphasized something she felt strongly about? Had she ever thrown it in anger? Had she ever made a major life decision while staring down at the soothing, rhythmic turns of the old spoon?

While I thought about culinary anthropology, the gorgeous man in my kitchen sneaked his hands around my waist and cuddled me close as I stirred. "Smells good," he said once more. "And I'm not talking about the food." He dipped his nose into the crook of my neck, inhaling deeply. "Honey." He sighed.

"Yes, dear?" I replied, laughing at my joke as I rolled a lemon under my palm.

"That fucking honey scent that's all over your skin, it's driving me crazy," he murmured, his breath hot on my skin. "I can't keep my hands off you—it's like they have a mind of their own." His lips traced the shell of my ear, his hands slipping underneath my shirt. His callused fingers, worn rough from hours of hard work, felt natural on my skin. Natural and amazing.

I pushed my hips back against him. "Pretty sure I know which mind is guiding them." Unbelievably, after everything that had gone down, ahem, on the porch and upstairs, he'd be ready to go again with just an invitation and quick squeeze.

Instead, I squeezed the lemon. Dodging his roving hands and very determined hips, I added a handful of fresh chopped parsley to the pan, then lifted big forkfuls of linguine into it, stirring until each strand was coated with the heavenly sauce. "Go grab the plates, please."

Frowning, he gave my backside a swat, but went to get the plates. A moment later our plates were on the table, piled high with pasta. He sat down and I stood next to him, grating a little fresh locatelli on top as his hand curved around the outside of my thigh and higher toward my hip. I enjoyed his hands on my body more than I cared to admit, and not just during the sexy times. I squashed the thought. "There we go—try that," I said, with a final sprinkle of cheese.

I watched him twirl a forkful, lifting it to his mouth. He chewed, once, twice, a third time before his eyes closed in bliss. That was The Look—the look that every chef craves. What I'd made, crafted with my own two hands, was bringing him pleasure. The rumble from deep in his throat, which I'd heard only an hour before when my tongue did something he really liked, matched the look on his face. He liked my linguine.

I sat down in my chair, already satisfied, and I hadn't even tasted it yet. To be fair, I'd been satisfied more times than I could count already this evening. The aglio olio? Was just icing on this very sexy cake.

We ate in silence, no sounds but the clinking of forks and slurping of noodles. My mother always used to say the test of a good meal is how quiet the guests are: if they're quiet, they're enjoying. I'd found that to be true time and time again. Leo sighed through a mouthful here and there, smiled if I caught his eye, but otherwise just ate. It was nice, sitting in a darkened kitchen with him, my knee brushing his occasionally. His foot tapping mine. In the middle of the night, in the middle of the kitchen, sharing a quiet meal was as intimate as what we'd shared one floor above.

Twirling one last bite around his fork, he stared mournfully at it. "There was a chef in the city who used to cater a bunch of my parents' parties; he used to make something just like this." He studied the fork. "Not exactly the same, I don't remember any green in it." He ate the last bite and moaned out loud. "Fucking hell, that's good. His was good, but this is better. His had a slightly different taste, almost, I don't know, a little nutty? Does that make sense?"

"It probably had anchovies in it," I said, sucking down my last noodle.

He made a face. "Nah, I don't like anchovies."

"No one thinks they like anchovies, but you've probably eaten them more times than you think. I put them in pasta dishes all the time." He didn't look convinced, so I continued, "The trick is to put them in the pan early, right before the garlic. They're so tiny and thin, they dissolve right into the hot oil. That's the nuttiness you were talking about."

Still looking a bit disturbed, he poked at the little bit of garlic left on the plate. Checking to see if it was a tiny fish perhaps? "Anyway, yeah, the chef. He'd come over, make some super fancy stuff for the guests, but once things were under way he'd make a pan of pasta just for me. Sometimes he'd throw in something extra, if there was lobster or crab, something like that. But good god damn, it was incredible." He smiled a little at the memory.

"Did they have a lot of parties?" I asked, thinking about what a party at the Maxwells' must have been like.

"All the time," he said, his expression changing a bit as he moved away from the pasta memory and onto something else. "There were always people in town on business, or families who were on holiday, deals to be brokered—some kind of bullshit. My family hardly ever ate dinner together. They were either out with friends, or we had friends over, but just our family? By ourselves? Not often. A lot of nights, it was just me and my sister, Lauren. And Angela."

"Another sister?"

"Nanny. Gabriela was there in the morning, but Angela was there afternoons and evenings." He smiled as he said it, but there it was again, that fleeting sadness. Maybe there was something to the "poor little rich boy" cliché.

"Where's your sister now?" I asked.

"She's still in the city, works with my dad. She heads up our international division. I don't see her much." He looked lost in thought.

"When we had parties at my house we made ice cream out back with a hand crank, and whoever my mother was dating grilled hot dogs or sausages. Someone brought potato salad, we'd bring coleslaw from the diner, and the adults would play horseshoes until everything was ready to eat. It was all sticky fingers and mosquito bites and half-burned hot dogs and enough Kool-Aid spilled to bring every ant east of the Hudson into our backyard."

"Sounds fantastic," Leo replied.

I thought back to those lazy days. The sun baking down and everything as bright as a crayon box, and the entire world boiled down to a skinned knee or a stubbed toe. And I realized something all of a sudden. "You know what, it kind of was." My gaze traveled around the well-worn kitchen: the scratched linoleum, the little bit of peeling paint, the height chart that was still on the doorframe from when I grew up. I slid my foot across the floor under the table and covered his foot with mine.

We sat in silence again, this one a little different, heavier. We each seemed lost in our own memories. He, perhaps thinking of a childhood filled with nannies and fancy. Me, thinking of a childhood filled with nothing fancy and full of love, not knowing how rich my life had been.

Now my world boiled down to a warm foot tucked under mine. And when he rose and pulled me into his arms, then led me back upstairs to my creaky twin bed, I didn't even think about giving him my standard speech about my insomnia and not being able to sleep with someone else in my bed. I just let him tuck around me and spoon.

And color me the most surprised when I slept five whole hours that night.

Chapter 14

$\mathcal{F}$ive whole hours was luxurious. Equally luxurious was the way those hours ended. Soft lips tracing a path across my shoulder, a deliciously callused hand pulling me back against a warm chest, and then—oh!—as Leo thrust into me from behind.

I came back to this memory over and over again while I worked in the diner, trying to concentrate on steak and eggs, when all I could think about was the way his eyes burned into mine as he fucked me on my front porch. I poured coffee, I flipped burgers, I did what I could to not think about the night before—and the fact that I'd *slept* with a man for the first time in my entire life. As in forty winks. Mr. Sandman.

I was deep in piecrust, not thinking about this at all, when Chad Bowman sidled up to the counter looking like he was headed out to Montauk for some boating. Pleated navy shorts, spiffy white Sperrys, and a salmon polo shirt. Not pink, not peach, not sunset or orange. Salmon, for pity's sake. All that was missing was the knit cardigan around his shoul—And there it was. He tied it into a perfect loop around his broad shoulders and popped a pair of silver aviators onto his blond hair.

"You look like something out of a catalog," I said, tugging on his popped collar. The. Popped. Collar. "J. Crew called, you're wanted on page sixty-nine."

He preened, his tan skin pinking under my praise. "As Queen Bey says, I woke up like this." Smirking, he gave me the once-over. Then he gave me a twice-over.

I smoothed my hair automatically, straightening my apron. Could he see? Could he tell? Surely he couldn't—

"Mmm-hmm," he said, settling onto a stool and giving me a knowing look.

"Mmm-hmm what?" I asked, smoothing my apron again.

"Oh, you know exactly what, Little Miss Crushing on a Farmer."

"I am not crushing on a farmer!" I snapped, loud enough that the entire diner fell silent. Which *never* happens. Forks hovered, mouths hung open, and every pair of eyes was on me. I'm pretty sure they were all picturing me naked.

Judging by the glint in his eye, Chad was picturing *Leo* naked.

A wave of embarrassment flashed over me, hot and fast. I didn't like my business being put out there. And I was pretty sure Leo wouldn't like his business out there either.

"Mmm-hmm." He lifted up his menu, which shook as he laughed quietly.

"Don't start rumors, Bowman," I said quietly, straightening the tines of his fork to line up with the paper placemat. "It's just . . . it's not like that." I looked around to see if people were still watching. And listening. . . .

Ninety-nine percent of the diner's customers went back to their breakfasts, busily gossiping and doubtless passing it through the town's phone tree. But one older fellow at the counter was glaring a hole into the back of Chad's shirt.

I blinked. Surely he couldn't have a problem with Chad?

"Pay the bigots no mind, lovey," Chad said, turning me to face him. "That's Herman." He smiled and tipped his coffee toward Herman, who looked irked that attention was being volleyed back at him.

Throwing back his coffee, the man tossed a few bills onto the counter, then stormed out of the diner. Unfortunately, the door did *not* hit him in the judgmental ass on the way out.

"A good friend, I see." I leaned my elbows on the counter across from Chad. Though he'd brushed it off like it was no big deal, I could see that it bothered him. "Do you get that a lot? The nasty staring?"

I hoped that the answer was no, that most people were accepting, and only a few were assholes. Especially in this town, where half of the businesses flew rainbow flags outside.

Chad shifted on his stool. "No, that doesn't usually happen here. That's a big part of the reason we decided we could move back. And I can handle that crap now, but just after high school, that kind of thing would have killed me." He smiled. "I would have panicked and said nothing, and then thought of ten great comebacks an hour later."

His admission gave me such a new perspective on him. I couldn't imagine how hard it would be to hide that big a secret. To pretend to be something I wasn't.

"I wish I knew then, in case you wanted someone to talk to or whatever."

"Enough about this," he said dismissively. "I want *all* the explicit details about last night!"

"Phone for you, Rox," a voice rang out from the kitchen, and I grinned in relief.

"Gee, looks like I have to take a call."

Chad pointed two fingers at his eyes, then at me, telling me he that knew something was up and he'd be watching me.

I grinned and grabbed the phone off the wall. "This is Roxie."

"Hello, Roxie, this is Mrs. Oleson, from the mayor's office."

"Oh hello, Mrs. Oleson, how are you?"

Chad's eyebrows went up. Mrs. Oleson had worked in the mayor's office for as long as anyone could remember, no matter who the mayor was. She had her hand in nearly everything that happened in town. Huh. Not unlike a Mrs. Harriett Oleson from Walnut Grove. I allowed myself a few seconds of Almanzo fantasy.

"Roxie, are you there?"

"Yes, I'm here. What can I do you for, Mrs. Oleson?"

"I'm in a bit of a pickle, dear, and I'm hoping you can help me out."

"I'll do what I can. What's up?" I replied, confused but intrigued.

"Well, you know I always bring cakes to the ladies' luncheon, and this year I've just totally overextended myself. Linda and Evelyn were positively raving over the walnut cake they had at the diner last week, and I wondered—"

"You want a walnut cake too?" I finished.

"Actually, I'd need four. And maybe . . . do you have something different you could make? They've already had the walnut cake, so I thought maybe we could surprise them with something new," she said, her voice getting quiet and sneaky. "Eleanor made her famous sponge cake last week, and I need to step it up a notch or two."

"Something new," I repeated, glancing over at the barren cake display case with worry. Not about how I was going to bake more—but because I *wanted* to do it. "When do you need these?"

"Tomorrow?" she asked hesitantly.

Yikes. I looked again at the display case. This morning it had held eight cakes, each sliced in eighths, individually for sale. Now there were only crumbs.

Did I want to do this? *Could* I do this was a better question, adding another thing to my already packed schedule.

"What did you have in mind?" I asked, decision made, grabbing the yellow order pad out of Maxine's apron pocket as she passed by. She frowned, eyeing me from under the beehive hairdo that held a—

"I need this too," I chirped, plucking the pen from the hairspray-stiffened swirl. She cracked me on the ass with a dish towel in complaint.

"Carrot?" I parroted back to Mrs. Oleson, my mind immediately racing. "Traditional? With *nuts*?" I was giddy at the thought of shopping at Leo's for the ingredients. Mmm, I could do a cream cheese frosting. I'd seen tubs of it at Maxwell Farm from the dairy next door. What else could I pick up there? Oooo, maybe he'd pick *me* up. Maybe he'd finish what he started that day in the silo—

Shit, I was on the phone. "Pick them up tomorrow morning," I instructed Mrs. Oleson, flustered.

As I hung up the phone, the Scott family walked in. Mom, Dad, and two kids, with the point-five bun in the oven and ready to pop out.

"Have a seat anywhere that's open," I called, leaning over the counter to see if there was a booth or table free. There was one in the back, and Mrs. Scott was able to waddle uncomfortably over and sit down.

"Looks like someone is making a name for herself in this town," Chad said over his menu.

"I don't even know why you're pretending to look at this— you always get the same thing. Tuna melt, potato salad, cherry Coke." I rolled my eyes, smacking the top of his head lightly with his menu.

"She knows her customers' orders, she's becoming famous for

her sweet treats, she's emphatically *not* crushing on a farmer—what a summer Roxie Callahan's having," Chad said.

I smacked him again, not trying to hide my smile.

After sending his order to the kitchen, I started rifling through one of the old cookbooks my mother kept behind the counter. An old Betty Crocker from the fifties was chock-full of American classics: sponge, angel, devil, coconut, pound . . . And then came the mother lode: the European Dessert section. Tiramisu, Black Forest, Pavlova, and Irish Mousse. I was about to read the recipe for the boozy take on mousse pie when Mr. Scott approached the counter.

"God, I haven't seen that in twenty years!" he exclaimed, pointing to the picture of an Apple Amber pie. According to the recipe, it was a whiskeyed-up meringue pie. Fresh farmyard apples sweetened with cider, sugar, and lemons, blanketed with rich, brown meringue piled high.

As Mr. Scott leaned closer to stare at the cookbook, he looked like he was about to drool. "Are you making this?" he asked hopefully.

"I don't know—maybe. I've never made it before." But I could, easily, and the regulars would love it. Hmmm. Apples weren't in season yet, but peaches would be soon. I mentally started converting the recipe from apples to peaches: maybe less cinnamon, a splash of bourbon. Did Leo have peach trees? Hmmm, sweet, luscious peaches. And sweet, luscious Leo.

Zombie Pickle Class. A phrase never before uttered in the history of phrase uttering, let alone printed on a sign. But there it was in the diner's front window, propped up by a ten-gallon plastic pickle tub. Which was high art apparently, according to Chad. "It's ironic, it's homey, it's perfection!" he'd said when he'd dropped it off earlier that day and strong-armed me into letting him put it in.

Though I tried to insist that teaching him and Logan hardly constituted a "class," he'd insisted more. So here I was, surrounded by cutting boards, cucumbers, garlic, and a few dozen jars, waiting for my first class to start. The diner was quiet, the front lights turned down and jukebox off, just the faint hum of the fridges audible in the kitchen.

I yawned, leaning on the countertop. I'd only managed about three hours of sleep the night before, and it'd been a long day. One of the line cooks had called in sick, so I'd worked both the breakfast and the lunch shifts on the grill. My back creaked, my shoulders ached, my finger was burned by a sauté pan.

But I was also surprisingly . . . exhilarated. I'd worked a hard day, did everything I needed to do, put out fires—literally, and made sure every single person who came through the door enjoyed the hell out of their lunch. I'd made a new version of tomato soup today. I'd slow roasted the tomatoes with basil and a bit of chervil before pureeing them, rather than using the standard canned. I'd used crème fraîche instead of half-and-half. Then I added brioche croutons, tossed with gruyère and black pepper. Did we sell out of that soup before 11 a.m.? Possibly. Did we get way more take-out orders for soup than we'd had since I'd been home?

Yes! Tons of take-out orders!

Along with the exhilaration, I also felt a sense of . . . comfort? Belonging? That would seem a perfectly natural reaction, since it was my hometown—yet I'd almost never felt it before. And along with the exhilaration and the comfort of belonging, add one dash of . . . butterflies?

No, that's not it.

A heart murmur?

Pretty sure you're healthy, cardiacwise.

Indigestion?

With your cast-iron stomach? Hardly.

So what is it?

Hopefulness? Joy? Intrigue?

Indigestion. That's it. Too many croutons.

Croutons are giving you butterflies?

Mmm-hmm.

I pondered this while I held a cucumber in my hand. Which naturally brought up other thoughts. Thoughts I didn't have time to explore, because the owner of the cucumber I *wished* I was holding came through the front door, his eyes searching for mine. Cue the butterfly croutons.

When Leo saw what I was holding, his face broke into a movie star grin.

In that instant, all of the air left the room. In that instant, all I was aware of was his face and those eyes and that grin . . . and a quickly warming cucumber. In that instant plus one second . . . I realized I was in deep trouble.

Because this guy was incredible.

Because this guy was real and sweet and kind, and he knew about the kinds of things that could wiggle through every chink in my armor and into my heretofore unbreakable heart.

Food.

Orgasms.

Food.

Sweet.

Food.

Strong.

Orgasms.

Oh boy.

And funny.

Caring.

Kind.

Not afraid to get his hands dirty.

Not afraid to talk dirty.

And the surprise of all surprises: I already missed him in my bed.

"Hey, Sugar Snap," he said. "What kind of plans do you have for that cucumber?"

Officially, I came up with a clever comeback. Officially, I offered some witty banter to keep things light and flirty. Officially, I shot down every butterfly crouton that was fluttering around inside me.

But unofficially? The feeling of being somebody's Sugar Snap made me grin widely. Nothing witty came from my mouth; it was too busy smiling. And then the smiling became a kiss, then two, then three. Because I nearly vaulted over the counter, ran to Leo like a fool in a Nicholas Sparks film, and threw myself into his strong arms, kissing him as if someone had threatened to take his mouth away from me.

His arms enveloped me, his surprised chuckle quickly muffled by my face. Which he covered in equally urgent kisses, his lips pressing against my forehead, my cheekbones, the tip of my nose, and finally my mouth again. Lifting me right out of my clogs, he set me on top of the counter, coaxed my legs apart with no resistance from me, and stood between them. I wrapped my legs around him, crossing them high on his back as he let his head tip forward, resting on my breasts, his hands digging into my hips, hard.

"You drive me crazy, Sugar Snap," he groaned.

"Call me that again, and I'm canceling pickle class." I ran my hands through his hair and kneaded his scalp, getting a satisfied moan in response.

"Sugar Snap? That's what brought this on?" he asked, and I tilted his head up toward mine.

"That's it. Class is canceled." I was about to tell him to lock the door and ravage me up against the Fryalator when I heard a slow clapping, à la every movie from the eighties.

"Well done. Will all classes begin this way?"

Chad and Logan stood just inside the door, wearing enormous grins and bearing cucumbers.

I slumped down against Leo's chest, breathing in his heady scent, and breathing out my frustration at being interrupted. When I looked up again, Logan made a decidedly ungentlemanly—okay, totally juvenile—gesture with a cucumber, and I snorted in spite of myself. The moment broken, Leo helped me down off the counter, and I faced my peanut gallery.

"You boys ready to pickle?"

They were in fact ready to pickle. And pickle we did. They were surprisingly good students, once they got all the jokes about pickle size out of their systems. They paid close attention, they followed directions, and within about ninety minutes we had several jars ready for the fridge. It was fun, and I'd forgotten how much I enjoyed teaching people how to do things like this.

Leo kept close to me most of the night, refusing to answer Chad's unsubtle questions about what was going on with us, changing the subject smoothly each time. It was frustrating for Chad, amusing for me, and it kept the evening focused on the food. I did wonder how far things would have gone if Chad and Logan hadn't shown up . . . but no matter. I was enjoying the evening with three gorgeous men, and I might get to see one of them naked very soon. Zombie Pickle Class was a total success.

Zombie Pickle Class was also noticed by several passersby. How could you not stop to read a sign like that? Though the door was locked, that didn't stop people from peering inside. Interesting . . .

"We should make more! I want enough to last the entire winter," Logan proclaimed as he labeled his jar of hamburger dills.

"These are fridge pickles, so they'll only be good for a few months. If you want pickles that will keep longer, that's a whole different ball of brine. You have to cook them a bit, same as making jelly or jam."

"Yes! Let's make jam too!" Chad chimed in enthusiastically.

"Okay, everyone settle," I said as Leo smothered a laugh. "We can definitely make jam, but not tonight." I smiled at their eagerness as I scooped up a few jars of my own concoction—baby cucumbers in a zesty brine of spicy peppers and the tiniest drizzle of honey—and headed for the fridge.

"How about next week? Same time, same place?" Logan asked, and I nodded in agreement.

"Blackberries just came in, and by next week we'll have raspberries too," Leo said.

Mmm. I did love raspberry jam.

"Do you know how to make apple butter?" Chad asked as he cleaned up his station. "My nana used to make it every October, and I ate half a loaf of bread every day after school just for that apple butter. Can we make that?"

"No can do—sorry."

"Why in the world not?" Then his eyes lit up with a wicked gleam. "What if I put on my old letterman jacket?"

Logan's head popped around the fridge. "Let him wear the jacket, Rox. It's hot as hell."

"Oh, I remember. But apple butter making is in the fall."

"So?" Chad asked, and Logan gave me an inquiring look.

"I won't be here in the fall," I said quietly, feeling Leo's stare on the back of my head. It's funny how a gaze can be physically felt from across the room. "I'm leaving once my mom gets back from her *Amazing Race*, remember?"

A silence fell on the kitchen, all the good humor of the evening seeming to fall away.

"Besides, the Jam Lady is going to kill me as it is, teaching you guys how to make jam. I can't take away her apple butter clients too—she'd never let me hear the end of it."

"You won't be here to hear her. *That's* kind of the end of it," Logan muttered.

I rolled my eyes. "Okay, zombies, class is over. Next time jam, same time, same place," I said, forcing my voice to stay light and bright.

Chad nodded, pulling me against him in a quick hug. "Tonight was fun—thanks for the pickles." He dropped a quick kiss on my forehead before ushering Logan and their jars out the door.

Leaving me with Leo, who dropped his gaze when I turned around. "I'll get a broom, help you get this place cleaned up," he said, moving toward the utility closet.

There was nothing I could say to ease the sudden tension, because I *was* leaving. This . . . thing . . . was just for the summer. So he got the broom and I wiped the counters, and within a few minutes we began to chat about what other fruits might be ready soon for jam. Light and bright.

Light and bright means no expectations. No demands on time, no hard feelings, and certainly no tears. Which is why when he left with just a quick kiss on my forehead, I didn't feel a suspicious prickle inside my eyelids, or notice that my chin wobbled at all.

I locked up, drove home, and didn't sleep. Because officially, it was just a fling. And a fling made no demands on where he spent his nights.

Light and bright.

Chapter 15

$\mathcal{I}$ couldn't believe the Fourth of July was almost here. It seemed like I'd barely arrived, but the bunting going up around town said the summer was half gone.

I swear to God this town kept the bunting business in business more than any other small town in the country. If it was a holiday, you can bet your sweet apple pie that Bailey Falls was dragging out the red, white, and blue and lashing it to anything that would stand still. Quaint. Homey. Pretty great, actually.

Finished at the diner for the day, I drove my big old American car down the middle of good old American Main Street, and thought about fucking my good old American farmer while holding two sparklers. Now *that's* how I'd like to celebrate our country's founding.

I pondered this while waving to familiar faces along the main drag. People I used to know and had come to know again, new people I'd met since coming home. With some I knew names; mostly I knew orders. Hey look, Scrambled with Rye Toast is coming out of the hardware store with cable ties. Wonder if he's planning on using those on Miss Steel-Cut Oats with Nonfat Milk and Hold the Raisins. I just bet she liked her raisins held . . .

The thermometer on the bank said it was near ninety degrees, and I was glad of the breeze coming through my window. Turning on the radio, I head the strains of "Mysterious Ways" and snickered at the thought that *Achtung Baby* was being played on an oldies station. My mother would flip out if she knew that. Where was she right now? Brazil? Italy? Minnesota? Wherever she was, I hope she was enjoying herself.

As I drove home I saw a few teenage girls walking into the woods behind the high school, carrying towels and a beach ball. And I suddenly knew exactly where I wanted to spend my afternoon. And whom I wanted to spend it with.

I sped back to the house, stopping only to send a text to Leo.

> Can you play hooky today?

He texted back right away, and I snorted out loud.

> Will you be naked? I can only consider naked hooky requests.

> It's very possible. Come on, come and play with me.

> Isn't that a line from *The Shining*?

> You should take me pretty seriously then, right? Also, don't pay attention to that ax behind my back.

> You're lucky I like dangerous women. When?

Now. Drop your hoe and
grab your swim trunks.
I'll be there in fifteen.

Swim trunks? Now I'm in-
trigued.

Intrigued enough to play
hooky?

Make it twenty and bring
snacks and you've got me.

Done.

Also naked. Remember the
naked.

I'll do my best.

I threw on a bikini, making sure to double knot the strings. Because, Leo. I grabbed a cooler, threw in ice, beer, the sandwiches
I'd made at the diner that were originally going to be my dinner,
and then grabbed my mom's old CD boom box. It was big, square,
covered in knobs and switches and dials, and exactly the kind of
thing you want for playing hooky at the old swimming hole.

Every town in the Catskills either had a swimming hole or was
within a few miles of one. There were so many creeks, streams,
ponds, and small lakes—if there was water, we'd swim in it. It
was how you survived the hot summers when you were a kid, and
where you learned how to French kiss when you were a teenager.

There were multiple great places to swim around Bailey
Falls, but The Tube was my favorite. Close to the edge of the
Bryant Mountain House hotel property there was a small spring
and pond that fed the larger lake on the hotel's grounds. Clear
cold water, rocky bottom, and lots of outcroppings if you were

feeling daring and wanted to jump. It was a cool respite on a hot day, and it was exactly where I wanted to take Leo today.

When I pulled up to the big stone barn, it occurred to me that I still didn't know where Leo lived. He'd said he didn't use the main house, as it was used for tours and tended to be the domain of his mother when she visited. Which I gathered was rarely. So where did he sleep at night? There were guest houses that he'd converted into dormlike quarters for the summer interns in the apprentice program, but I doubted he stayed there.

But before I could think too long on it, there he was. Taller than the rest of the group, his sandy blond hair shining in the sun, getting lighter by the day.

He waved good-bye to the group he was chatting with, then jogged over to my Jeep.

"So mysterious," he said, sidling up to the window. Looking left and right (to make sure no one was looking?), he leaned his head in to kiss me once, twice, three times. "Where are we going, Sugar Snap?"

My toes pointed involuntarily and the engine revved, a consequence of being called by my nickname. Chuckling, he backed away, hands held up in an *I give* gesture.

"Get in," I said. "And buckle up."

"So *this* is where you brought all of the boys to have your wicked way with them in your younger days."

We'd turned off the main road into the woods, onto a dirt path barely large enough for my Wagoneer to fit down without snapping off a few branches here and there. I was pleased to see no other cars here when I parked, and I led him a few hundred yards or so to the clearing above the clearest, and coldest, swimming hole for miles.

Starting as an underground spring, the water forced its way up through the rock underneath, creating this beautiful little pool ringed with huge craggy boulders, some rough and pointed, some flat like giant platters. The pool was somewhat oblong, more like a tube than a circle, hence the name. Since it was smaller than some of the other swimming haunts near town, it usually wasn't as crowded.

And today, we had it all to ourselves.

As we admired it from above, what he'd said finally registered. His eyes were full of fun and mischief as he gazed down at me, waiting expectantly for my answer.

"I never brought boys here, mister. Not for wicked ways or *any* ways." I punctuated my statement with a smack on his buns.

"Oh, I find that hard to believe," he teased, returning the buns smack. "Come on, you can tell me. Teenage Roxie, with her legendary culinary skills, must have made a helluva picnic to tempt the boys out to skinny dip."

I thought about it for a moment. How perfect that version could have been. Snapping a red-and-white checkered tablecloth onto the grass and wildflowers. Sitting with The Chad Bowman crisscross applesauce while we ate tiny sandwiches and talked about . . . whatever we would have discussed.

It was hard to put myself in an imaginary memory with my former A-number-one crush, when I had my current A number one here in the flesh.

"That wasn't me," I explained, pulling him close and tucking his hands around my lower back. He slid his palms into my back pockets like they did in every eighties music video on MTV. Back in the day when MTV actually *ran* videos. "I was shy. A people watcher who kept to myself. I didn't turn into a brazen hussy until after I left Bailey Falls."

I nipped his chin with my teeth, earning two firm bum squeezes. "And speaking of brazen hussy, I'm down with creating some wannabe superhorny teenage memories right here and now. Interested?"

A deep, searing kiss was the answer. *Interested.*

We climbed carefully down the rocky path. He was all chivalrous with his "Oh, let me help you down" hands that landed and lingered on my backside. Or the casual lean-in that brushed against the side of my boob, which I didn't immediately lean away from.

We just couldn't keep our hands off each other. And I was quickly becoming addicted to that comfortable sweetness mixed with steadily growing passion. It was going to be hard to cut myself off cold turkey at the end of the summer.

I leaned into his shoulder to smell the summer on his skin.

Wella, wella, wella, huh.

I was addicted to all things Leo. Right now, as we picked our way down across the rocky shale, I settled on his fingers. Tan, strong, and all man. Not the manicured, pristine, hand-creamed-to-hell fingers that most of the guys in Los Angeles had. These were callused and hardworking, and of the earth.

And at the moment, they were toying with the hem of my shorts. The frayed bits that dangled against my legs were a particular favorite of his. He wound them around his index finger as we walked, and the contact points became little fiery spots that sent tingles up my spine and down my shorts.

And lately, his hands had been coming into contact more often. For obvious reasons, sure, but it was more. When he wasn't playing grab ass or boobie graze, there'd be the lightest brush here. The softest touch there. It felt like he was unaware that he was doing it too, like the zing he got from making contact surprised him just as much as it did me.

We carried on until finally we cleared the trees, where the stillness reined in our silliness.

"This is perfect," he said, pulling me in front of him to rest his head on my shoulder.

A dragonfly bounced along the water, sending tiny ripples through the blue, inviting water. We had the place all to ourselves. Suddenly seized by inspiration, I smiled. Brazen hussy reporting for duty.

I turned within his arms, blinking innocently up at him. "Stay," I instructed with my index finger in the center of his chest. Curiosity shone in his eyes. He looked like he wanted to ask what I was doing, but he didn't, letting me run the show.

I kicked off my flips, sending them sailing under a nearby tree. My thin white tank was next, sliding over my head. Leo's eyes narrowed as he took in my barely there bikini, red and white polka dots that tried, almost unsuccessfully, to cover my sudden inspiration. Slipping out of my shorts to expose another part of barely there, I was delighted when his face changed from expectation to deep satisfaction.

I turned away toward the water, peered over my shoulder with a secret smile, and saw Leo standing stock-still, answering my smile broadly. His hands fisted at his sides as he watched me tug at the string on my bikini top, exposing myself to God, country, and dragonflies. I let the tiny triangles slide down my heated skin into the gravel and dirt, and his breath caught. He took a tiny step forward before catching himself. He was letting me do this at my pace, and looked like he was enjoying every single second of it.

I took a step toward the water. I heard him take a step behind me. When my toes hit the water, I almost jumped out of my skin. I'd figured it would be warmish given the time of year, but this was downright nippy—and visibly nipply.

I moved deeper into the water, the coolness slipping up over my shins, my knees, halfway up my thigh—then I stopped and took another look back at Leo. It was like a game of Red Light, Green Light. For every step I took into the water, he stepped further down the rocks. When I stopped, he stopped. When I turned this last time, letting him sneak a peek at what the trees were already familiar with, he stopped so short he had to pinwheel his arms to keep from falling. Jesus, if tits could do this to a grown man, what would happen when I . . .

I took hold of the strings on either hip and tugged.

I'd seen Leo move quickly before, but he was about to break the land and sea record for getting naked and into the water. Jeans and boxers were gone together in a tangle as he hopped on one foot while he toed off his boots simultaneously.

He winced when he hit the water, but didn't lose momentum. His shirt was still on, as if he'd forgotten he was wearing it. Ripping it off, he threw it behind him, landing on a rock with a wet *thwap*.

"You shouldn't tease a guy, Roxie," he warned, pulling me to him so quickly that the water splashed up between us, wetting his face and eyelashes.

Now pressed together, very wet and very naked, he gave me a very specific once-over. The kind that you give someone you want to devour. I'd volunteer for a devouring. As he smoothed his wet palm over my hair, my eyes closed at the light touch. I leaned into his warmth, unable to stop the smile that took over my face. My eyes flittered open, blinking against the sunlight, and I sighed in contentment.

He was just leaning in to kiss me when something buzzy flew past my ear. My body went stiff. So did his, and not in the good way. Though that particular part was still bobbing against my leg.

"Just ignore it, Rox, it'll go away," he coaxed, trying to shoo it away.

"No. Bee. Bad," I stuttered through clenched teeth, trying

to flee but unable to escape his hold, his arm banded across my bottom, his hand over a cheek for good measure. I tried to breathe. "It's like some kind of call goes out across the forest: 'Hey, Roxie's here; she's naked in the pond and trying to get it on with Almanzo—let's get her!'"

"You really have a thing for Almanzo, don't you?"

"You have no idea. Remember the episode when Nellie Oleson made him cinnamon chicken, his favorite dish? But Nellie didn't know how to make it so she made Laura do it? Only Laura hated Nellie, so she switched out the cinnamon for cayenne pepper?" I babbled, burying my head in Leo's chest while trying to get us as low in the water as I could.

"Cinnamon? What?" he asked, confused, almost losing his footing as I scrambled against his stomach, hunching down.

"You said ignore it, I'm trying to ignore it. Is it gone yet?"

I'll never know what his answer was going to be, because just then I was buzzed in stereo by Bee Number One and his asshole cousin, Bee Number Two.

"Good-bye!" I chirped, and went under. His hands splashed after me as I wriggled down to the bottom, where not even an asshole bee could follow. I swam a few feet, surfaced, saw Leo waving his hands over his head trying to shoo the motherfuckers away, then submerged again, this time with lungs full.

This went on awhile, me popping up in different spots, Leo trying to communicate with me in the 2.2 seconds I was above water before diving deep again, determined to wait it out. He waded this way and that, trying to find me, only to see me shoot up like a dolphin to catch another breath. The poor guy was playing Whac-a-Mole with a lunatic with exceptional breath control, and I caught little snatches of words between inhales.

"Roxie they're—"

"—gone, you can—"

"For God's sake Rox, can you—"

"Dammit, Sugar Snap, would you just—"

It was the Sugar Snap that got me. It always would. I swam closer to him, and even underwater I was mesmerized by his person. I couldn't resist giving it a few strokes. His hands plunged under the water, grasped me by the shoulders, let me get in at least one more good stroke, then brought me back above the water.

"Gone?" I spluttered as he put me on my feet. Then he quickly picked me up under my knees and wrapped my legs around his waist.

"Gone," he said, and pulled us gently into deeper water.

"What are you doing to me?" he said, holding my face delicately while he was decidedly not so delicate with my lips. It felt fevered, out of control. I answered his question with actions. Totally caught up in each other, our bodies molding to each other, skin heating even surrounded by the cool water. Blissful. Wanton. Unaware.

So much so that we didn't notice the high schoolers along the rocky bank with their towels . . . and grins.

"You bet, Mrs. Montgomery, two dozen cupcakes for your Fourth of July picnic. You want them all cherries jubilee, or . . . Okay, I can do some with blueberry. Yes, that's very patriotic of you. Cherries and blueberries, and I'll pipe some vanilla buttercream on top. All the colors of the flag." I wrote everything down, calculating how much to charge, and how much time I'd need to get this order in. Mrs. Oleson's Carrot Cake had been a hit, and I was the talk of the ladies' luncheon. Everyone wanted a piece of me. Of my cake.

When the bell dinged above the front door, I looked over my shoulder and grinned when I saw Leo.

"There she is," he whispered, seeing I was on the phone. He gently set some bags on the counter stools, then braced his hands on the counter and pulled himself up, looking like he was about to start a pommel horse routine, resting his hips against the chipped Formica. Leaning in, he gave me three quick pecks on the lips, pulling away just enough to watch me smile, then zooming back in for a fourth. I almost dropped the receiver when his lips left mine to concentrate on my neck, making me shiver deliciously. My neck continued to receive this attention until he saw the empty dessert case.

He looked back at me in such a woebegone fashion that I had to bite back a laugh, and I wrote "I saved you some blue-berry pound cake" on the notepad where I was writing Mrs. Montgomery's order. Delight crept over his face like a sunrise. So easy was this guy. I held up a finger, indicating I just needed another minute, and he nodded.

He peered inside the dessert carousel and saw the crumbs and icing remnants, and a few errant blueberries. With his body balancing on one arm, which the pommel horse judges would have given him fill marks for demonstrating his innate strength, he popped the door open and plucked up the crumbs, smiling wickedly while he did it. He began to press sugary crumbly kisses along my collarbone, causing me to inhale rather quickly, almost gasping into the receiver.

"What, Mrs. Montgomery? Yes, I was listening, sorry. There was . . . something."

He grinned, pulled himself up and over the counter, and now sat right in front of me as I attempted to carry on a conversation. He was determined to keep kissing on me. He snickered and nipped, licked, and sucked his way across my shoulder into the hollow of my clavicle, before his hand slowly traced down my stomach. Wide-eyed, I shook my head no. Wide-eyed, he nodded yes. He leaned in and down, and began kissing a path straight to my tummy, deftly slipping under my apron, unzipping my shorts, and had his hand inside before I could even gasp. And he was now inserting himself right into the conversation, by inserting himself right into my drawers, and—oh!

I dropped the phone. Right on his head. "Serves you right!" I mouthed, trying not to laugh as I watched him rub the goose egg.

He bounded away with the supplies he'd brought, still smiling as he disappeared into the kitchen.

As I brought the receiver back up to my ear, Mrs. Montgomery was asking what time she should pick up the cupcakes, and what in the world was making me sound so out of breath?

"Sorry, I just dropped the phone. And come pick them up the morning; we're closing early for the holiday. Good-bye to you too."

Revved up and ready to go beyond belief, I took off in the direction Leo had gone, pushing him up against the ice machine and kissing him until he was breathless too.

I also rubbed his goose egg.

Ten minutes later I was still breathless, and decidedly glowing. Our quickie had come to a screaming (me) end just before the front door dinged open, announcing the first arrival for Zombie Class Number Two. You've never seen someone straighten out an apron faster in your life—trust me.

And the door kept on dinging as more and more people poured in: some I recognized and some I didn't. What in the world?

It seemed my class was a sleeper hit; everyone wanted in on it. And as I started counting how many people were here, I felt a weird sensation in my stomach.

I was carving out a niche. In the town I swore I'd never niche in again. And worst of all, it felt . . .

Strange? Not entirely.

Familiar? Not really. Though the setting was familiar, this summer was anything but.

Nice? Perhaps.

Too much? Perhaps.

Quickly getting away from me? Oh, *perhaps!*

I sighed. It didn't help that my mind was still a bit scrambled by the ice machine boning.

Misinterpreting my sigh, Leo kissed the tip of my nose. "It's totally normal to have butterflies, Sugar Snap."

From the kitchen, we were peeping through the window in the swinging door. We'd needed an extra moment to collect ourselves. After all, he'd been inside not two minutes before. Even thinking these words made me clench. Mmm . . . aftershock.

"Not really nervous," I said. "I just didn't expect this many people."

Chad and Logan's Realtor, Mary, was here with her boyfriend, Larry. Mrs. Oleson and Mrs. Shrewsbury from the Ladies Auxiliary. I recognized a few of the younger interns from Maxwell Farm. And the woman from the farmers' market whom I'd seen fanning herself with a leaf of romaine and making eyes at Leo. And one very tall guy with wavy black hair caught back in a leather tie, who was very tattooed, very loaded-for-bear in the muscles department, and looking very uncomfortable to be attending a jam-making class.

"Who is that?" I whispered.

"Which one?"

"*Game of Thrones* guy back there." I pointed to tall, dark, and fuckhot.

Leo looked, then snorted. "Oh, he'll love that. That's Oscar, the dairy farmer next door."

I pushed him out of the way and took another look. He was so tall he'd just bumped his head on the Drink Local Beer sign that hung over the front door.

"*That's* Oscar?" I asked, incredulous.

"Yep," he nodded.

"The *dairy* farmer?"

"Yep."

I shook my head, watching as the young girls, no doubt lured by Leo, were now giggling stupid in the presence of Oscar. "Fuck me, the other men in this town don't stand a chance."

"Pardon?" Leo asked.

"Forget it." I pushed the door open into the diner. What the hell had they started putting in the water since I'd moved away?

After welcoming everyone, I hurried about, setting up everything they'd need to make jam. Since there were way more people than planned stations, I paired everyone up two by two like a jam-making Noah. Except for Oscar. He'd been drafted onto Chad and Logan's team, and looked relived to be there.

Once everything was ready, I got their attention. "Hi, everyone, thanks again for coming tonight. We're making jam!" God, I loved teaching!

"Do we get to drink beforehand?" Chad asked Logan with a giggle.

I fought back a grin. "As you can see, I wasn't expecting so many of you, so you'll be sharing jars. Next time we'll have more. You'll find everything you need in front of you: jar, funnel, pectin, sugar, and lemon juice. I've already washed the fruit, boiled the jars, rings, and lids, so you get to do all the fun stuff. For the fruit portion of tonight's activities, you have a choice of delicious fresh berries courtesy of this guy here and Maxwell Farm. There are blackberries, boysenberries, raspberries, and even a few gooseberries."

As if on cue, Leo put his arm around me and popped a gooseberry into my mouth.

Oh. Public Display of Affection—our secret was out!

The truth is, no one cared except for the mooning interns, who quickly shifted their attention to Oscar's direction. As I realized the town wasn't going to implode just because I'd come home and was getting it put to me good by Leo Maxwell, I realized that there were some nice advantages to living in a small town after all.

My smile filled my face. "Okay, everyone come choose your fruit!"

⌖

"Maybe jam wasn't such a good idea," I said, washing off the countertops one last time. The blueberry syrup had gone everywhere, and the class stayed to help clean up—stacking pots, hanging spoons on their racks, and setting measuring cups back in their places.

"Are you kidding? This was the most fun I had in ages," Logan said, affectionately blotting the blackberry juice on Chad's Key Lime Pie polo shirt. I'd love to see the lineup of J. Crew polos in his summer closet.

"Did you have fun, Oscar?" I asked.

He was at the sink, cleaning out a bottle with a brush, thrusting it in and out. I'd really like to say I heard his answer, or anything he'd said all night beyond, "Hi, nice to meet you," but it'd be a lie. Because . . . *so* hot. Chad, Logan, and I all stopped to stare as he thrust and talked and thrust. Sweet merciful God.

Eventually he put on his hoodie and left, tossing a wave to Leo on his way out the door. Which *he had to stoop to clear.*

"You know, Miss Roxie, you could easily get a thousand a class in the city for these lessons," Chad said.

That brought me back down to earth. A thousand a class? Wheels started turning and ideas started churning in my brain, pinging off the synapses like a pinball machine.

I'd be lying if I said I didn't have the beginnings of a mental checklist of reasons to stay in Bailey Falls vs. reasons to run screaming back to Los Angeles. And a weekly class was a solid checkmark in the Stay column. It'd take me a while to establish such a willing audience in Los Angeles—especially since there was no predicting how long the culinary hit would be out on me by Mitzi and her crew.

Leo was watching but trying to be inconspicuous about it, sweeping the floor.

"I see the gears working. Tell me you're considering it," Chad pressed in a lower voice, leading me to the corner to have some semblance of privacy.

My eyes found Leo, who was still watching closely. He'd laugh at something or join in a conversation, but I could tell one ear was tuned into us.

"Mmmmaybe?" I clapped my hand over his mouth before he could squeal.

"Wow, Leo must really have a magical beanstalk on that farm to get you to consider staying."

He meant to tease, but I recoiled and verbally struck out. "That's not why! I mean, yeah, it's a great summer thing, but that doesn't mean I'd . . . I mean . . . Just because its only for the summer doesn't mean that it doesn't *mean . . . Fuck!*"

Whatever this was, it was the kind of fun that could quickly kindle into something beyond. That's what my instincts were telling me. But with the hopeless romantic gene pool I came from, I didn't know whether to trust my gut. Whichever way my heart told me to go, I usually ran in the opposite direction.

But how was *he* feeling? He seemed to be enjoying this just as much as I was. And like me, he went into it with his eyes wide open. He was counting on three months. But what if—

"The amount of internalizing you're doing right now is going to give you an ulcer." Chad patted me gently on the back. "This isn't something you need to decide tonight. Get through the next class first," he said, laughing and joining the rest of the group.

"What are we making next week, Roxie?" an intern asked expectantly, and the diner fell silent as the group waited for my answer.

Leo stopped sweeping, the broom beneath his chin as he leaned against it, waiting.

I glanced to the counter, spying a stack of cooking magazines that my mom ignored monthly in favor of the diner usuals. On the cover was a big blue bowl filled with linguine, clams, and tomato sauce.

"We're canning tomatoes," I blurted, my eyes on Leo.

Who was beaming.

Chapter 16

My best friend Natalie moaned. "Do you know what I'm having right now?" It sounded like she had a mouth full of something. "Guess."

"Judging by the moaning, I'm going to guess a big, beautiful dick." I laughed when she starting choking.

She'd called as I was taking a break between the breakfast and lunch rush, and I was eager to get caught up with her. I slid into the corner behind the unused coat rack for privacy, balancing the phone between my shoulder and my ear. The diner had been busier than usual, the lull between breakfast and lunch getting shorter each day.

We always closed early on the Fourth of July and stayed closed on the fifth, a minibreak for the staff. I was eagerly looking forward to putting my feet up and relaxing. Or perhaps putting my feet up, and around, a certain green-eyed gorgeous. Mmm. But back to Natalie . . .

"Ass, I could have died. Death by pot sticker!"

"Natalie! You're at House of Wong without me? *I'm* the one who should be saying ass, ass! You know those are my favorite pot stickers—how could you tease me like that! I'm so jealous."

"Girl, please—you've been in Bailey Falls for how many weeks, and you haven't once popped into the city. I don't feel bad about this at all. Hear that?" Cue slurping. She didn't. She wouldn't.

"Are you having their soup dumplings?"

Slurp. Slurp, slurp. "I'm sick of waiting for you to get your cute little ass down here. What the hell is going on up there?"

"Oh, you have no idea." I groaned, imagining the bamboo steamer filled with perfectly shaped dumplings, chewy yummy dough, and rich, gorgeous broth.

"You're still thinking about my dumplings, aren't you?" she asked.

I grinned. "Caught. You make it sound so sordid."

"I make it sound so lonely. Get your ass on the train—you can be at Grand Central in ninety minutes."

"I've still got lunch service. Get *your* ass on the train—you can be in Poughkeepsie in the same amount of time."

She hooted. "Yeah, but then I'm in the sticks. What the hell am I supposed to do there?"

Natalie suffered from the Manhattan belief that nothing worth doing existed off her island. Normally I'd immediately join in, agreeing with city good, country bad. But . . .

"The sticks? Not so bad." Hello, what's this?

"Sticks schmicks. That doesn't explain why I'm enjoying a delicious dumpling crawl, and you've still not told me why you haven't come in to the city to play."

"I've been . . . busy." I felt terrible about not being honest with her, but how could I, when I wasn't fully being honest with myself? I had a day off here and there, and where had I been spending it? Under and over someone dreamy.

"I'm just busting your chops; I know the diner must be exhausting. But I miss you, Rox! What's happening? Lay it on me."

"Now's not really a great time," I said, seeing more and more customers filing in. It was going to get real busy real quick.

The town always had an influx of visitors for the holiday weekends. The New Yorkers who didn't hit the Hamptons escaped to the mountains for a hint of the country life. All the businesses were swamped; Leo said the tours around the farm were booked solid for days. Not for the first time, I wondered when I'd get to see him next. We'd talked about watching tonight's fireworks together, but—

"Did you just dreamy sigh?" Natalie asked, her tone teasing.

"What?" I thought back a few seconds and realized that yes, I'd thought about Leo and sighed. Dammit, now I'm swooning.

"You *never* dreamy sigh—ever! Tell me right now what's happening!"

Oh shit. "It's not just the diner . . . I met someone when I got here. We're Summerly Involved."

"Summerly Involved? What the hell does that mean?"

"It means that I've got someone I'm seeing. For the summer. And . . . well . . ."

She gasped. "And . . . well? You never *and . . . well.* It's condom on, condom off, wahoo, back to work. Don't tell me Miss No Fuss, No Muss is falling in—"

"Shah-ha-hut-it! Shut it right now. Don't put words in my mouth."

"What's *he* putting in your mouth?"

I hid my face in my hands. "Oh boy."

"I can tell you what I'm putting in *my* mouth. A entire plate of soup dumplings. Grab your summer love, get thee on a train, and get your ass here!"

"He can't really leave during the summer; he's a . . . well . . . he's a . . . ." I cupped my hand around my phone and quietly said, "farmer."

"He's a what?"

"A farmer," I whispered.

When she finally stopped laughing, she told me all about the farmer *she* crushed on at the Union Square Farmers' Market. Farmers were the new It Boy, it seemed.

Eventually I was able to get off the phone, promising her that I'd get into the city just as soon as I could. But for now, I had a diner to run. I headed back into the kitchen, offering a high five to Maxine as I passed, who congratulated me on getting off my feet for a change.

Nice to be needed.

"I can't believe you didn't want to go to the parade. Who doesn't like a parade?" Leo said.

We were in the kitchen of my house, washing dishes after dinner. I'd made fresh corn on the cob, Mexican street style with lots of chili powder, salt, and lime, tiny roasted fingerling potatoes with fresh chives and crème fraîche, and buttermilk fried chicken. Which was not just finger-licking good, but apparently Roxie-licking good. After one bite, Leo had pronounced it the best fried chicken he'd ever had, and then made out with my neck for a while. I couldn't wait to find out what he licked when he found out I'd made pie . . .

Now we were discussing the town's activities for the night, and my lack of interest. "I like a parade just fine; it's just that I've been to that same parade every Fourth of July since I was a kid. I know everything that will happen. The high school band plays, the cheerleaders cheer, the prom queen waves from her toilet paper float, and the mayor gives a speech. Which is usually accompanied by heavy sweating and a little slurring, due to the fact that he's already in his cups a bit. Usually from Mr. Peabody's homemade hard ginger ale, which is rotgut in a plastic cup. The fireworks go off over the town hall, everyone oohs and ahhs, and then they rush to get to their car and be home by midnight." I set down the plate I was washing and waggled my eyebrows at him. "I'd much rather stay home and enjoy some oohs and ahhs of a different kind, if you know what I mean."

He promptly set down the plate he was drying and moved behind me. Hands sneaked around my waist, drawing me close to his body. "I do know what you mean. And if you're ready for the oohs and ahhs, I've been ready to salute our country's birthday since you came to the door in that stars-and-stripes bra." He bumped his hips into mine, sharing his "salute" with my backside.

"How did you know?" I asked, turning my head to see his bashful grin.

I'd picked out this bra especially for the occasion after spying it in a window on Main Street. The local lingerie shop specialized in themed underthings. Want to make sure your stocking gets stuffed next Christmas? They'll fix you right up with a nightie that looks just like a sexy chimney. Want your boobs to look like birthday cakes for someone special? They've got a bra for that. Want a pair of panties with a strategically placed bush to commemorate Arbor Day? You betcha.

But I'd hidden my red, white, and blues under my clothes, planning to reveal them to Leo while listening to faraway booms from the town fireworks show.

"When you were shucking corn earlier, your middle button came undone. I saw it all. And by the way, I'd prefer that all corn shucking now take place naked, or at least stripped down to your skivvies. Because holy shit, you shucking corn is hard to watch without wanting to get immediately involved." His lips were on my shoulder now, nuzzling my shirt aside and exposing a star and a stripe.

"You wanted to help me shuck?"

"Let's be clear," he murmured, nipping at me a bit. "I wanted to bend you over that barrel out back and shuck you until there was corn silk everywhere."

I closed my eyes at the sudden image of Leo, strong and naked, glorious and naked, and also naked, thrusting into me from behind as he tipped me merrily over a rain barrel, while fireworks lit up the night sky and corn silk blew lazily across the yard. Instant heat bloomed low and my hips arched backward, seeking contact with anything that resembled a cornstalk. As one of his hands slipped under my shirt I felt my heart pound faster, my blood racing around my body.

My lips felt lonely. My breasts felt heavy and full. My hips felt in need of very specific guidance, mostly of the back-and-forth kind. And other areas felt achingly empty. I tipped my head back onto his chest. As his mouth moved against my neck, his scent surrounded me, earthy and grassy and salty sun-browned. I looked down as he started popping open my buttons, and saw his hands on my body. Wide, strong, and a little dirty, the line of dirt embedded underneath his nails persisting even though I know he scrubbed before coming over. Coarse, callused, hard-working hands, which were gentle as they eased my shirt from my shoulders to pool on the scuffed floor that was used to long, hot, dirty days. I wanted the same thing from him.

Long, hot, dirty days. And nights.

I spun around, letting him surround me as he leaned me back against the sink. His eyes burned as he took in my red and white and blue, and he grinned, realizing that I'd planned to celebrate this holiday with him in the naughtiest way possible.

"Look at you, Sugar Snap," he whispered, lifting me as easily as he might lift a kitten, setting me on the edge of the counter, spreading my legs in one swift move. He stood between them and pulled my legs around him as I balanced right on the edge. Then with one finger, placed exactly in the center of my stomach, he poked me. And I fell with a splash into the sink.

"What? Seriously—what?" I sputtered, legs flapping and water flying everywhere.

Leo held me at arm's length and just laughed and laughed. But when his eyes met mine again, they were less mischievous and more devious. His hands, which had been keeping me from climbing out of the sink while he laughed, now slipped under the water, sliding along the inside of my thighs, underneath my shorts and—

"You're wet," he remarked, his gaze heated.

"Well, yeah," I replied, gripping the edge of the sink as his fingers dipped lower against my—

"Not just from the water." He moved closer, flush against the counter, as I found myself leaning into his hand, bobbing in the sink. My breath caught. The passion that was always bubbling just under the surface was now catching fire, sending tingles to the tips of everything.

"Did you know your eyes change color?" he murmured, his gaze heated as looked at me closely, so closely.

"Hmm?" I tried hard to keep my eyes open, when all I wanted to do was close them and relish these feelings.

"They change. When you're excited." His fingers slipped inside my panties. My back arched involuntarily, and I held so very tight to the edge.

"I know they change . . . color when I'm . . . frustrated . . . fuck, that feels good."

"They're usually this light hazel color, maybe a little blue, maybe a little brown, but when they go green . . . mmm." He sped up his fingers. Which sped up my breathing. He leaned closer, pressing his lips to my neck, kissing a path upwards to just below my ear, where he whispered, "Did you know they go full green? Right before you come?"

I groaned. This man knew me; knew me so well. He stood back a bit, studying me.

"Look at that, they're turning even more green by the second."

All I could do was moan at the onslaught of sensations breaking across my body. He watched my eyes, his fingers slipping across my skin as I began to come apart on his hand. But just before I did, he hauled me against his chest, getting him just as wet as me. As he backed through the kitchen and out the back door, my hands immediately dug into his hair, and I kissed him wild. My legs went to wrap around him, but before I could get purchase he set me on my feet in front of the rain barrel and spun me like a top.

"This is just too good an idea to pass up." He dragged my shorts and panties down my wet legs; seconds later, I heard his zipper. Mmm. "Grab the other side there, Sugar Snap."

I leaned across, feeling the night air on my bare backside. "Like this?" I asked, looking back over my shoulder, arching my back. What I saw was the stuff of legend. Leo, face buried inside his vintage Screaming Trees tee as he pulled it off. Torso, long and lean and strong as he tossed away the shirt, then popped open the button on his jeans. Which were swiftly pushed down. I shivered as I watched him tear open the condom wrapper with his teeth, then watched his hand disappear inside his jeans. The butterflies in my tummy flew in a thousand directions at once as I saw him holding himself in his hands, rolling the condom down his thick length. Now, *this* was parade worthy.

His right hand holding himself at the base, his left hand slipped down my spine, splaying wide on the small of my back and pushing me further across the barrel. "Spread your legs a bit further, Rox—just like that," he murmured, his voice molasses thick. What is it about being told what to do while naked? It thrilled me to no end.

I held my breath as he pushed into me. He let his breath out while he pushed into me. In one long . . . slow . . . exhale. When he was buried deep inside, he said my name. His hands ran up and down my back, not moving inside me yet, just holding so very still, and yet, his hands. Soothing. Stroking. His said my name over and over again, in this gorgeous, raspy whisper that was as sexy as it was intimate. I felt, in a word, worshipped.

Then one hand closed around my shoulder. The other gripped my hip, then he thrust. It felt delicious. "God, I wish you could see how you look right now," he said, his words pouring down on me. I rolled my back like a cat, pushing back against him. I peeked back over my shoulder once more, turned on even more by the intensity on his face, how he bit down on his lower lip as he thrust, the cords on his neck tightening as he moved my body with his own.

"Tell me." My breath caught in my throat as he pulled me powerfully back against him.

The corner of his mouth tipped up in a sweet grin. "Your skin is glowing, and it's not just the moonlight."

"Yeah?"

"Every time I push into you, you tip your hips back, and Christ, I can feel you all around me."

"Mmm-hmm." I sighed, squeezing him tightly. I got a groan in response.

"And fuck, your ass looks fantastic like this." He gave me a light swat on the rear, and I cried out. Not just in surprise. "Duly noted," he murmured, slipping his hand up my spine to bury it in my hair, twisting a handful around. Tugging slightly, my neck arched, my back arched, and I was perched right on the edge, literally and orgasmically, especially as his other hand slid underneath me, just above where we were connected.

"I wonder what color your eyes are now," he groaned, his own hips speeding up, punishing, hungry, desperate. Strung out and fevered, I could feel the low ball of tension pulsing through my body, lights flashing before my eyes, his moans thick behind me. I was going full green, coming apart under the night sky, with Leo hard and slick inside me.

Happy Birthday, America.

❧

"Hey, what's that?" Leo asked.

"That's my boob."

"I'm aware of that," he said, leaning down to drop a sweet kiss on my breast. "But what's *that*? The big thing out in the bushes?"

"Clarify, please—or I'm running into the house and leaving you to deal with whatever big scary thing is in the bushes."

"That," he said, pointing toward the—

"Oh, that's the old Airstream" I said, relaxing back into his arms. Which were suddenly no longer there.

"One of those old trailers?" He was already on his feet, leaving my breast unattended. Grumbling as I buttoned my shirt, I followed him across the yard to where he stood. "Wow, look at that! How long has this been out here?"

"Hard to say. When was Nixon in office?" I replied.

He turned from where he'd been poking around the underbrush. "You're kidding."

"I never kid when I'm half naked," I answered, primly holding together my shirt. Which was mostly unbuttoned.

His eyes roamed across my body in a cursory way—almost as if, as a boy, he was unable to *not* look at a half-naked girl—but then quickly returned to the trailer. I tried not to take it personally.

Pulling a few branches off, he thumped on the metal. "Any idea of the last time it was on the road?"

"Still waiting for you to remind me of when Nixon was in office," I answered.

"Woman. You're killing me," he moaned, using his phone flashlight to try and peer inside. "People use these for all kinds of things, you know. Not just camping."

"That may be—but I'm sure critters have been camping in there for years."

"Food truck." He turned to look back at me, his flashlight shining right in my face.

Temporarily blinded, I shielded my eyes. "You want to shine that somewhere else?"

"Seriously, Roxie, this could be a food truck. They're everywhere these days."

"Dude, I'm from LA. Food trucks are a dime a dozen there."

"Dude," he said, suddenly right in front of me, flashlight turned off. "You're *from* Bailey Falls. And they're not a dime a dozen here yet."

My mind instantly ran through my culinary Rolodex, sorting through dishes that would work well in a mobile environment. Then it moved to the farmers' market—and the food-truck-free parking lot.

They say when an idea strikes, it's like a flashbulb goes off over your head. In my case, it was fireworks from city hall. Going off right over the back of my property, where an ancient Airstream gleamed in the moonlight through decades of overgrowth. And a farmer, backlit by stars and spangles, wearing only his faded jeans and a giant grin.

From up here, the town was spread out like a postcard,

nighttime lights twinkling, the Hudson River unseen in the dark but suggested by the darker smudge on the horizon. And over all of it, big splashes of fiery red, white, and blue, as the faintest hint of the high school band could be heard.

Leo's hands wrapped around my hips, standing me right in front of him, facing the fireworks, the Airstream, the town. I allowed my head to fall back against his chest, soaking in the warmth of his skin. His arms crossed in front of me, a sigh of contentment escaping as his chin settled on top of my head. And as we watched the fireworks, and I relaxed into him, I realized that the sigh came from me. And that the contentment was mine.

And for just one moment, I allowed my imagination to run wild. A food truck filled with old-fashioned cakes. A line around the block of loyal customers ready to place their orders. And Leo, there at the end of a long, hard day, ready for a long, hard night.

And I shivered, though I was very warm inside his arms.

Chapter 17

$\mathcal{I}$ slept in. Until ten in the morning. A feat unheard of in the history of Roxie Sleep. I rolled over, stretching deliciously and reaching for Leo. We'd gotten to sleep late, after spending the night postfireworks tangled up on the back porch. It hadn't escaped my attention that when Leo was in my bed, I slept longer and more deeply than I ever had before. Did he just wear me out that well? It's possible; the man gave great orgasm.

It's not just the orgasm . . .

No, it wasn't. It was just Leo. Who took up too much space in my twin bed. His hands were rough, his feet were cold even on the hottest night, and the hair on his chest tickled my nose something awful.

And I loved sleeping with him. Back to front, head to chest, butt to butt—it didn't matter, I loved it.

My hands groped across his side again, searching for a handful of warm Leo, but he was gone. My eyes opened sleepily, and I saw that he'd left me a note on my pillow.

Sugar Snap,

My heart went pitty pat to see my nickname written down. Why was that so thrilling? Anyway, back to the note.

Sugar Snap,

Got a busy day today. I'm helping Oscar move some cows onto a new field and I'm replacing the sink in my kitchen. Should be done by five though—dinner tonight? I'll bring you some of those strawberries . . .

Leo

P.S. Looking forward to getting you green in less than one minute.

I blushed, thinking of all the things he could to do to make my eyes change color. Then I blushed again when I realized I was holding the note close to my face, as if I would kiss it. I rolled over in bed, squealing like a schoolgirl with her first crush. I sighed into his pillow and breathed in the lingering trace of his scent. I giggled out loud, kicked my feet into the air, and realized again that I was moving beyond a crush.

I reread his note, eager to see his nickname for me again, and I noticed at the bottom that he'd made a little drawing.

A loose interpretation of an Airstream trailer, with a girl smiling wide, hanging out of the side window. And a line of customers leading up to it. A thought bubbled up, the same thought I'd had last night while watching fireworks from within the circle of my Almanzo's arms.

My Almanzo?

Shush. Trying to daydream here.

I coaxed the thought back up again.

A food truck. Could I do that? Could I actually decide to stay here, instead of heading back to Los Angeles? It was no longer out of the realm of possible. The cakes were certainly selling. I'd have ready access to Leo, and all that would entail. And I was very fond of his entail.

I flopped over on the bed, rereading his note for the fourth time. He was going to bring me strawberries. I could bake a strawberry pie. I *should* bake a strawberry pie. I had the day off since the diner was closed.

. . . *I'm replacing the sink in my kitchen* . . .

I'd never seen his kitchen. I'd never seen his house. I knew the way, though; he'd pointed out the side road that led to his part of the property, on a quieter part of the farm. Hmmm.

I could head over early, surprise him, get him to pick me some strawberries, and bake him that pie while I watched him replace his sink. I'd love to see him holding a wrench. The image of him holding himself last night popped into my head, and I shivered.

I headed into the shower, creating a mental list of everything I'd need to bake the surprise pie. And anything I wouldn't need . . . like panties. God willing.

Two hours later I was driving down the country road, my favorite pie plate on the seat next to me, along with all my ingredients. U2 was on the radio, "So Cruel." I'd been smiling since I woke up, and the realization made me smile even bigger.

As I drove through the gates to the farm, I marveled once more at the hustle and bustle of everything he'd created here. I was starting to get to know the farm, and could see the changes that had taken place since I first came out here for my tour. The pole beans were climbing higher and higher on their stakes, full and green and lush. The lettuce rows were thinned out, some bolting and going to seed, as Leo had explained would happen once the sun grew too strong for the cool-weather crops.

I turned onto his side road, which turned to crushed gravel as I neared where his house must be. The trees thinned, and I could feel my heart race a little. Racing just to see Leo? Rather than pushing the feeling down, I let it bloom a little. Simple happiness rolled across me, lighting me up and *lightening* me up, the wall I kept between me and men crumbling a tiny bit.

My happy fingers tapped out the tune on the steering wheel as I hummed happily along. Two more turns through the woods, and I could see a house beginning to take shape. Leo's Jeep was standing next to the house, and my heart jolted. He was home!

I pulled alongside his truck off to the side of the house, gazing up at the beautiful home. Fieldstone, soaring windows, charming shutters, and a massive chimney poking through the roof. It wasn't big, it wasn't small; it was lovely and very Leo.

And speaking of, there he was, coming down the steps of the wide front porch, laughing. He was always quick to find merriment in any situation, and I wondered what was making him chuckle. As I climbed down from my Wagoneer, I saw the source of his amusement.

Riding piggyback, with sandy blond hair and eyes that matched his, was a little girl, six, maybe seven years old. Leo took off at a gallop through the front yard as she giggled and squealed.

Just as I was trying to figure out what I was going to say, he caught sight of me, standing there with my mouth no doubt wide open. He stopped cold.

The little girl wasn't having it. Kicking at his side like she was wearing spurs, she shrieked delightedly, "Go, Daddy, go!"

I was so caught off guard that I didn't even notice when a big fat bumblebee buzzed in, flew underneath my skirt, and stung me right the fuck on my thigh.

Which hurt just as much as I was afraid it would.

For the record, I didn't run. And I didn't swear. I did swat at my leg rather violently, killing the bee and causing it to fall right on top of my foot, where it lay for all the world to see. A world that included Leo *and his daughter*. Who were walking toward me now.

"Roxie," he said in a soft voice.

I'd heard that softness before. The softness triggered a panic that ran through my whole body, and my gaze dropped away from Leo and his daughter—*his daughter*! It landed on the bee on my foot, and pain began to bloom somewhere midthigh. Two fat tears formed in my eyes and spilled down my cheeks before I could stop them.

"I got stung," I said, feeling the tears slip down my chin and onto my dress. I'd been *stung*! I kicked off the bee, watching it fall to the grass. It was a *huge* bee. And I was crying? What was happening? "I got stung," I repeated as I rubbed my leg, making it worse.

"You got stung by a bee?" the little girl asked, and I looked up into those familiar green eyes, blurry because of my tears. Bees *are* assholes! Why didn't anyone listen to me! "Yes," I sniffed, wiping my face, which was growing hotter by the second.

Leo looked concerned, but also a little bit guarded.

"Let me see, let me see!" she said.

Leo crouched down and she swung off his back in a practiced way, then ran over to me and looked up expectantly.

"Um, you want to see my bee sting?" I asked, confused.

"No, I want to see the bee. Where'd it go?"

"Oh. There it is." I pointed, seeing it in a clump of grass.

She squatted down next to it, studying it carefully. Leo came to stand by me, his eyes searching mine. I had so many questions, but right now, all I could feel was the hurt.

In my leg.

"It's a bumblebee," she said matter-of-factly. Suddenly she drew herself up straight and turned to me in horror. "You killed it."

Surprised at being put onto the defensive by such a short person, I answered, "Yes, I did. So? Don't bees die after they sting, anyway?" What the *hell*?

"Nuh-huh, only honeybees. There was no reason to kill it."

"I had a reason," I grumbled, and looked to Leo for help. Who was watching the two of us, fascinated.

Whether it was the sting, the surprise, or the fascination, my knees buckled and suddenly I was in the grass, next to a dead bumblebee, a disapproving child of indeterminate age, and a farmer with how many more surprises hiding behind his sweet face.

"Shit," I muttered, then clapped my hand over my mouth.

Leo knelt down, patted me on the shoulder, and turned to his daughter. "Polly, this is my friend Roxie."

"Hi," she said, eyeing me up and down.

"Hah," I said through my hands.

Leo smothered a laugh. "Oh boy, how 'bout we get you cleaned up?"

I nodded. Polly nodded. Leo tried to smother another laugh.

"Are you sure this is what you're supposed to use? There's not something else that actually came from the pharmacy? In a tube that says bee sting medicine?" I was sitting on the kitchen counter, next to a half-installed sink, with my leg perched on the back of a chair. I'd gotten stung on the inside of my leg right above my knee, and it was puffing up nicely.

"Baking soda and water is the best thing for a bee sting," Leo soothed, mixing up the paste with his finger.

"Baking soda neutralizes the acid from bee stings, so it's the best thing." Polly tapped her finger against her lower lip. "Unless it's a hornet sting—then you need vinegar. Did you know hornet and wasp venom is actually alkaline? The acid in vinegar counteracts the venom."

"I didn't know that," I said, hissing as Leo's finger dabbed the paste on my sting.

"Baking soda is good for lots of things around the house. You can use it to brush your teeth, and to clean pots and pans. Daddy uses it all the time. Especially on his hands when they're really dirty," Polly said, counting off the ways.

"It's good for baking too," I said. "Ever seen cake batter before it gets baked?"

She nodded. "My friend Hailey's mom bakes all the time, and sometimes she lets me lick the beater."

"Okay, so you know how it goes into the pan all gooey and flat?" I flinched as Leo patted another wad of paste on my leg. He mouthed "Sorry."

"Yes," Polly said.

"And after if comes out of the oven it's taller, right?"

"Right."

"That's what baking soda does in a cake: it makes things rise and get fluffy. But its alkaline—you used that word earlier."

"And I know what it means," she said, rolling her eyes.

Wow. Tough crowd. I looked to Leo, unsure how to proceed with this one.

"Polly, what have I told you about rolling your eyes?"

"That it's incredibly rude," she sighed, looking in my direction. "Sorry I rolled my eyes, I just read a lot." She studied me carefully. "If you say something else I already know, I won't roll my eyes."

Leo coughed. His shoulders were shaking a little too.

"Right, well, it's alkaline and doesn't taste very good. If you've brushed your teeth with it, you've probably noticed that. So if there's baking soda in a recipe, the other ingredients have to counteract that—kind of like the way vinegar counteracts the alkalinity in hornet venom."

After staring at me for a few moments, she said, "Dad, can I go play?"

"I'd like it if you'd unpack first," he said.

She jumped down off the counter and started for the front door. "I did already."

"And sorted the dirty laundry into piles?"

"Define piles," she said, and this time it was me who smothered a laugh.

"Mounds of white clothes. Mountains of dark clothes. The definition of piles does not include shoving it all into the closet and covering it with a blanket."

She headed for the stairs. "Right. On it." As she ran up the stairs, her head popped back over the banister. "Sorry about your bee sting, Roxie."

"Thanks, Polly."

"But next time don't kill the bee, okay? So goes the colony—"

"—so goes the earth. Yeah, yeah, I know," I finished, rolling my eyes. Under my breath, I said, "They're still assholes."

She grinned, disappeared, and a few seconds later I heard a door slam shut.

Alone, finally, I turned to Leo, who was sitting there with an amused expression and a pasty finger.

"You can brush your teeth with that, you know," I said, not meeting his eyes quite yet and leaning down to inspect his handiwork.

"I've been told." He also leaned down. The skin around the sting was still puffy, but the fire had begun to cool under the baking soda paste. "How're you feeling?"

"Blindsided. You?" My voice had an edge I didn't like.

"Blindsided." His voice had the same edge. "What are you doing here, Rox?"

"I came over to bake you a pie—" Omigod, the ingredients were still in the truck, in the hot afternoon sun! "Shit, I've gotta go get—"

"Whoa whoa whoa, just hold on a minute," he said, stopping me from jumping down from the counter. "Where do you think you're going?"

"There's probably butter melting all over the front seat!" I tried unsuccessfully to jump down again. "It'll be a huge mess."

"I'll get it—you stay here a minute. That paste needs to harden or it'll run all over the floor." He looked pointedly at the gooey paste. "Don't move."

I let out an exasperated sigh and tossed him my keys, then made a great show of not moving. Except for my eyes, which I rolled hard. A smile slipped out from him, and then he was gone. And I was alone in his house. With his daughter.

What. The. Hell.

The multitude of occasions he could have mentioned that he had a kid ran through my head like a newsreel. In the next reel, all the occasions where anyone in town might have mentioned this little nugget. Seriously, how could no one have *mentioned* this before?

And his daughter had just unpacked, which meant she'd been away. With her mother? Was Leo divorced? Separated? Still married?

Dread struck low in my belly as I wondered if I'd been sleeping with someone's husband. But no—Chad would have told me if he was married.

"Bleagh," I muttered, clutching my stomach. What a fucking mess. So much for summer flinging.

Just ask him.

Yes, I would do just that. But now I wondered what else Leo might have been hiding. Now that I thought about it, it seemed strange that I'd never been here. Everything had always happened at my house. Or my diner. Or my swimming hole.

I felt a sharp pang inside my chest as I thought about all the things I'd done with Leo, and wondered if it was all over now.

Get the intel.

Right. I took a deep breath, then looked around.

The house was as beautiful inside as it was outside. The chimney was the focal point of the entire lower level, stacked fieldstone with a gorgeous firebox made of deep green glass bricks. Rich chocolate brown wood floors, wide planked and shiny smooth. A two-story great room, anchored by deep built-in bookshelves, and comfortably plush couches and chairs scattered about in conversation areas. The kitchen, which was filled with high-end appliances and work surfaces made of stunning poured concrete, was wide and open; the island counter I was sitting on was big enough to seat six comfortably. The fridge, a Sub-Zero large enough to store a year's worth of food, was covered top to bottom in schoolwork. Tests, homework assignments, pictures drawn with crayon and marker.

And pictures of the two of them were everywhere. Leo holding a tiny Polly, who was wrapped in a pink blanket, one clearly wailing and one absolutely beaming. Leo holding Polly by the very tips of her fingers as she took what looked like her first steps. Leo and Polly at the farm, her hands buried in the dirt with a flat of seedlings next to her, her very own spade sticking out of the earth. Leo's face was split by a wide grin in every one. He was clearly over the moon for his daughter, and rightly so. She was a pistol.

Then I heard Leo come in through the front door.

"Butter's soft, but not too bad. Fridge?" he asked, carrying in my bags and pie pan. I nodded. "Did you stay put?" he asked, his back to me.

"Yes, I stayed exactly where I was told to."

He turned from the fridge, his expression warmed up some since he'd left. "Roxie, I—"

"Dad? My laundry is sorted. Can I go play now?" a voice called down from above.

"Come on down," he responded, eyes still on me. He offered me a sheepish grin, and I couldn't help but smile back. That grin always got to me.

"I want to go see the pigs, see how big they got while I was gone, and—what's that?" Polly had come running down the stairs, flew into the kitchen, and was now staring at the baking supplies.

"Roxie brought those with her. Something about a pie?" Leo answered, looking at me with a twinkle in his eye.

"Oh yeah—a pie," I said. "Someone was promising me strawberries, so I thought I'd—"

Polly burst out, "I *love* strawberry pie. Can I watch you make it? Is it hard? Do you make your own crust? Sometimes strawberry pie has rhubarb, will this one? There's a diner in town that makes cherry pie, but I really like strawberries better. Daddy has a new variety of strawberries this year called brown sugar strawberries. I haven't tried them yet, but he told me all about them. Are you using those? Can I help? Can I—"

"Hold on there, Pork Chop, you're talking a mile a minute. Let's slow it down a little, let Roxie catch up," Leo interjected.

He called her Pork Chop.

"Catch up to what?" she asked, totally unaware. "I can help, you know. After all, I'm seven years old."

"Well, then, you're practically driving," I joked.

She looked at me seriously. "I can't drive for another nine years."

I blinked. "Of course." I looked to Leo for help, but he was unpacking my bags. "Wait a minute—baking a pie here obviously isn't the best idea."

"Why not?" he asked.

"Why not?" Polly echoed.

"Um, well . . ." I looked around wildly. "The sink! It's out of commission, and you can't bake without having running water. Beside the fact that . . ."

Leo had grabbed some tool, disappeared under the sink for thirty seconds, popped back up, and turned on the faucet.

"Right. Well—"

"You need strawberries, right?" Leo said, lifting a small bag from the counter and spilling the world's sweetest, juiciest, most perfect brown sugar strawberries into a bowl.

"So, pie?" Polly asked, bouncing a little as she clapped her hands.

Oh, for Pete's sake . . .

"So, pie," I said, squashing my flight reflex.

Leo's phone rang and he raised his eyebrows.

"Sure, go ahead," I answered, climbing down off the counter and testing my leg. It barely hurt.

Leo had gone into another room, so I asked Polly, "Where does your—" *Good lord, I can't call him* Daddy. "Where does he keep the mixing bowls?" She was only too happy to show me.

In minutes, we had an assembly line going on the countertop: bags of flour and sugar, measuring cups I'd brought from home, a cutting board, and my best paring knife. I decided to start with the crust, and put Polly to work.

"You know how to measure flour?" I asked as she dragged a step stool over to the counter.

"I know fractions." She didn't say *duh,* but it was implied.

"Right." I may have also implied a *duh*. A point for her, though, for not rolling her eyes.

"Can you hand me the apron hanging next to Daddy's?" she asked, pointing toward the hooks by the back door.

There was indeed a small apron and a large apron. All that was needed was a medium-sized apron to make it the perfect Three Little Bears house.

I limped over to the apron, realizing after a couple of steps that I didn't need to limp. That baking soda had really done the trick. Since Polly was watching me, I turned the limp into a little sashay.

"Do you always dance when you bake pies?" she asked.

"You don't?" I asked her right back, deadpan.

"I've never baked before." She thought a moment. "I like the pie dance."

I grinned and handed her the apron. "Okay, here's what we're going to do. I'll tell you what goes into the bowl, and you can measure. I'll cut up the butter since the knife is very, very sharp, but you can add it in when we're ready. Deal?"

"Deal," she said excitedly. "Where's the recipe?"

I pointed to my head. "It's all up here."

We got to work, and after a while we had a bowl full of sliced strawberries with some lemon juice, another bowl filled with perfectly measured flour, salt, and sugar, and now Polly was adding my uniformly cut-up butter to the dry ingredients.

She questioned everything: Why was there salt in a piecrust? Why did the butter need to be so cold? She also seemed to appreciate the way I made each cube even and straight, all looking the same. Good girl.

"Okay, now press down on everything with this pastry cutter. It'll mix the flour and butter together, and then we can add the ice water."

"Ice water? In a pie?" she asked.

"Remember what I said about using cold ingredients for pastry dough?"

"The colder the ingredients, the flakier the crust," she repeated, with my exact inflection and tone.

I had to smile.

"How're we doing in here?" Leo asked, filching a strawberry from the bowl. I swatted his hand, making him laugh. As he ate the berry, he made a face. "Why are these so sour?"

"Because I haven't added the honey yet. That's why you can't sneak a bite till the chef says you can," I said, reaching for a jar of local honey.

Polly watched it all with wide eyes, then returned to her pastry cutting. Her little wrist turned over and over again in the bowl, her tongue peeking out the side of her mouth as she worked. I was suddenly struck by a vision of Leo doing this exact thing, when he was packing up a farm box on a busy Saturday.

"Bees make honey, you know. You sure you aren't scared?" Polly asked with a cheeky grin.

I felt my face heat up.

"Can it, Pork Chop; quit making fun of Roxie," Leo said. "Say you're sorry."

She looked down at the bowl. "Sorry," she said, her voice meek.

"No big deal," I answered, drizzling some honey over the berries. After tossing them a bit, I told Leo, "Try another one; see what you think."

He closed his mouth around a berry. "Mmm."

My cheeks heated again. The last time I heard him say mmm, he was enjoying something else entirely.

"My arm's tired. Is this almost done?" Polly asked, rubbing her shoulder.

I peeked over her shoulder to look in the bowl. "Looking pretty good. See how those in the corner are the size of peas?"

"There are no corners in a bowl—it's a circle." She must have caught a glance from Leo then, because she changed her tone. "Oh yeah, pea sized. I see."

"Make them all that size, and we're good to go." I began to tidy up. "A good cook always cleans as she goes."

I got a big thumbs-up from Leo on that one. He seemed more relaxed than he was earlier, more at ease with having me in his home, and around his daughter. I wished I felt the same way.

Outwardly I was calm, but inside I was still coming apart at the seams. Processing. Thinking. Second-guessing. Imagining.

And as Polly concentrated on her pea-sized dough blobs, Leo and I had a silent conversation across the island counter.

What the hell, my face said.

Later, his face replied.

Oh, you can count on that, my face assured.

His face responded with either, *We can talk later*, or *We can fuck later*. Oddly, they both looked the same.

In the meantime, however, there was an *After all, I'm seven years old* in the room, and we had a pie to finish.

In the end, a pie was made. Polly was great with a rolling pin, and when the crust tore a little bit, which was normal, she listened patiently as I taught her how to wet her fingers and pinch and smooth it back together. She asked if, when that happened, if it was a good time to dance, and I agreed. So we paused for thirty seconds for an impromptu dance break, to Leo's great delight. Polly didn't understand why he laughed so hard, and told him, "Daddy, dancing helps sometimes." How could he argue with that?

He stayed in the background mostly, fielding phone calls on occasion. I was getting the sense that his taking the day off was unexpected, and I wondered for the millionth time where Polly had been, and why she'd suddenly appeared. The note he'd left in my bed this morning referenced moving cows, gathering strawberries, and getting me green. Nowhere was anything mentioned about daughters piggyback riding.

After the pie went into the oven Polly went out to play, stopping just shy of the back door to thank me for letting her help bake. Now, alone in the kitchen with Leo, maybe I could get some answers.

"I'm hungry—you hungry?" he asked, turning away and rummaging in the pantry. Answers would not come quite yet, apparently.

"I'm not so much hungry as I am confused."

"Confused?" he repeated, seeming to be determined to make me say it all. To put my shit right out there before he did.

"Confused, as in, what the hell, Leo? Why didn't you ever tell me you had a—"

The front door slammed. "Can we go down and see the chickens? I want to see if they remember me." Polly came running into the kitchen, and stopped just short of plowing into me. "I mean, when the pie's done, of course."

I knew my limit, and I'd just about reached it.

"You know what, I think I'm gonna take off now. Don't worry, the timer is set, and remember what I said about seeing the juice bubbling up? When the timer goes off, if the pie is bubbling, it's ready to come out. If not, just give it a few more minutes. You can help her check on the bubbling, right, Leo?"

"Rox—" he started.

I spun for the door. "I'll get the baking stuff later. Nice to meet you, Polly."

I all but sprinted for the door, hauled ass across the lawn, and was backing out of the driveway in the time it takes to say *there she blows*.

All things considered, I thought I'd handled it pretty well. Until I realized I'd forgotten my purse.

I slowed down to the speed limit. There was no way I was going back now.

Chapter 18

$\mathcal{I}$ slammed the pan down on the burner. My knife cut angrily through the butter. I tossed a pat or two into the pan, watching it instantly sizzle.

Dammit.

I added olive oil, swirled the two together, then pressed a sixteen-ounce rib eye into the hot pan. I let it char on one side, while I chopped the parsley as if it had done something personal to me.

Dammit.

I listened to the steak sizzle, trusting my ears to tell me when it was time to flip it as I murdered the parsley. The familiar rhythm of chopping distracted me from the thoughts that were rolling around inside my brain like bowling balls, heading down the alley toward my very firmly ensconced pins.

Pin 1.   Don't get involved.
Pin 2.   Enjoy the penis. Engage no other organ.
Pin 3.   Attachments are for suckers. *See also* Mom.
Pin 4.   Falling in love sucks.

Whoa, whoa, hold the phone there. Falling in love? Who said anything about—

I mentally picked up the bowling balls and threw them through the plate glass window in the bowling alley in my mind.

Dammit!

After I'd left Leo's I'd driven home, circled the driveway, headed back into town, dropped by the butcher shop, and asked for the biggest, most beautiful cut they had. The Flintstones-sized rib eye was perfect. I scraped my parsley into a bowl and started pulverizing a perfectly innocent clove of garlic.

Innocent, my foot—let's see what *you're* hiding. I pounded and smashed, added a sprinkle of kosher salt, and mashed it all into a beautiful little paste, which I stirred into the parsley, which was glad to no longer be the object of my . . . anger? Was I angry?

Did that parsley just snort at me? I drowned it in olive oil, squeezing a lemon over the entire mixture until it yelled "Uncle!" then whisked it into oblivion.

All to avoid feeling the . . .

Steak's done! I forked it onto the cutting board, covering it with foil to let it rest while I looked around the kitchen for something else to massacre. Tomatoes. Oh, look at that—tomatoes. Harvested by hand, from plants nurtured in perfectly tilled soil by perfectly bearded hipsters, in the land of organic milk and asshole honey, where everyone was happy and in tune with the earth, and the entire world narrowed down to slow, sustainable, and the concept du jour—local.

Fuck local. I'd *fucked* local, and look where it got me. Angry/not angry, listening/not listening for a phone call or text, feeling/not feeling overwhelmed, confused, betrayed, and slightly . . . used?

I grabbed the goddamned tomatoes by their stupid vines, tore the door almost from its hinges, and threw them as hard as I could across the backyard, splashing through the tangle of vines to spatter against the Airstream.

"Nice shot."

Dammit! The last tomato in my hand became gazpacho. I whirled around to find Leo standing next to the house, and I had to resist two simultaneous urges. To mash the tomato into his face. And to then lick it off.

I chose neither, opting for calm and neutral.

"What are you doing here, Leo?" I asked, throwing the dripping tomato into some bushes and stalking back into the house, knowing he'd follow. As I rinsed and dried off my hands, I was surprised at how much they were shaking. So much for neutral.

I could feel his eyes on me as I moved around the kitchen, and I avoided his gaze, tidying up, restacking plates that didn't need it.

He didn't answer my question, so I finally looked up at him, raising my eyebrows. His face was cautious, tinged with something a little like . . . hope? I steeled myself.

"I wanted to talk to you," he finally answered, watching as I uncovered the steak that had been resting.

I picked up a carving knife and began to slice. "So, talk," I replied, arranging the steak on a plate and drizzling the parsley and lemon mixture over it. No way was I going first here. I wasn't playing my hand until I saw what else he might have.

He said, "You ran out of there so fast this afternoon I didn't have a chance to—"

"I've been here for *weeks*, Leo—weeks! And you never *once* thought to mention you had a daughter?" I jammed a bite of steak into my mouth and chewed it furiously. "Like, hey, Roxie, here's some of these strawberries you like—my kid loves them too," or, "Thanks for showing me this swimming hole; I'll have to bring Polly up here sometime," or, "Hey, Roxie, before I fuck you senseless, did I mention the fact that I've got a secret daughter?"

I cut the steak so hard that half of it went flying to the floor, and the other half streaked across the platter. I blinked up at Leo, who wore an expression that I imagine someone who's just been slapped might wear.

"You're kidding me, right?" he asked softly.

I dug into the remaining half of my steak, sawing back and forth with a vengeance. "Not sure what I'd be kidding about here, Leo. You lied to me."

"I never lied."

"You want to talk *semantics*? A lie of omission is still a lie." I forked up a big bite of steak and shoved it in.

Leo scrubbed his hands down his face, as if he couldn't believe what he was hearing. "Did you really just Bill Clinton me?"

"Call it what you want. But you and I both know that you chose not to tell me about your daughter, and where I come from"—I paused to swallow—"that makes you a liar."

"Where I come from, it doesn't make me a liar. It makes me cautious about who I trust with my family," he replied evenly, crossing his arms and leaning back against the counter.

Before I had a chance to send over the next volley, he looked straight through me. "And you and I both know that you made it clear from the beginning that you wanted nothing to do with me beyond this summer."

"I didn't . . . that's not . . . you make it sound like . . ." I spluttered, trying to form a sentence.

"You did, it is, and it's exactly what it sounds like," he replied.

"You agreed! I asked you, and you agreed! We *both* went into this knowing exactly what this was, and haven't we had a grand old time?" I snapped, kicking my chair back into its place and dumping my plate into the sink. "This, right here, is the reason I don't get involved."

I glared into the sink, the room now silent except for the *drip drip drip* from the old faucet. Then a shuffle, and then the hairs on the back of my neck stood straight up. Because he was behind me, and my stupid traitor skin knew enough to be thrilled.

"That night you made me dinner, here, with the beets? What did you tell me?" he asked, his voice low, his mouth only inches away from my ear.

"I told you lots of things," I hedged, trying like hell to resist the muscle memory that was aching to lean my head back, onto his chest, which I knew was steady and strong.

"You told me love was messy, painful, and emotionally draining."

I winced to hear my words thrown back at me. But then he went on. "Do you remember that first night I had you, on the porch?"

The memory came so fast the moan was out of my mouth before I could stop it. Leo, strong and beautiful, sliding in and out of me, gazing down at me with something like wonder. I nodded, biting down on my lip to stop from moaning again.

His hands were on either side of me now, his heat all around me. "And I told you it'd been a long time for me?"

I did remember. That first time, it'd been frantic and furious and incredible. Then he'd fucked me again upstairs, this time slow and sure, with more of the same incredible. I nodded again, wondering where this was going.

"My daughter is seven years old," he whispered, his lips nearly touching my ear.

My brow crinkled. What did that have to do with—oh. Oh now, wait a minute. He couldn't mean . . . *oh*. Realization dawning, I spun around, confused but not really that confused anymore.

"You mean that you hadn't— Not since—*Really?*" I asked, my hands automatically going to his chest, looking him dead in the eyes. "But that's . . . You're so . . . That's criminal!"

"Criminal?" he asked, the corner of his mouth lifting the tiniest bit.

I smacked his chest for emphasis. "Have you *seen* yourself? More to the point, have you *fucked* yourself?"

And that, ladies and gentlemen, brought to mind imagery that would keep me warm on cold winter nights for the rest of my life. Not to mention the heat that flared in his eyes. I felt my own cheeks flame, and I knew I was losing credibility here. "I just mean— hell. I don't know what I mean." I patted his chest absently, grounding myself in the feel of him. "I guess the question is, why?"

"Why I hadn't had sex in so long? Or why I didn't tell you about Polly?" he asked, his arms still on either side of me. One hand came up easily to my hip, settling there, his thumb stroking the skin exposed.

It thrilled me no end to have his hands on me once more. And it scared me beyond belief that his hands could thrill me so. Did I have the courage to push past that?

"Answer both," I ventured, my hands no longer patting but smoothing, soothing. Touching just because I could? Okay, we'll go with that.

"I *will* answer both; they're actually linked. But it's a bit of a story—are you up for it? It's all the things you say you don't like: messy, painful"—he bumped his hips into mine—"and emotionally draining."

He was giving me a choice here. Not just to hear his story, but to take this next step with him. To hear his story, and let him in. To hear his story, and he'd trust me with it. Was I up for this?

I chewed on my lip. He stroked my hip.

"Okay," I said carefully, then placed a kiss in the exact center of his chest. "Let's hear it."

We sat on the front porch on opposite ends of the old wicker sofa, separated by a pillow I'd unwittingly erected between us. Probably not the most receptive-seeming way to listen to his story, but I needed this small distance.

These strong emotions were exhausting. I now understood why, when my girlfriends complained about how stressful relationships were, they said they were *tired* of all the back and forth and arguing and feeling let down.

Frustration, elation, being determined and driven—I knew those feelings inside and out. But the emotions of being involved with someone romantically? I had no primer except my mother's—hence the determined, driven, and avoidant.

After telling Leo okay, I went straight for the scotch, and he accepted my offer of a highball. So here we sat, just us and our highballs, and Leo told me his story.

"I was born in Manhattan, Lenox Hill hospital—"

"A poor black child?" I just couldn't help it.

He smiled, but arched an eyebrow. "Pretty sure you agreed to hear my story, not embellish it."

I mimed zipping my lip, locking it, then throwing the key over my shoulder. I then had to fish around in my pocket for a second key to unlock it so I could take a sip of my water, as I was thirsty.

He watched all of this with an amused expression, then waited for me to get settled. "You done there, squirmy?"

I nodded. "Proceed."

He did. Being born into a family of extreme privilege brought its obvious perks, but also a side of life that I'd never given much thought to.

"What elementary school did you go to?" he asked.

"Bailey Falls East Elementary."

"And why did you go to that school?"

"Because we lived closer to it than Bailey Falls West Elementary."

"Mm-hmm. Easy. Simple. Not the same for me. The name Leopold Matthew Maxwell was on the list for Dalton two weeks after I was born. Unofficially, even before I was born, there was a Baby Maxwell on the list. My whole life, I was brought up according to the best things that particular life had to offer. When it came time for college, there was no question about where I'd go."

"Adirondack Community College?" I asked, earning a grin.

"My father went to Yale, my grandfather went to Yale—guess where my great-grandfather went to school?"

"Adirondack Community College?" I repeated.

He gave me a shocked look. "How'd you guess?" He rubbed his chin thoughtfully. I could hear the rasp against his fingertips, and I'd come to associate that sound with Leo and that sandy-blond gorgeous. "My great-grandfather was even a legacy student: we Maxwells go back six generations in New Haven.

"Everything was preset. Parties, trips, vacations around the world. There was a circuit I was on—we all traveled together, pledged the same clubs and fraternities together. And the girls—wow, they were everywhere. I was a dick back then. Girls and women all wanted a piece, and I was only too glad to give them one. My friends were all exactly like me: just going through the motions, enjoying the extremely easy lifestyle until we could get on with the business of real life. And the definition of 'real life' to us? Of the guys I went to high school and college with, there are at least three congressmen, four CEOs, an ambassador, and one host of a very important political talk show on CNN."

I threw back the last of my drink. My head was starting to spin. "Okay, so life of a young rich boy, I got it. When did you get off the train? Where did you deviate?"

"Funny you should mention that," he said with a rueful look.

As he went on, the picture of charmed life began to have a slightly darker underbelly. After Leo graduated from Yale he went to work for his father, going into banking as he simultaneously pursued his MBA.

"I was learning a little bit of everything, trying to find my place within the system. Each generation of my family tries it all, works in almost all sectors of our business, before finding their particular niche. I bounced around longer than most. It wasn't that I didn't have an appreciation for what my family had built. But nothing was ringing any bells for me. Nothing was interesting beyond the paycheck. What I was interested in was partying, enjoying the good life that, frankly, I hadn't earned. But try telling that to a twenty-three-year-old."

I kicked back on the swing, the movement soothing as I listened to Leo's story—the parties, the women, the coke. I can't say I was ready to pronounce him a poor little rich boy, but it certainly seemed there was a pressure that came with the extreme wealth he'd been born into. He *did* bounce around within his family's company, although it was clear when your last name was Maxwell it wasn't a hard forty-hour work week, like some. Forty hours, *pfft*. My mother worked fifty to sixty my entire life, and that was a *hard* fifty to sixty.

"Remember the financial crisis a few years back? All those mortgage loans, all those foreclosures, all those people who lost their homes because they couldn't afford their balloon payments?"

"I sure do. My mother almost lost this house," I replied, and I watched as he winced. "She'd been dating a mortgage guy who talked her into refinancing. And not thinking that the loan would surely outlast the relationship, she was completely surprised when the payments increased—something about an adjustable rate?"

"Yep, tons of people got suckered into new loans called ARMs: adjustable rate mortgages."

"We were lucky. We knew the president of the local bank and were able to get her moved back into her original loan, but she lost a ton of her savings to do so." I stopped swinging. "Was your family involved in that kind of banking?"

"My family is involved in all kinds of banking. My family *is* banking." He looked stricken.

"So, yes then."

"Yes. Of course yes. Did you know there are probably less than twenty people in the world who can actually explain the cluster-fuck that happened, how many arms and legs that entire mess had, and the effect it had on literally everything? The statistics of it, the advanced mathematical theories that need to be employed to truly understand what happened, and how truly fucked up it was, are staggering."

"I don't need to understand the math to know it was fucked up. My mother was considering moving into the diner. I get it." I started to swing again, my foot angrily kicking at the porch, keeping up the pace.

"I started to think twice about the family business, how thoroughly linked it all was, and what it stood for. And around that time, as I was beginning to question my place within the company, I met Melissa."

It's amazing how quickly an opinion can be formed. All I knew about this woman was her name, and I was instantly on guard. I had an almost physical reaction to another woman's name on Leo's lips. And that told me more about my own feelings that I cared to admit, at least for the moment. I kept up the swinging, needing the rhythm.

"At first, she was just another girl, one of many. Melissa had just filtered into the group I was running with at the time, a friend of a friend, and as she began to be at the same places I was, an attraction happened. And other things happened. But as I got to know her, she seemed . . . hmm," he paused for almost the first time in his story, seeming almost lost in thought. "Different. She was different from everyone else. She came to New York from a small town in Wisconsin, she wasn't at all concerned with money and last names and who everyone was or might become one day. Anyway, we started dating, and then dating more seriously, and just like that, I was head over heels. I introduced her to my parents, stopped dating anyone else, and we became exclusive." He paused to look at me carefully. "You okay?"

"Why wouldn't I be okay?" I asked.

"You're about to swing us right off this porch," he said, and I noticed for the first time how much air we were catching. My body had a *very* definite reaction to this *Melissa*. Dragging a foot, I slowed us down to a normal pace.

"Sorry about that. You and this *Melissa*—I mean, you and Melissa—exclusive. Go on." I forced my foot to just barely graze the porch every so often.

He did. They dated for months, she met everyone he was close to, she was welcomed thoroughly into the family. A junior partner at an accounting firm, she was knowledgeable in many areas of finance, and could hold her own in most conversations. *She could kill it at a cocktail party*, he said, and he was proud to have her on his arm.

But as the economic recovery was still struggling, Leo began to voice some of his concerns over the practices that not only the Maxwells were employing, but the banking world in general. "She'd encourage me to speak up, share my ideas, but I began to notice that she'd always add in something about it not being the right time, or to maybe keep some of it to myself until the climate had shifted, things like that. She knew I was unhappy with things at work, yet when we'd talk it out, I'd always come away feeling more confused than I was before, unsure about my position and how vocal I should be."

He suddenly looked into my eyes, intense and a bit haunted. "Have you ever gotten so totally thrown by someone, you have no idea how it could have happened?"

"Honestly? No." I paused, chewing on my lip. "But that's because I never let anyone get close enough." *Very dramatic gulp.* "Until you."

We stared at each other, the emotion between us shimmering in the air in giant waves of *ohmygodthisguycouldwreckmeforalwaysbutImightbeokaywiththat* until a noisy jaybird startled us.

Lifting one corner of his mouth in that adorable way, he went on. "Well, until Melissa, I'd been the same way. But she snuck right on under the fence, under everyone's fence—and my entire family was born with a gold-digger alarm."

"No," I breathed, and he nodded.

"Oh yeah. She was so good, I didn't even see her coming. I continued to waffle back and forth about how involved I wanted to get at work, whether I wanted to make a shift into a different division, try something new—and then we spent a weekend up here in Bailey Falls. I hadn't been up to the farm in years, but we both wanted to get out of the city for a long weekend, and she seemed fascinated by all the properties my family owned, and away we went up the Hudson. She seemed impressed by the overall size of the house, and the grounds of course, but a bit disappointed in the state of things up here. Especially since no one had lived on the farm full-time in years, things were a bit rustic."

"Rustic as all grand old country homes can be," I said in a simpering Upper East Side accent, and he grinned.

"Exactly. Anyway, three very important things happened during

236 ~ ALICE CLAYTON

that trip. One, I visited a nearby organic farmer, a farm that I'd been read about in *The New Yorker*, about how he was doing amazing things with an old property. That Saturday morning while she was still asleep, I took out the old caretaker's Jeep and ran around our property all day, following the old fields and seeing possibilities with the land I'd never seen before." His face lit up as it always did when he spoke about the land, and the way he tended to it.

"And the second important thing?" I asked.

"I heard the end of a conversation Melissa was having with her mother, bragging about how big the house was, but also how rundown everything seemed to be, and what she'd do to it if given the chance to be a Mrs. Maxwell."

My nose wrinkled, and my lips pursed together. Once more, he nodded in agreement.

"So did you tell her to pack it on up and take her *big but rundown* ass back to the city?" I asked, rolling my eyes when he shook his head.

"No, but I did tell her the beginnings of the idea that became Maxwell Farms," he said ruefully. "She wasn't too keen on the idea."

"I can imagine," I huffed, knowing already who this woman was. She seemed exactly like Mitzi St. Renee and the gaggle of size-zero assholes whom I used to cook for in Bel Air. But I was also seeing Leo in my mind's eye—younger, more citified, standing right on the edge of becoming the fantastic guy I knew, doing exactly what he loved, making the world a little bit better, and a lot sexier. "So, what was the third important thing that happened?"

"Right after I told her she shouldn't worry so much about how rundown the house might be, she told me she was pregnant."

The swing stopped so suddenly I almost pitched forward onto the porch, not realizing for a second or two that it was my own foot that stopped it.

Leo reached out to catch me, then set a comforting hand

on my shoulder as I reeled from the news he'd received almost eight years ago.

"You're shitting me," I said through my teeth.

"I'm not shitting you," he assured, rubbing my back in soothing circles. "Although I said something similar."

"Do you think she planned it? To get pregnant I mean, or is that too rude to ask?"

"It's not rude, and it's also the same question almost every person I know asked at one point. Whether she did or not, it almost doesn't matter."

"I suppose not," I answered, leaning into the circles he was painting on my back, which turned into an entire arm around my shoulder. I leaned into that, too.

"Anyway, we tried for a while to make it work, considered getting engaged, but my eyes were wide open now, and I knew it was just a matter of time before it all went to hell. What I *didn't* know was that it was also a matter of money."

"What does that mean?"

"We tried to make things work between us because we were having a kid. But it became clear very quickly that 'things working' wasn't going to be in the cards for us, and we began to fight constantly. Which made me nervous, because I knew all that stress wasn't good for the baby. But when I made an off-hand comment one night about giving her a bag of cash to just give me the baby after she was born, she jumped all over it."

"No, oh my God, no," I whispered, horrified.

"I couldn't believe it, either, but she was dead serious. Turns out all her contacts in Manhattan were a little shady. She wasn't nearly the big swinging dick she thought she was at her firm, and for an accountant, she had a terrible spending habit. So having a Maxwell baby?" He spit out the words, two red spots burning high on his cheekbones. "That was a payday she was pretty excited about."

"Leo. I'm so sorry," I said, turning in his arms and resting my head on his chest, wrapping my arms as tightly as I could around his waist.

"It's all good, Sugar Snap. Because I got that fantastic kid out of the whole deal." He held me just as tight, his chin resting on the top of my head, where he now dropped a kiss affectionately. "It was a mess for a while, sure—the gossip columns were brutal, and I wouldn't wish that hell on my worst enemy. But once the lawyers got involved and a settlement was reached, it was a done deal. She had the baby, she held Polly exactly three times, and we haven't seen her since. My accountant tells me the checks are still cashed monthly, and that's the only contact I have with her."

The backs of my eyelids prickled, wondering how this woman could give up her own child for a check.

"But after that, things got so much better. I quit my job after talking to my father, explaining that I just couldn't be a part of that scene anymore. And I'm grateful my name afforded me the opportunity to take over the farm and really grow something incredible."

"Pardon the pun," I chuckled quietly.

"Once Polly was a few months old, I started spending more and more time up here, getting things ready, building the house we live in now, and apprenticing at the farm I'd visited that weekend when everything exploded. I hired a few people to help me out around the property, started turning over the fields, and a year after Polly was born, we moved out of the city and into the country full-time. I didn't want her growing up the way I did, and with the Page Six mentality swirling around my family and speculation about where Polly's mom might have gone, I knew it was better to remove ourselves altogether. It rocked the Maxwell boat a bit, and I don't see my family as often as I'd sometimes like, but my family is really all about me and Polly now, and this life we're creating together."

"Sure. That's got to come first."

"Polly did really well here, and even though people in this small town read the same magazines as they do in the city, they seemed to kind of . . . I don't know, watch out for us. I found a great nanny, a few actually, and if I wasn't with Polly, she had really great people with her. It's a great town to raise a kid."

I smiled.

"Everything revolved around Polly, and the farm. And after everything that happened, the absolute *last* thing on my mind was getting involved with another woman."

"You never even thought about it?" I asked, twisting in his arms to look up at his sweet face.

"Sure, I thought about it," he admitted sheepishly, a different kind of pink coloring his cheeks now. "But never wanted to risk upsetting this life. Never wanted to trust anyone with Polly, after I saw her own mother throw everything over just for money."

"Mmm-hmm," I said, something low, and unexpected, twisting in my stomach.

"And then you showed up," he said, forcing my chin up to look him in the eyes, which were soft. "And Polly was away at summer camp for the first time. And I had a summer where I could just . . . relax. Be a guy. Get a little starstruck over some L.A. chick."

"And I made sure to tell you a thousand times I was leaving at the end of the summer," I sighed, as the last puzzle piece clicked into place.

"You sure made it easy for me to simply enjoy," he said, his voice heating up and heating me through. Nuzzling my neck, he pressed a kiss just behind my ear. "But something happened that I wasn't expecting."

I held my breath, waiting to see what he would say.

"It became more than just a summer thing—don't you think?"

"Yes," I whispered, answering his question as well as my own. It was out there now. We had gone beyond the simple pleasure and were into something deeper, unexplored on my end, and likely scary on his.

"And then Polly came home early, with almost no warning. I would have told you, Rox, but she came back while her nanny was on vacation. I had no one to watch her so I could come talk to you, and that's not the kind of thing you want to say over the phone. I was already trying to think of a way to tell you about her, about us, to make staying here a . . ." He trailed off, not finishing his sentence.

I finished it for him. "A possibility?"

"Is it?" he asked.

I sighed. "I don't know Leo," I admitted. I felt him exhale. "But I'll . . . I'll think about it."

"Really?"

"Yes. Obviously its gone beyond a summer fling for me, too. Dammit, why the hell are you so awesome?" I laughed, sliding off the swing and pulling him with me. He had baggage, Lord knows I had baggage, but maybe. Just maybe. "Just let me think a little bit, okay?" I said, letting my hands creep up his chest and around his neck, feeling his good heat soak through my shirt and into my bones. He killed me.

"We can still have fun, you know," he whispered, his hands sliding down to my backside, crushing me further into him.

"I'm going to need you to prove that, please," I laughed, bumping my hips against his, "because this day has been weird long enough."

He proved that we could still have fun. And that farmers are hot. But damn near *nothing* is as hot as Farmer Dad.

Chapter 19

"You are the best goddamn thing I've seen all day." I inhaled deeply, reveling in the fresh, earthy smell, even salivating a little. I looked around to make sure no one was looking, then I rubbed my cheek over the firm, thick loaf of artisanal sourdough rye that the bakery just delivered. Tender, crumbly, with a beautiful brown scored crust, I was delighted to find that it was still warm.

"Ahem," I heard, bringing me out of my doughy reverie.

"Oh, sorry," I said to the scandalized driver.

I signed for the delivery and paid the poor man, who backed out of the door, clipboard in hand, as I stood cradling the bread like a baby.

"Get a grip, Roxie," I told myself. But two seconds later, I smelled the loaf like I'd seen mothers sniffing their baby's head. Something about the smell of a newborn? Is it wrong that I feel the same way about a warm swirled rye?

Racks of gorgeous bread were waiting to be sliced for sandwiches. My mother had been ordering white bread from the local bakery since before I was born, sliced thin for toast and thick for sandwiches—which she almost endearingly called *sangwiches*.

I'd altered her order, keeping the traditional white bread but adding a few other varieties, mostly for the new line of deli *sangwiches* I'd premiered to great fanfare.

Swirled rye for the Reuben. I'd updated the classic by adding a little lemon to the Russian dressing, and a very thin slice of smoked Gouda hidden between the Swiss.

Dark, dense pumpernickel. I paired it with thinly sliced Vidalia onions, horseradish cream, and thick slices of Polish ham.

Caraway rye for the pastrami. Cut thick from whole briskets that I sourced from a local butcher in Hyde Park, the pastrami was reminiscent of that from 2nd Ave. Deli in the city. It was slathered with teary-hot deli mustard . . . and nothing else. Come on, I was still a New York girl.

I used other breads in other ways too. We still made our traditional French toast with thick-cut white bread, but I'd added a brioche bread pudding to the menu. Eggy brioche slices soaked in vanilla egg custard, then baked with currants and pecans in between, topped with powdered sugar and allspice? It might have sold out every day since I'd added it to the menu.

I admired this bread the way a sculptor might admire a piece of virgin marble. Just a block of rock, but what else might it be? What could it become under a master's hands? I rubbed the pumpernickel again.

"Would you rather we left you alone?" Leo asked from behind me. Starting a little, I turned to see him standing in the swinging door that led to the dining room.

I smiled, a little bashfully, full of feelings I couldn't name and wouldn't even try to explain. After last night, I was a bit unsure as to how we moved into this new phase of . . . whatever this was. I'd never been here before. Would it be weird? Would it be strange? Would we immediately go from being cool and happy-go-lucky, into some kind of now-we're-a-couple-and-

this-is-how-couples-behave-and-holy-shit-wait-a-minute-are-
we-a-*couple*—

A kiss broke me out of my incipient panic. It was just the
tiniest brush against my lips, but so warm and sweet that it cut
right through my bullshit and made me want another kiss. And
another one.

Leo's hands sneaked around to the small of my back as he
tugged me against him, little light kisses dancing off in a line
toward my neck.

"Hi," he murmured, speaking directly to my heartbeat, cur-
rently thumping against his lips.

I breathed in deeply, luxuriating in his scent. All that green
grass and salty skin. His beard rasped a bit against my collarbone, and I realized that the feel of him, rough and scruffy, was
something I'd also gotten very much used to.

"I've got a pile of bacon here that's getting cold, and you
know Mr. Beechum hates cold bacon. So eighty-six the kissyface
and get your buns back to work." Maxine cracked my buns with
a dish towel as she walked by with a crooked smile.

My kissyface had been noticed. My kissyface would be the
talk of the condiment station within minutes, and out on the
gossip wire within the hour.

Eh.

Eh?

Yeah, eh.

It's a new world order.

I dared to sneak in one more kiss, then smiled up at him.
"What's up?"

"We're here for lunch," he replied, his eyes dancing.

Riiiiight. Cue cold water bucket. Because Leo was already a
we. And would always be a *we*. And as someone who already had
issues with being a *we*, this would be tricky for me.

I smiled bravely, determined to see how this played out. I'd promised Leo I'd try.

Pushing through the swinging door into the hustle and bustle, I spied Polly sitting at the end of the counter. Taking a deep breath, I sauntered out like I owned the place—which technically, in my mother's will, I did—determined to show no fear.

"Hey there, Polly, how's it hanging?" I asked. I actually asked a kid how's it hanging. And I know this because the words were flashing in the air, enclosed in a bubble like in a comic strip. A comic strip titled "Things to Never Say to a Child."

I looked over my shoulder to see if Leo had caught it, and he was just staring at the ceiling, shaking his head.

Polly looked confused. "How's what hanging?"

Flailing, I said, "Your ponytail, of course!" I smiled so widely I could feel my lips stretch.

She smoothed her ponytail with her fingers. "Fine, I guess."

"Well, that's just great. So what can I do you for?"

"I'm starving," she announced, sitting primly on her counter stool.

"Then, you've come to the right place. I was just getting ready to make myself a grilled cheese. You like grilled cheese?"

"I don't like grilled cheese," she said. As I started to think of other options, she leaned across the counter and said in a dead serious voice, "I love grilled cheese."

"Fantastic," I replied, deadpan as well.

"Hey, Rox? She likes her grilled cheese with Velvee—"

"Hush," I said, which made Polly giggle. "You want the regular grilled cheese or you want the Roxie Special Grilled Cheese?"

"Roxie Special!" she shouted. Then, as though she'd caught herself having fun, she repeated "Roxie Special" in a nonchalant manner.

"Coming right up," I answered, shooing Leo onto the stool next to her.

"Aren't you going to ask if I want a Roxie Special?" he asked, just as Maxine came around the corner with a wet dish towel.

"*Another* one?" she asked with a wink and a snap of her towel.

Leo's mouth fell open, then closed when he saw Polly studying his reaction.

"What did she mean, Daddy?" I heard her ask as I backed into the kitchen, laughing to myself. Facing the grill, I commandeered a corner for myself from Forever Grumbling Carl, and went to work.

Ten minutes later, I slid three piping-hot grilled cheese sandwiches onto plates and carried them out front.

"Oooo," Polly breathed as I set the sandwich in front of her.

"Oooh," Leo breathed as he looked at the sandwich in front of her. "Wow, Rox, that's beautiful, but—"

"This doesn't look like my regular grilled cheese," Polly said, looking at the sandwich, then me, then the sandwich again.

"No, ma'am," I replied from my side of the counter. I picked up half of my sandwich, and a string of ooey gooey fontina followed.

Fontina, layered with mozzarella and English cheddar, topped with thin slices of Granny Smith apple, and the barest hint of fresh sage. The bread? Thickly sliced caraway rye, buttered on both sides and blackened with grill marks. I took a huge bite, rolling my eyes up to the heavens as I enjoyed the fuck out of my sandwich.

"What's that sticking out of the side?" Polly asked.

"Apple."

"On a grilled cheese?"

"Oh yeah." I nodded through a mouthful.

"My dad always says you're not supposed to talk with your mouth full."

I shot right back, "My mom always says to eat what's put in front of you."

She thought about that a moment, head tilting to the side in the spitting image of her father. "My dad says that too," she agreed, and picked up her sandwich. She sniffed it, wrinkled her nose, then took a tentative bite.

I noticed that Leo wasn't breathing. I noticed this because I was also not breathing. Which is why when Polly's face lit up with a huge grin, her bangs were ruffled in the breeze as we tandem exhaled.

Rather than make a big deal out of it, I just picked up my sandwich triangle, clinked it with Leo's, and the three of us ate lunch together. But every time he caught my eye, his eyes were smiling. By the end of the meal, I'd learned that Polly loved the color blue, she wanted to be a horse trainer or a meatologist (aka someone who did the weather on TV) when she grew up, and that the Roxie Special was her new favorite sandwich. It was "lots more grown-up than the sandwich Daddy makes. His favorite cheese is string. Mine was spray can but not anymore!"

Oh for God's sake, this kid was making me a little funny around the edges. By the time the sandwiches were just crusts, Maxine offered to let Polly pick out the next few songs on the jukebox, and Leo and I were left alone.

"So that went well," he said, reaching across the counter and stealing the last pickle from my plate.

"Yep, grilled cheese is my specialty," I said.

"Not just the grilled cheese; I meant—"

"Oh, I know what you meant," I interrupted, feeling a little funny around the edges now for a different reason. "You just happened to be in town, and just happened to come in here for lunch."

He dropped that slow grin on me, and I wobbled slightly. "Hey, we had to eat, right?"

Rolling my eyes, I nodded yes, they had to eat.

"You going to Chad and Logan's housewarming Saturday night?" he asked, changing the subject.

"Of course." I started clearing the plates, bending down to put them in the plastic tub under the counter.

He leaned across the counter a little. "Want to go together?"

I popped back up. "Wow—bringing his daughter around, inviting me to parties . . . look who's making things official all of a sudden?" I gave him a toss of hair over my shoulders to soften my words slightly, but no matter, the words landed.

"Hell, yes, a housewarming party makes it official," he said lightly, pretending to toss his own hair over his shoulder. He'd peeped my game, and wasn't having it. "It's a party, Rox. I'm just asking you to go to a party; it's not till death do us part."

Have you ever been in a room filled with ambient noise, and you know can have a private conversation that no one can possibly overhear, because of all the background chatter? But then suddenly—usually during the juiciest part—all the side noise falls away, and everyone hears what you're saying?

Now imagine that in a small-town diner, when there's a break in the jukebox playlist exactly as Leo Maxwell, the town's most eligible bachelor, says *till death do us part* to Roxie Callahan, runaway daughter and least eligible bachelorette?

Maxine and her cohorts had a banner day at the condiment station. A banner day.

Chapter 20

That week went from weird to weirder. I stayed super busy at the diner, was baking cakes after we closed for the orders that were pouring in, and was starting to realize that even with the artisanal bakeries, the mom-and-pop joints, and the local locavore diet, people were flat-out clamoring for cakes made the way their grandma used to make them. I was knee deep in red velvet, up to my eyes in bourbon cream, and more often than not, went to bed at night with coconut in my hair.

What I *wasn't* going to bed with was a certain farmer whom I'd become used to having at my disposal whenever the need (which was always) arose (which on him was always). But when you add a kid to the mix, especially one as precocious as Polly, it became less summer lovin' and more summer talkin'. And textin'. And oh my goodness, could Leo sext.

It wasn't like I'd seen him every night before Polly popped onto the scene. But more often than not, sometime around six I'd get a call asking if I'd eaten (code for "can I come over and will you feed me your delicious food"), or a text around ten asking what I was up to (code for "can I come over and will you feed me your delicious puss"—strike that, I'm keeping that code under wraps). And eventually, after the rocking and the rolling, he'd fall asleep and I'd fall asleep, tucked into his side or enveloped entirely, as he liked to do.

He didn't spoon. He ladled.

And I liked it. No, what's more than like? I adored it. And what's more than adored? That four-letter word that I was loath to use, but it was the only way to truly capture the way I felt about Leo. About *sleeping* with Leo, I mean. After years and years of insomnia, I was finally sleeping through the night, wrapped up in a cocoon of Almanzonian Awesome.

But now adjustments had to be made.

Because now, the calls and texts were to check in and chat about the day, and always ended with, "As soon as her nanny is back in town, you can bet your sweet ass I'll be over to fuck you and tuck you in."

But no actual fucking or tucking was happening. Consequently, no sleeping was happening—I was back to averaging three hours a night. Which I'd done for years and years, but I'd loved having more. And I was missing the ladle.

I saw Leo a few times that week, around town, for his regular delivery, and for what was becoming a daily lunch trip for grilled cheese. But alone time with him? Not so much.

I was adjusting to the idea that Leo had a kid. I mean, kids happen, right? What I was having more trouble with was adjusting to how I was adjusting to the idea. As the night of the Polly reveal . . . revealed, we had moved into some kind of in-between territory with no map.

I'd rallied when he'd brought Polly to the diner the next day, and rallied pretty well, based on her reaction to the sandwich, now proudly her favorite. But still, there was something about it that I couldn't put my finger on. An uneasiness, almost like the feeling you get five seconds before a lump forms in your throat.

You're pre-lump? Jesus Christ, is that the best you can do?

And speaking of the best I can do . . .

It was Saturday night, and I twirled in the mirror upstairs in my bedroom. I'd brought only one nice dress back with me this summer, and I finally had a chance to wear it. A deep bloodred linen shift, it was softened by a sprinkling of pale pink flowers here and there. V-neck and sleeveless, it was cool but quite elegant. Eschewing my usual twin braids or top bun, tonight I left my hair down and curly. I'd tamed it with a bit of coconut oil, and it shone a burnished copper. And though I'd applied sunscreen liberally every day, my skin was a rosy bronze, my nose and cheeks freckled.

But more than that? I looked relaxed and happy. The worry lines that had begun to appear between my eyes and across my forehead had smoothed out this summer, making me look young and fresh. Leo was like Botox.

I slipped into my lacy gold high-heeled sandals, then hurried downstairs to put the finishing touches on my housewarming gift. Tiny crème brûlée cupcakes, soaked in orange-scented brandy and covered with a crackly sugared crust, they were bites of heaven. I'd made some for the guests and a separate container for Chad and Logan to enjoy after everyone had departed. Cupcakes at midnight—not a bad way to ring in a new house.

I was just placing the last few in the container when I heard a car pull up outside. It didn't sound like Leo's Jeep, so I looked out the open door and saw a big black Mercedes in the dusty driveway.

It took me a moment to realize that it was Leo. With his vintage tees and his rusty Jeep, he flew under the radar so well that it was easy to forget that he was rich. And the guy, the man, getting out of the car was more than I was expecting too.

Clad in a white button-down, black blazer, runway worthy jeans, and some kind of adult shiny shoes, he was stunning. And . . . *oh!*

He'd shaved.

Hiding under that hipster beard? Cheekbones cut by Da Vinci. A jaw chiseled by Michelangelo. His green eyes were set in the most handsome face I'd ever seen. His sandy blond hair was swept back, tousled, but under new management. Pomade? Wax? It was perfection.

His gaze swept across me hungrily, taking in the dress, the heels, the legs. I knew how much he liked my legs. As he approached the porch, I could feel my skin pebble everywhere his gaze touched.

"You're beautiful," he said as he stopped below me, one foot resting on the bottom step.

"You're . . . what's better than beautiful?" I asked, going down one step, bringing me closer to him.

"Luminous? Radiant? Sexy beyond rational thought?" He stepped up once more, bringing me within pouncing distance.

I nodded. "You're all those things."

Before I could take that last step and pounce, he pulled me down to him, suspended in midair, crushing me into his chest and kissing me breathless. After five days of sexy texts and a lonely bed, this man had me in his arms, with one hand creeping up my thigh, and my heart nearly beat out of my chest.

When he finally let me catch my breath and I opened my dizzy, dreamy eyes, he nudged my nose with his. Dropping one more sweet kiss on my mouth, he set me back on my feet and winked.

"Let's go warm that house."

∞

With his hand resting on my knee, his pinkie traced circles over my skin as we drove through town. Tiny, imperceptible circles that were firing me up so much that I nearly vaulted over the center console and sat on his. . . *lap.*

"If you don't stop that, sir, you're going to have to pull the car over," I warned, setting my hand on his to stop the motion.

"I fail to see the problem with that." He carried on, ignoring my request.

Smiling back, I volleyed the one threat that I knew would get his attention. Leaning over, I brushed against his arm and whispered into his ear, "The faster we get there, the faster we get back home and I get to try out your clean, close shave."

He suffered through a full-body shudder. "You're not playing fair, Roxie."

No, I wasn't. But he wasn't either, picking me up and looking like the Wolf of Wall Street.

"What can I say? It's been a long and lonely week," I admitted, giving him a quick kiss while we were stopped at a red light.

He lifted my hand and kissed it gently, smiling and making my heart do a thundering flutter. "I missed you too."

Bomb dropped, he stepped on the gas as the light turned green.

Meanwhile, I was a bundle of *holy shit.* Breathe in. Breathe out. He missed me. He missed me!

Summer lovin', holy fucking shit . . .

Tonight felt like there was a lot riding on it. I wasn't nervous, per se. More like confused, excited, and a little apprehensive—this was an official coming out of sorts. He'd been much more open, more touchy-feely, more all-out-grab when others were around lately. A brush across my cheek here, a pinch and a tickle there, drawing every eye to us.

I wondered if it would be more of the same tonight. Judging

by the cinema-worthy kiss he delivered . . . I would wager that would be a yes.

As the car crunched over the gravel driveway, I barely felt a bump—a testament to the amazing craftsmanship of the Mercedes. Lines of cars were already here, and the driveway was lit up with solar lights that led the way to their newly painted bright red door.

When I came here for the painting party, Leo and I weren't a thing. Now we were, and were announcing it to the town. Shit, wait, what were we announcing? Were we a thing?

Leo pushed a button to shut off the car. This was some serious techno stuff—no key, just a button.

"Are you ready?" he asked, turning toward me. Tucking a strand of hair behind my ear, he twirled the end between his fingers.

"As I'll ever be," I answered. I moved in and gave him, one, two, three pecks on the lips.

He groaned when I finally pulled away, his lips chasing me halfway back across the console. "If I don't get out of the car now, I'm taking you into the backseat, and I don't care who witnesses it."

I looked at the number of people milling about the driveway. It appeared that most of the town would be getting quite a show. "Later. I'll make it worth your while."

Satisfied, he adjusted himself and hopped out of the car, then circled around the front to open my door. He held out his hand and helped me out, his eyes never leaving mine.

They said so much, held so many filthy promises, that I was tempted to toss him onto the front of the car and mount him like a hood ornament.

"You're here!" Chad shouted, coming down the stairs with two mason jars in his hands. Beautiful, fitting, and charming, they held some sort of punch with raspberries, mint, and ice floating around.

"We're here!" I answered, as full of enthusiasm as he was. I welcomed the interruption, before we were tempted to put on an X-rated movie of *Old MacDonald Had an Orgasm*. A movie that, based on how good Leo was looking tonight, I'd be proud to star in.

Chad led us into the house, taking my hand as we walked through the front door. But no one was looking at his hand. No, ma'am. They were all looking at the hand that Leo had placed firmly and succinctly in the small of my back, announcing our relationship more publicly than if we'd arrived with his tongue down my throat.

Eyes widened, hands covered open mouths, and elbows jabbed to alert others. And I'm fairly certain that those who couldn't attend were alerted via Facebook and Twitter, since people were snapping pictures of the happy couple.

The happy couple being us. Or at least one of us.

Don't get me wrong, it was great, feeling so wanted. And Leo had no problem letting me feel just how much he wanted me. He came up behind me while Archie Bryant, fifth-generation son of the Bryant Mountain House, was telling me how much he'd enjoyed the coconut cream cake one of his chefs had purchased the other day from the diner, and he wondered if there might be an opportunity for us to work together.

An opportunity to work with the Bryant Mountain House? The place was legendary, iconic!

I nonchalantly told him yes, I'd be interested in talking about it, trying to keep from squealing. It was also hard to keep from squealing as Archie was incredibly cute. Wavy auburn hair, dancing blue eyes, and a quick smile made him easy to squeal over.

But beyond the squealing, I also had to keep from swooning, as Leo was behind me, announcing his presence with a very specific and very hard part of him pressing into my backside.

Fighting a blush, I thanked Archie for his interest and promised to go see him sometime.

Leo was good at this. I'd go left, and he was right next to me with the hand brand on my back. I'd go right and, you guessed it, he fell right into step with me. And no one was the wiser that he was rocking a silo in his pants while he was shaking hands and laughing at jokes.

This all should have annoyed me. I waited for the prickly sensation at my neck or between my shoulders when he'd run a finger down my spine . . . but it didn't come. Only a deep desire to have him naked and underneath me at the earliest possible moment. And yeah, there was a part of me that liked being claimed so publicly too.

Feeling hot, almost feverish, I finally separated from Mr. Happy Hands to visit the ladies' room, which was designated by chalkboard saying No Dicks Allowed. Cooling the back of my neck with a wet towel, I looked at myself in the mirror. Flushed and wild-eyed—oh, Lord, I had it bad.

And when I exited the bathroom, I stepped right into my own John Hughes movie.

There stood Leo, leaning against the wall across from me, one leg bent at the knee. His head was down, and he did a slow, knee-bucklingly sexy look up to see me. Then he kicked off from the wall and walked—no, stalked toward me like the sexiest predator you've ever seen.

He pinned me to the wall. To the wall! His body covered all of mine, his hips positively owning me. Just around the corner, the rest of the party was just a canapé away from finding us up against a wall and out of our minds. But with this much Leo pressed against me, it stayed on the edge of my mind. Lost in a fog of hormones and pure carnal need, I focused on Leo's lips running up my neck as he whispered the filthiest promises I'd ever heard. *Lick. Suck. Bite. Lift. Spin. Turn. Spank. Fuck. Fuck. Fuck.*

A glass dropping startled us both and we turned our heads at the sound, the tinkling of glass followed by a muffled giggle. It was enough to snap us out of it, and we peeled ourselves off the wall and headed back to the party, where everyone seemed to know exactly what we'd been doing.

"I need a drink. You need a drink?" I asked, flustered. I needed a moment without the intoxicating Mr. Maxwell so close and under my skin. And very nearly under my dress.

He licked his lips, grinned at me, and headed into the fray to get our drinks, smiling and chatting like a pro.

Then I heard a voice that had haunted my high school days.

"Well, well, look whose back in town and turning all the heads." Krissy Jacobson—Class President, Prom Queen, and Most Likely to Succeed at Being a Bitch for the Rest of Her Life—clicked over to me. Behind her trailed her faithful four lemmings. How many years since high school, and they still followed her like baby ducks?

I braced myself for the catty quips and jabs about High School Roxie and the backward mess that I was.

"Hi, Roxie!" Maureen chirped. She was always the friendliest of the bunch.

Loren pulled me into a hug. "It's so great to see you!" she cheered, kissing me on the cheek before passing me on to Paula, who repeated the embrace before passing me on to Lece.

They oohed and aahed over my dress and my hair and my "sun-kissed" glow, which I'm pretty sure they all knew came from making out with Leo, not the sun. None of them had left Bailey

Falls, choosing to raise their 2.5 kids here, and my head swam as they told me about their families, husbands, and kiddos.

Then they riddled me with questions about California. Did I go to the beach every day? Did the Kardashians go to my gym? Did I cook for any famous people?

I never ever cook and tell, but these were the girls who made life miserable for me back then. So I *might* have showed them the picture of me and Jack Hamilton, his arms around me in his kitchen, his hands full of my pound cakes. They all squealed, staring at my phone.

"And Leo . . ." Krissy let his name float out there for me to catch it.

"Yes, Leo," I replied, sipping my drink and avoiding eye contact.

"You're so lucky," Lece said. "Women have been trying to snag him for years!"

I nodded, taking it all in. How invested he was in the community, how cute he was with Polly.

"Nothing is sexier than a doting father," Maureen said, throwing back a shot.

"You're the talk of the town, being Leo's girl," Paula said.

Smiling politely, I chewed on Leo's Girl while they moved on to Oscar the Dairy Hunk.

For as long as I could remember, everyone saw me as Trudy's Girl.

Now I was Leo's Girl.

What did it take for me to just be Roxie?

California.

I kibitzed with the girls for a few more minutes, sucking on olives with Lece, doing a shot with Maureen, then another shot with Maureen, then finally a third shot with Maureen. I confessed to Krissy that I'd been the one to sabotage her strawberry shortcake in home ec class by switching her sugar for salt—as you do. And then there was one more shot with Maureen.

When I finally excused myself and headed back into the swing of things, I was a bit in my cups and wondering how long it would take for Leo to get into my cups when he got me home. My cups being my bra. *Hiccup.* Oh boy, I was even cupping in my braaaaiiinnn . . .

In the time it took me to walk from the drink station to the living room, I'd moved from "a bit in my cups" to "holy shit in my cups." I spied Leo in the kitchen, sitting on the granite countertop and sipping on a bottled water, talking to Oscar the Giant. Who was dressed in a clean white T-shirt that was nearly popping at the seams to contain his enormous tattooed biceps. His shiny black hair was tied back again with a leather tie, and I tipsily wondered what had to happen to make him take his hair down. I bet someone really gorgeous. And speaking of gorgeous . . .

Leo met my gaze and oh, the burn, that sweet fire that'd been kindled by that kiss on the porch reared its beautiful face again. I made my way across the bumpy tile floor (it was smooth and straight), stumbling only slightly on my mile-high shoes, and ended up standing between Leo's legs, grinning stupidly up at him.

"Almanzo, you wanna go for a buggy ride?" I purred (slurred), reaching around to put my hand in the small of his back, making sure everyone saw my claim. Which would have been more effective if his blazer wasn't covering it up, but who cares? I was going to get laaaaaid tonight!

"I'll talk to you later, Leo," Oscar grouched (see how funny I am?), and made for the back door, dipping down to get through.

"I saw you doing shots over there with the girls," he said, laughing as I tipped my head forward onto his chest, breathing in his earthy scent.

"They hated me in high school," I informed him. "But now they love me. Because I'm with you? Because I'm California Cool now? Hard to say. And whyyyyy aren't you riding me in a buggy right now?"

"Sounds like you're ready to go home, Sugar Snap." He dropped a kiss on the top of my head while I played with his shirt buttons.

"Oh, God, do you know what it does to me when you call me that?" I sighed. "It makes me want to do the splits."

"The splits?" he asked, that corner of his mouth lifting.

"On your face." I patted his cheek as his jaw dropped open. "Okay, time to go."

Calling a quick good-bye to Chad and Logan, he hurried me out the back door, down the sidewalk, and into his car before I had a chance to say, "Hey, nice house, hope it's thoroughly warmed now!"

I yelled this particular gem under Leo's arm while he fumbled with my seat belt.

"Leo, Leo, Leo—God, I love saying your name," I said, under his arm and up to the sky. He knelt by my seat, sweeping my hair back from my face and looking deeply into my eyes. Because he was searching for answers there? Or because he was checking to see how drunk I really was? "I thought about you all week, you know."

"You did?" he asked, his pleasure evident even through the concern.

"Stop looking at me that way. I'm drunk, but I'm not too drunk to know some things."

"What things do you know, pretty girl?" His palm swept across my cheek, cradling my face, his fingers resting lightly on the back of my neck.

"I know what you were up to in there, with your big sexy

hand on my back all night, marking your territory." I tugged at his shirt, bringing him in closer, then kissed his nose, his eyelids, his forehead, and finally his chin.

"What if I was?" He inhaled quickly as I nibbled his jaw. A muffled groan escaped him as I wound my hands into his hair, then kissed a path straight toward his mouth.

"I know a much better way to mark your territory," I breathed, then covered his mouth with a hot, wild kiss, thrusting my tongue into his mouth as his hands became rough and unsteady.

"Tell me," he said, his voice full of need and want, and I luxuriated in the knowledge that I could make him this way. "Tell me what you want."

I pulled him close to whisper in his ear. "I want you to fuck me raw, then come all over me. I want to be covered in you, slippery and wet and filthy dirty."

Leo froze. Then pulled back to look at me. And sucked in air like he didn't have nearly enough.

I'd love to tell you we made it back to my house. The most I can say is we made it just barely of town, and defiled a country road in the most glorious way.

Chapter 21

"Order up! I've got scrambled with dry rye, two Reubens, one with pickle, and a black cow. Let's get a move on, shall we, ladies?"

I laughed as dish towels from all four corners of the diner came flying in my direction. Maxine and the others trooped over to retrieve their orders from the window, and I earned a wink from her. I'd spent the morning in the weeds when Carl called out sick. I'd handled the grill, prepped for tomorrow, and started on the cleanup, staying ahead as best I could.

"How's it going, Mrs. Oleson?" I called out as the bell tinkled, alerting me to a new customer.

Mrs. Oleson waved and called out, "Roxie, will you be here tomorrow morning? I need to order something for the mayor's luncheon next week. Can you do a pineapple upside-down something?"

"How about pineapple and orange, with a brandy glaze?"

The entire diner oohed and aahed, and she gave me the thumbs-up. Giving a little curtsey, I turned back to marrying the ketchup bottles behind the counter, whistling along with the jukebox as I combined the half-bottles. Hearing the bell tinkle once more, I called over my shoulder, "Welcome to Callahan's! Grab any open seat; a waitress will be right over with . . ."

My voice trailed off as the scent of patchouli reached me. No way. I turned to see my mother standing just inside the door, Aunt Cheryl right behind her. She was tan, healthy looking, and positively beaming.

"You're not supposed to be— What are you— I mean, you're home!" I blurted. Oops.

"Well, welcome home to you too," she replied, her voice warm and happy. Her arms and hands were covered in henna tattoos, she had a new piercing in her nose, and her wild hair was in two frizzy braids.

Overcome with the need to hug her, I rushed out from behind the counter. A wave of patchouli washed over me, strong and earthy, and for the first time in a long time, I was very glad to see her.

But how odd that my first thought was, damn, was it time for her to come home already?

"A little help here?" Aunt Cheryl was struggling with what appeared to be both sets of their luggage.

"Oh, Aunt Cheryl, I'm so sorry, let me help you with that," I exclaimed, snatching up duffel bags and tote bags filled to the brim with Spanish flamenco fans, Chinese New Year masks, a bamboo—

"Ma! You can't just carry a bong around like a purse!" I threw a dish towel over the bamboo pipe.

She was waving to everyone like a celebrity. Oh boy. She'll be milking this for the next ten years.

"It's a ceremonial bong, Roxie. I got it from Laos. Your uptight is showing," she said, walking further into the diner and taking a good long look.

Something tightened in my stomach as she sized up the

changes I'd made, no doubt weighing how quickly she could change them back.

Shaking my head, I sprang into action. Maxine and I set all the bags off to the side by the door, while my mother was greeting everyone as if she'd been gone for years.

Someone at the counter asked the million-dollar question. "So, did you guys win?"

Mom and Aunt Cheryl passed a look between themselves before shaking their heads. "Sorry, can't say anything. Contractually bound to be silent," Mom explained.

"Aunt Cheryl, are you okay? You look exhausted," I said, pushing a stool behind her.

"I've never been so tired in my entire life." She sank onto the stool gratefully, resting her head on the countertop.

She was half asleep by the time I looked around for my mother, who was making the rounds, greeting her regulars, making conversation. She grew up in this town, she knew everyone, and she was well liked by all. Her return provided some excitement for this sleepy town, and she was getting her moment's worth. As she walked around she continued to check out the changes I'd made, but there were no comments or questions so far. If she *was* irked by the changes, she didn't say anything. Maybe because we had an audience. Or, maybe because she was happy with it. Unlikely, but stranger things had happened.

As I continued with my side work, the restaurant started to clear out from the lunch rush. And as I cleaned, I kept waiting for the feeling of relief to wash over me. That she was back, that I'd done my time, and I could return to my life in California. And I kept on waiting for that feeling.

But it never came. Funny.

When the last of the lunch crowd left, Mom locked the door.

Making her way over to me, she sat on the stool next to her snoring sister, laughing. "Should we let her sleep?"

"She seems pretty tired." I chuckled. "I say let her sleep."

"Speaking of sleep—"

I jumped. Who'd told her about Leo already?

"How have you been sleeping, with all this fresh country air?"

I breathed in relief. "Oh, um, I've been sleeping pretty good, actually. "

"And you look really good," she said, examining me carefully. "You look rested. You skin is good, your eyes are bright, and your hair looks nice and strong."

"Thanks, I eat a raw egg every day for a shiny coat. You want to check my teeth?"

"Don't sass your mother, Roxie," she said absently, still looking me over too carefully. Could she tell? Did she know? "Mmm-hmm," she finally said.

I felt the same way I had when I was a kid and I tried to lie about whether or not I'd done my homework. She always knew.

"You're free to go, Rox," she said.

"Um, thanks, but I've still got ordering to finish up before I can leave today. I'll see you back at the house. I'm sure Aunt Cheryl would prefer to nap on the couch rather than on the counter." I smiled, and patted her on the hand. "Good to have you home, Mom."

"I meant, you're free to go back to California."

I was halfway through the swinging door when I heard her words. I swooped back out to the diner.

"I'm home! You're released!" she cried, making a grand gesture toward the front door. "I'm surprised you didn't run for the hills the second we walked in."

I sat down beside her, toying with a loose thread on my apron. The setting was much as it was when I was a little girl.

Sitting side by side, not looking at each other, but at the yellow order tickets that flapped against the steel strip.

"I was thinking," I finally said, spinning my phone on the counter as a distraction, "I sort of have to stay a bit longer. You see, you're home sooner than I planned. I'm glad you're home, but I'm not prepared yet. I um . . . still have cake orders to fill. I need to tell you about the cake orders I've been taking. And I've got these zombie classes I'm teaching. We've still got canning to learn, and I was hoping to get to pureeing and freezing before the last of the tomatoes go."

Then my phone lit up with an incoming text. And on the screen was Leo's name, and a picture that I'd taken the day he showed me his walnut . . . trees. He was grinning lazily, looking every inch the poster boy for Hot Farmer—it was my favorite picture of him. And though I quickly turned it over, I wasn't quick enough.

My mother saw the picture. And she might have even seen the text. Oh man.

Her lips rolled in as she tried to hold back a grin. "I see."

"You see nothing. This isn't what it looks like."

"I'd love to know what *you* think it looks like, when the most eligible bachelor in the state of New York is texting my daughter things like, 'Hey Sugar Snap, last night was incredible and—'"

"Stop talking! Oh my God, make it stop!" I wailed, dropping my head onto the counter just like Aunt Cheryl.

"You've been making more than cakes this summer, Roxie Callahan!" My mother leaped up from her stool and ran behind the counter, grabbing two mugs and the coffee. Pouring us each a cup, she propped her chin up on her hands and arched her eyebrows. "Spill it."

✺

I spilled it after dinner, after Aunt Cheryl was sawing logs in the guest room, and my mother and I sat on the front porch. That front porch was seeing some action this summer, between the floor sex and the storytelling. My mother partook of a bowl of Colorado's finest leaf, while I stuck with an iced coffee.

I kept the spill light and disclosed no real substance, admitting only to seeing Leo occasionally, casually. A few juicy nuggets easily distracted her, and with only the slightest nudging, I was able to turn her focus away from me and my love life, and on to how her trip had been.

Officially she couldn't tell me whether they had won, but based on the fact that she was home early, and an artfully timed wink when I said, "Oh, for fuck's sake, just tell me, you lost, right?" I put two and two together.

And as easy as it was to distract her with something shiny (talking about herself), she could be distracted even more by something shiny and rose petal filled (*her* love life).

My mother had met no less than three men on her trip. First there was Hank, an auto parts salesman from Akron, Ohio, traveling with his son for the show. An early favorite, he and Mom had shared one night of drunken kissing in San Francisco's Chinatown after the Welcome to *Amazing Race* cast party. His son and Aunt Cheryl had intervened, explaining to each in turn that getting involved with the competition was a recipe for disaster. When my mother caught Hank with his hands down the pants of another competitor (Sabrina, a yoga instructor from Tallahassee), she agreed, and off Hank went into the discard pile.

Next up was Pierre, a French expat who'd been the instructor on a South Seas pearl diving expedition. After trying to free dive after only ten minutes of training and zero breath support, my mother had been hauled up out of the water and onto Pierre's lap, whereupon she was resuscitated by the smitten

Frenchman. She actually came around several moments before she publicly came around, so as to enjoy a little more mouth-to-mouth. My mother and Pierre enjoyed a night of oceanic skinny dipping, where she urged him to try to set a new world record for holding his breath underwater while otherwise occupied . . .

I nearly had to get the scotch to listen to that story.

And finally, there was Wayne Tuesday. Yep, his actual name.

Wayne was a cameraman for the production company that owned *The Amazing Race,* and his unit had been assigned to my mother and Aunt Cheryl. Late one night on the island of Tahiti, after a limbo contest that my mother won, the two of them sneaked away from the rest of the crew and shared a frozen pineapple daiquiri. Was it the pineapple? Was it the limbo? Was it the bendy? (Pretty sure it was the bendy.) Who knows, but she was quite taken with Wayne.

Now, typically when a reality show contestant gets involved with a member of the crew (they frown on that), one of two things happens. The contestant is removed, or the crew member hits the bricks. Wayne and my mother were able to hide their budding romance from everyone until the final location in Rome, where they were caught playing a spirited game of hide the salami. He was fired, and a few weeks later, my mother and Aunt Cheryl had been eliminated.

For the record, this was how hard it was for my mother to keep a secret. Did she ever tell me, "Hey, I didn't win the *Amazing Race*"? No, but she circumvented the rules, quite handily in her mind, by using words like *eliminated.* No one, and I mean no one, who knew Trudy Callahan longer than an hour told her a secret.

But as she recounted story after story of her adventures, I was caught up in the excitement, the silliness, her carefree come-what-may attitude. I was enjoying her company, I laughed at her tales, and I sympathetically patted her shoulder when she told me of the perils of getting sunburned *down there* after a stint at a nude beach.

And so we sat, watching the fireflies dance lazily through the backyard, chatting about this and that and everything. I was convinced she'd forgotten about the text when she suddenly said, "Leo Maxwell is exactly the kind of man I can see you with. See this through, Roxie."

I was so taken aback that I remained on the porch, sitting stone straight, thinking about what she'd said long after she went inside.

Chapter 22

The next morning, my mom told me that Wayne Tuesday was arriving today; he was driving up from DC to spend the week with her. Aunt Cheryl had left for home early the next morning, telling my mother to never, ever call her again for any kind of reality show. Or any traveling of any kind.

My mother was pleased as punch that I'd be staying around for a bit, but it was going to make for close quarters around the house. I was used to my her having her boyfriends over, but it'd been years since I'd actually had to see it. I shuddered as I pressed down on a burger patty, thinking about what I might have to endure once Wayne arrived.

Mom and I had driven into work together today. She was eager to see the books and see how things had run while she'd been away. I was anxious, now that she was back and settled in, to see how what I'd done would be received.

Though it shouldn't have mattered. I was leaving . . . right?

Perhaps? Perhaps not? If Chad Bowman were in my head right now, he'd have done a cartwheel. I was entertaining the idea of . . . staying? It seemed so.

I pondered this as I cooked up some cheesesteaks and got

ready to throw a new kielbasa on the griddle. The butcher shop I'd gotten the pastrami from had a new line of German sausages, and I'd been steadily working my way through them. The kielbasa was fantastic, perfectly spiced and a little squeaky with good fat here and there. I was mentally working on a recipe with grilled onions and a splash of apple cider vinegar when I heard Maxine call out that I had a visitor.

Looking at the ancient clock over the hood, I saw it was just about lunchtime, which could only mean one very specific visitor. I grinned, setting the cover down on the cheesesteaks to let the cheese get nice and gooey, wiped my hands on my apron, and pushed through the swinging doors.

I immediately spied Polly sitting at the counter, her menu in front of her, looking very grown up.

"Drinking soda isn't illegal. That's just silly, Daddy," she argued, giving Leo one helluva a sideways glance.

I leaned against the doorframe and smiled as Leo calmly took the menu and closed it, setting it down between them.

Behind them I saw my mother with the coffeepot, bopping from table to table, chatting it up, making sure everyone had what they needed.

And a flash forward suddenly struck me—or maybe just a daydream. Clear as day, I had the sharpest vision of a slightly older Polly helping me at the diner. She snapped gum and took an order from a boy who wasn't much older than she was.

I gazed out at the scene before me: happy people, in a happy town. All the hap-hap-happy—could it be real? Could this be real for *me*?

Just then Leo noticed me, and as always, his eyes traveled over my entire body, heat flaring in his eyes before he gave me a wink.

I grinned instantly. Maybe this *could* be real. I waded into the argument with that same grin.

"Pork Chop, you can't have soda. White milk or apple juice are your choices. Take it or leave it," Leo said, in a firm voice.

"Grandmother, please," she whined.

Grand*what?* I stopped so fast I left skid marks.

Sure enough, there sat Mrs. Maxwell. And she looked so profoundly out of place I had no idea how I hadn't seen her.

Maybe I was distracted by the little family fantasy of me and my very own Almanzo raising Polly on the farm.

Her severely chopped bob was so silvery it would glow in the moonlight. And she had green eyes like Leo and Polly, though hers were the color of money and power.

She was dressed sharply in cream colored trousers that were tailored within an inch of their life, and I silently applauded her for having the balls to wear them into a place that served chili seven days a week. The crisply pressed navy blouse was capped off with pearls that probably cost what I'd paid for culinary school. Or more.

Mentally cataloging my outfit, I cursed, thinking about the rice pudding that had splotched onto my capris earlier. Not to mention the smear of cranberry on my apron.

"Hi, Roxie!" Polly chirped. Smoothing her napkin over her denim shorts, she continued, "Grandmamma, this is Roxie. The girl I was telling you about. She makes the best pie! And we make a superfancy grown-up grilled cheese with fawnteeni cheese and apples and rye bread with these weird little sticks in it. It is sooooooooo good!"

"It's a pleasure to meet you. Roxie, is it?" she asked coolly.

No handshake. She probably couldn't even lift her hand, due to the weight of the diamond as big as a skating rink.

"My Leo tells me that you have been helping out your mother here until you move back to . . . where is it?"

"C-C-California," I spluttered, seeing my mother heading toward the counter with two empty coffeepots and a wide grin.

Oh boy. My mother and his, in the same place and time, could be the stuff of legend. It could also be the stuff of epic train wreck.

"Hey there, Polly, you're home from camp early, aren't you?" my mother called out, scooting around the counter in a swoop of sandalwood and leather fringe to stand in front of Leo's daughter, reaching out and tweaking her nose. Polly giggled, and answered my mom's high-five offer with a resounding smack of her own.

"Hi, Ms. Callahan! Camp was just okay, and Daddy missed me so much we decided I should come home early."

"We're glad to have you home. And, Leo, you just get better looking every time I see you!" My mother moved down the counter. "How've you been this summer? It sounds like you and Roxie have had a grand old time! Goodness, look at you, turning as pink as a pig's butt."

If you say the word *butt* in front of a seven-year-old, no matter how brainy they are, they will laugh until their head pops off. Hearing her father referred to as a pig's butt sent Polly off into a gale of giggles that rolled on and on and on, no matter how Leo's mother tried to kindly quiet her down. She giggled so hard she likely missed the comment about me spending the summer with her daddy, but his mother sure didn't.

"And this must be your mother, Mrs. Maxwell. You know, I think you've been coming here all these years and never once made it into my diner. Now, how is that possible?" My mother moved across from Leo's mother.

"You know how summers can be, so busy with guests and parties. I always mean to get into town when I visit, but Leo keeps me so busy back at the house," she replied in that nasal, Northeast monied voice. A little bit Boston, little bit Hamptons, a lotta bit Upper East Side. "And I don't think I quite caught your name, Mrs . . . ?"

"Just call me Trudy."

Mrs. Maxwell smiled evenly, likely wondering how she'd suddenly become on a first-name basis with some hippie. She extended her hand across the Formica, a gesture that my mother ran away with.

"Say, look at that lifeline!" she exclaimed, turning Mrs. Maxwell's hand over and examining her palm. "Unbroken, but this curious line here . . . hmmm . . . were you in an accident when you were a child?"

"Mom, lay off, huh?" I urged, placing my foot on top of hers behind the counter and pressing down. "Mrs. Maxwell, what can I get you? Cup of coffee? Cup of chili?" I'd just asked the equivalent of a modern-day Mrs. Rockefeller if she'd like a cup of chili?

Before she could answer, my mother stepped in. "Roxie, go brew Mrs. Maxwell a cup of my special black tea. I'm going to read your tea leaves!" My mother moved around the counter and tucked her arm through Mrs. Maxwell's. "Come take a look at our jukebox; I bet you'll know all the old classics from your teenage years—which were hopefully misspent."

As Leo and I watched, our mouths ajar, my mother led his mother off to the old Wurlitzer. And Mrs. Maxwell, with years of good breeding, went politely along, smiling and nodding and likely thinking she'd indulge the townie for a little while before beating a retreat.

And as they were going one way, Chad and Logan came the other way, heading straight for the counter.

"What is happening?" I asked as Polly played unconcernedly with the buttons on Leo's sleeve. As I looked closer, I noticed he was wearing very un-Leo clothing. White polo shirt, long sleeves rolled up. Khaki shorts. I peered over the counter to get a look at his feet. Sperrys. "What's up, preppy?"

He grimaced. But before he could answer, Chad and Logan arrived.

"We need ice cream sodas, stat," Chad announced, sinking onto the stool next to Polly and offering her his fist. "Hey there, Pollster, what's going on?"

Polly bumped his fist. "Just hanging out with Roxie. Daddy, I also need an ice cream soda, splat."

"Can you make mine chocolate?" Logan asked. "You have no idea the day we've had!" He leaned across Chad to offer Polly his own fist bump. "What's up, little miss?"

"You have no idea the day *I've* had!" Polly echoed. "First, I almost flushed my Barbie down the toilet. Then, Grandmother and Daddy almost got in a fight about whether I should be allowed to try on her lipstick. And even though it's probably not my color, it should be still my choice whether I get to try it on, right?"

"I totally agree," Chad said.

"And then," Polly said, knowing she had all eyes on her, "we get here, and Daddy says I can't have a soda! And now the boys are getting ice cream sodas—how is that fair?"

Seven years old, just to remind you.

Polly, Chad, and Logan all looked at Leo.

"Ice cream sodas all around, please, Roxie," he said with a sigh. "You still have that bottle of scotch hidden back there?"

"Roxie, how's that black tea coming? Hop to it!" my mother called out from the front of the diner.

I escaped to the kitchen, where I was greeted with smoke pouring from the grill, the cheesesteaks now fried, and a burned-beyond-belief kielbasa.

"What is happening?" I asked the world one more time, and someone finally answered me.

"Crazy has come to Bailey Falls," Leo said in a deep movie

announcer's voice, peering around the swinging door, coughing slightly at the smoke.

I nodded in agreement. "And its name is Mother."

Once the smoke cleared and the sausage was put out of its misery, Leo reached out and tilted my chin up toward him. "You doing okay with all this, Sugar Snap?"

"I'm trying, Almanzo. I really am." I sighed. I let him pull me into his arms, wrapping mine tightly around his waist, feeling his good strength seeping into me. Resting my chin on his chest, I gazed up at him, losing myself in the eyes I'd first looked into in this very kitchen, only two months before. I sighed, rising up onto my tiptoes. "A kiss would help."

"Coming right up." His lips pressed against mine, hungry and hot.

And when Maxine opened the door, asking where the black tea and ice cream sodas were, the entire world could see us.

I heard a gasp and we both broke the kiss, turning to see my mother and his, one with a look of delight, the other with a look of distinct displeasure.

Chad and Logan with big grins.

And Polly. Her eyes widened. Then filled with tears. Her face crumpled. She climbed off her stool, ran to her grandmother, and hid her face in Chanel N° 5.

Leo's hands fell from my skin like he'd been electrocuted. And the look on his face . . . oh.

He left the kitchen without a word, running across the diner and scooping up his daughter, holding her close as she cried, as his mother tried to comfort her as well. He backed out of the diner, his arms full of his family, his eyes meeting mine.

Now I knew.

He mouthed, "I'm sorry." His mother looked backed at me with absolute ice in her eyes.

Now I knew.

I stood in the kitchen doorway, dumbstruck.

Now I knew why they called it falling in love.

Because the fall was so very, very bad.

Moments after the Maxwells left, while I was sitting quietly next to Chad and Logan, my mother handing me the tea I was supposed brew for Leo's mother, the bell tinkled and we all turned at once, hoping to see . . . I couldn't say it.

A tall, good-looking man in his fifties came sailing through the front door, more salt than pepper in his hair. He held a bag in one hand and a map in the other. "I'm looking for Trudy Callahan? I'm Wayne Tuesday."

My mom patted my hand made her way over to Wayne, and he kissed her full on the mouth, right in front of everyone. Jesus, everyone was getting kissed stupid right out in the open today. Like no one in town had anything better to do than watch people smooch it up?

As the kiss became two, then four, I felt that damn lump in my throat, and try as I might, it just wouldn't swallow down.

"You know what, I think I'm gonna get out of here." Pushing off from my stool, I untied my apron, grabbed my bag from under the counter, and nodded to Chad and Logan.

"You want some company? You can come over; we've got *Beaches* on Blu-ray," Logan offered.

"That does sound nice, but I think—" I looked over their shoulder and saw quickly where this was going with my mother and Wayne Tuesday. "Ugh. I just need to get out of here."

Because the lump, I was discovering, was quickly followed by tears, and they were already stinging, preparing to march down my cheeks. The guys both looked at me sadly as I headed out the front door.

My truck looked blurry through the tears now starting to spill. I jumped into the giant Wagoneer, which had carried me all the way across the country and back again, and as I started up the old familiar rumble, U2 came blaring out of the crackly old speakers, singing "One."

Is it getting better . . .

Oh can it, Bono!

I pulled over on the side of the road, threw the car into park, and pressed eject. I had no patience for U2 today, and the way their words never failed to highlight exactly what I was thinking, exactly what needed to be said. But still Bono sang, words about having someone to blame. I pressed eject again. *Still* nothing. I pressed eject a third time, and when nothing happened, I punched the stereo.

Which still did nothing! Bono sang about asking me to enter but then making me crawl, and I slapped at the CD player, yelling and crying, trying to get the damn thing to stop.

And then I heard a very familiar Wrangler pulling up behind me.

Before Leo could get to my window, I grabbed my bag and slammed out of my car, walking up the road.

"Hey, Roxie, where are you going?"

"Leave me alone, Leo," I said, not wanting him to see me crying, not wanting to see his face. He had a power over me that I'd never felt before, and I was weak with it. I was angry at myself for letting things get this far, but Leo was going to feel the brunt of my anger.

"Stop, please—Jesus, Rox, would you stop already!" he

shouted, his footsteps loud on the hot asphalt as he ran after me, because that's what happens in a romantic comedy, right? She walks, he chases, she protests, then they kiss and all is well—ha.

He caught up to me and I turned around, my face wet with tears.

"Where do you think you're going?" he asked.

"I don't know yet. Where's Polly?"

"She's with my mom. I dropped them off at the house, and then I came back for you. Your mom told me you took off, and I guessed you'd gone this way. Polly's fine. She's—"

"Polly's *not* fine," I countered. She's not fine at *all*—she was crying."

"Rox, she's had me all to herself for seven years. Don't you think seeing me kissing a woman, especially one she just met, would be a bit weird for her?"

"Are you crazy? It's a *lot* weird! You have no idea what she's feeling right now," I snapped, wiping at my tears angrily. I stomped past him, heading back for the car.

"What do you mean? How can you know what she's— Hey, would you stop running away from me?" Leo called, hot on my heels.

"She's wondering if you're going to marry me. She's wondering if I'm going to kick her out of her house. She's wondering if you're going to stop paying attention to her. She's wondering if I'm going to start making her eat boiled carrots every night. She's wondering if you're going to forget her one day, because you've got *me* now!"

I reached the car and opened the door, but he slammed it shut before I could get in. I whirled around, sheer anger flowing out now. "And worst of all, she's wondering if she's going to love me and I'm not going to love her back!"

He rocked backward as though I'd slapped him.

The lump . . . oh, the lump. I was choking on it.

"Don't you see, Leo? You can't just bring a girlfriend home when you've got a kid. It's not fair to her, it's not fair to you, and it's sure as hell not fair to me."

"Oh come on," Leo said, his voice angry. "That's bullshit." He advanced so that I was pressed back against my Jeep.

I pressed back. "Don't tell me what I feel is bullshit! Don't you dare do that! I let you in, and I don't do that with *anyone*! You give me this incredible summer, and then I find out you've been hiding a kid from me this whole time, and then you expect me to just become Miss Susie Homemaker and be exactly what you need, what she needs, what everyone needs? What about what *I* need?"

"What *do* you need, Roxie? What exactly do you need? You say you let me in, but that's not true. I still don't know how you feel about me, how you feel about us. You think you know what I want? How the fuck could *you* know that, when *I* don't even know what I want!"

He dragged his hands down his face, scrubbing. "I want you. I know that. But how that happens and what that looks like, I have no idea. And if you'd stop fucking running away from me, and just let this happen—Christ, Roxie!" He stepped closer to me, reaching out across the divide, and caressed my cheek. How could a hand so rough and tumble be so gentle?

I leaned into his hand, unable to stop my body from responding the way it yearned to.

"Just let this happen, Roxie, and we'll figure it out."

I wanted to. Truly. But I couldn't.

"I have to go," I whispered, my throat raw. "With what I went through with my mother, all those broken hearts—I can't do that to you, or to Polly." My voice broke. I steeled myself, then looked him in the eye. "I won't do it."

"Your past is legitimate." He looked back at me, pain in his eyes, but resolve as well. "But so is your present. And so am I. And what's right in front of you. And if you're leaving to prove a point? Then you should go—but not for the reason you think."

His hand caressed my cheek once more, then he pulled away. And I climbed into my Jeep and drove off.

I didn't look back. I couldn't. I knew if I saw him, with our hearts broken all over the dusty country road, I'd never be able to leave.

I drove to my mother's house, stuffed some clothes into a bag, drove my car to the Poughkeepsie station, and jumped on the Metro North into Manhattan.

I needed to see my best friend.

Chapter 23

When I was a kid, everyone referred to Manhattan as *the city*. We never said *Manhattan*, and we certainly never said *New York City*. And though as a kid I thought I had to go to California to make a name for myself, I know now that *the city* was far enough away and large and fabulous enough to have been able to lose myself in it entirely.

Natalie *was* the city. She grew up in the Village, the daughter of a real estate developer and an art dealer. Other than dabbling in culinary school her freshman year, when we met, she stayed firmly on her island, venturing off only to head to the Hamptons . . . if she must. She had concrete running through her veins.

It surprised the hell out of her when I texted her from the train station, saying I was on my way and to cancel her Friday night plans. And now, here I sat. On a large, comfy couch in her apartment, while she mixed up a batch of margaritas in the blender. Since her father owned several townhouses in Manhattan, she was the beneficiary of a very specific kind of rent control. Occupying the ground floor of a three-story building, her apartment was the kind one might see on an episode of *Million*

Dollar Listing. Tall ceilings, intricate millwork, flawlessly gleaming wooden floors—the apartment was stunning.

Like Natalie. She was the kind of girl you looked at, whether you were into girls or not. If you were into humans, she appealed to you. She was statuesque, at least five eight in her bare feet—and she was never in her bare feet, preferring the latest, highest teeter-tottery heels. With strawberry blond hair, she was supermodel beautiful—and had the foulest mouth ever heard on land. She could even make a sailor blush, then tie himself into knots trying to get with her. She was loud, always the first to crack a joke, or make an indecent proposal—which was never turned down.

The girl personified curves, having a natural hourglass figure with an extra hour or two at each end. I've actually seen men nearly crash their cars when she walked down the street—the girl was a *brick house*.

She owned every room she was in without even trying. She was equally at home in the fanciest restaurant, ordering wines even I'd never heard of, or in the diviest dive bar, snort-laughing and throwing peanuts on the floor.

She dated politicians and cops, artists and firemen, a butcher, a baker, and while not technically a candlestick maker, one guy she dated was the president of the largest supplier of flashlights on the East Coast. She never got her heart broken; she *was* the heartbreaker.

After her year as a culinary student she enrolled at Columbia University, majored in advertising, and was now blazing a trail for herself in one of the hottest boutique ad firms in the city. She worked with Fortune 500 companies, putting together campaigns that everyone knew—you've probably hummed the song from a commercial she created.

Plus, she made a fucking killer margarita.

"Explain to me this," she said, peeling the lid off the blender and pouring the frothy lime wonderful into two glasses. "He's gorgeous."

"Off the charts."

"And you've got chemistry?"

"Off the charts," I groaned, flopping facedown in a pillow. I could hear her click clacking her way over to where I lay, starfished. I heard the clink of a glass, then the sound of her getting settled across from me.

"And the sex?"

I pumped my hips up and down. "Off. The. Charts."

"Yeah, I don't see the problem here." I could hear her sip her drink. "Also, that couch was really expensive, so quit with the humping."

I sat up and frowned at her. "He wants me to, like, *be* with him."

Now, a statement like that to anyone else would have resulted in a sarcastic *Oh, poor you*. But she got it. She knew me. She knew my bullshit.

Like the bullshit Leo was calling you on?

"I wondered why all of a sudden you run into the city," she said. "Not that I'm not thrilled that you're here."

The door buzzer sounded. "Thank God—I'm starving." I face planted into the pillow again, unable to get rid of the vision of me leaving Leo in the middle of that road. Hopefully the extra-spicy laksa would help me purge that, and most of my taste buds, right out of my head. Only in the city could you order Indonesian take-out delivery.

"Why the hell is she suffocating herself in your couch?" I heard, in a voice that didn't remotely belong to a delivery guy.

"Clara?" I said, lifting my head and seeing our other best friend, standing in the doorway with a small rolling suitcase and a big grin.

"She said you finally got your ass on a train, so I got on one too!"

✍

"My mouth is burning. I think. Is my mouth still where it used to be?" Natalie asked.

"Why do you order such spicy food if you can't handle it?" Clara asked from her perch on the arm of the sofa. She hoovered up a bowl of chicken curry that I couldn't even get within two feet of, and I had a pretty strong palate. She tipped up the edge of her bowl and slurped the rest of the sauce, smacking her lips.

"I love it. It's so spicy, but I love it," Natalie replied, moving toward the kitchen and stopping to check her reflection in the mirror. "But look how puffy it made my lips! It's like a lip plumper!"

While she preened, I rolled toward Clara on the couch. "I still can't believe you're here."

"I needed an excuse to get out of Boston for the weekend; things are positively stale there right now." She looked toward my bowl of laksa. "Are you going to finish that?"

"I'm stuffed. Hit it." As I passed her my takeout, I marveled that someone could eat so much and never gain a pound.

Clara and Natalie couldn't be more opposite, and I wondered, not for the first time, that if we hadn't all been away from home for our first time, if we ever would've become friends.

Clara was petite and athletic, with an almost boyish figure. A long-distance runner since high school, she walked with a powerful stride. She had an economy of movement that served her well as she competed in marathons and triathlons all over the world. With closely cropped blond hair and caramel colored eyes, she was a quiet beauty.

The most well traveled of our trio, Clara had a job that most people envied but few can actually do. After leaving culinary school, she enrolled in Cornell's prestigious hotel management program. Rather than spend her nights and weekends working the front desk at the Brookline Marriott, though, she parlayed her keen eye and analytical mind into a position with a branding agency in Boston. She helped failing hotels in the United States and abroad get back on their feet, specializing in older historic hotels. So she traveled almost nonstop, sometimes spending weeks on site.

"Stale? Why? What's going on?" I asked as she shoveled in the last few bites of food.

"I don't really know. Work just seems a bit off at the moment. There might be some changes up top, and it makes for a weird vibe. I'm heading out of town next month, though, which will be nice."

"And what glamorous city are you off to next? London? Amsterdam? Rio?"

"Orlando." She sighed. Then burped slightly, which she apologized for with a sheepish grin.

"Orlando? That's a little . . . different for you," I replied, crinkling my eyebrows.

"It's a little awful for me. What the hell do I know about magical mice?" she snorted, pushing the bowl away from her and patting her nonexistent tummy.

"What's a magical mouse? Is that like a Rabbit?" Natalie asked, swooshing back in from the kitchen and depositing herself on the floor on front of me.

Clara looked at her sideways. "No, it's—"

"Because let me tell you, nothing beats a Rabbit. Not a hand, not a dick, not even those little remote-control ones that fit right inside your panties. Nothing beats a Rabbit." Natalie paused. "Although a tongue is a close second."

"It has to be the right tongue, though," Clara interjected. "Attached to the right face."

"Not always. Some of the best sex I've ever had is with ugly guys. That guy I dated last year who worked on the trapeze, down at South Street Seaport? Face like a shovel, but holy shit, could he give fantastic head," Natalie said, examining her pedicure. "I mean, some guys just get *so* into it—like, you're ready to black out, it's so good, and it's almost too much, and you're like, hello, I just came, like, eleven times in a row. But they keep on going; they could keep that shit up all night long. I swear, some guys just live to be facedown in it twenty-four-seven; they're not happy unless they've got some girl's thighs wrapped around their head and a tongue full of pussy. I've always wondered, when you clamp down around their head, y'know, lock on when you go full freeze, if it plugs their ears, kind of like when a plane reaches cruising altitude? And when you finally let go, do their ears pop?"

She looked up to find Clara and me staring at her. She'd said all of this in one breath, by the way. "What?"

Silence. Then, "Do their *ears* pop?" Clara repeated.

"Oh please, like you've never wondered that!"

"Nat, I can honestly tell you, I have never in my life wondered about that," I said, hand on my chest.

"Oh, so Leo never made you nearly pass out? No wonder you hightailed it out of there," Natalie said in sympathy.

"No, no, that's not at all what I said. Leo is—"

"Is Leo the farmer she told me about?" Clara asked Natalie, who nodded.

"—amazing in bed. Incredibly amazing. No complaints there. But—"

"Yep, Farmer Leo Maxwell, who apparently paid more attention to his ee-eye-ee-eye instead of making her scream the more important *oh*!" Natalie replied, looking at Clara in a conspiratorial way.

"That's not true! Leo made me very *oh*, all the time with the *oh*, nonstop *oh*s, and—"

"Wait wait wait, did you say Leo Maxwell? The farmer is Leo

Maxwell? Blond guy? Early thirties? Drop-dead sex on a silo?"
Clara asked, fumbling for her phone.

"Yes, he's blond, and we didn't have sex on a silo, we didn't
even have sex *in* the silo, but we were in a silo when he licked
my spine and—"

Natalie interjected, "Atta boy, Leo! Did he keep going and
lick your—"

"Okay, shut up. Is this your Leo?" Clara asked, shoving her
phone in my face.

Oh yeah. That was my Leo. The picture showed a more City
Leo than I was used to seeing, but even in this grainy picture
you could see the gorgeous. Climbing out of a limo, wearing a
black suit tailored perfectly to his strong, lean frame. Striking
green eyes that were sharp, calculating, assessing. A little hard?
I swiped to the next image. Another City Leo pic, this one in
front of a publicity backdrop on some red carpet. Maybe some
fund-raiser? This time he was dressed in a gray suit, looking all
Billionaire Boys Club and Your Penthouse or Mine?

But while I could appreciate these pictures, in my mind's
eye he'd always be dressed in well-worn jeans, a vintage concert
tee, two weeks' worth of scruffy beard that felt *incredible* on the
soft skin between my thighs, and kind green eyes. An easy grin.
Peaceful and happy and so content in his world. City Leo was
obviously good-looking, but I preferred Country Leo.

I came back to the conversation, where Natalie and Clara
were talking animatedly.

"So wait, he left New York when—"

"Exactly, after the baby was born. She disappeared, and then
he all but disappeared. He was gone, no parties, no trips—he
sank everything he had into making that farm his life," Clara said.

I blinked. "Okay, wait. So you guys both knew Leo?" I asked,
confused.

"Knew him, no. Knew of him, of course. I just never put two and two together that Leo *Maxwell* was your Farmer Leo," Natalie said, lying back on the floor and kicking her legs up in the air. "There was no one in this town who didn't know Leo Maxwell. Everyone was trying to land that guy—what a fucking catch!"

"Seriously, Roxie, he was a young Mr. Big. Until he met Melissa. And once she sank her claws into him, that was it. No one ever really knew what happened; just that they were together, she was pregnant, there was a rumor they were getting married, then they weren't together, and then once the baby was born he took his daughter and headed upstate. She bounced around town for a while, but eventually took off for Europe. I think she married some Russian guy. No idea what happened between her and Leo, though. It was just . . . over."

I knew what had happened. Leo had told me the story. And I think some of the people in Bailey Falls knew what happened, or had guessed. Because no one really ever talked about Polly. Not that she was a secret, but they were . . .

Protective? Of both of them?

Yeah. Maybe. Small town, taking care of their own.

No wonder Leo wanted his daughter to be a country mouse.

"Please tell me you and Leo never dated," I said, looking at Natalie.

"No, I never met him. Though I probably would have hit that, if I had. Hey, how weird would that be?" She laughed, rolling onto her side and looking at me carefully. "If I'd banged the guy you were in love with."

"Hey, how weird would that be if I killed you until you were dead?" I replied.

Natalie and Clara dissolved into giggles, but all I could think about was Leo.

And the fact that when she called him the man I was in love with, I hadn't corrected her.

Shit.

That night something specific kept me awake instead of the usual insomnia. I Googled Leo after the conversation with the girls, and I was swiping away at two in the morning, looking at a slice of his life that'd been captured by publicity photos.

This was a Leo I didn't know. He seemed cool, more detached, very blue blood. I saw nothing of the Leo I knew.

Who would rather be riding in an open Jeep than in a town car. Who would rather have his hands full of sweet-smelling earth than martinis. Who was made happy by wet-with-morning-dew sugar snap peas. Who was caring sweet kind loving tender gasping panting moaning groaning rocking thrusting slipping sliding living life to the fullest, because it was a life he'd created exactly the way he wanted, and he wouldn't live for anyone other than his daughter.

I tossed and turned most of the night, wondering if I'd made a terrible decision leaving Bailey Falls the way I did.

"Coffee. I require coffee," I mumbled as we wove down an already crowded 17th Street.

"We'll get it, don't worry. We just need to get there before it gets too busy."

"When did Natalie start getting up so early on a Saturday morning?" Clara whispered to me.

"Better question, when did she start caring so much about where her produce came from?" I whispered back.

Natalie turned around to make a face at me. "I heard that," she singsonged.

"I meant you to," I singsonged back.

"Seriously, Nat, what's the rush? I don't remember you ever being so concerned about getting 'farm-fresh produce'—although I understand the draw of eating local as much as possible."

"Now, when you say eating local, I assume you're referring to Leo enjoying a trip *downtown*?" Natalie replied with a grin, leading us into the fray of the Union Square Greenmarket.

Clara laughed. "You have a one-track mind."

I didn't laugh. I was thinking about Leo's eyes as he watched me, when he did in fact enjoy a trip downtown. And I Kegeled right there, just thinking about it.

"I have a multitrack mind," Natalie said. "I just make sure one of those tracks is always on sex with guys who like to take a taste."

A very good-looking man who was heading away from the farmers' market with a bag full of leafy greens did a double take, then a complete about-face. Was he aware that he was licking his lips?

Natalie didn't notice; she was on a mission. She consulted a map, smoothed her already perfectly messy hair, and took off across the market.

"Hey, hey! Can we *please* get some coffee before stocking up on your suddenly-so-important groceries?" I asked.

She slowed. A bit. "Yes yes, there's a stall just around the corner from where I'm going. We can get coffee afterward."

I hadn't been here in years, and the place was humming. Stall after stall was packed with beautiful produce, eggs, poultry, meat, flowers —everything you could ask for. Many of the stalls were from farms in the Hudson Valley, and I wondered if Maxwell Farm had a stall here. And then I wished I'd brushed my hair before we left.

"Let me see that map," I asked, and she handed it back to

me. I quickly scanned the list of producers, and breathed a sigh of relief when Leo's farm wasn't mentioned.

As we made it to the end of the first row, Natalie suddenly slowed down, pulled out her linen drawstring bag, and started to . . . strut.

I knew that strut well. I'd trailed behind it in many a club and restaurant when she was on the prowl. Something she mentioned on a call weeks ago bubbled up in my memory, and I realized exactly what was going on.

"You got us up at the crack of dawn on a Saturday to go cruise for some cute farmer?" I asked.

She whirled around. "I don't know what you're talking about," she said, eyes wide and innocent.

"*You've* got the hots for a farmer too? What the hell is going on? When did Old MacDonald become the new Hot Guy archetype?" Clara asked, her face full of amusement.

"To be clear, he's not a farmer; he's a dairy guy. He has a bunch of cows upstate and makes the best fucking triple-cream brie I've ever had. He melts in my mouth." Natalie sighed, arching her back. I'd say without knowing it, but she knew how good it made her boobs look. The guy who'd been trailing us since we got there actually gasped.

"You mean his *brie* melts in your mouth, right?" I asked, arching my eyebrow.

"Well," she said, with a twinkle in her eye. "For now."

"Oh boy," I replied as she set off in her strut again.

And imagine my surprise when she strutted right over to Bailey Falls Creamery, run by none other than . . .

"Oscar? The hot dairy guy is Oscar?" I exclaimed.

"What are you talking about?" she asked, nonchalantly looking at a display of homemade churned butter. We were at the edge of the stall, surrounded by gorgeous wedges of cheese, beautiful glass-bottled fresh milk, and yes, some pretty delectable-looking butter.

And behind the counter, a head taller than everyone else, was Oscar. Leo's neighbor, winner of Bailey Falls's Conversationalist of the Year, and the man making Natalie's cheeks blush.

And *no* man made her blush.

"I know him; he grazes his cows on Leo's land sometimes."

"I'm going for coffee," Clara announced.

I went to stand next to Natalie in line, with her mouth-melting brie.

"So his name is Oscar?"

"Mmm-hmm, and that's all I know about him. He's very—"

"Intense? Mysterious?"

"Nonverbal."

"Mmm." Her throaty groan made several men, and three women, turn around with lust in their eyes. "He's the strong, silent type—I knew it."

"So how long has this cheesy flirtation been going on?" I asked as the line moved forward.

"I've been coming here for a while. You know how much I love my cheese."

I did know. It was her love of cheese that made her enroll in culinary school.

Everyone has a secret dream, a secret unfulfilled life that they imagine they'd live if they won the lottery. They'd quit their job and . . .

. . . sail around the world.

. . . open a luxury resort in the Maldives.

. . . sing on Broadway.

And in Natalie's case . . . become a cheesemaker.

Seriously. The woman who lived for concrete and yellow cabs wanted to run away from it all, simplify everything, wear cardigans, and make cheese.

She threatened to do this at least twice a year, usually when some ad campaign had her tied in knots and ready to scream. But then she'd remember the posh fund-raisers at the Guggenheim, the magic of Central Park in October, Malaysian takeout delivery at anytime o'clock, and she remembered why she would never leave her city.

But the girl still loved her cheese.

"Some coworkers had been going on and on about this new cheese guy at the market on Saturdays, so I had to check it out. First my taste buds fell in love, and then my eyeballs did when I caught a look at him. I mean, he's gorgeous, right?" she said, slipping her arm inside my elbow as we got closer.

"He totally is," I agreed as I watched Oscar interact with his customers. Leo was all smiles and hi-how-are-you with *his* customers, remembering names and kids' names, and which berry you liked best.

Oscar? Barely grunted, filling orders with efficiency and not much else.

Gorgeous, yes. Friendly? Um . . .

"How well do you know him?" Natalie asked, color coming high in her cheeks as we moved to the front of the line. She was patting my arm in an almost nervous way, moving her weight from one foot to the other.

"Not well at all. The few times I've seen him, we've barely said— Hi, Oscar! How are you?" I chirped, putting on my game face.

He looked blandly back at me. Natalie's skin began to burn; I could feel her heating up beside me.

"So, um, you come in each week to the city? I didn't know the creamery had a stand here. That's great!"

More with the bland.

"So, this is my friend Natalie—she loves your brie. Right, Nat? Hey—Natalie?"

My friend, who could talk a priest down off the pulpit with one button undone, had absolutely clammed up. Could have been a mannequin, for all the life that was in her.

Oscar turned his eyes from mine and looked at Natalie. He slowly took her in, taking his time as he scanned her from head to toe, then focused on her mouth. Which was pinched into a tight line, her lips almost white with tension. He finally looked into her eyes, and the snap crackle pop of tension between them made me feel a little dizzy.

Under her eyes, he came alive. But he still said nothing. Except . . .

"Brie?" His voice was deeper than I'd heard it before, scratchy and thick.

Natalie just nodded. He wrapped up a wedge, leaned over to set it in front of her, and moved on to the next customer.

Spell broken, Natalie flew over to the cashier, paid for her cheese, and continued her flight away from Oscar, away from the Creamery.

I caught up to her and tugged on her arm. "What the hell was that?"

"What?" she asked, all calm and cool again. She flung her hair over her shoulder and stood straight and tall, beautiful and in control once more. Clara was coming toward us with coffees, and Natalie's eyes asked me to drop it.

"We'll revisit this," I said, and she nodded. The only way anyone would know she had a killer crush on Oscar the Grouch was the bloom of color still on her cheeks, and the tiny secret smile that was toying at her lips.

But I saw Oscar leaning out of his stall to take in the magnificent sight of Natalie's backside as she strutted away.

Chapter 24

We walked home from the market, Clara taking her usual measured steps, Natalie appearing to glide on air, and me plodding. It was already eighty-five degrees well before noon, and would soar into the midnineties. Which in a city made of steel and concrete was borderline ovenlike.

In spite of the heat however, people were out in droves, walking fast and purposefully. I seemed to go left whenever they did, right when they did, and as a result was bobbing and weaving like a boxer. I caught three purses in the chest before I finally started walking behind Natalie, who at almost six feet in her heels acted as a natural crowd breaker.

The city felt like a physical being, wrapping around me warm and thick like a wool blanket. Not exactly what you want in the dog days of summer.

And the smell! It was garbage day, and thousands and thousands of plastic bags were piled onto the sidewalk's curb, three to four feet high in some places, since the city had been constructed essentially without alleys. And in the heat of summer, the smell could be unbearable.

How much of this could be composted, I wondered as I held

my breath walking by the bigger stacks. *How much of this could be donated and worked into a nutrient-rich mulch that could augment summer gardens and winter fields?*

Leo could figure this out, he would . . . *thunk*! Dodging yet another person who was intent on getting somewhere five minutes sooner than everyone else, I got shouldered into the wall of garbage, pinwheeling my arms to keep from going headfirst into a mountain of gross.

"Oh my God, Roxie! Are you okay?" Clara pulled me back just in time.

"Fucking dick!" I called after the guy with the shoulder, who didn't even pause, didn't check to make sure I was okay.

I was hot, I was sticky with humidity, my nose was filled with the stench of garbage, and I could feel my stomach giving a warning rumble. "Fucking dick," I repeated to myself. "I'm fine—thanks."

"Want me to smack him? I can catch him," Clara said, bouncing lightly on the balls of her feet.

"No no," I said, pulling at my T-shirt and trying to get some air. Suddenly everything seemed too close: the air, my clothes, the people, even my friends. It was all too loud, too much. My throat tightened, and a curious lump formed in the back of my throat as I realized in a great whoosh that I was . . . homesick. For Bailey Falls.

For the peace and quiet, for the good country air, for nosey gossipmongers, for the swimming holes, and the wind through the trees. For hills covered in funny little chicken coops on wheels, for brown sugar strawberries, and oh my God, I want Leo and every single thing that comes with it. *Everything*.

"You look like you're going to be sick." Natalie swept my hair back from my face.

"What's the fastest way to Grand Central?" I asked, digging

in my purse to find my phone. Dead. Dammit. That's what happens when you run off to the city without packing a bag. I was wearing Clara's clothes today, for goodness' sake.

"Wait, what?" Natalie asked.

"I'm going home. Metro North runs all day, right?" I asked frantically.

"Mmm-hmm." She raised a hand and grabbed a cab instantly. "Grand Central," she told the driver.

"Thanks, I gotta go. I'll send you your clothes," I said to Clara, getting into the cab, already feeling better. Lighter.

"Where are you going?" she asked.

Natalie patted her hand. "I'll fill you in."

Riverdale.

Ludlow.

Yonkers.

As the train sped up the Hudson, it was as though everything was suddenly clicking into place, like a giant game of Tetris tilting on end and every piece found its home.

The moment I decided I didn't want to be in that big city anymore, my heart cracked open and began to long for a small town—*my* small town. For mosquitos and sweet tea, for bare feet and gentle hills that led to craggy peaks. For spring-fed pools and glacial lakes. For nosy neighbors and cranky waitresses and sweet former quarterbacks. For flaky hippie mothers who made falling in love seem easy and wonderful, even when it wasn't, and always made sure their daughters had adequate fiber content.

For a farmer who groaned when he came, and grinned when I did.

For a farmer who wanted me desperately, but came as an already matched set, a set I'd never try to come between, but would be honored to someday join.

Irvington.

Tarrytown.

Philipse Manor.

I began to list all the reasons I had for never wanting to move back home and live a small-town life like my mother.

1. *You don't want to run the family diner.* I've run the family diner. I don't want to continue doing it forever, but it wasn't nearly as bad as I'd always thought it'd be.

2. *You think small towns are small for a reason, in scope and in size.* The size was small, but I'd found this summer that small didn't mean limited.

3. *There are no opportunities in Bailey Falls for a classically trained chef who doesn't want to work in a traditional restaurant environment.* Zombie pickles. Jam Class. Potential opportunity at Bryant Mountain House. And the idea that'd been percolating since the Fourth of July: an Airstream food truck.

4. *If you don't go back to Los Angeles and redeem your whipped cream disaster, that town wins.* This one was tougher. Did LA beat me? Worst-case scenario? Yeah, it beat me. And?

The *and* was the tough part. I'd never shied away from a fight. But it couldn't be a fight if one corner wasn't willing to participate, right? I'd likely always wonder what if, and what would have happened . . . But who didn't look back, revisit, and wonder about past decisions? The question was, could I live with knowing that Mitzi St. Renee and her Mean Girls had won?

Cortlandt.

Peekskill.

Manitou.

Somewhere between Manitou and Garrison, I had a sudden realization: someone like Mitzi St. Renee always wins. And you can't live your life fighting against everyone else's expectations. And sometimes the deck is stacked, and people with power over your career are assholes, and there's nothing you can do about that.

Excited for the first time in a very long time, I sat forward in my seat, pushing my right foot against the floor as if that would speed the train along faster. The Hudson sparkled blue on my left, sailboats and kayaks dotting its surface. Huge homes high on the ridge and smaller, simpler homes shared the gorgeous view.

Picturesque towns with tiny train stations, within easy distance of the grandest city on the planet, filled with people who chose to live a world away just an hour up the Hudson. The bright lights and the fast pace were close enough if you wanted it, but far enough away that you could never miss it.

My thoughts danced on, seeing endless opportunities that I'd never bothered to see, to an opportunity with a certain farmer and his daughter. I only hoped that opportunity was still available to me.

The train pulled into the Poughkeepsie station.

I got off. And drove straight to the farm.

When I got to Maxwell Farm I parked, raced inside the main barn, and started looking for Leo's long and lean frame everywhere. I thought I spotted him when a Screaming Trees T-shirt came around the corner, but it turned out to be one of his interns.

People who knew me and knew of my relationship with Leo said hello to me, and judging by the way they said only hello and kept on walking, they knew I'd left him standing in the middle of the road. They were protective. I got that.

I headed into the farm store, but no Leo. I checked the barn, I checked the silo, and I checked the kitchen garden out back. No Leo.

"Looking for my dad?" I heard from behind me, and I turned to find Polly sitting on a wheelbarrow, sorting seed packets.

"I am, yeah. How are you, Polly?" I asked, kneeling down.

"How are *you*?" she asked pointedly. I reminded myself that she was only seven years old. But based on my actions lately, likely years ahead of me emotionally. "I heard you went away."

"You did, huh?" I asked, wincing a bit. "I'm back, though. I just went into the city for a day or so."

"You mean Manhattan?"

"Exactly. Have you been there?"

Shuffling the seed packets, she finally answered, "I have—it's nice. Grandma's apartment is pretty, you can see really far up that high! It's fun running up and down the hallways and riding the elevator, but she was mad when I pressed every single button."

"Oh, I bet. I did that too once, when I was a kid."

"And I like going to the museums, especially the dinosaur exhibits. But . . ."

"But?"

"But I like it here lots better. Daddy grew up in the city, you know."

"I did know that," I replied, watching her look carefully at me.

"He loves it here. He says we'll never leave here and live somewhere else."

I swallowed hard. "It's pretty great, isn't it?"

"I saw you kiss my daddy." She looked at me, unblinking.

I blinked. A bunch. "Um, yes. You did. Was that weird?"

"Yeah, at first it was. But now, I think . . ."

I held my breath.

She laid out some of the packets face up, arranged like a vegetable full house.

Leo was in for it with this kid. I smiled, hoping that I'd get to watch it happen.

The smile from me was what she needed.

She smiled back, her pensive face turning bright. "I'm going to go see the hogs. Daddy's in the apple orchard."

And then she was off, running pell-mell across the field.

And I was off to the orchard.

∾

Parking next to Leo's Jeep, I peered through the rows of trees, looking for him. I thought I saw something moving several rows down, so I entered the orchard and made my way toward him.

As I walked, I became aware of two things.

One, my skin tingled. I was excited to see him! I wanted to see his face and kiss his lips and hold him close and hear his voice in my ear and feel his hands on my skin, after I told him, 'I'm here to stay if I can still be yours.'

Two, my skin crawled. I became aware of the second thing as I wandered through the Macouns and the Empires, the Honey-crisps and the Sansas. And when I moved into the late-summer peaches . . . that's when I felt it.

First came a low, droning hum, almost like feedback from a very low bass speaker. I called out to Leo, who I could now see moving a few rows away. My call changed the hum to something more recognizable, a familiar sound that bumped into the corner of my brain. Something familiar enough to make my skin pebble.

And then I saw them.

Bees.

Everywhere.

The droning hum was a collective buzz, which announced itself to my brain in a wave of awful, realization crashing across my body in a cold sweat and an absolute sheer terror. I wanted to run. I wanted to freeze. I wanted to—

"Roxie?" a surprised voice asked, and I saw Leo underneath a peach tree, oblivious to the million-bee chorus announcing that I was here and ripe for the picking. To those who are about to die, we salute you.

"Oh!" was all I could manage—and then the internal screaming began. One buzzed my ear, one buzzed by my nose, and several bopped around my head. Their bee noses must be drunk on the fear coming off me in waves. My eyes flashed to his, and he saw I was surrounded.

But . . .

I came to this orchard to get my guy.

Or at least tell him I'd like to be his girl.

I took a step.

I took another step.

The bees went with me, a cloud of nightmares hovering just inches from me, talking among themselves about how best to torture me. I had a sudden vision of the flying monkeys carrying away Dorothy, her legs kicking in the air. I only hoped that when the bees carried me off, someone would make sure my mother got my chef's knives.

Steeling myself, I tried to speak. "Hi. Leo." My voice was cracked and shaky, bordering on panic. "I wanted to talk to you . . . oh! I wanted to tell you . . . shit, that was close! . . . I, I'd like to—"

"Jesus, Roxie," Leo said, marveling at the sight of me standing in a bee cloud, trying to carry on a normal conversation. "Just breathe, okay?"

"Yeah, trying to do that, not working so well," I said shakily. "Anyway, I'm here because I wanted to tell you that . . . Motherfucker!" I got stung. So much for the theory that if you ignore them they'll ignore you. Fucking rogue bee. "Ow!" Annnd there's another sting. One landed on my shoulder, another landed on my ear, and though I held it together through all of that, when one had the balls to land on my nose, that was it.

I ran. But instead of running away, I ran toward Leo and his shocked face, which finally had the sense to show some healthy bee fear, and the two of us ran through the orchard, high-step running through the tall grass, swiping at our heads and windmilling our arms.

"Left, go left!" he shouted, and I followed, swatting as I went, feeling stings on the back of my calf and my elbow.

In a haze of screaming and twitching, slapping and jumping, we burst out of the orchard and into a clearing. And just beyond that? Water.

We plunged into a deep, cold pond, splashing out into the center where we could submerge, the stings instantly cooling. I grabbed for his hand underwater, and we took turns popping above to grab a breath and see how SwarmWatch was going.

Eventually the bees got bored and headed back to the orchard, to continue gorging themselves on fallen fruit. Leo coaxed me back up to the surface, and we treaded water in the middle of the pond, in the middle of Maxwell Farm. My hair was plastered to my face and a bee sting was swelling up in my eyebrow. I was covered in pond algae, twigs, and sticks, and I was hoping like hell that whatever kept wrapping around my ankle was my shoelace.

"What the hell, Rox—"

I wrapped both arms around him, kissed him until we both

went under, and then kissed him again as soon as we popped back up.

"I love you—I love you so much! I want you, I want everything. I want small town and home grown. I want this—without the bees preferably, but if the bees come with this life, then I'll take the fucking bees. I just want to be your Sugar Snap."

Leo silently treaded water, one arm still holding me close, not pushing me away but not pulling me closer.

I ached to be closer. I ached to just *be* with him.

"I want to live here—not just for the summer. I want fall and winter and spring, and hayrides and hoedowns and being bent over a rain barrel on the Fourth of July. I love you, Leo—and—I want it all."

I grinned, no fear left. It felt so good to tell him this, to tell him everything.

"I want to start a food truck, and cooking classes, and get to know Polly, if you're okay with that, because I think she's amazing and I think you're amazing. And—Jesus Christ, I *hope* that's my shoelace!" I pulled my leg up to the surface, slapping at it underneath, splashing Leo in the surprised face.

But the surprise became hopeful. And the hopeful became happy. And the happy became heated. But before the heated could escalate, concern crowded in.

"You sure about this, Sugar Snap?" *Butterflies!* "Because it's not just me I have to consider. If you want me, you have to want us both. I can't have someone temporary in my life. It's all in, or . . ."

The late afternoon sun shone down, casting a golden light on the landscape, the water, the algae in his beard.

I wrapped my leg around his and pulled him closer with a smile. "I'm all in, Farmer Boy."

Epilogue

Farmer Boy. She called me Farmer Boy.

I thought about this as I walked through the fall wheat, running my fingertips along the tall grain. The air was crisp today, not quite chilly, but with a hint of the winter that was only a few months away now.

The fall wheat was usually the last crop harvested; the apples already picked and stored for the winter. She'd made apple butter after all.

Polly loved apple butter. She ate it every year, but this year she learned to make it. I smiled as I thought of the afternoons spent in the back kitchen of the diner, jars spread out everywhere, a spicy cinnamony scent heavy in the air, and my girls in matching braids, laughing as they filled containers with the sweet treat.

My girls.

Roxie was adamant about keeping her own place, and rightly so. Once she made the decision to move back to Bailey Falls, she was determined to live away from her mother, but close by. The old farmhouse she found was about halfway between my place and her mom's, only a few minutes from the town she claimed was too small, but she secretly loved.

When I flew out with her to Los Angeles to pack up her apartment, I noticed there wasn't a lot there that made it . . . well . . . homey. It was functional, and of course the kitchen was impressive, but there was nothing about it that really said . . . Roxie.

As much as she claimed to have a full life out there, it took us less than a day to pack her up, and less than an evening to say goodbye to her friends. Sure, her Hollywood friends Jack and Grace were sad to see her go, but they assured her that anytime they were on the East Coast, they'd be sure to get together.

Driving back across the country, Roxie seemed excited to be getting home, to her new old life. And quicker than anyone expected, she'd cleaned out the Airstream, equipped it with the necessary items to turn it into a food truck, and Zombie Cakes was born. And killing it. She sold out each and every time she showed up to a farmers' market, a county fair, or a private event.

I smiled, thinking about her leaning out of the side of the truck, passing a slice of mile-high coconut cake to a happy customer. I smiled wider when I thought about what her tits looked like in her V-neck Zombie Cakes shirt.

I came to the end of the row, satisfied with the feel of the plump grains on the stalks. We'd harvest soon, maybe by the end of the week. When I heard the Jeep roaring up the dusty farm road, I turned, catching the faint sound of U2 through the open windows. Turns out Polly was a big fan of the band as well, and she and Roxie listened to the old albums by the hour while they baked. *"It's good for dancing, Daddy,"* Polly had informed me one afternoon, when I caught the two of them busting a move while sifting flour.

I agreed.

As they made the last turn and pulled up beside me, I raised a hand in greeting. Roxie turned off the motor as Polly wrestled with her seat belt, eager to get out and race up and down the rows, like she did every time she came out here.

"Hey, Daddy!" she cried out, as I helped her unbuckle and swung her high.

"Hey, Pork Chop! Did you finish your homework?"

"I did; Roxie helped me. We stopped by the diner after school, and Miss Trudy gave me some pie."

"A small piece," Roxie explained with a sheepish look. "And who gives seven-year-olds homework, by the way?"

"I don't mind, though. I learned all about the difference between cumulus and cumu . . . cumula . . . what is it called?" Polly asked, looking to Roxie.

"Cumulonimbus," Roxie prompted, and Polly nodded her head vigorously.

"Yeah, cumulonimbles. They're different types of clouds."

"I see. And what are those over there?" I asked, pointing at the western sky, watching as she wandered and muttered to herself, trying to decipher exactly what was overhead. I took the opportunity to pull Roxie into me, stealing a kiss.

"Watch yourself, Farmer Boy," Roxie sighed, the faintest bit of green showing in her eyes. "I'm not above groping you in front of the wee one."

"She'll be busy with her cumulonimbles for at least twenty minutes." I grinned, my heart beating a little faster at having her in my arms again. "At least let me take a peek down your shirt. I'll pretend a bee flew down there."

"You'll do no such thing. Besides, we need to save something for later," she said, but her breath was coming faster.

"I can't come by tonight, Sugar Snap. Mrs. Nyland had to go take care of her sister down in Yonkers, so I'll be on Polly duty tonight."

To keep things as routine as possible, there'd been no

overnights at my place. Roxie was insistent on that. She came over all the time, but she never spent the night. I was hoping to make a change in that department sooner rather than later, but that was a conversation for another day. In a fancier setting.

"Oh no, I called in a few favors. My mom agreed to come over tonight and stay with Polly, so feel free to come stand outside my window anytime after eight. If you're not there," she breathed, more green appearing in now, "I'll start without you."

"Dangerous," I groaned, kissing her lips and wrapping my hands around her hips, feeling those curves underneath my fingertips. She got breathy, like my girl always did when I kissed her gentle like this. Her hands slid down the front of my shirt, tugging me closer. As I bumped my hips into hers, her eyes popped open in surprise.

"Are those nuts in your pocket, or are you just glad to see me?" she asked, her soft brown curls blowing wildly around her face.

I dug into my pocket, producing a handful of walnuts, which made her toss her head back and laugh in the way I loved. "Both." I started to lean back in for another kiss.

"Roxie! I think I found a serious!" Polly pointed excitedly at the sky. "And kissing is gross, by the way."

"I think you mean cirrus," Roxie said with a chuckle, squeezing my hand. Then she ran into the field after my daughter, kneeling down next to her and looking up at the sky where Polly was pointing.

My heart felt like bursting as I watched my Pork Chop and my Sugar Snap study the clouds.